THE SHADOW OF IQUITOS

BY
JOHN R BEYER

If Jonas was right, the bombing had nothing to do with any terrorist group, but how could he prove it?

"No one has claimed anything?" Jonas asked. "You're not even hearing a hint out there?"

"No, nothing of substance," Smythe returned. "Sure, we got the regulars who are claiming it, but so far, it's a big zero. We've had people claiming to be members of ISIS, Al-Qaida, and Hamas, but they probably don't have a lot of interest in our little city. Anyway, NSA checked the hot ones and found they came from local numbers and after checking them out we patted the idiots on the ass and said not to call us again. Loonies! It seems the real bomber did his thing and disappeared into thin air."

Jonas nodded. "That's awfully strange."

"Everything seems a little strange, wouldn't you think?"

"I guess so." Jonas stood up from the desk and pocketed his cell. "I need to get going, Lieutenant, but if I think of anything, I will let you know."

"Jonas, make sure it's in a timely manner?"

Jonas looked down at Smythe. "Of course, I will."

As Jonas walked out of the department and onto Orange Street, he realized he hadn't liked lying to his former boss but believed there was nothing else he could have done at the time. If Iquitos was the key, then it was up to Jonas to learn why, and that germ of an idea in the back of his head was growing by the hour.

Jonas Peters and Frank Sanders team up to solve a string of murders, starting with the intentional and fatal bombing of a local coffee shop in downtown Riverside—a usually calm city in Southern California. Dozens are dead after an explosion rips apart the Coffee Grind, leaving dozens of others gravely wounded. Frank soon finds himself up to his elbows assisting the bombing victims, especially when he discovers that Jonas was walking to the Coffee Grind to meet up with his fiancée, but he never made it. In an instant, all their lives are thrust into a trail of death and destruction carried out by an unknown psychopath.

ACKNOWLEDGMENTS

The author would like to express his gratitude to the Peruvian Navy for their assistance in exploring the Amazon River near the city of Iquitos, and especially to Commander Carlos Garrido (retired). And a special thanks to our good friend Paul K. Bakas who followed us into the hinterlands of the Peruvian Rainforest in often miserable conditions for indepth research for this novel.

GENRE THRILLER MYSTERY-DE-TECTIVE POLICE PROCEDURAL

SHADOWS OF IQUITOS ~

Copyright © 2025 by John R. Beyer

All Rights Reserved

Print ISBN:

First Publication: April 2025

DEDICATION

*To Laureen—who has always been there for me
and been my guiding light.
She has made me a better man.*

TABLE OF CONTENTS

PROLOGUE

Jonas Peters grinned at the slightly older man standing on the second step of the entrance to the brick building while reaching out his right hand. "Thanks for the help on the case."

Frank Sanders shook his head. "I should be the one saying 'thank you' a few times, as many cases you've helped me on."

"How's business, seriously?" Jonas asked.

"It's good, Jonas. Some cases really make me some money, and some just pay the bills. Sure, I miss the days when you and I would bump into each other at the department on a juicy murder or burglary, but those days are gone. Retirement pay isn't substantial, but this gig gives me plenty of traveling money."

The two men had spent the previous forty minutes in Frank's office on the second floor of the Wright building just northwest of the Mission Inn in downtown Riverside, California. They had been going over the final paperwork on a joint case they had been working on together, albeit somewhat apart.

Frank had gone from a crimes-against-persons detective to private detective when he retired from the Riverside Police Department. Jonas Peters had gone from homicide detective to falling into a bottle of Jack Daniels and then resurfacing to finish a case which cost him a dear friend, along with many innocents. Fortunately, that story had a happy ending, with the killing of Zachary Marshall, the psychopath who had started it all. It should have meant the release of the demons Jonas had felt for so many years, but instead, it just reinforced the negativity of the world in which he had lived for so long. He wanted out, but did not know how to exit.

Jonas had turned in his badge for the Riverside Police Department where he worked, and moved to Scottsdale, Arizona, believing his life might take a one-eighty. It hadn't. Jonas eventually found himself on a pension, living on twenty acres of desert near a small town named Phelan in Southern California and working a few cases here and there as a private detective. Not a glamorous job but one, like Frank had responded, that helped make the financial side of life a bit more comfortable.

Jonas also liked the solitude of the High Desert. Seemed fewer ghosts circled there.

He also liked to cry where no one would see him.

"How's your life really going?" Frank asked while stepping down a step and looking his friend squarely in the eyes.

Frank had known Jonas for over two decades while working at the Riverside City Police Department but had never gotten to know the man very well. Jonas had always been friendly enough, but to dig into his personal history was not a door a fellow officer ever tried to venture through.

Jonas had always been somewhat aloof. Not aloof like a head-in-the-sky sort of fellow but one who always questioned himself and thus never allowed anyone from the outside to look inside.

"Actually, Frank," Jonas stated. "Things are looking up for me recently. The cases I take are ones that I want, and the ones I don't, I don't."

Frank nodded his rather large square head. "Any women?"

Jonas smiled. "There was in Scottsdale for a while. A great lady by the name of Samantha—I called her Sam—and we hit if off well after I retired from the force. You know, after Steve's murder, I just had to get out of here, but after a year or so I needed to come back. This is where I grew up and all I really know."

"You know, John Steinbeck wrote that you can never truly go home."

"Yeah, well, he was right. That's why I live out in the boonies in Phelan. Just me and my three dogs."

Frank grinned. "I like dogs."

"You have any?"

"Nope, I'm just gone too much to feel like it would be fair to them."

"That makes sense."

"What happened to Sam?"

Jonas shifted his weight from the left to the right. "She could sense I wanted to move back near here, and we sort of went our own ways. We reconnected a few months back—you know, sort of a long-distance affair with texts, phone calls, and the like. She called me the other week to let me know she would be in Riverside on business. It coincided with my meeting with you."

"Serendipitous, I would say." Frank clapped Jonas on the shoulder while giving him a wink.

Jonas smiled in return. "Yes, we've spent the last couple of days together, and things were just like they were. We may even try the relationship again—even if it means some traveling for both of us for now. I truly love that woman, Frank."

"And I'm sure she feels the same way about you."

"I hope so," Jonas said. "Well, I gotta get going. I promised to meet her at the Common Grounds in a few minutes. Thanks for helping me on the case."

"And vice versa." Frank held out his hand and shook his friend's. "Go and enjoy your cup of coffee."

I hope she does love you, Jonas—you could use it.

CHAPTER 1

Entering the late morning sunshine, Jonas looked across the wide street and marveled at the impressive architectural splendor of the Mission Inn looming above. The massive structure was so awe inspiring he was surprised that Hollywood had not used it for more backgrounds in films. The city of fantasy was only forty or so miles to the west and this historical landmark would be just a hop, skip, and a jump for the industry.

The historic hotel had plenty of excellent rooms to put up any number of crew members who may need a spot to retire for the evening after a day of shooting. He had spent the last couple of nights in the inn, but it had been more than memorable, especially, with Sam by his side.

When he had drifted back toward the Southern California area early the previous year, he knew that Sam would not, or could not, follow him. A good career, lots of clients, and the dream of continuing to build her business allowed her to let him go.

It had been a hard decision for the both of them. They were deeply in love.

Jonas explained he had to return to near the locale he grew up in since his daughter was buried there, and living so many hours away in Scottsdale made him wake at night with feelings he had abandoned her.

He knew he had murdered his young daughter.

No one else thought that, but a father feels what a father feels and, to Jonas, if he hadn't taken his only child to a convenience store for some milk, she might still be alive. It wasn't his decision to have a hyped-up junkie try to rob the store while the both of them were there, but it was his choice to reach for his off duty weapon. It was that movement the robber saw and shot Jonas's daughter in the face.

Not a night went by Jonas didn't regret that evening or that he didn't wish he'd been killed instead of his baby.

So, Jonas had said goodbye to the woman he loved and moved back to within an hour of his daughter's gravesite. He missed Sam, but he loved sitting most Saturdays at the cemetery reading a story to a child he would never hold in his arms again.

He was alone, but he was never lonely. He had the memories of his precious sweetheart, but as the year wore on, he noticed he missed Sam more than ever.

She was there in his thoughts day and night and, as hard as he tried, Sam's smiling face was the last image he saw before nodding off to sleep.

Whether he wanted her or not, Jonas's sister, Maggie, decided to get involved as she always had, and suddenly Jonas was texting, emailing, and talking with Sam again.

Her business was flourishing with many new clients, and things were nothing but positive for her.

Jonas decided not to ask if Sam had a new love in her life. He had no right. He knew that better than most since life had slowly moved on after his daughter's murder. He couldn't be angry if Sam had moved on faster than him. Jonas always felt there was someone much more worthy than himself for Sam to be involved with.

But Sam hadn't found anyone else.

Maggie was ecstatic, Sam hesitant, and Jonas was not sure.

Three months later, they were in a long-distance relationship.

Now he had spent a wonderful couple of days making love to the woman he truly adored and knew he was ready to settle down. Sam meant everything to him.

Jonas walked across the street toward the Common Grounds, a block and a half ahead of him as he strolled down the cobble stoned walkway.

He felt great. A case closed with Frank Sanders with a hefty check in his right pocket and the woman he admired so sipping her favorite herbal tea just a minute or two from him. How could it not be better than this?

Jonas smiled. He did not do that very often.

They had checked into the Mission Inn a couple of days ago. Jonas had chosen a rather expensive suite but knew it was worth it. As he and Sam had entered the room overlooking the pool below, both knew this was what luxury meant.

"Oh, my God," Sam said as the bell person left their room. "Jonas, the view is gorgeous."

Jonas tossed the plastic room key cards onto the top of the credenza and firmly grasped Sam by the waist. "And so are you."

The view for the next hour was lost as they both eagerly and hungrily enjoyed the other with caresses, kisses, and deep groans of sexual satisfaction. This was not pent up energy but the love each felt for each other and the reckless abandon that it brought.

They were meant to be together.

Now, Jonas relived those moments as he walked by an antique store on the west side of the mall and wondered if he should pick up that piece of jewelry Sam had spotted the night before after a wonderful dinner they had had at Duane's. It was a three hundred dollar broach, but Sam had loved it so. It was a lot of money but not much if it pleased her, he thought.

It took Jonas a couple of minutes to enter the boutique and get the price down to two hundred and change from the clerk, who seemed more interested in getting the deal finished so she could get back to a very important twitter debate going on.

I like this technology if it gets me deals all the time.

He exited the store and, with bag in hand, walked toward where Sam was waiting for him, knowing she would scold him for such an expensive gift but would love it anyway.

Jonas grinned, stepped onto the walkway just across from the coffee shop, and raised his right arm as Sam gestured she had garnered a table right outside of the entrance to Common Grounds.

God, she was beautiful.

The crosswalk light changed. Jonas had started across the street when his cell buzzed, and reluctantly he grabbed it off his belt and, while watching the traffic, glanced down at the message he had received on his text.

~ Remember Iquitos?

Jonas continued on his path, wondering what the message meant. Then a second popped up.

~ Of course you do.

Jonas looked at his phone and then up at the coffee shop where he was to meet Sam.

In an instant, the entire south-western block where Jonas had been walking became nothing but a terrible ear-splitting explosion. Building fronts disappeared within seconds, sending tons of concrete and debris onto the unsuspecting. The blast sent Jonas flying through the air, painfully landing sprawled across a water fountain.

"Sam," he moaned as darkness engulfed him.

CHAPTER 2

The casualties mounted during the late morning as city workers and emergency personnel cleared away the wreckage caused by the explosion. More than a dozen dead, with three times that number seriously injured. The death toll would certainly climb by late afternoon, according to the first responders.

A heavily muscled man rubbed his chin with his right hand while pointing with his left. "It's a hell of a mess over there."

"That it is, Captain," replied a paramedic dappled with dust and soot.

Fred Midfield had been one of the first responders once his station had received the call about the explosion. Like his fellow fire fighters, Midfield believed a gas main had exploded, causing the disaster.

It had only taken a few moments to realize this was not a pipe which had suddenly decided to blow up.

Fire Captain Guy Kennedy had arrived in his department sedan only moments after Midfield's crew and noticed the cratering on the upper north half of the building which once housed the coffee shop. "That's no gas line," he grunted while tearing off his tie and getting busy pulling people from the wreckage.

Forty minutes after the explosion, all of the seriously injured had been transported to the three closest hospitals while dozens of fire personnel and volunteers were working on the less injured a block from the explosion site.

Teams of canine units were combing through the rubble looking for survivors. Instead, they turned up more and more fatalities.

Kennedy was exhausted. He made it a practice to hit it hard at the gym, especially with the heavy weights, four days a week, but moving blocks of cement, overturned tiled tables, planters, and the like had worn him to a frazzle.

"Captain," Midfield started as he walked up to his superior. "How did you know it wasn't a gas line rupturing almost as soon as we got here?"

"Not a hundred percent sure until the bomb squads are finished along with our arson crew, but that building cratered inward by the looks of the damage."

Midfield waited a moment while scanning the building where Kennedy was again pointing. The paramedic was also using this conversation as a chance to catch his breath. Even though he was only twenty-six, he felt about a hundred at this moment. He was covered from head to toe in grime and ached in every muscle.

"That sort of cratering tells me that an explosive was placed on the outside of the building instead of a pipe erupting from the inside. An inside explosion would have blown the interior walls outward but there shouldn't have been as much damage as we're seeing here."

Midfield listened to the older man and didn't interrupt. Not many people did when Kennedy was speaking and only then at their own personal risk. The captain was a nice enough person, but when he was on the job and explaining this or that, a person was wise to listen quietly. That calm person persona could disappear in an instant.

Besides, Kennedy knew what he was saying. The man had served two tours as a reservist in Iraq back in two thousand eight and nine, scouting out potential suicide bombing sites and defusing IEDs. It was those improvised explosive devices which had been the real classroom for his boss's vast knowledge of the world of explosives. That and losing his best friend when Kennedy missed one on the side of the road while doing a sweep before the regular troops came through.

Kennedy missed, it but his friend hadn't.

"Without all the reports, I'd say it was a simple pipe bomb, perhaps two and as many as three, which caused this much damage." Kennedy stopped and patted a fireman on the left shoulder as he was walking by. "Black powder and potassium nitrate can cause a pretty nasty surprise for the unsuspecting. Pressure builds up inside the sealed pipe rather rapidly once the detonation has been started. They're usually filled with shrapnel, but I haven't seen any evidence of that sort of damage."

Midfield nodded. "Why wouldn't they use shrapnel then?"

"A person can pack a heavier charge in a pipe bomb without the nails or screws generally used. A much bigger wallop for the buck, I would guess. And they already had all the shrapnel they needed."

That didn't sound right to Midfield. "How's that?"

"The huge glass windows would be more than enough shrapnel to blow out and kill people." Kennedy muttered. "Let's go. You and I have caught our breath, and there's still a lot of work to do here, unfortunately."

CHAPTER 3

"What a fucking mess," yelled Lieutenant Randall Smythe who was now, against his wishes, leading the investigation for the Riverside Police Department. There were others, but since his rise in rank a couple of years ago to chief of detectives in homicide from a sergeant in patrol the assistant police chief had made it very clear who was in charge of this fucking mess.

Smythe followed orders. He was good at what he did and was well respected. But as he viewed the massive destruction of the former bistro, he wanted to be as far away as possible.

"Number of dead?"

A shorter officer in uniform looked quickly at a small notebook in his right hand. "At this time, there are a confirmed thirteen killed. As you can see, the teams are still searching but are pretty confident all those accounted for are."

"Never assume, Johnson." Smythe shrugged. "We're still not sure how many were lost at ground zero in 2001. Things get overlooked."

Johnson looked up at his supervisor. "But surely this can't be compared to New York."

"And not meant to be, but the point is a blast can do very strange things to people. This was pretty powerful, and if a person was standing at the ignition point…well then, who knows?"

Johnson looked back to his pad of paper. He didn't want to delve any further and let the matter drop since the thought of a fellow human simply disintegrating was a little hard to swallow.

"Injured?"

"Thirty-three, twenty-two seen and released at the site, seven more in serious but good condition, with another four in critical condition. The badly injured were shipped around to area hospitals to lessen the load in the ERs."

Smythe kicked at a piece of mortar by his right foot. "Funny, three hours ago that piece of brick with the mortar was in place on the building's façade. How and why did it get here in such a violent manner?"

"The explosion, sir," Johnson replied.

Smythe patted the young officer on the shoulder and smiled. "Yes, I know that, but what I don't know is how and why. Until that is answered, we simply have a deadly puzzle to put together, don't we?"

Johnson nodded and then followed Smythe across rubble toward a make-shift command post just north-west of where the coffee shop once stood.

Frank Sanders was sipping on a cup of coffee while listening to an investigator provide the known details of what had happened hours ago two blocks from his office. The younger homicide detective was someone Frank helped train when he was on the department before retiring six years earlier.

The explosion had nearly knocked Frank out of his desk chair and, when he got his wits about him, he bounded down the steep flight of stairs to the front of the red brick building.

Instead of entering into what should have been late morning sunshine, he found the light blotted out by a thick ceiling of dust blowing from the south a couple blocks away. Instinctively, he sprinted the distance to lend a hand to any injured.

After nearly an hour working the site with first responders and civilian volunteers, it dawned on him that his friend, Jonas Peters, had been walking in the direction of the explosion to meet his girlfriend. It was then that Frank started hounding every uniform he came across for any information as to Jonas's well-being or his whereabouts. To his consternation, Frank had come up with nothing.

Frank finished his coffee, nodded at the detective, and then saw Randall Smythe walking toward the command post. Frank had worked for Smythe when he was in homicide, and though he believed the lieutenant was a little anal, had always respected his quality of professionalism. Every T crossed and every I dotted used to drive Frank crazy, but Smythe knew his stuff, and ninety-five percent of his cases cinched putting the bad guy away for a long time.

"Sanders," Smythe started while eyeing Frank. "What brings you out here?"

"Trying to help."

Nodding, Smythe looked Frank up and down. "By the looks of you, I'd say you were there moments after the blast."

"Just about."

"Well, thanks for all you did," Smythe replied.

"Should have seen the civilians, Randall," Frank stated. "They came out of the woodwork to help. Made me proud."

Smythe took a cup of coffee from a police cadet and nodded his appreciation. "Americans have that wonderful habit, don't they? When need arises, they arise to the need."

"Yeah," Frank said. "How bad?"

"Bad, I'm afraid, and nothing yet."

"If you can't talk about it, Randall, I understand," Frank commented. "I don't carry the badge any longer. I'm just Joe Citizen now."

"You'll always be a cop, Frank, but honestly, we have nothing. No one claiming victory over this crap, and we don't even know how much explosive was used to cause the damage. A lot that's certain, but we're not anywhere close in determining how much or how it was set off. We have our hunches, but I'll leave that for the experts."

Frank nodded. "By the way, do have a list of the victims handy?"

"Johnson," Smythe called over to the officer who had been walking with him. "Where's that list? Why, Frank?"

"Jonas stopped by to see me earlier, just before the explosion but, for the life of me, I can't locate him."

"Peters? Why did he come to see you?"

"A case we worked on together. We privates do that sometimes to cover more territory in an expedient fashion."

"Yes, I had forgotten that Jonas had taken up after you in the private investigation field." Smythe smiled. "Johnson, do you have a Jonas Peters on that list?"

With his finger going down the names slowly Johnson suddenly stopped and looked at the two men. "His name is here."

The lieutenant grabbed the clipboard from the officer's hands. "Why didn't you tell me?"

Johnson simply looked at Smythe. "I don't know any Jonas Peters, sir. The name didn't ring a bell."

"Of course, how could it?" Smythe handed the board to Frank. "You weren't here when he was."

"No, sir, I just transferred in from Redondo Beach PD last summer."

Smythe nodded, watching the expression on Frank's face.

"He's listed as injured, but that's it," Frank explained, handing the clipboard back to Johnson. "Do you know where he may have been taken?"

"Give me a minute, sir, and I'll find out," Johnson stated, moving away from the two men and walking over to a table where a lap top was available.

"Frank," Smythe said. "Why did you think Jonas may have been in the accident?"

"He said he was meeting his girlfriend at the coffee shop where the explosion took place."

Smythe remained silent a moment. Then he sighed. "Really?"

"Now, come on, Randall," Frank stated. "You can't believe that, just because Jonas is in the vicinity, he had anything to do with what just happened?"

"Remember the last case he worked on?"

"Zachary Marshall was a psychopath and, thank God, Jonas was there to put an end to him."

"It nearly tore this town apart, let alone the department."

Frank stared at his former boss with disbelief. "Jonas is now a civilian who investigates low-level stuff like I do. I doubt some guy is going to blow up a building because Jonas caught him in bed with a mistress and advised the spouse of the infidelity. That sounds like paranoia to me. Besides, as far as we know, it could still just be a horrible accident."

Smythe shook his head. "It was no accident, Frank."

"How do you know?"

"My gut tells me so."

Officer Johnson returned and handed Frank a slip of paper. "Mr. Peters was taken to Riverside Community, and it appears his injuries are not life threatening."

"That's good news," replied Smythe. "Frank, what was the name of Jonas's girlfriend? The one he was to meet after leaving your office."

Frank thought a moment or two before answering. "Sam—Samantha, that's it, but I don't have a last name."

"Johnson?" Smythe asked.

"Got her," Johnson replied stopping his right index finger beside the only Samantha on the list.

Smythe didn't like the look on the young officer's face. "Well?"

Silence and then Frank was handed back the clipboard. "It's not good."

CHAPTER 4

Frank drove over to Riverside Community Hospital to check on the status of both Jonas and Samantha not knowing what he'd find. The couple of scratches on the sticky note given by Officer Johnson weren't enough to supply any details, but it was all he had at the moment.

Lieutenant Smythe stayed behind as Frank sped off in a westerly direction toward Magnolia and then spun south on the major thoroughfare for the short two-minute drive to the hospital. There was just too much work ahead to allow Smythe the luxury to leave the scene. Too many questions to answer, so he nodded at Frank and told him to check on the status of Jonas for him.

Frank would let him know what the prognosis on both victims were in a short time.

Nearly taking out the curb at 4445 Magnolia Avenue, Frank slammed his car into park behind a black and white, flashed his ID at a uniformed officer, and started for the doors to the emergency and trauma unit.

"Hell of a mess in there," stated the uniform.

Frank nodded. "Bet it is."

That was an understatement. Frank crossed through the double-wide automatic glass doors and was instantly belted by the cacophony of noise within the long hallway. Gurneys were lined up on both sides, people laying on them in obvious pain and shock, orderlies and nurses checking vitals, and doctors covered in bloodied scrubs yelling out strict orders on who was to be seen first and where. Triage was in full swing.

Frank had never seen anything like this in all his years in law enforcement.

It was certainly a mess but, after a moment or two, he realized what superb professionals he was watching. The chaos, and it certainly was, seemed orderly and precise. Glancing at the wounded from the explosive blast, Frank saw that a system had been set up in the emergency room with those severely injured being seen first and the lesser injuries being tended to quietly and respectfully, calming their natural fears of what they had just experienced.

Frank slowly walked through the crowd and nodded here and there at the familiar faces he knew from previous trips to the hospital in the past, keeping his eye out for someone, either hospital staff or law enforcement, who may be able to direct him to where either Jonas or Samantha were.

He moved back a few steps as a man on a gurney was slowly pushed by him being led by an orderly who was also holding onto an IV bottle.

The man expertly routed the gurney through the throng of busy people and was calmly telling the young woman with bandages around both eyes that everything would be fine and her family was being contacted at the moment.

The great thing about being one of the largest emergency facilities and level-two trauma centers in the Inland Empire was that the folks who worked here treated every patient as though they were the only patient.

Frank almost smiled as the gurney slid past him on the linoleum, remembering the countless times he had been there with gunshot victims. The hospital staff had always impressed him with their professionalism and kindness.

He had almost smiled—it didn't seem appropriate, though, at this point with so many human tragedies all about him.

"Who could have done this to so many innocents?" a man in his early thirties asked while cupping a bloody towel in both of his hands.

Frank glanced at the obviously distressed male and shrugged his shoulders. "There are evil people in the world."

"Evil," the man returned but then continued walking toward the exit of the emergency room as if in a trance. "How is that supposed to explain to my children why their mommy won't be coming home?"

In his many years patrolling the streets of Riverside both as a patrol officer and a homicide detective, Frank had seen brutal things. So many horrific episodes between humans that he knew he could never discuss with his family, not knowing if they would even believe him. Mothers killing their own children, fathers raping their own daughters, fiends hunting other humans for sport without regard for the victims, and the rest of the sick and perverted criminals he had come into contact with in this rather large but seemingly peaceful city in Southern California.

How many showers had he taken to try and rinse off the scum he felt covered him after talking with those animals? And always, when the tap was turned off, the filth was still there.

Of course, Frank hadn't discussed his average day with his family or friends. There were no average days in a cop's life but simply the understanding that there was indeed a very thin line protecting the sheep from the wolves.

The men and women who wore the uniform knew what they were getting themselves into when they hit the streets. Frank never whined about it but knew it was the job of the sheep dog to do their best to protect those who wouldn't, or couldn't, protect themselves.

The job was never easy but had to be done. Even Frank's older brother had publicly referred to him as a murderer in the social media after Frank had to take the life of a man who had just beaten his sixteen month old child to death with a frying pan. Frank hadn't wanted to, at least not consciously, but the rules called for taking the man into custody. The father must not have read the same rule book since he decided to pull out a knife and lunge at Frank when he was told he was under arrest. Frank didn't hesitate and pulled the trigger four times.

The last thing he had ever said to his brother ten years ago was that at least babies were now safe from that piece of shit.

He turned and watched as the glass doors slowly closed behind the grieving man. How he grieved for that father who had to go home and tell his children that their mother was brutally murdered by strangers simply because she had wanted a cup of coffee.

There was evil in the world.

"Aren't you Detective Sanders?"

The voice brought Frank to the present. A tall uniformed officer stood before him.

"Yes."

"Thought so," replied the officer with a worried expression over his face. "A Jonas Peters has been asking about you."

"Really?"

"Ordered me to go and find you more like," the officer said while shaking his head slightly. "Who is that guy?"

"Someone who, when he tells you to do something, you do it," Frank replied. "Take me to him, please."

The officer guided Frank down two separate hallways and out of the organized chaos to the rear of the critical care tower. Rooms were divided into what appeared to be, for the time being, areas for the victims who had not received life-threatening injuries but severe enough that they were being held at the hospital for an undetermined amount of time for observation. This section was a few yards from the more seriously injured in the ICU. Frank followed the officer and looked down a long corridor marked for the surgical intensive care unit. The SIC section was for the really life-threatened victims. The ones who needed to go under the scalpel immediately.

"Rather busy," Frank mentioned as the officer pointed to a small and sterile room equipped with two beds.

"Yeah. He's in the second bed."

"Thanks," Frank replied and then slowly entered into the room, passing the first bed where a woman was crying softly to herself with her head completely bandaged. No one was sitting in the chair beside her.

"You'll be fine," Frank said while stopping a moment and grasping the trembling hand of the woman. "Your family is on the way."

Frank wasn't sure that was true or not, but she obviously needed something. He hoped it hadn't been false hope.

He stopped at the foot of the other bed as he gazed at his friend lying with his eyes closed. Jonas's face was deeply bruised and a large gash had been sewn shut on the right cheek, making his friend look somewhat like Frankenstein.

"Frank," came a voice barely above a whisper. "How bad do I look?"

Frank was silent a moment, taking in the almost surreal image of a man who he thought had been invincible. It was difficult to see Jonas in such a condition. Almost hopeless it would seem.

"You look like hell."

"I've seen hell before," Jonas croaked out. "And I will send those responsible there personally, even if I have to go with them."

Frank moved closer to the left side of the bed and sat down on a pale brown cushioned chair for patient visitors. "Investigation has just started, Jonas. No idea what this was all about and Smythe hadn't heard anyone take claim for it yet."

Jonas tried to open his eyes but, with the attempt, only the left one peeped out a bit. His eyes were nearly glued shut. "Goddammit! That's why I asked for you and not any one on the force."

Frank felt his stomach flop a bit, and it wasn't the sight of Jonas making him suddenly queasy. Out at the command center, Smythe had mentioned that bad things happened when Jonas was around. Frank had dismissed it as just a statement made by a suddenly overtaxed officer in charge of what could be the worst manmade disasters in Riverside's history. There was no doubt, and Frank knew Smythe felt the same, that the explosion at the coffee shop was deliberately set. The only question had been by whom.

Now, as Frank stared at Jonas, he wondered if the lieutenant had been correct in his assumption. Was Jonas somehow linked to the explosion and thus the reason for the unsettling feeling in Frank's stomach? He was afraid he was going to learn something he may not want to learn.

"I'm not going to like this, am I?" Frank asked.

Jonas forced himself into more of a sitting position on the bed and groaned loudly at the sudden shot of pain that ran from his spine to his shoulders. "Damn, that hurts."

"Not surprised."

"Yeah," Jonas replied. "Where are my things?"

Frank didn't move nor look around. "You're not leaving here anytime soon. You look like shit."

"Feel worse but, no, I realize I've got some mending to do but just want to know where my personal belongings are."

Frank walked over to a small narrow closet on the other side of Jonas's bed and opened it up. "Well, there's some dirty clothes that smell like smoke, your wallet, some change, and oh yeah, your cell phone."

"That's it," Jonas said. "Take out the phone and look at the most recent text messages I've received."

Frank really didn't like the sound of this and wondered why his friend hadn't asked about Samantha. It wasn't like Jonas to forget about the woman he said he was madly in love with.

Standing by the closet, Frank grabbed up the phone but stopped and turned to face the one-eye-opened man on the bed.

"I already know about Sam," Jonas mumbled. "Took a bit of time but finally a doctor came in here and explained what happened to her."

"Well, I don't know."

"She's not dead, Frank. At least not now, but she's in extremely serious condition down the hall in surgery. She was almost on top of the blast. Thank God a brick pillar was between her the explosion. Still serious enough, but I think she'll live, or at least I'm praying she will."

Frank remained silent, remembering looking at the clipboard in the officer's hand at the command center and recalling it had listed Samantha as deceased.

Jonas caught the look on his friend's face. "Yeah, they thought she had been one of the fatalities, but as they had laid her body down, she gasped for breath and the paramedics worked on her and brought her here as one of the first arrivals. A lot of injuries but that pillar may have saved her life."

"That's good," Frank said. "That's real good, Jonas."

"Yeah, real good," Jonas replied sluggishly, suddenly feeling the exhaustion slam back into his whole being. "I don't want to be rude, Frank, but I think I need some rest."

Frank stayed a moment without moving and just watched as Jonas slipped into a much needed rest. He did look awful, and Frank said a silent prayer for his friend that he would heal quickly and the love of his life down the hall would do the same.

Frank wasn't much on praying but this day seemed a good one to say a few.

CHAPTER 5

Frank parked himself in the cafeteria of Riverside Community Hospital for the next, hour sipping on decent-but-cold coffee and wondering what the hell had happened in his city this day.

A tremendous explosion ripping apart a brick building and leaving more than a dozen fatalities and three times that many wounded. Who could have done that? Why would someone want to destroy a coffee shop? Who could be capable of manufacturing such an explosion?

The questions bounded through his brain like a loose locomotive without a track. Sure, he had seen bad things through the years, but this was the worst. Jonas once had a serial killer coming after him who left dead bodies spread through two different states, but that was one crazed man with a simple mission on his mind. To kill Detective Peters—luckily it was Zachary Marshall who ended up dying and not Jonas. But this was totally different.

Acts of terrorism happened in other places in the world, not here in the United States. Yes, he knew there had been instances since 9/11 but, overall, somewhat rare, considering the bad players in the world. There had been the tragedies in San Bernardino, Orlando, and Dallas to name just three, but today in Riverside would rank right up there with the others.

Who would claim responsibility for this newest terror?

He was brought out of his reverie by the orderly he had met while exiting Jonas's room a little over an hour earlier and had asked the woman if she wouldn't mind advising him when Samantha came out of surgery.

"Excuse me," said the pretty, but obviously tired, woman.

"Yes," he replied.

"Ms. Williams is out of surgery and has been moved to ICU."

Nodding, Frank stood up. "And?"

The woman stared back at Frank and then offered a slight grin. "She's in an induced coma and the surgeons are pretty certain she will recover but won't know for—a while. But I really shouldn't be telling you this since you are not family."

Frank hated doing it but he withdrew his wallet and showed his detective badge. Not his private detective badge but the badge he had carried while on duty with the Riverside Police Department. When a cop retired, they still carried a badge, though it did state retired on it.

"You're a detective?"

"Was and now am private, but as a courtesy, I'm doing some work for the department and need a few questions answered."

The woman mulled over what Frank had said and then rubbed her eyes. "What the hell?"

"Thanks," he replied while putting his wallet back into his pocket. "What injuries does she have?"

"Let's see, broken ribs, a fractured spine, possible neck injuries, and she had internal bleeding in her chest, but that was stopped. She'll be out of commission for quite a while, I'm afraid. Amazing, though."

"What is?"

"With all that damage she was able to talk a bit when they brought her in to the hospital."

"Yes."

"Sorry," she said while rubbing her eyes again while yawning. "Ms. Williams kept saying, actually mumbling— I hope Jonas is okay."

True love, he thought. "That's her fiancée or is going to be if I know the relationship. He's down the hall, badly hurt but not life threatening."

"That's good to hear."

"Can you take me to her?"

"She's in a coma and can't talk or hear you."

"I understand but I'd like to see her, if that's okay."

The woman looked around a bit and nodded. "I don't see any harm in that."

"Thanks, Jonas would want me to look in on her."

Frank nodded at the orderly, listened to the regulations of the hospital about visitors, and told her that he fully understood and that he would only be a moment or two. Regulations were regulations, and Frank, more than most, knew them like the back of his hand. How many witnesses and suspects had he watched and interviewed in the various intensive care wards in Riverside County during his years with the department? Too many to count, but one thing he had learned—a cop couldn't be a hard ass with hospital staff.

That might work in the Hollywood world but, in real life, when a doctor, nurse, or a pretty orderly like he was just talking to told you bye-bye, you found the exit.

Badges meant nothing in the workings of a hospital. Their job was to prolong life and not be lackeys for law enforcement. That said, Frank knew he had been offered a moment he was not entitled to. This was a favor by a tired, over-worked, and stressed young woman who only wanted this nightmare of a day over and realized, with his concern, Frank wanted nothing more than just to look in on a friend's fiancée.

It worked for both of them.

"I'll be a minute or two."

"Take your time, she's not going anywhere," the woman answered but immediately placed her right hand to her mouth. "God, that sounded awful, I'm so sorry."

"No, no apologies needed. You're tired and your day is not over by a long stretch and, in fact, Samantha is not going anywhere soon, is she?"

There was no reply but simply the young woman placing her left hand on Frank's right shoulder and nodding. In a moment, she was gone down the hallway to assist other patients or inquisitive family members over the day's events.

He wished her the best for whatever else this horrible day would wrought.

Walking toward the glass door of the ICU, Frank braced himself, not knowing what the view might be. He wasn't, in the slightest, weak-stomached like some of the cops he had worked with had been. In fact, he was the iron pit of the department. If an officer didn't want to see an autopsy, then they sent Frank in and he'd record, video, and take personal notes as the ME sliced and diced. He would then hand the information to sensitive-stomached detectives with the idea they would, in turn, buy him lunch after some pretty gruesome autopsies.

This was not one of those moments. As he entered the room and saw the outstretched unconscious woman before him, he momentarily lost his breath.

There were monitors all around the bed but only a small plastic mask over Samantha's nose and mouth. Frank couldn't help but realize how beautiful she was.

"No wonder Jonas loves you," Frank uttered then felt ashamed. "Sorry, I'm sure it's not just your looks. You have made my friend whole again—I thank you. He needs you more than you will ever imagine."

Frank took the next five minutes standing in the room, wishing the young woman would wake up and talk with him. No bruises, no blemishes to mark that she had been in a horrific accident. She simply seemed slumbering in a peaceful bliss.

He knew she wouldn't awaken. Her internal organs were in shatters, according to the orderly who had guided him to Samantha's room. This was touch and go for the next forty-eight hours and, no matter how excellent the surgeons and staff were at Riverside Community Hospital, this woman could also be dead very soon.

The blunt trauma from the explosion had caused intensive damage internally, even though the pillar she had been sitting in front of her had softened the blow externally. That was the good side of the event for Samantha. The bad side was that the surgeons had done their best, and now it was up to her own body to figure out the rest.

Live or die.

Doctors were not God but simply trying to mimic his work. He had the patent—they did not.

Frank walked back down the hallway, slowly pondering what his next step would be. Seemed simple enough—tell Jonas he had looked in on his girlfriend and give him an overview of her condition.

It wasn't going to be as simple as it seemed. How did you tell your friend, who was pretty badly injured himself, that the love of his life was in an induced coma, and the next forty-eight hours would determine if she would live or die?

Not simple at all.

"I'll tell you, Jonas, she is one beautiful woman who deserves better than you," Frank muttered to himself, knowing a sad attempt at humor would not be the way to open the conversation.

Within minutes, Frank found himself standing in front of Jonas's hospital bed and, a few moments later, Jonas opened his eyes to a narrow slit.

"Well?"

"You're awake."

Jonas slowly nodded his head. "Barely, some nurse just stopped by and added something to my IV. I think I'll be going off to slumber land soon."

"No problem," Frank replied softly. "I checked in on Samantha, and I have to tell you Jonas that if I didn't know any better, I would just think she was asleep."

"Beautiful, huh?"

"Stunning would be the word I would use to describe her—sorry."

A slight smile and then it was gone. "Can't be upset over a man clearly seeing what was in front of him, Frank."

"She's in an induced coma, Jonas. Pretty severe internal injuries—next forty-eight will be telling."

"Is she going to make it?"

Frank wasn't sure how to answer that, but the truth would have to do. "Not sure. The surgeons have done what they can, but there were a lot of injuries…"

Jonas was softly snoring so Frank just stood and watched his friend a few minutes and was somewhat glad the conversation didn't last longer than it had.

He wanted to believe the woman would recover fully, but only God knew if she would or not, and God wasn't telling anyone at this time.

Frank made a point to travel back to the command center to report to Smythe the physical and mental state of Jonas and Samantha. As he passed near the coffee shop where the explosion had taken place, he stopped and stared. Cadaver dogs were making the final walks through the debris but, at this point, the authorities were reasonably certain all victims had been identified and either sent to the hospitals or to the coroners. Rescue personnel were packing up their gear and getting ready to leave the scene. Taped off with thick yellow caution tape, the building and surrounding areas would be a crime scene for at least a week if not longer. Soon the site would be swarming with detectives and fire inspectors, looking for any clue possible to learn the identity of the fiend who delivered this disaster to Riverside. It would a time-consuming but necessary venture to bring justice to the victims.

Smythe wasn't at the command post.

"He drove back to the department for a briefing with the chief and the commanders of the other agencies. Not sure when he'll be back," Sergeant Chandler stated.

"No problem," Frank said. "I'll leave him a quick note and my number in case he wants to get a hold of me."

Chandler shook his head. "What a damn mess today."

Frank only nodded while handing the man a quickly jotted note. "Yeah."

"Worst part of it all is that no one has taken credit for this. Usually these assholes can't wait to contact us and tell us all about the reason they decided to take innocent lives."

"Nothing?"

"Not a peep."

"Thanks," Frank replied while slowly walking back to his office just a short distance from the command post.

Suddenly, Frank felt as though he was carrying a ton of bricks on his back. He was so tired—exhausted—but knew anyone would feel the same after the day he had experienced. Panic, dismay, cries of pain, and bleeding bodies were nothing new to the ex-Riverside Police Detective but never had he seen anything as horrific as what he had seen this day. The total wanton destruction of innocents was beyond the pale, to steal a saying from the Irish. What sick pieces of crap would bring down a building on top of people who were just enjoying themselves on a rather pleasant morning?

He knew the answer, but his mind was having trouble keeping up, and as he entered his office, the only thought he had was to close his eyes for a few minutes. A power nap was what he referred to those moments in the afternoon when things were quiet and he could catch up on some sleep.

Most of the time, sleep eluded Frank, and if he got three hours in a row during the night, he felt very fortunate. Once awake in the wee morning hours, it could take another two before dozing off again.

His demons were thick and many, as with most cops. Moments of doubt invaded his awake and not awake times—no cop ever wanted to kill another human being, but sometimes that deed had to be done and, when it was over, it wasn't over.

Two shootings in nearly thirty years was all Frank had done, but one ended in a man's life. It was one killing too many. Sure he had received slaps on the backs and a commendation, in reality, but when the darkness encroached in his bedroom, so did the self-doubts. Did he have to have pulled the trigger? If he had waited one more second, would the gunman have surrendered? The questions never went away, and neither did the guilt of killing another human.

Of course, as Frank took out his 9mm from his waist holster, placed it on top of the bureau, and sat back into the large leather chair behind his desk, he realized why sleep never was his ally. He could never forgive himself for the greatest loss of his life.

Alone at the age of fifty-four was not where someone wanted to find themselves but an incident nearly ten years previously had not given him a choice.

While on duty in Indio, just east of Palm Springs working a rock concert for extra pay as security, his wife and two children had decided to join him for some relaxation around the many pools and water parks.

That plan went awry when a drunk driver decided to enter Highway 10 west bound into the east bound traffic just east of Desert Hot Springs. Forty seconds later, the Ford Explorer was right into the path of Frank's family Honda.

In the wink of an eye, the Sanders family went from four to one.

He was alone, and thus why sleep was not a normal activity for him any longer.

Reaching into the desk drawer for the ever present bottle of Jack Daniels, he poured a short shot, enough for perhaps a nap, and then found himself suddenly awake.

The jolt of recognition came like a bolt of lightning. Instantly, he forgot about the glass of spirits and reached into his right front pants pocket. Taking out the cell phone he had gathered from Jonas's belongings at the hospital, he turned it on and then stared at it.

"What the hell did he say?"

He kept staring at the Android and tried to get his muddled brain back onto the conversation he had had with Jonas. Of course, it had not been much of a conversation but simply Jonas making somewhat understandable statements while drifting in and out of consciousness.

He mulled the thoughts over. "What about the cell phone?"

Hesitantly, Frank looked at Jonas's emails and felt like a voyeur.

Nothing of importance there, or at least nothing out of the ordinary registered as he scrolled down through a few business emails and the typical barrage of advertisements.

Punching up the text messages he stopped at the last two received.

"What the hell?" he exclaimed. "What is an Iquitos and why would Jonas seem to know."

The time of the received messages was mere seconds before the moment of the blast at the coffee shop earlier in the day. Frank had a piece of the puzzle but was not sure where it fit in the larger scheme of things.

Glancing down at the untouched shot of whiskey, Frank knew he had to drink it. A quick gulp and the fiery brown liquid was up and done his throat. Grimacing for just a second, he knew it was time to go to work. The nap would have to wait.

So would the demons.

CHAPTER 6

Iquitos, what the hell does that mean?" Lieutenant Smythe asked as he passed the phone back to Frank.

"It's the largest village in the world where the only way you can get there is by boat or by plane. On the Amazon River or something like that. No roads in or out."

Smythe stared at the man sitting across from him wondering what all this had to do with the bombing. "So, you came in here to tell me that on Jonas's phone you found those two text messages and that is the clue we may need to catch the perpetrators?"

Frank nodded. "Yes."

"But you don't know what it means."

"No I don't."

"And Jonas is still under sedation."

"Yes."

Smythe felt like shit. His desk was elbow deep with reports, the captain was chewing his ass for not having more information about who had done such a hideous thing, and now Frank Sanders was here with less than nothing.

"Perhaps Jonas was interested in a trip there."

Frank remained silent a moment before speaking. "Come on, Smythe, I'm not here to waste your time, but don't you think it's rather odd that Jonas would get these messages just moments before the blast? It was as though someone was blaming him for what was about to happen."

"Sorry, Frank, I know you wouldn't be here if you didn't have a good reason, and perhaps you're right. Jonas does seem to have a knack in being in places where dead turn up in ample numbers." He waved his hand just as Frank sat up straighter and was about to say something. "I know he's your friend, and I like him too, but you have to admit that trouble seems to follow Jonas."

Without being able to stop himself, Frank felt a small smile creep across his face. "Yeah, Jonas does know how to get in deep, doesn't he?"

"So, your theory?"

"Nothing yet until I can talk to Jonas," Frank responded. "Do you know anything he may have been involved with down in Peru on the Amazon."

Smythe shook his head. "I didn't even know a place called Iquitos existed until you came in and told me, let alone that it was on the Amazon. Sounds like a B-rated movie."

"Oh, I don't think this will turn out like that. This may be truly serious and give us answers on what happened to-day."

Rubbing his temples with both hands, Smythe closed his eyes. "God, I hope we get something before my ass is ten pounds lighter by all the chewing it's getting."

Frank stood to go. "I'll see what I can do."

"Frank."

"Yeah," Frank replied while heading for the door.

"Keep a leash on Jonas if it turns out he knows who did this, will you?"

"A muzzle is more like it."

Smythe didn't smile. "If he learns who did this to all those people and especially his girlfriend I'm afraid there will be a trail of dead bodies all leading back to our friend."

Frank nodded as he left the lieutenant's office.

Frank hated hospitals but then again who liked them? Perhaps doctors, nurses, and the rest who made their living here, but the average person hated them—what was there to love? A person didn't go to a hospital because they were feeling fine and dandy.

He toyed with the cell phone in his hand, looking at the two messages Jonas had received moments before downtown Riverside had changed forever. Over the past two hours, news came from the cities structural engineers that the buildings, one of which had once housed the Common Grounds coffee shop, would have to be razed.

Like many buildings in downtown Riverside they were old—some over a hundred years or more when the city was the center of one of the largest citrus belts in the nation. Of course, this was all because of a woman with a persistent personality and the understanding of how to grow plants. In 1873, Eliza Tibbets decided to experiment with two plantings of the seedless oranges grown in Bahia, Brazil. The results were outstanding and, in 1879, these oranges went on display at a public fair and received award after award, besides the fact the public wanted these oranges because of their shape, color, and the fact they were seedless. Within forty years, the now-named Washington Naval Orange was a booming thirty-million-dollar-per-year industry in the small city a scant fifty miles east of the Pacific Ocean.

With the influx of so much cash, the city grew very prosperous, and the downtown, along with the neighborhoods lining the nearby Santa Ana River, saw a building boom. Red brick buildings lined the boulevards, and the rich drove their horseless carriages in and around in a show of wealth.

And it was all because of a woman with a dream.

Frank looked down at the cell phone and wondered whatever happened to Tibbets—a few streets named after her that was all. His hobby was the history of his city, but that part he hadn't explored much. Sometime in the future he would look into it.

"Frank," a tired-sounding voice said, bringing him from the past to the present.

"Too bad about the building coming down," Frank said.

"What?"

"Never mind," Frank replied, knowing he had confused centuries for a moment. A nap would have done him some good.

Jonas forced himself up onto the larger of the two pillows behind his back. Surprisingly, he felt better than earlier but how much earlier he had no idea. "How long have I been out?"

"Not sure," Frank responded, truly not knowing. It was nearly ten in the evening, and even he had no idea how long he had been sitting by his friend's hospital bed. The growl from his stomach let him know that dinner had long been missed.

Jonas nodded. "I feel better."

"That's good."

"I'm ready to leave."

"That's bad." Frank held up his left hand. "You have some injuries, my friend, and I don't think your doctor will sign you out."

Jonas let a small smile cross his lips. "And you think that would stop me?"

Jonas was a very good-looking man of five feet eleven, probably bouncing in at a hundred seventy-five pounds, and was pushing every year of fifty, but Frank knew Jonas moved like a person twenty years younger. There was something about Jonas that people admired and feared.

Jonas was a good man, but not a nice man.

He'd give you the shirt off his back but would peal it off your dead body if you crossed him or a loved one.

That's why Frank never feared for his life while working with Jonas on the beat, but that changed when Jonas's partner Steve was killed during a bank robbery gone sour. Jonas was still the same sort of friend but now he had a dangerous edge to him that made even good acquaintances like Frank a bit wary.

No doctor would be able to stop him from leaving the hospital if he chose to. It would simply be Jonas's choice when he would leave or if he stayed. The plastic wrist band would not be a deterrent.

Frank shook his head. "Of course not, but, Jonas, you are hurt and not twenty-two anymore. As we get older, we need more time to heal."

"Thank you, Dr. Drew." Jonas smiled and Frank relaxed. "I'll be a good boy, but only for another day or so. I need to get on this and find out who's responsible."

"You know, the Riverside Police Department is pretty good about this sort of thing, and I hear the feds are now involved, believing it was a terrorist activity. Let them handle this and you take care of yourself and Samantha."

"She's okay then?" Jonas responded.

"Still in a coma but by my watch the next thirty-six hours will be the deciding factor."

"Sam's tough."

"Has to be to love you," Frank said.

"She's so beautiful and smart, Frank." Jonas closed his eyes. "I don't deserve her."

"Now, that is the most logical thing you have said to me all this time," Frank agreed.

Slowly, painfully, Jonas reached out his left arm for the small clear plastic cup filled with water and ice.

"Want me to get it."

Jonas shook his head, gritted his teeth, forced himself over to the edge of the bed, and shakily grasped the cup. A few sips and he smiled. "That was tough."

"It's a test."

"Did I pass?"

"We'll have to wait for the results since everything here is recorded and being watched."

"Damn NSA." Jonas chuckled while taking a sip of the cold water. God, he was thirsty. He drained the cup and placed it back on the ridged plastic table which slipped over the edge of the bed during meal times. This time, the movement didn't bother him much. "How is Sam really, Frank?"

Frank looked down into his lap. "She's doing the best we can hope for, Jonas. I actually spoke with her surgeon a little over an hour ago, and he seemed very pleased at her prognosis, given the severity of her internal injuries."

"Don't sugar-coat it."

Any other person would have been offended with Jonas's bluntness, but it was just his way. It didn't faze Frank at all.

"Tomorrow morning there will be more X-rays and a MRI, but he seems pretty optimistic about Sam's recovery. She's young, healthy, and probably wants to hang around a bit and maybe get hitched to this dufus of a private eye named Jonas Peters."

"I'm the medicine, all right," Jonas said while sitting up a bit straighter on the bed. The talking was doing him good and he was glad Frank was there to go back and forth with.

A few moments of silence followed while Frank stared at Jonas who had closed his eyes. "Are you feeling okay?"

"Yeah," Jonas said while looking at Frank. "You check my cell phone?"

Frank had been waiting for this but hadn't wanted to push the questioning until he knew for sure Jonas was up to the task. The surgeon might have been optimistic about Samantha but the doctor who had worked on Jonas had told Frank that, if he had struck that water fountain an inch or two to the right, Jonas would be in the morgue. A sharpened steel art work of a dolphin barely missed his main artery in the left leg. He would have bled out if a passerby hadn't used his own belt to cinch the wound. The doctor said Jonas needed bed rest for at least two weeks.

Frank hadn't had the heart to tell the physician that wasn't going to happen.

"I glanced at it and am confused," Frank replied. "What's this all about? This Iquitos obsession—"

"It's in the Amazon, Frank Sanders, and if you don't leave my brother alone right now, I will personally boot you there myself!" a woman's voice interrupted the two men's conversation.

"Ah, Jesus," Jonas moaned.

"The Almighty will not help him, Jonas, so don't even bother asking," the woman's voice continued.

"Maggie just entered the room, didn't she?" Frank asked while placing his hands over his face.

"The one and only," Jonas said while looking over Frank's shoulder at his younger sister who had entered the hospital room like a bull in a china shop.

"I tried to stop her, Jonas," stated Roger, Maggie's husband, who had stopped at the entrance to the room with both hands in the air as if to surrender. "Hey, Frank."

"Roger, Maggie," Frank said while standing up. "I'm outta here."

"Not yet, mister," Maggie said, walking up to Frank and throwing her arms around his neck. "Thanks for looking after this idiot."

"Somebody had to." Frank felt a sense of relief as Maggie let go and stared into his eyes.

"Do I get a hug?" Jonas asked.

Maggie ignored her brother and walked Frank to the door. "Will you two look in on Sam while I have a word with Jonas?"

Roger gently grabbed Frank's arm. "Best idea yet."

"Thanks," Maggie whispered as both men left. She turned toward her older brother and tried to put a stern look on her face.

It didn't work.

"I love you, little sister," Jonas said, smiling.

Maggie stood there a moment before the tears fell like a waterfall. "I am so mad at you!"

Jonas was nearly overwhelmed by the emotions from his sister. "I didn't blow up the building."

A snort and sniff from Maggie. "No, but I bet you know who did."

"Maggie." Jonas stared at his younger sister. "I'm not sure I'm strong enough to have this conversation." He knew what to expect next. Maggie Schmidt may be a petite woman, but she pulled no punches with her only sibling—she was not someone to take lightly.

"You really want to start there?" Maggie asked.

Jonas simply moaned, hoping it may lessen the barrage coming from the woman standing over him.

"Moan and groan all you want, mister but that doesn't impress me. As soon as we were notified of what had happened this morning, Roger hired a private plane for us to get out here as quickly as we could. Luckily, we were able to land at the Riverside Municipal Airport instead of Ontario."

"Lucky indeed."

"Now, Jonas," Maggie said, brushing away a sweep of her shoulder-length hair. "I was terrified when we heard about the explosion. The children wanted to fly out with us but I wasn't sure what to expect so I wouldn't let them come."

Jonas nodded. "Good."

Maggie was a very attractive woman in her late-forties who maintained her athletic body like a well-oiled clock. No diets for this woman. She simply watched what she ate and worked out at the large and very well appointed gym she had professionally set up in their rather upscale home in Scottsdale, Arizona.

Of course, the house had to be totally renovated a few years back when Jonas was still on the force in Riverside and a simple comment to a local news reporter about a murderer started an avalanche of killings which stretched across two states.

A bomb placed strategically near the front door of the Schmidt residence had done so much damage that the city engineers deemed the property uninhabitable. Roger wasn't thrilled at the costs of rebuilding, but Maggie was beside herself with the task. She made the house even more elegant and beautiful than it had been previously, if that had been possible in the exclusive neighborhood where Maggie resided with her husband and two children.

Jonas had seen the house a few times after the total remodel and knew his sister had done a marvelous job. He lived alone in a small house in Phelan, and his sister lived in nearly a mansion now.

No jealous feelings existed since he adored Maggie and her husband was a wonderful provider with his very well paid job as an investment broker.

No, Jonas was proud of both his sister and brother-in-law for their accomplishments.

"Good, do you know how hard it was for Tim and Annie not to come? There were tears and almost tantrums when I had to tell them what had happened. They adore you."

"And I them," Jonas responded, truly meaning it. His niece and nephew meant the world to him since he had no children. At least none alive.

Maggie sat down on the edge of the bed and held her brother's hand. "What happened?"

"I don't really know except I was walking from Frank's office to meet Sam when all of a sudden there was an explosion." He shrugged. "That's it."

"That's it?"

He nodded in return. "That's all I remember."

"Who did this, Jonas?"

"How would I know?"

"You know."

Maggie gently rubbed the back of Jonas's right hand. "My darling brother, if there's trouble, you're the first to figure out who did it."

"I will," he said softly.

"No idea yet?"

Jonas remained silent and looked into his sister's beautiful blue eyes. "Not yet, but there are things running through my brain and, when I figure it out, I'll know for sure."

"You look tired." Maggie patted his hand and laid it back onto Jonas's chest. "I'm going to check on Sam. We already spoke to her doctor, and everything is looking better than a few hours ago I guess. She's young and strong."

"That's what Frank said earlier."

Maggie dropped a million-dollar smile on her brother. "Better keep that hound dog away from her, Jonas. She's way too good for him."

Jonas sighed. "And me, too."

"No, you're a good man, but you just don't know how good."

"Thanks," Jonas replied, feeling his eyelids starting to fall. *What sort of drugs are they giving me that I can't keep awake more than a few moments at a time?*

"Jonas."

"Yesssh."

Maggie stared down at her brother as she heard his breathing start to get softer and deeper. "When you find out who did this to you and us, you kill all of them. You kill them all for what they have done, and then you get some peace."

Maggie felt a single tear roll down her cheek as she turned and left Jonas's hospital room.

CHAPTER 7

Frank needed a nap, big time. Glancing down at his watch, he realized it was nearing five in the morning and, for a guy like him, going nearly twenty-fours without sleep was not recommended. He tended to get a bit sour around the edges.

Grinning over at Jonas's sister, he felt every edge of tired.

"You're tired?" she asked.

"Exhausted, Maggie," Frank replied and nodded over at her husband, fast asleep on one of the waiting rooms sofas. "I think Roger has had it."

"Perpetually tired," Maggie said as she looked at the father of her two children. How she loved that man.

'He's a good guy."

"The best."

Maggie leaned across the chair she was sitting in and touched Frank's hand. "I really do appreciate what you've done for all of us, Frank."

"It wasn't anything."

"That's where you're wrong. You're a good friend to Jonas, and that makes you a better one to me."

Standing up, Frank knew it was time to go. An hour earlier, they had checked in on Jonas who was still fast asleep and on Samantha who was still critical but the words spoken by her surgeon were very encouraging. The woman was responding well to the surgery and medications, though still in an induced coma, and that was very promising. Even though the forty-eight hours were still a ways off, the doctor believed the worst was behind Samantha, and that had made them all breathe a sigh of relief.

This day needed a happy ending for someone.

"Leaving?"

"I've got to, Maggie," Frank said. "It's been a tough day and night, and I need some rest. I'll stop by later this afternoon to check on Jonas and Sam, but you two should take off also. Nothing can be done now, and you'll need your strength when Jonas gets up and about."

"He'll find them, won't he?"

"Who?" Frank asked but knew exactly the "who" Maggie was talking about.

In the hours they had spent together, not once did Maggie bring up the subject of who had been behind the explosion, and Frank had not offered any information, though that was easy with him not knowing anything really. The cell phone had not been mentioned.

That would have to wait until he had a chance to speak with Jonas—strange that the department hadn't been that interested in it, but Frank felt that might have to be put down as an overwhelmed lieutenant with too many things on his plate at the time.

He was sure Smythe would remember their conversation, and the questions concerning Jonas's phone would come. Until then, Frank wasn't about to say a thing to anyone except Jonas.

Maggie only winked and held out her hand. "I'll talk to you later. Boy, you law enforcement guys really hold things tight to the chest, don't you?"

Frank held onto the pretty woman's hand a moment and then smiled slightly. "Not sure what you mean, Maggie. I'm as open as a book."

"Yeah," she replied, watching the detective leave the lobby and head for the entrance of the hospital. "A book written in a pirate's code."

The rising sun through the lobby windows reminded Maggie of how tired she suddenly was. Frank had been correct about everyone needing rest if they were going to be functional in the upcoming days and, as she looked at her lightly snoring husband, knew he had been right. She would look in on both of Jonas and Samantha before waking Roger and suggesting they head over to the Sheraton to grab a room. A hot shower, quick phone call to check on her children, and a few hours' sleep should go a long way, she thought, getting up and walking down the hallway to the critical care section where Samantha was located.

"You're not just getting here?" came a familiar voice over Maggie's shoulder.

Turning around, Maggie saw Doctor Scarlet Rose looking fresh and proper with her white jacket and stethoscope around her neck. She was actually quite an attractive woman, Maggie thought, smiling. She knew this surgeon must turn every male head when she walked into the room. Seeing how poised and together the younger woman was made Maggie feel a bit self-conscious.

Maggie shook her head. "No, been here all night just in case I was needed."

"Looks as though you could use some rest," replied Scarlet Rose as she picked up a clipboard from the nurses station in the critical care wing.

"You read my mind. Going to head for a hotel right after checking on both Jonas and Sam—my husband is already camped out in the lobby, but I just have never enjoyed being in a hospital enough to be able to sleep."

"I don't think anyone is ever that full of joy to be here." The doctor smiled then suddenly stopped. "Look, it's none of my business, but you should get some rest as soon as possible. You have been put through a lot of stress, and that is very unhealthy for an individual."

Maggie felt insulted for a moment and was about to shoot something rather catty back at this beautiful surgeon but bit her tongue. The woman was one-hundred-percent correct. "Yes, I realize that, but I would feel guilty just leaving while Jonas and Sam are both here."

"Come back later…say around three this afternoon…and I'll have a complete update for you on both patients." Scarlet Rose stated. "You're not going to do them any good being an exhausted mess—they'll need someone chipper, if I may say so."

"If I wasn't so tired, I could almost get angry with that statement but know you are one-hundred-percent correct. You seem so cool and collected, besides being young and beautiful, while I feel so tired and just a mess, but I will abide by the doctor's orders."

"Good." Scarlet Rose held out her hand.

"Thanks," Maggie replied, shaking the doctor's hand. She turned and headed back to the lobby to wake up Roger.

"Oh, Mrs. Schmidt?"

"Yes," Maggie answered, while turning around.

"I'm not really that young," Scarlet Rose said.

Maggie laughed. "Now, I really hate you."

Roger didn't bother with a shower but simply climbed beneath the coverlet of the king-sized bed in the room he had rented at the Sheraton and was soon asleep.

"Of course, within seconds." Maggie glanced over at the bed, astonished time and again at how her husband could fall asleep as quickly as he did. "To have that power."

Fifteen minutes after speaking with her children whom she left in the care of friends in Scottsdale, Maggie found herself standing beneath a blazing hot stream of water within the floor-to-ceiling-tiled shower of the suite. The pulsating droplets felt good and almost as though they were washing away the strain of the past day from her very person.

Suddenly the water she felt on her face was her own tears. She slowly sank to the floor and gave in to the torrent she had been holding back ever since they had received the first phone call involving her brother. She just couldn't lose him. Except for Roger and the children, Jonas was the only family she had left.

The crying jag continued and, within moments, Maggie thought back to the words spoken by Doctor Scarlet Rose about the stress she had been under.

Maggie sobbed louder. "And she's smart too."

CHAPTER 8

Five hours later, Maggie stepped back into Jonas's room and saw her brother's bed empty. Fear instantly ravaged her.

"Your brother is one tough guy."

Turning, Maggie smiled as Dr. Scarlet Rose entered the room quietly behind her. "That he is."

Shaking hands, the two women stared silently at each other for a moment. "So are you."

"You wouldn't have said that a few hours ago when I was crying myself into hysteria in the shower at the hotel."

Scarlet Rose let go of Maggie's hand and smiled. "We all need that once in a while—sort of balances the hormones, I think."

"Is that a professional opinion?"

"Nope, simply one female to another," Scarlet Rose said, walking over to the chart at the foot of Jonas's bed. Making a quick notation, she turned and faced Maggie. "He's taken to sitting beside Samantha's bed at this time. I had an orderly try to stop him about two hours ago but he simply got out of bed and hobbled down the hallway, taking his IV with him."

"The orderly didn't stop him?"

Scarlet Rose shook her head. "Not once he saw the look in your brother's eyes."

"Smart man," Maggie replied. "How's he doing?"

"He'll be fine but sore for a while and waiting for good news."

"Yes." Maggie breathed. "We all are."

"It will take longer, but I've spoken to her attending physician, and there shouldn't be many complications in the healing process. She's one lucky person."

"Yes, she is," Maggie said, feeling an overwhelming sense of peace suddenly overtake her. The two most important people outside of Roger and the children were going to be fine. She couldn't have asked for any better news.

"Of course, there will be physical therapy for both of them."

"At least for Sam," Maggie returned. "Jonas won't go along with it."

"Then he won't mend very quickly, I'm afraid, and could suffer with long term stiffness in the damaged tissue on his left arm."

Maggie nodded. "I'm glad it's not his other arm."

"Why is that?" Scarlet Rose asked.

Maggie grinned. "He shoots with his right."

"I see. Would you like me to take you to him in Samantha's room?"

"No, you're busy, Doctor. I know the way and thank you so much for what you have done for both of them."

"You're welcome, but with Jonas—I'm afraid he doesn't follow doctor's orders very well."

"That's my brother, but don't think for a moment he doesn't appreciate all you did for him—I know he does."

Scarlet Rose watched Maggie walk out of the room and head toward the Intensive Care Unit wondering if she may be working on Jonas Peters again sometime in the near future.

Frank looked at the cell phone again and cursed his luck at not being able to trace the text messages Jonas had received just prior to the explosion. He knew they were the key, even though it was downplayed by the department. Jonas would know who had sent them and why, but Frank hadn't had the time to return to the hospital yet since he had been busy all afternoon, trying this contact and that contact to get the information he needed.

Finally, a friend of his at Verizon told him the hard truth.

"Frank, I've gone over this a dozen times with you. There's no way to trace the messages back to the sender. Sorry, but what I found out is that whoever sent them knew how to bounce across the towers like a professional. That person could be anywhere in the world."

"Not possible, Tony." Frank had sat up straighter in his chair. "The guy had to be on the scene to know my friend was nearly at the coffee shop to ignite that charge. There's no other way."

"Well, if he was, I can't determine where he may have been and, yes, that makes sense, but again, I can't get a lock. Maybe he used a remote camera on the building and knew when to ignite the explosive."

"Nah, nothing like that was found," Frank replied. "Thanks, though, for everything."

"I wish I could have been more help than I was just now.

"Yeah, me too," Frank replied, hanging up the phone.

Tony Hawkins was one of the best in the business, and if he couldn't locate and lock onto a signal bouncing here and there, then no one could. Frank always wondered why Tony had left working for the National Security Agency and gone the private route, but it could have been the Snowden fiasco. Tony didn't seem to like all the information the government kept on its own citizens. He believed in the privacy of citizens—period.

"Well, if I'm going to stay in the field then I may as well get paid better than working for a governmental agency," Frank remembered Tony telling him at the time he made the move from the NSA to Verizon as one of their top trouble-shooters.

Frank wasn't sure that Tony had left the agency completely. The NSA weren't exactly thrilled when one of its own left and went into private practice. Perhaps Tony still moon-lighted for his previous employer—looking for true bad guys and not just the everyday man or woman on the street. That would be more Tony's style. Who knew how much a corporation like Verizon might have to do with the government behind closed doors? Probably nothing, but who knew in this new world of non-transparency transparency?

Frank stared at Jonas's phone as if the inert object would suddenly come alive with all the information he had wanted to glean from it.

It just stared back at him.

"God, I hate this," he said, laying the phone down and picking up his office phone as it started to ring.

"Frank, it's Maggie. Jonas is doing well but a little stubborn about going back to his room and leaving Sam alone. Any chance you can come back to the hospital?"

He wanted to reply that he had a hot date and couldn't make it, but he had to be serious with himself and knew he had nothing on his plate. The few dates he had had since his wife and children were killed in an auto accident years ago had never turned into anything of significance, and he was glad. Alone but never lonely was his motto. It wasn't as if he felt he was cheating on his spouse, but no one had ever come close to her qualities. A glass of wine here and there, and that was it.

He was not a romantic but had truly loved the mother of his children and the next Mrs. Sanders had a high hurdle to overcome. In a way, he hoped no one would be able to jump that high.

"I'll be there within fifteen minutes and try to put a lasso around that brother of yours."

"Sure, easy for you with the carefree life of a bachelor and no worries about family," Maggie replied. "Jesus, Frank I didn't mean that—I mean—"

Frank shrugged his shoulders but still felt the hole in his heart. "It's been a long time, and we all forget—no problem."

"I'm so sorry."

"Be there in a shake," Frank replied.

As he was locking his office, Frank silently wished sometimes he could forget but silently scolded himself. *I could never forget my wife and babies. Never!*

Frank found Jonas sitting on the edge of his bed, desperately trying to tug on a pair of Nike's. Maggie was standing beside him with anger in her eyes. Roger was simply sitting in a chair on the opposite side of the room.

"What are you doing?" Frank asked after taking in the scene for a moment.

Jonas swore and then threw the tennis shoe onto the floor. "Trying to put on these damn shoes, but it seems my feet have swollen."

"You pick up an accent while I've been gone?" Frank asked.

Maggie turned to face him, and Roger silently shrugged his shoulders.

"What?" Jonas snapped.

"You sounded like you had a mouthful of marbles just then."

"Damn medication, I guess." Jonas sighed and then let his shoulders sink. "I need to get out of here."

"I've tried telling him he can't until the doctor says it's okay," Maggie stated.

"I've echoed that," Roger said from his side of the room.

"And I've heard you both, and now I suppose I'll hear from Frank just as well," Jonas replied.

"Not if you don't want me to," Frank said as he walked over and picked up the discarded shoes. "Here, I'll even help you put these back on. May be a tight fit, but with both of us trying, we should be able to slip your Manatee foot in there."

A slight chuckle came out of Jonas as he waved his arms in the air. "I got it from all of you, and know I should wait to be released, but there are things that need to be done."

"The department is handling the investigation."

Jonas stared hard at Frank. "Do they know everything?"

"At this point they don't know anything."

"What about my phone?"

"What about your phone?" Frank replied, nodding at both Roger and Maggie.

Maggie stomped her right foot. "What the heck is going on here? Roger, can you make sense out of what they are saying or implying?"

Roger stood up, brushed the wrinkles out of his slacks, and calmly walked over to his wife. "Yes, my dear, they want to talk alone. How about I purchase you a cup of coffee downstairs and give these two men a chance to speak?"

"I don't want to leave," Maggie snapped. "I want to know what's going on."

Roger gently grabbed Maggie's right arm. She looked up at him but didn't yank her arm away as she felt like doing. "Maggie—please."

"What is going on?"

"I believe, if I may play psychologist for a moment, is that they are trying to keep us safe by not spilling the beans. Correct, gentlemen?"

"Yeah," Frank responded while Jonas looked over at his brother-in-law and nodded slowly.

"I will never understand this constant need for secrecy with cops," Maggie uttered, turned on her heels, and walked from the room.

"And neither will I, my love, but I do appreciate it."

"Thanks, Roger," Jonas stated.

"No, thank you two."

When they were alone Frank went over and closed the door to the room for a little added privacy. "I have your phone and already gave the information to a friend of mine at Verizon, and nada."

"You have it? I thought you would give it to the department," Jonas replied.

"I started to but the lieutenant seemed awfully busy and uninterested, so I decided to keep it a while for a little private snooping. Don't hate me, Jonas."

A slight smile spread across Jonas's face. "Your buddy couldn't find anything at all?"

Frank shook his head. "The signal could have been local or in Africa—who knows with this sort of technology? But the one thing for sure is that whoever set the explosion off did not want to be found. We'll give the lieutenant a call, and I'll deliver it early this evening."

"Good," Jonas responded. "Are you going to help me with those shoes?"

"I only said that to make a point."

"And that is?"

"For you to stop being an asshole and realize you're too banged up to leave and possibly get into more trouble."

"My nature."

"Well, natures can change," Frank responded. "Maggie loves you and wants you well and, by the way, you have a wonderful woman down the hall who needs you around to help take care of her once she's released also."

Jonas shifted his weight and settled against the pillows. "Okay, one more night, and then I'm out of here."

"Your face will still be red and puffy, but your eyes do look clearer and not so swollen as yesterday."

"It's been over twenty-four hours, Frank, and I heal quickly."

"And the doc wanted you to stay at least three to four days until she was sure you were ready for the real world."

"Are any of us ready for that?" Jonas questioned.

"Point taken," Frank replied. "Now, just because my guy couldn't figure out the perp who did this, you probably have an idea, or you wouldn't have told me to take your phone yesterday morning."

"I was pretty fuzzy, and I'm not a hundred percent at this moment either."

"But enough percent to know the key was the phone, correct?"

Jonas remained silent a moment. "Did you check the text messages?"

"You told me to but it made no sense to me," Frank said. "Iquitos—looked it up and it's in Peru by the Amazon. What's that got to do with blowing up a building and killing people?"

"What about the second text?"

Frank thought a moment. "You mean, 'Of course you do'?"

"Yeah, that's it."

"What's it mean?"

"Not clear, but I have an idea."

"You going to share that idea or not?"

Jonas looked at his old friend for a few moments and then shook his head. "I don't think so, Frank. Not now least wise."

"Jonas for God's sake—"

Jonas interrupted. "Frank, listen to me. If it turns out to be what I think it could be, then it will be too dangerous for you to know."

"There were a lot of its in that sentence, Jonas."

"Frank, I may know what this is about perhaps—not sure though, and I don't want to get you tangled into a web. I promise once I find out, I will let you know."

"You promise?"

Jonas nodded. "Of course, if it's what I think it may be, then I will truly count on your help."

"You know you can do that."

"I'll need to, Frank," Jonas said. "I'll be putting those I love under your care to keep them alive."

"Jesus," Frank hissed.

"I hope he'll help, Frank, but I'm going to end this before it gets too out of control."

As Frank promised he dropped off Jonas's cell phone to Lieutenant Smythe—of course after Jonas made sure to clone it to another phone.

"Never know how long they may keep it before giving it back," Jonas had said, handing the phone back to Frank at the hospital.

"You do know this stuff," Frank replied, suddenly very impressed with his friend's ability to simply clone a phone within seconds. "Where did you learn to do that?"

"YouTube and other places."

Frank eyed his friend. "And other places?"

"Yeah," Jonas said. "I'll stay the night here, but I need to get moving to find out who is behind this tomorrow."

"How do I get in touch with you?"

Jonas looked Frank in the eyes and shook his head. "I'll get in touch with you and not vice versa. Remember what I said about keeping my family safe?"

"This is getting to sound like some damn Tom Clancy novel."

"Perhaps, but I have to do it my way. Besides, Clancy would have a protagonist a lot smarter and better looking than me."

"Probably right, but you never cease to amaze me, my friend."

"Me neither," Jonas said, patting Frank on the right shoulder. "Now get out of here and deliver that phone to

Smythe and perhaps they can come up with something your buddy at Verizon couldn't."

"Doubt it but I told him I would drop it off."

"So, how's he doing," Smythe asked, tossing the phone onto his desk top.

Frank looked at the tall and thin man in front of him and shrugged his shoulders. "He's getting better by the minute—man, that guy heals quickly, and he's determined to get back to work as fast as he can."

"You mean he's ready for some more divorce cases or whatever you private eyes work on."

That was an unusual tone for Smythe to use with Frank. Normally, he was friendly but, at the moment, Frank felt he was being dismissed as just another license-carrying private detective who had no business doing police work. Perhaps, he was tired and took the lieutenant the wrong way. "Well, I think he wants to make sure Samantha is better before stepping out and trying to find out who was behind this explosion which nearly took both their lives."

"And over two dozen citizens, as well as those injured!"

"That's what I meant," Frank defended himself. No, Smythe was definitely acting very strange at this moment.

"You advise Detective Peters that this case will be handled strictly by this department and the appropriate federal agencies. He is not to get involved. I have his cell phone, and if it turns out that the person who texted him that strange message had anything to do with this tragedy, then at that time only will I be calling Jonas into the office."

Frank had nothing to say but simply stared at his old commander. Smythe said nothing further. He simply sat down behind his desk and picked up the phone.

"Is there anything else?"

"Nope, that's all I needed," Frank stated and turned on his heels.

What the hell is going on around here?

Frank found himself sipping a cold Shock Top at a local watering hole, wondering what was going on in the city of Riverside. A little over forty-eight hours and he felt as though he knew less than when the explosion first ripped the city apart. The blast had been carried on nearly every news-paper front page for the past two days and vans from CNN, FOX, and other cable outlets—besides the local television stations—had been hovering about city hall, the police department, and the hospitals where the victims were recovering just to grab a line or two from anyone willing to talk. Glancing up at the flat screen behind the bar, he recognized the pretty brunette from FOX News discussing the very thing that was currently on his mind.

"A local reporter from Riverside has stated to our very own Roger Newcomb that the bomb blast which killed more than two dozen people and injured twice that number has not yet been claimed by anyone or any organization."

''That's right, Cynthia,'' the tieless-but-suit-jacketed reporter replied. "In a case like this, the authorities are quick to mention who planned and pulled off such an explosion, especially one that tragically killed so many innocent civilians, but no such information as of now."

"Why is that, Roger?"

"That's the rub, Cynthia," Newcomb responded. "It seems that no one has taken credit for the explosion. That itself seems rather strange. I've covered these sorts of terror attacks from around the world in the past dozen years, and almost immediately some group has laid claim to the destruction."

"And why hasn't anyone taken responsibility? Is it terrorism or a simple but horrific accident, like a gas leak explosion?"

"No, the idea of an accident has been ruled out with the explosive experts combing the wreckage and locating the remains of the explosive device. No doubt it was purposefully set to explode with a triggering device like a cell phone but the question still remains on who did it and why. It is very strange, to say the least, that no credible source is able to say who conducted such a barbaric act on innocent people simply having a coffee."

"Strange doesn't seem to be the half of it," finished the television anchor.

Damn good looking woman, Frank thought while taking another pull on the amber-colored drink in his mug. And right on point.

He had worked some odd cases in the years he had been on the police force but never an intentional explosion of this magnitude. During those years, part of his duty was attending different conferences around the United States and Europe where discussions of possible home-grown or foreigner-involved terrorist attacks took place. Most experts concluded, and he concurred with them, that these sorts of acts would occur in the United States on an ongoing basis and would probably ramp up over time. Not a hopeful scenario but one he knew was becoming truer and truer with each passing year, especially with the groups running ram shod in the middle east and Africa. It seemed the suicide bombers and bloody militias were everywhere when one read the newspaper or turned on the television.

It had only been a few years since a middle school in Victorville, not fifty miles north of Riverside, had been taken over by a group of Islamic terrorists, leaving a lot of bodies in their path before being killed by law enforcement. That was a shocker for every American to know that even a school was a target by these crazed barbarians. Luckily, it hadn't turned out as bad as it could have been but it still tragic enough with the few deaths that had visited the small city to the north.

Soft targets are abundant for those looking.

Still though, at least there, it was quickly known who the perpetrators were and even their illogical demands dictated to the authorities were out in the news before the terrorists' bodies were cold. But this was different.

No one claimed responsibility. As the FOX News anchor had stated—strange doesn't seem to be the half of it.

"Frank, another round?" asked the bartender as he casually wiped the counter top.

Frank stared down from the television and into his beer. "Yeah, I think so, but let's try something a little different."

"A Stella?"

"That's good," Frank returned, trying to puzzle something out in his mind.

"You're quiet tonight, Frank. Does it have anything to do with the explosion the other day?"

He looked up at Benny and nodded his head. "Yeah, actually it does."

Benny stood there wiping the counter after placing the new glass of beer down in front of his only customer for the moment. "What's that?"

"I'm not privy to the investigation but doesn't it seem like someone would have taken credit for the bomb blast by now?"

"I own a tavern, Frankie-Boy, and don't know the world of the cop mind."

"Come on, Benny," Frank responded. "You've been around cops all your life—your old man was a detective and so was your uncle back in New York. This bar has had more flat foots walking through here than most beats, so don't tell me you don't know anything about law enforcement. You know what I'm asking."

"Yeah, suppose I do," Benny said, suddenly stopping with the wiping.

Frank eyed him carefully.

"With all the crap in the Middle-East still going strong and those ISIS assholes not being put away for good along with the Taliban or Al-Qaeda and the rest of the fuckers who only want to put Americans in the grave, it does surprise me no one has laid claim. Not that I like it but from what I heard, the explosive device was pretty sophisticated to do the damage it was supposed to."

Not quite, since Jonas is still alive.

"So why hasn't anyone?"

"You tell me, Frank."

"I don't know."

Benny wiped the top once more and then headed down the bar where two new customers had just seated themselves. "And that's the strange side, Frank—neither do I."

CHAPTER 9

Jonas had seen and felt so much misery in his life that, for a moment, he wondered why his cheeks were suddenly wet. Reaching up his right hand, he remembered the droplets touching his fingers were tears.

I think I've forgotten.

He stared at Samantha lying almost lifeless upon the hospital bed.

She reminded him of a story he used to read to his daughter before he lost her. Sleeping Beauty. Stacy loved the story of a beautiful princess waiting for her knight in shining armor.

How many times had Jonas read and read and read that story to his own little princess before finally the fairy would drop the right amount of dust into her eyes lulling her into a young child's sleep?

He couldn't remember and never wanted the exact count. He lost her to a crazed addict's bullet when she was eight years old, and though he only tried to recount the happy times, the vision of half her head being blown away haunted him day and night.

Jonas swore then when she was killed he would never forgive himself for not protecting her as a "real" father would have in that convenience store, and to this day he hadn't.

He had kept his promise.

A raspy breath of air brought Jonas out of his usual visions of the past and a razor shot of concern ran through his spine as he bolted up in his seat and found himself on his feet.

"That's a good sign, so relax," a voice said from behind him. "It means she's trying to breathe on her own, instead of letting the machine do it for her."

Jonas didn't turn. He nodded but the adrenalin was pumping through at an accelerated rate.

Doctor Scarlet Rose stopped by Samantha's bed and stared at Jonas. "That is if you know what it means to relax."

"Never had much time for that."

"You should try it some time."

"You ever killed a person, been shot at, or watched loved ones die in front of you?"

Scarlet Rose shook her head slowly. "Luckily, no."

"The problem is when you have, then there will be no relaxing," Jonas replied. "And I hope forever."

"You'll give yourself a heart attack."

"If that were only true."

The doctor looked at Samantha's chart, quickly read over the latest results written down, and turned to Jonas. "You know, your fiancée isn't even my patient, but because you are mine, her surgeon has allowed me to spend a lot of time down here checking on her. Trust me, as I understand in your own profession, us professionals don't like sharing with others in the same field. Is that true?"

"Not if we want to share information."

"He's her surgeon," Scarlet Rose replied. "He doesn't have to give me anything."

"Then why?"

"I'm wondering at this point why myself," she said. "I don't want you to die of a heart attack. I wished you would have stayed in your bed instead of stumbling down the long hallways to see Sam. I don't know—I'm your damn doctor and want the best for you. Seems simple, doesn't it?"

Jonas thought a moment, just staring at the woman lying on the bed who had brought him back to life after the terror Zachary Marshall had caused, and then turned to Scarlet Rose. "I don't belong here," Jonas stated. "I'm fine and need to get on the road to find the fiends that did this."

"You read a lot?"

"What?"

"Do you read a lot?"

"I guess for the average guy," Jonas responded, wondering where this was going.

"There are no average guys. At least an average guy that reads. But most people don't use the word 'fiends' unless they are well read," Scarlet Rose responded. "They would say bad guy, perpetrator, killer, or many other descriptions, but you used fiend."

"I got lucky using an educated term."

"You're not lucky," she stated. "You don't believe in luck but just getting out there and finishing the job. That's good, but luck has nothing to do with it. You're educated—be that college or self-taught—but you are educated."

"Doctor," Jonas said with his voice rather low. "Where is this going?"

"Where this is going," she replied, "is the fact that I have spent the last few hours with your sister."

"Oh, God."

"No, she is not but, like you, she is very smart and probably well read."

"Her nose was always between the covers of some book," Jonas stated, giving Samantha another look before turning his full attention to the doctor.

"Ah, a woman after my own heart," Scarlet Rose said with a smile. "And also very astute when it comes to her only sibling, which is you."

He didn't say anything. He didn't need to, just like when Maggie started talking and got an interested audience such as this Doctor Scarlet Rose.

"Ah, silence," Scarlet Rose said. "Let me tell you that you are very fortunate to have a sibling who loves you so much that she shared just about everything about you to your doctor. Maggie, if I may call her that, loves you more than you can ever imagine, and all she cares about is your happiness."

"I know that," Jonas snapped. "I love her too and would do anything for her and her family to keep them safe."

Scarlet Rose nodded. "You don't see how lucky you are, do you?"

"What do you mean?"

"I have a sibling." Scarlet Rose's voice dropped suddenly lower to the point that Jonas hoped he could hear her over the respirator attached to Samantha. "I had a sister once, she's still alive but she died when my mother died."

Jonas didn't reply but only stared at the very attractive woman before him. He knew not to interrupt a person when they started speaking freely and not encouraged by another party. It was just plain sensible detective work.

"We had been close once," Scarlet Rose said, "I think, but in the past couple of years I am starting to doubt my recollections about that closeness. You see, she was ten years older than I and we lost our father when I was young.

I was devastated since I adored my daddy but I saw my sister change over the past ten years. My mother who was developing Alzheimer's at a relatively young age along with other health issues relied more and more on my sister to pay her bills, do her grocery shopping, and the other things that make an everyday life every day. Unbeknownst to me, my sister was stealing money from my mother's bank account each month. Later, I learned she had taken over seventy thousand dollars out in one year. I should have been suspicious since my sister was divorced, didn't have much money as far as I knew, but yet was traveling the world. I didn't question it until she went for full legal custody of my mother and her finances."

"A red flag, huh?" Jonas asked.

"It was like being kicked in the head by a mule." Scarlet Rose shook her head. "If I had only paid attention to what was happening more fully than being so interested in my new medical practice, I would have been able to stop what was about to happen."

"And that is?" Jonas asked turning back slowly to see Samantha's face. *I don't deserve her.*

"That my sister killed my mother to get the remaining amount of her finances."

That perked Jonas's ears up. "Killed her?"

"Well, nothing a detective like you could claim since as far as I am concerned it was gross negligence to her health issues but, by the time, mother had passed and was cremated, not my choice but my sister's, there wasn't much I could do."

"Did your mother die at home?"

"No, my sister had placed her in a home in Corona after her Alzheimer's and other issues had gotten worse. I blame myself but had trusted my sister to do the best for my mother. She lasted less than a year."

"Trusting isn't always the best thing, is it?"

"It should have been."

"But it wasn't."

"You are blunt," Scarlet Rose responded. "Just as Maggie said you would be."

"I hate that term, but yes, I tend to be brutally honest." Jonas nodded. "Your sister sounds like a peach and, hopefully, she will get what she deserves. So, good Doctor, what was the point of this story? I mean, I am sorry that you had such a worthless and rotten sibling but, unfortunately, it's simply a game of genetics that determines who we have or not have as a brother or sister."

"Educated," Scarlet Rose said, nodding. "The point, Detective, is you have a wonderful sister who loves you and wants you to take care of yourself. That's all, and something that I never truly had but simply a sibling who was selfish, egotistical, and a liar. You are very lucky."

"That's all?" Jonas asked.

Shaking her head, Scarlet Rose leaned against the door-frame to the room and grinned. "She also asked if I would release you so you could attend to business."

"And that business would be what?"

Scarlet Rose did not respond but went to the head of Samantha's bed and looked into the young woman's eyes. "You know, at this point she is only asleep. Induced perhaps but what I've learned from the surgeon and her charts is that she is one extremely fortunate woman. She will wake up soon, perhaps in a week and will have to be told what happened to her."

"That's great news, "Jonas responded, feeling as though a thousand pounds of steel had been lifted off his chest.

"Medical procedures are terrific, Jonas," she stated. "But there's one thing we can't do for her when she wakes up."

Jonas let a few moments slip by before he spoke again. "What's that?"

"To explain why this happened to her. Only you can."

"How?" Jonas asked, rather confused at this point.

"By signing the hospital release forms for you," Scarlet Rose replied.

Jonas didn't respond.

"Yes, Maggie said you wouldn't say a thing at that news," Scarlet Rose said. "She knew you would simply take the release as an affirmation of the job ahead."

"Affirmation?"

"To find those that did this to us and bring them to your justice."

"What about your Hippocratic oath." Jonas could even hear his own voice take on a tone of revenge.

"As a physician, I will do my utmost to heal those within my reach," Scarlet Rose replied. "Those out of reach of my arms will have to deal with God or you first."

"Where's Roger?" Jonas asked as he walked up to his sister who was sitting in in the lobby of the Sheraton where she and her husband had been staying for the past four days.

"Jonas!" Maggie squealed as she jumped up from the sofa and gave her big brother a tight hug.

"Not too tight, sis." Jonas grimaced a bit when the very athletic woman nearly broke his backbone in her grip.

Maggie released her hold on Jonas and stepped back a foot, looking him up and down. "Okay, a few telltale bruises and some bags under those blues of yours, but beyond that, I'd say you're almost back to your fighting prime."

"Yeah," Jonas said. "Tell me that again in another day or so after a real bed and some good old starchy food instead of the stuff the hospital calls a nutritional diet."

"Come on," Maggie replied. "I've practically eaten every meal there since Roger and I arrived from Arizona, and I think it's just fine. Perhaps not as fine as Duane's at the Mission Inn, but far more suitable then most places I've visited. And by the way, Roger sent his love but had to get back to be with Tim and Annie who also send their love."

Jonas nodded and slowly sat down on the upholstered chair next to the sofa where his sister had been sitting only moments ago. "What sort of tea?"

"The usual, simple green tea. It's the best for getting rid of oxidants," Maggie replied. "Want some?"

"Nah, probably nothing right now, just wondering," Jonas said, staring over to the tiled bar area of the lobby, and watched a young couple laughing quietly as they leaned in a bit to each other. The familiar tug was what he felt—he missed Sam.

"Really, you look good." Maggie tried to distract her brother, knowing he could go to dark places in his mind if he wasn't careful.

There was no one else on the earth she loved more, besides her children and her husband, than her older brother. He had always been there for her, especially after their parents had died in a car crash when she was still in her teens. He took care of her. Made sure she finished college and gave his blessing to the man who would later become her husband and the father of her children. Maggie believed she had a wonderfully idyllic life and made every effort to do her best every day to be grateful for what she had.

Jonas, on the other hand, had not finished university until she had settled, and then he went back to night classes, finishing his bachelor's in police science while a detective with the Riverside Police Department. He had married a woman Maggie hadn't really liked but never let Jonas know, and he had a beautiful little girl whom they named Stacy. For eight years, Maggie prayed that Jonas's marriage would work out and he'd be safe on his job chasing villains and putting his life on the line like all law enforcement did each day, but that prayer hadn't been fulfilled.

Her darling niece had been murdered by a lone gunman at a small market in Riverside one night while she was with her father. Unexpectedly, a man had entered the store, pulled a gun, and demanded money from the cashier. Jonas, who had been stopping by with Stacy for some milk, instinctively reached for his off-duty weapon to subdue the robber but instead Stacy became the victim. In front of Jonas, the man had calmly turned his weapon to the scared little girl and pulled the trigger.

Jonas's pride and joy was dead, the marriage over, and Maggie had seen Jonas change instantly into a dark and brooding man whom, though she loved him, she found it difficult to spend time with him.

It had been years in the making for Jonas to return to his old self but she knew there were places within his mind that he never let her or anyone else enter.

It was probably safer for everyone that way.

"Maggie," Jonas was saying, and suddenly Maggie turned back to her brother. "Did you hear what I was asking?"

"Sorry." She shook her head. "I was someplace else right then."

"Hope it was pleasant."

"Just hoping Roger remembered to leave a check out for the cleaning service this morning before dropping the children off at their school."

"Ah, the dilemmas of the rich."

"Jonas Peters." Maggie pretended to sound upset. "You know we're not rich or that rich."

"My loving little sister," Jonas responded. "I am so happy for you and know that Roger is a whiz in the financial markets and should reap the benefits of his long hours at the office. I hold no evil thoughts for his success but instead am so overjoyed at how he takes care of you and my nephew and niece. Besides, how many times have I been to that very large home and very exclusive neighborhood in Scottsdale?"

"You mean the house you nearly blew up years ago?"

"Not fair," Jonas said. "It wasn't me who laid the explosives but, in the end, we made him pay for all the destruction, didn't we?"

Maggie was silent, remembering the horrifying incidents which nearly cost her family their lives less than a decade earlier while Jonas was still actively working as a detective for the Riverside Police Department. They tried to make light of it, which had taken years, but those insidious days were nothing but terrifying, and a lot of people had lost their lives at the hands of an insane spree killer.

"Sorry," Jonas said, seeing the look on his sister's face. "That was rather a bad thing to try to make sound funny."

"At least we can now talk about it," Maggie replied. "That's a good sign since we didn't for years."

"Perhaps we shouldn't now either," Jonas said softly

"Perhaps you're right." Maggie nodded. "Now what were you saying?"

Jonas remained silent for a moment, studying the younger woman before him. He knew his sister better than anyone and realized she had not been worrying about money for a maid but he also knew better than to delve to where she really had been in her mind. They respected each other that much. If she had wanted to tell him, she would have.

"I was wondering if you would stay by Sam until I sort things out."

Maggie stared at her brother in disbelief. "Stay by her? Jonas, Sam's my best friend and there is no way I am going to leave until she is out of the hospital and recovered completely. I owe her that alone for being my friend and for her being your fiancée. Though I wonder how you convinced her to come back to you after you had broken up with her."

"It was a mutual break up two years ago, and you know it, Maggie." Jonas pouted. "And then it took a lot of begging and chocolate from me to have her finally see the light."

"Dim at best."

"Need a flashlight in there," Jonas said with a large smile. "I'm a lucky man."

"You don't know how much you are but, of course, I'll be staying while you sort things out. I shouldn't ask what that really means, should I?"

Jonas shook his head. "Not sure right now what it means myself."

"But with each passing day the trail gets colder, doesn't it?"

"Always has in the past and this shouldn't be any different."

"You will be careful, won't you?"

Jonas continued to smile. "Aren't I always?"

Maggie shrugged her shoulders. "You're definition of careful and the rest of society's have two opposite meanings, I'm afraid. Tell you what—just come home to us soon."

"That I can promise," Jonas agreed. "It will take a couple of days before I'm ready to leave and then it shouldn't be too long, I think."

"Any ideas who did this?" Maggie asked.

"I have a couple of hunches, but that's it at this point."

"Well," Maggie said, leaning forward and placing her right hand on Jonas's left forearm. "Get those hunches figured out, take care of business, and come home and marry that woman who loves you so much."

Jonas placed his hand atop of his sister's and smiled. "That will be the end game, and the sooner, the better."

The smile felt good.

Jonas spent the better part of an hour staring at Sam at the hospital and then leaned over her and kissed her forehead. "I love you and will be back soon, my love. I just have a few things to take care of before we can be together again."

He closed his eyes and said a silent prayer for the woman he adored and for the personal mission he was about to start on. It wasn't like him to be a religious man but something inside him at that moment advised that the path he was about to start on might be fraught with danger, and he alone might not be enough.

That was different—he thought as he turned and walked from Samantha's intensive care room.

CHAPTER 10

S mythe looked up at Jonas as the man walked into the office. "You up and about, are you?

"The doctor signed my official release about two hours ago. Said they were getting nervous with me hanging around there," Jonas replied, taking a seat.

Smythe nodded. "I can understand that when it comes to you, Jonas. You do have a way of creating havoc when you're around."

Jonas didn't reply.

"How's your girlfriend?"

"Still the same, but her doctor said she's doing much better, and there shouldn't be any complications when they bring her out of the coma. She's strong and resilient, which is helping her."

"I'll keep her in our prayers," Smythe returned, looking down for a moment at some paper on his desk. "So what does Iquitos have to do with all this?"

"Nothing," Jonas replied rapidly.

"Well, your old buddy Frank came in here the day after the explosion with your phone and said that was the ticket to solving this mess."

Jonas thought a moment before answering. "I was out of it, Lieutenant, and really can't recall what went on between anything I said or didn't say to Frank. Maybe he thought it was important."

"You don't recall?" Smythe said, staring across his desk. "That's the oldest cop way of saying I know but don't want to tell you."

"That's all I have," Jonas said. "If I really thought that text message was the answer, I would tell you. You've had my phone the past few days, anything else come up?"

Smythe shook his head. "I found a charger for it and kept it here in my drawer but nothing more has come across the texts and, pardon me, but I did keep an eye on your emails and such. I didn't find anything of substance. Hope you don't mind."

"Never need a warrant for an innocent man." Jonas smiled. *Anything of substance—makes it seem like I have no life at all.*

"Seriously, why would Frank make such a fuss about the text?"

"Well, it did seem rather suspicious to me at the time also, if I can remember through the haze of pain meds the hospital had me on. I was pretty banged up, still am, as you can tell by the bruises on my face, and trust me you don't want to see the rest of my body either."

"That is a true statement."

"I must have had a foggy idea it was a clue but just late yesterday I thought about it more seriously and a lot more clearer and believe it's just a message from someone I had contacted recently about a possible tour of the Amazon for Sam and me when we get married."

Smythe eyed him suspiciously. "You'd take a honeymoon on the Amazon? I looked this Iquitos up, and though it sounds adventurous, it also sounds downright muggy and hot with lots of flying and crawling bugs. Not the typical place a man would want to start a marriage at. It didn't sound very romantic. Why not go to Paris?"

"I don't like the French." Jonas smiled. "Seriously, we had talked a while back and two things she mentioned were to see Machu Pichu and the beginning of the Amazon River in Peru. I don't know what to say except she is the adventurous type."

"Okay," Smythe said, tossing Jonas's phone back to him over the desk. "But didn't you do some things down there in the nineties with other agencies?"

Jonas wasn't sure how to answer that so he paused for a few moments. "A long time ago, there was a multi-agency task force sent down near that area, closer to Columbia, actually, going after a drug cartel. It's when cocaine stopped flowing in from spots like Cartagena and the cartels started hauling it through the backdoors of Peru and down the Amazon, using the native population, or forcing them to act as mules. "

"And that has nothing to do with this strange text message?"

"I don't see how, Lieutenant," said Jonas. "That was a long time ago, and I'd hazard a guess that anyone alive down there twenty years ago sure isn't now. Like I said, it's probably got something to do with my requesting bids for the tours and this guy, whoever it was, decided to text me instead of email."

"Perhaps," Smythe replied. "Do me a favor, and if you get anything else strange on a text or anywhere else, keep us informed. This disaster has the mayor sending nasty messages every few hours to the chief, and no one is pleased we're not one step closer to finding out who set the explosives and for what cause."

"No one has claimed anything? You're not even hearing a hint out there?"

"No, nothing of substance," Smythe returned. "Sure, we got the regulars who are claiming it, but so far, it's a big zero. We've had people claiming to be members of ISIS, Al-Qaida, and Hamas, but they probably don't have a lot of interest in our little city. Anyway, NSA checked the hot ones and found they came from local numbers and after checking them out we patted the idiots on the ass and said not to call us again. Loonies! It seems the real bomber did his thing and disappeared into thin air."

Jonas nodded. "That's awfully strange."

"Everything seems a little strange, wouldn't you think?"

"I guess so." Jonas stood up from the desk and pocketed his cell. "I need to get going, Lieutenant, but if I think of anything, I will let you know."

"Jonas, make sure it's in a timely manner?"

Jonas looked down at Smythe. "Of course, I will."

As Jonas walked out of the department and onto Orange Street, he realized he hadn't liked lying to his former boss but believed there was nothing else he could have done at the time. If Iquitos was the key, then it was up to Jonas to learn why, and that germ of an idea in the back of his head was growing by the hour.

"Are you sure you're okay with this?" Maggie asked Jonas who was standing by the window of her hotel room overlooking the Riverside Raincross Conference Center.

He nodded. "I just spent the last two hours drilling Sam's doctor and was reassured over and over again that she is healing better than expected but won't be released from her induced coma for another week or two. They hadn't been sure how long, at first, but since she's healing so well, they aren't about to bring her out just yet but promised to notify me right away. Besides, her parents are here as you are, and that's plenty of family and friends when she awakens, even if I'm not."

Maggie stared at her brother's back. She admired him so much and loved him so deeply that she just wanted to wrap her arms around him and whisper that everything would be just fine. Though, knowing Jonas, that wouldn't do the trick.

He would know when everything was back to normal when he decided it was.

Her older brother was not so narcissistic to believe he was in control of all that surrounded him, but he did have an uncanny sense of some kind that, when he believed things were calm, they generally turned out that way. She had always counted on him as her anchor in case of a storm.

Maggie trusted her brother whole-heartedly.

"If she awakes, and you're not here?"

"Tell her I'll be right back."

"You went out for coffee?" Maggie asked.

Jonas smiled and turned from the window, glancing at his sister. "I wanted South American coffee beans. I felt it would be a real treat for her."

"South America?"

"Maggie," Jonas said, walking over to his sister and softly grasping her shoulders. "I have a few trips to take to unravel whatever happened the other day. Just trust me."

Maggie reached up and held her brother's strong forearms. "You know I always will, but you're leaving the country?"

"Just for a bit," Jonas replied. "The answers we need are not here in Riverside but farther south—say about four thousand miles."

Maggie released her hold and took a step back from Jonas. "When are you leaving?"

"I have a flight out of Los Angeles tonight at ten."

"Need a ride?"

"No, Frank's driving me."

Maggie knew before she asked but she had to anyway. "Will you tell me what is in South America that is so important that you need to leave?"

"The past." Jonas smiled. "Maggie, isn't it always our pasts that catch up to us eventually? We move on, we hide, we find religion, but, in the end, the past is just the past which shaped us to who we are today. The past isn't really the past but just the present in suspended animation. It thaws when we least expect it."

Maggie just looked at her brother in a moment of silence before responding. "You've turned into quite the philosopher, haven't you? But you're still not telling me exactly where you are going and why, are you?"

A slight chuckle came out of Jonas. "I'll tell you this, you busy body of a younger sister. I had to get malaria pills and yellow fever shots."

"Heck, that could because you wanted to try a new restaurant," Maggie said.

"It's not a food fetish," Jonas said.

Maggie shook her head. "Well, that makes me feel better."

"And that's what I counted on," Jonas replied. "Look after Sam until I get back."

"And when will that be?"

"Soon," he responded with a bit of uncertainty in his tone.

Maggie ignored it. "Will you have a gun to protect yourself?"

"I'll be fine, Maggie," Jonas responded.

Maggie moved in and hugged her brother so tightly it brought out a quick whimper.

"Your strength," Jonas hissed. "I still have bruised ribs you know."

"You'll have more than that if you don't come home to all of us."

Jonas kissed his sister on the forehead, gently undid her grip on him, and walked from the hotel room without another word.

It was time to go to work.

Jonas hadn't been totally truthful with his sister. He had a plane to catch and had work to do but he had one more stop to make before Frank would pick him up for the drive to the airport.

He held her hand firmer than he had planned, but he couldn't help himself. Jonas had lost so much in his life— his parents when he and Maggie were young, never knew his grandparents from either side, and the loss of his daughter Stacy had left him emotionally empty for much of the past ten years or more.

Samantha had come into his life because of a psychopath killing machine. Jonas prayed that murderer was in hell but couldn't stop a small feeling of thankfulness that, because of him, he and Sam were together.

He hated the thought of it.

He couldn't help it as he stared at the woman he loved more than his own life. She was lying there fighting for another chance of mortality.

Jonas knew, if it wasn't for Zachary Marshall, he would never had met Samantha.

That was an example of irony his high school English teacher had never taught.

"I love you so much," Jonas whispered. "And I am so sorry for all of this—seems I am not good to be around for those I care for. Sam, I promise you that I will find out who did this, and they will not be able to repeat that action again. I also promise I will be back and, hopefully, someday make you proud of me."

A few tears flowed their way down Jonas's face, but he ignored them. He didn't want to release Sam's hand.

A shuffle behind him told Jonas he was no longer alone with Sam. "I'm sorry but we need to take her in for some tests. You can stay and wait—shouldn't be more than an hour."

Jonas ignored the nurse for a moment, bent down, placed a loving kiss on Sam's hand, and finally released his hold. "I love you."

Standing up, he turned and nodded at the nurse. "That's okay—I have things to do."

The nurse smiled at the handsome man, wondering if he knew he was crying.

CHAPTER 11

"I hate airports," Frank said, pulling into the unloading zone in front of Star Peru at the Los Angeles International Airport. Though his dislike of most airports was universal, he did have a smidgen of respect for LAX—especially the international flights out of the Bradley terminal. It was all in one space and usually pretty efficient.

Jonas looked over at his friend from the passenger seat of Frank's SUV and smiled. "Frank, no one likes airports just like no one likes hospitals. It's just the way of life—to travel you deal with TSA and the crowds, and to heal you go to a hospital. It's as simple as that."

Frank shook his head, staring straight ahead through the windshield at a police officer walking the vehicles to ensure no one overstayed the allotted time in dropping off passengers. "Yeah, I knew that, but why do you always bring in comparisons?"

"What?" Jonas responded, checking his passport and the medical documents he needed when traveling into potential malaria hotspots.

Frank continued to look out the windshield. "You have a habit of trying to equate one thing to another."

"It's for the benefit of the unwashed and unlearned," Jonas said.

"I showered and am pretty educated."

"Yes, I know that and am reminded whenever we talk to each other. But you made a statement, and I just added that an airport is where you go to travel and a hospital is where you got to get healed. It is nothing more but the obvious, obviously."

"I got it," Frank whispered as he smiled at the officer and flashed his police badge. He got a nod but no smile as the woman walked down the line of traffic.

"I'll say it if it makes you happy—you are very smart and I appreciate everything you are doing—especially with Sam and my family. Frank, I don't know what's coming, but it will probably not be pretty. I'm following memories, thoughts, and the like—oh, hell, I don't even know anything and wonder if I'm just being stupid and should just check myself back into the hospital and mend properly. Let law enforcement handle this thing."

"Then you wouldn't get the answers you want."

"Answers? Ah shit, I don't even know what questions I'm chasing—could be my tail for all I know," Jonas responded.

Frank nodded and turned off the car, knowing no one, even at LAX was going to hassle a retired cop. Especially if Jonas Peters's name was mentioned—his buddy had quite a history in the golden state, and not too many people would question him twice—not even once, for that matter.

"How long have I known you?" Frank asked.

"Way too long," Jonas responded, looking down at his watch and realizing he had plenty of time to catch his plane. He was a man of integrity and knew that if the airport wanted him two hours before an international flight, he would make sure he was there three hours ahead. A good book, a bar, was all he needed to break up the departure time.

"Have I ever questioned you about your wisdom or ideas?"

"Nope and neither did Steve when I sent him to his death," Jonas responded.

Frank shook his head and just wanted to reach across the distance and slap the shit out of his friend. Jonas was probably the worst pain in the ass he had ever known—that included, in Frank's case, hemorrhoids that had persisted for over three weeks. Agony beyond agony, but Jonas was right there next to the cream he had to use to slather on those bulges daily.

"Jesus, are you going to bring Steve into this and your purported guilt? He was a detective, just like you. He made a decision to go up those stairs after a murderer. You weren't there, and he was a big boy. I loved Steve, but he went up and confronted the asshole—unfortunately, it didn't turn out as it should have."

"Steve was murdered."

"A lot of people get murdered daily in this country, Jonas," Frank responded. "We live in a free country, and that means free people are free to kill each other."

"Now who's making comparisons?" Jonas replied with a grim look on his face, knowing the lecture he was about to get from Frank.

"Doesn't take a genius to know this but we're different," Frank said. "You, I, and all those patriots who wear the uniform are convinced we are doing the right thing. When cops on the street get killed, does it really matter where the incident takes place? People murder us while doing our duty—plain and simple. Most times no one gives a damn unless someone makes a mistake or people lie. We've seen it over and over again on the news—someone gets killed by a cop, and suddenly, the officer is the guilty party. It doesn't matter if someone was trying to kill the cop first. It's just the crap the media and the public make without the facts. People have the attention span of a gnat with no skills in researching before opening our mouths. It's a shitty world sometimes, but without us—those in uniform—the world would be a lot shittier."

"You're rather passionate about this, Frank," Jonas said, forgetting his departure time.

Frank looked out the driver's window. "Sorry, in my old age, I'm getting dramatic. Just got news that a kid I knew about twelve years ago had just graduated college, got a job at Google, and had a baby with a girl who I swore he didn't have a chance of winning but did."

Jonas watched his friend. "Sounds like the perfect story."

"It was." Frank's voice lowered. "The kid was trouble when I first met him during my Rubidoux beat days, and I popped him a couple of times for nothings, but it did end him up doing nine months in juvenile hall."

"Not a nice youngster, huh?" Jonas commented.

"No, actually he was very nice, but the typical story of nobody being home and all that."

"And you took him under your wing," Jonas said with a smile, knowing Frank's true self.

"Yeah and with a lot of ass kicking," Frank responded.

"What happened?"

"I got a text from his mother that Bobbie had been murdered just a mile from his office in Irvine. Seems he stopped at a convenience store to pick up some pampers for the newborn and some guy decided the Lexus was worth more than Bobbie's life."

"I'm sorry," Jonas said.

"That's the problem," Frank replied. "It doesn't seem anyone else gives a damn. Here's a kid from the wrong side of the tracks making a break and graduating college, obtaining a hell of a career, marrying a good girl, and was a brand new father and then gets murdered. They caught the punk two blocks away when he couldn't figure out running a red light is a dead giveaway to the cops something is wrong, especially in a stolen vehicle."

Jonas looked over at his friend and remained quiet a few moments. The hustle and bustle on the sidewalk by the terminal seemed to fade in the distance. "What's really troubling you, Frank? It's deeper than someone you know getting killed—we all have that experience, and it's tough, which I will give you."

"He was African-American."

That puzzled Jonas for a moment. "Okay."

"The killer was also African-American," Frank replied, bringing his hand to his eyes and rubbing them. "The issue is there were witnesses at the market, and they heard the killer say, you must be a black hater to be wearing those fancy clothes and driving a white man's car."

Jonas sat watching the human traffic and thought a moment. "People are ignorant, Frank."

"Yeah," Frank replied. "A little deep, isn't it?"

Jonas wanted to admit that he was about to embark on a very long trip with no results guaranteed, and they were discussing race relations. Two retired cops could not sit at an international airport and find the solutions haunting this country for centuries. It would take a lot cooler and wiser heads to do this besides the two sitting in a SUV with an ever-diligent traffic officer walking by their vehicle.

"I'm sorry, Frank," Jonas said. "People are bad, in my opinion, and do bad things. Sounds naive, I know, but how many cases of homicide did we cover to learn the killer was jealous, mad, or just didn't know why they killed the other person? I hate to say it but we will never truly know the cause for all the murders we investigated. We just investigate, that's all we do."

"That sounds rather dismal."

"No, Frank, it sounds reasonable," replied Jonas. "It's not a race thing but a jealous thing that drives people to kill. I want what you have and if I can't have it right now, then I will get it by removing the obstacle in my way—that being you."

"So, the kid murdered a couple of weeks ago wasn't killed because he was black?" Frank asked.

"Probably not." Jonas shrugged. "Though I wasn't there, I would think the scumbag saw a successful young guy and got pissed off. Throwing in the race crap was just an excuse for the killer to make himself feel better. Hope he remembers that when he's on death row."

Frank nodded and glanced out the windshield. "Thanks, I knew I could dump this on you, and you'd come up with a reasonable explanation for the feelings I've been having about this young man."

"I lost my daughter to a piece of fuck years ago, Frank," Jonas replied. "I've had plenty of time to come to conclusions about the beasts living among us."

He looked across at the man in his vehicle and smiled. The smile was for his own benefit since, at this moment with the terminal lights bouncing off of Jonas's eyes, he knew his friend was thinking of his own demons.

The deaths in Jonas's life were not an accident but calculated acts of murder. But yet, Jonas moved on—dangerously but he moved on.

"No more wonderment about the frailties or insanities of the human race this evening. I don't want to have you late for your flight."

"Plenty of time," Jonas said, smiling at Frank. "Not sure how long I'll be gone but I'll call you as often as I can to see how Sam's doing."

"I know you will," replied Frank.

"You remember what we talked about?"

"Oh, you mean in the nearly three hours to get here? Yeah, I recall some of what you said."

"I'm a man of few words, Frank," Jonas said. "Almost a monk, most would say."

Frank shook his head. "A monk who couldn't keep his mouth shut during the drive."

Jonas grabbed a small duffel bag off the rear seat and stepped out of his door onto the curb. "I really have plenty of time, Frank."

"I thought you said your flight was fifteen minutes from now," Frank said. "I was really worried."

Jonas closed the car door and leaned in a bit through the window. "As Steven Covey would have said, be proactive and think ahead. I always count on a crap of a drive to LAX—just guarding my flight."

"You, my friend, are a genius."

"Nope, just flown more than I like," Jonas said, standing up and moving a step away from the Hyundai.

"Jonas," Frank yelled out across the passenger seat and through the open window. "Take care of yourself."

Jonas didn't reply. Just held up his right arm and waved.

"You better or Maggie will have my ass," Frank said while smiling at the airport security officer who was about to give him an earful.

"Traveling light for time in Peru?" asked the ticket agent as Jonas verified his seat on the Star Peru airline.

"Yeah, anyway, I never know the temperature there—you know, summer here winter there and vice-versa. I can always buy clothes to match the weather when I get to Lima."

"So, you've been to my beautiful country before?" the young female flight agent asked, checking Jonas's credentials.

He knew he could have checked through faster just using the e-ticket kiosk but, no matter how much he flew, Jonas enjoyed doing it the old-fashion way, eye to eye. Too much technology left him feeling hollower than he already felt in his life, and though he wasn't a great fan of the human race, sometimes a real live person was more real than touching a monitor screen.

"A long time ago," he said.

"Well, enjoy your trip, and I have upgraded you to business class."

"I didn't ask for the upgrade," Jonas stated. "Why then?"

"Because we have an open seat on this flight, and you have pretty blue eyes," the agent stated, smiling.

"And you are an angel," he replied, returning the smile. "Thank you."

"Yes, sir, and enjoy your trip."

"It's better already."

By the time Jonas had gone through the TSA checkpoint, gotten himself rearranged into a presentable status after nearly undressing in front of an airport full of strangers, and found the closet bar, he noticed he still had nearly two hours before his flight.

Ordering a Shock Top with orange slice from a very shapely brunette, Jonas settled back on the tall leather bar stool. He realized he must have sounded foolish to Frank waiting curbside a bit earlier. "But I don't what I'm looking for," he muttered aloud just as the young woman returned delivering the room temperature glass and beer. "Thanks."

"Most want a frosty mug," the waitress replied, laying the tab on the bar.

The place was empty and Jonas knew she was just being polite, as well as a bit bored. She wanted to kill some time. "I never liked the frosty mug thing. Beer gets too cold and the flavor seems to leave rather quickly."

The woman nodded, setting her right foot up on the lower rung of the bar stool next to Jonas. "So that's why they drink warm beer in Europe."

"England did, but it was slightly chilled in reality. Just above room temperature, actually." Jonas declared. "They make their beer differently than here where we expect near freezing, which actually reduces the effectiveness of the proteins within the beer, or ale, as they prefer to call it. I like my beer cold, but not having ice build-up on the glass is rather nice. Sorry, that sounded rather boring, didn't it?"

"Not at all," replied the woman. "So they like it cold then?"

"Again, not like we do, but yes, the times I've traveled there over the years, it seems the beer in the pubs is getting a bit colder. But not so cold it ruins the flavor."

"Got ya."

"Then again, I'm not a beer expert but simply a traveler who enjoys the taste of a good beer."

"You seem to know enough, though," she said, looking over her right shoulder and noticing an older couple had come into the bar. She didn't want to leave this solitary customer since he seemed very interesting. And he certainly was not like the other men who only wanted to watch her walk and perhaps make inane conversation with her while ogling her breasts. This man was different. She could see it in his eyes—almost haunting but still a great deal of spark deep down.

She wanted to stay but her job was serving. "I'll be back."

"And I'll still be here," Jonas replied.

His mind instantly wandered back again to the unknown plans ahead of him.

Another mouthful of beer, a wipe of his mouth, and Jonas glanced down at the manila envelope before him.

Besides his shoes, watch, belt, emptying of the pockets, and loss of his dignity, Jonas had silently watched the plastic bin pass through the X-rays without a hitch. Twenty-seven single-spaced typed pages simply was scanned, considered non-threatening. Jonas collected the envelope, along with all his other personal items, and left the TSA area to rearrange himself.

A nondescript pile of papers, which if made public could start an international incident of political finger wagging and, for certain, the downfall of a few politicians' careers as well.

All he wanted as he started to unclasp the envelope was the answer to who had tried to kill him so dramatically.

Maggie sat beside Samantha's bed silently reading from the latest novel by Daniele Steele. She wasn't a huge fan but even Maggie had to admit it was a page turner and Steele certainly could turn a phrase when it came to writing.

She also had to admit some of the steamier paragraphs she had just read truly made her miss Roger.

Two children or not, she and her husband always found time for each other. Busy schedules be damned, they both realized that, to keep a marriage happy and fulfilling, there had to be a line drawn with a huge sign which read:

The world can wait—we need time alone together.

For nearly two decades, Maggie and Roger knew it had worked for them.

"I hope you'll have the same with Jonas," she said aloud, glancing over at her sleeping friend.

"Another Beer?"

Jonas glanced at his watch and weighed the options. "The gate is sixty feet away, I have forty minutes to kill, so I have plenty of time for one more beer."

"Thought so," the waitress replied. "I already ordered another for you."

"A psychic, huh?" Jonas said. "Tell me the winning lotto numbers for tonight, will you?"

"If only," she said with a smile and then turned and headed back to the bar. In a flash, there was a Shock Top in a room temperature glass sitting in front of her customer.

Jonas nodded at the efficiency. "Bet you get good tips."

"Yes and a lot of lame pick-up lines."

"Sorry, but I have a fiancée," Jonas said with a slight grin.

The waitress looked down at the man and returned the grin. "I didn't mean to imply anything about you."

"No implication taken."

"Where is the bride to be, if I may ask?"

Jonas took a pull of the beer, wiped his mouth with a napkin, and stared into the young woman's eyes. "She's in the hospital."

"Oh, I'm sorry," she said. "That was none of my business—just trying to make small talk."

"No problem," Jonas replied. "But now you probably are wondering what sort of man would be heading out on a plane while his girlfriend is lying in a hospital bed and not there by her side."

She nodded. "Who is the psychic now?"

"I'm off to find out who tried to kill her."

The woman visibly blanched. A few moments of awkward silence drifted between the two of them.

"Sorry," Jonas stated. "A little too blunt."

"Uhmmm, I have customers," she said, moving away slowly.

Jonas nodded, took a rather long drink of the beer, and placed two twenties on the table top.

Ten minutes passed while he studied the documents he had brought with him. Names, dates, locations, and reasons, all reminded him of days long in the past. But suddenly that past was as current as the nearly empty glass in front of him.

He didn't really concentrate but just looked at the paperwork. He wasn't ready yet to completely delve into the written material in front of him. The flight to Lima would offer ample time for a serious perusal.

"Sorry about my abrupt departure."

"No, you had other thirsty customers," Jonas said.

"Yes."

"And my last statement must have been a bit unsettling."

She smiled. "Not an everyday conversation starter to say the least."

Jonas handed the pair of bills to the waitress. "No change."

He finished the beer, packed his paperwork into the manila envelope, and stood up.

She hadn't left the table. "I hope you catch whoever did that to your fiancée."

"I will."

"And bring them to justice."

He stared at her for a moment. "Oh, I certainly will."

"Frank Sanders," Frank stated after he slid his finger across the screen on his Galaxy in his left hand.

"Frank, it's Jonas. Do me a favor, will you?"

Frank glanced at his watch and knew Jonas should just be about boarding the plane. "Shouldn't you be belted in by now?"

"We're loading now," Jonas responded.

"Okay," Frank said. "What do you need?"

Frank could hear Jonas speaking to someone and, from what he could make out, it was probably someone with the airlines near the boarding desk. "Sorry about that," Jonas said. "Talking with the gate keeper."

"No problem."

"Hey, I sent you a couple of emails, and if you could look into a few things, I'd appreciate it."

"Okay."

"Also, I put in a guy's name I met a couple of years ago out of Ontario. Do me a favor and see if you can find a contact number. He's on the anti-terrorist speaking circuit, a Russian—maybe get a hold of Grossman—he seemed to know the guy."

"A Russian?" Frank asked. "You changing political parties, Comrade?"

"Yep, that's me." Jonas laughed. "Vodka and communism."

Frank smiled. "Wouldn't say that too loudly at an airport.

"I'm in the plane now and, besides an odd glance from a fellow passenger I just walked by, I think I'm safe."

"Jonas, I'll check my email and will get back to you when you arrive in Lima. What's the time?"

"If there's no delays in San Jose, then I should be there by ten in the morning your time."

Three hours in time difference would have Jonas landing in the capital by one in the afternoon.

"Okay, got it," Frank replied. "Have a safe trip."

"Thanks."

"Jonas," Frank said. "I spoke with Maggie, and nothing has changed with Samantha."

There was silence for a moment on the phone. "Yeah, I spoke to her a few minutes ago. Thanks for caring, Frank."

"That's what friends are for," Frank replied, ending the call.

The flight from LAX to San Jose was rather uneventful, allowing Jonas more than enough time to scour the contents of his envelope. Jonas had not looked in the package on his lap for decades. The past should stay the past, but perhaps this time, it was worth revisiting.

Memories, some uplifting and some disturbing, came back to him while he was sitting in the window seat in business class. He had made a lot of friends during the two months with the task force in South America, but unfortunately, contact had been lost through the years. Jonas had never been one to have many long term friends, not that he didn't enjoy the company of others but life just seemed to get in the way and contact would be lost.

Sir Arthur Conan Doyle's character Sherlock Holmes once stated to Dr. John Watson: "John, I don't have friends. I have one."

Skimming over the pages laid out on the food tray attached to the back of the seat in front of him, Jonas wondered if he had one.

Samantha was his lover, confidant, and the person he wanted more than anyone else to spend the rest of his life with but his best friend? Of course, in the aspect of family building, but did he have a true friend outside of family? Someone he could confide in about any aspect of his life without worrying about being judged?

The question went unanswered in his head and a momentary sadness crept over him.

"Man, I gotta work on getting a friend," he said quietly to himself but then he remembered Frank's comment just before he took off for Peru and smiled. "Perhaps I don't have to look far."

Frank looked over his calendar, which was mainly empty spaces on a very nicely illustrated yearly dog calendar that he received from a secretary he knew at the police department. Marla Gaines was a wonderfully dedicated and special person that Frank and the rest of the detectives loved working with. She was playfully rude, conspicuously inattentive, but more than anything she would cover any officer's back.

Frank always thought if there was ever a television show made about a police precinct, Marla would be there with her short "man-cut" hair, quick retorts, and never-ending devotion to those she worked with. She was a peach but a hardened peach—she had lost a father in the line of duty, though that memory seldom surfaced. But when it did, Marla could be rather emotional. Everyone knew Marla and knew the only interest in her heart was for the men and women in uniform. She had loved her father, and she loved those whom she worked with.

Not quite a cop but more a cop than many—a daughter of a fallen brother. That alone set her on a pedestal with the men and women within the Riverside Police Department and that pedestal would never be shaken. If so, whoever shook it would have to deal with over four hundred pretty pissed off cops—not anything one would want to deal with.

Marla Gaines was an original.

Frank looked down at his phone and wondered if he should make the call. Marla had retired just five months earlier. Perhaps he should allow her a chance at some peace and quiet?

Memories surrounded Frank, but as he looked down at the phone in his hand the call had to be made.

After the second ring, the old familiar voice said, "Frank, I'm retired—get someone else to get your coffee."

"Very funny, but when did you ever do that?"

"Not once I am proud to say," Marla responded. "You were out protecting the streets but I was the one who told you the streets to protect."

"You were the best, Marla," Frank responded. "I've been thinking of you."

"Frank, I'm happily married in Texas," Marla continued. "You should move here—you don't have to worry about state taxes, high crime rates since everyone has a gun and conservatives are the major players. It's heaven on earth for an old gal like me."

"Sounds really good but I'm not calling for a recital on real estate in Texas. I just have some questions I was hoping you—if you have the time—would look into for me—"

"Frank," Marla interrupted. "Everything is recorded—please be careful in what you say—I do not believe in conspiracy theories, but I do believe in conspiracies."

"I got ya," Frank replied—recalling that's how he felt. "Okay, do you remember Jonas Peters?"

"Those blue eyes and sultry look?" Marla replied.

"Yeah, I guess."

"Frank, no offense," she said. "Which woman in the department didn't want those eyes gazing at her?"

"The smart ones."

"Oh, Frank."

"Come on, Marla, he was good cop but that was it," Frank said.

"Really," Marla continued. "For you, a good cop but Jonas was a dream boat for most of us."

"Perhaps this phone call was a mistake," Frank stated, though he couldn't help the smile crossing his face.

"What do you need from a retired overweight secretary?" Marla asked. "Is Jonas single again? I can lose weight and perhaps dump my husband."

"No, he's happily engaged but a simple question he asked and I thought you would be the one to get the answer for me."

"Of course."

"I need you to track down a Russian by the name of Yuri Shakirov."

There was a moment of silence. "Really, Frank, that's the guy who helped take back the middle school in 2014 in Victorville. "

"Crap, I didn't forget, but when Jonas mentioned the name, it didn't click and now it does," Frank replied. "Not sure what this has to do with anything but Jonas asked me to ask, and I knew instead of just searching Google I could come to you."

"Jonas knows this guy."

That didn't make any sense to Frank. If Jonas knew Yuri Shakirov, why did he want Frank to find him? "Nope—that wouldn't make sense," he said.

"It does, this guy is a bad ass," Marla stated.

"How do you know this?"

"I have two screens up at the same time," Marla responded. "You should try it some time."

"That's way too technical for an old codger like me."

"Yuri was there in Beslan when the school taken over in 2004. He's the real deal—a regular terrorist hunter." There was a slight drop in Marla's friendly tone—Frank caught it instantly. "There are no connections between Jonas and this Yuri, but obviously if Jonas asked you to contact him, there's something."

"Nothing that has been shared with me, and he's my friend. Why the secrecy?"

"That's Jonas, isn't it?"

Frank was suddenly upset. "And wouldn't it be nice if he were to let us know what is going on? And, Marla, you seem to be a little distant at this point. Remember I was the detective who could tell a person's mood by the tone of their voice?"

"I just spent the last three minutes on a secured department website, Frank," came the reply. "I need to end this conversation."

"What?" Frank asked as the phone went dead.

He redialed but got nothing but ringing into empty space. Not even a message to leave a message.

"What the hell is going on?" Frank said, not expecting an answer.

He didn't get one.

CHAPTER 12

The text offered a meeting at the Embarcadero 41 restaurant and bar in the Surco area of Lima. Less than two hours in Peru's capital and Jonas found himself staring at a bartender busy working a silver shaking blender.

Within a few seconds, two fresh pisco sours were poured and placed before Jonas and a man he had not seen nor spoken to in two decades.

"Seems as though I live in bars lately," Jonas said, reaching out for the drink.

"Not a bad way to live, my friend," his drinking companion stated, sipping the slightly frothy drink and smacking his lips appreciatively. "Especially with such libations as these."

Jonas stared across the table at Carlos and was once again impressed with the man's command of the English language. If it hadn't been the slight Peruvian accent and rare slips at idioms, Jonas would have sworn English was Carlos's native language instead of Spanish.

"The secret to the sour is the pisco and to ensure only egg whites are used. My favorite is the Gran Cruz Mosto Verde for a pisco—they seem to have the aging down to a science. No oak barrels like the Chilean variety. We us only copper containers for the distilling, which really allows the grapes to ferment with no bad taste. Of course, as soon as it is fully distilled, it is bottled immediately and never diluted."

"Unlike the Chilean pisco."

"Exactly, theirs has fewer flavors and an unappealing amber color most times."

Jonas had to admit the drink was refreshing but what he didn't admit was the first sip was very similar to a margarita on the rocks back home. He let that observation lay flat since the second taste was as unique as the drink itself.

"Very tasty," Jonas conceded readily.

Carlos nodded his balding head. "Of course, but do be careful, it is, as you Americans like to say, a high-octane drink. One is good, two okay-dokey, but three and you are on the floor."

"I'll remember that," Jonas said, not recalling that American saying about drinking but again he left it alone.

Jonas looked across at Carlos and smiled but then a strange feeling came over him while seeing his friend's eyes this close. He wondered if his own had that look. Though clear and bright, there was a vision of darkness and loneliness. Not soulless as his ex-wife had shouted about his but more like eyes which had seen too much damage during their years on earth.

He didn't feel sorry for the man sitting across from him in the airy and comfortable restaurant. There could be no sympathy for people like Carlos or himself. They had chosen this life and had to accept the consequences, no matter where those consequences fell.

Jonas had never been fond of the Blaming Others Disorder.

He and the likes of Carlos owned their lives and what came of it.

"Enjoy the pisco and do not think about the life you could have had," Carlos said, swirling the glass in front of his face and marveling at the tint to the drink. "Beautiful."

"How do you know what I was thinking?"

"It has been a long time since we saw each other," Carlos said. "Much too long but I don't forget the talks we had in the jungle night after night."

Jonas shrugged his shoulders. "Hell, all I remember are the damn mosquitos."

Carlos laughed and waved his hand a bit in front of his face. "Just little birds that liked to lite on sweet-smelling American's."

"They were the size of eighteen-wheelers and about as dangerous," Jonas replied, taking another sip of the pisco sour.

"Did I not advise you to eat a couple of sulfur match heads? Just two every day will keep the mosquitos away."

"I had Deet," Jonas replied.

"And you smelled quite badly all the time."

Jonas laughed, took another drink, and found that he was starting to enjoy this pisco sour drink. Common sense reminded him that two would be his limit.

"Anyway, we would often talk—you me and the others camped out there below the canopies—and discuss if we hadn't been soldiers. What would our lives had been if we had worked as bankers, teachers, or the like."

"Boring as hell," Jonas responded. "But I wasn't a soldier—you were."

"You fought by my side as law enforcement personnel and that made you a soldier," Carlos corrected Jonas. "Yes, those other trades would be very boring for the likes of us but then again we may not be haunted in our dreams with the things we have seen and done, yes?"

"Perhaps."

"No perhaps, Jonas Peters," Carlos said. "It was our fate to do what we did, and we did it while making our lands safer."

Jonas didn't reply as he thought about Carlos sitting across from him and wondered how haunted he was in his own right. Carlos had been in the Peruvian military for nearly twenty-five years when he was forced to retire due to a change in the political scenery of Peru. He was once a highly distinguished and highly decorated military officer who had suddenly, along with many others in the military, become a pariah to the new government. The war against terrorism had been called a success, even though innocents were murdered. Sometimes killed by the terrorists and sometimes by the military. It was referred to as collateral damage.

What really mattered was that innocents had died for a cause that most involved in the fighting could not remember now.

War was hell—remembering it worse.

"Do you like the pisco?" Carlos interrupted Jonas's thoughts while taking another sip of his drink. "Tasty but the flavor is hard to explain and the reason it is one of the most favored drink in South America."

"And yours is the best?"

"Of course." Carlos shrugged. "Why would I ever give the Chileans any good graces like you people like to say?"

Jonas took a drink, smiled, and replied, "We wouldn't say that but it is a good drink."

"You know." Carlos stared at one of the dozen large LCD screens lining the walls. "Do you know the difference between a good game of futbol and your professional football?"

"I'll bet you will tell me."

"Not the protective pads or the recognition of advertising companies who will pay millions for a few seconds of one of your best players on the television but the love of the sport."

Jonas took another sip of the pisco sour—perhaps two drinks wouldn't be the limit this day. He suddenly recalled that his friend Carlos loved to talk and talk—a philosopher in his own right.

"Blood, injuries, and the hatred of the audience sometimes is all the players have to stand up again to kick, block, and run," Carlos stated.

"That would make me want to get back up and hit the field," Jonas said. "But oh, come on, some of your soccer, as we call it, players are the most handsomely paid athletes in the world. They love the game, sure—but millions per year makes the hits that much more endurable."

"True, but overall, I live in a poor country but you American's do not understand the poverty around us. I'm not blaming you or your country, but we are poor compared to your poorest. I'm a retired commander in the navy and make less than someone in our country on welfare. Poverty in one country does not equal the poverty in another country—"

Jonas hated doing it but he interrupted his friend before this could turn ugly. "I've been here before and what's the point? I feel like a student in a university class you are delivering in Lima about the mistakes of Western expansion. I can't do that since I believe each country has the ability to be successful or not and it is up to their people but honestly after two of these piscos, I feel I will only start sounding like something out of a bad novel."

Carlos gently waved his hands in the air. "I apologize, our first meeting in so long and I have nearly caused an international incident."

"Not so much," Jonas responded. "What is truly on your mind?"

"How many people have you killed?"

That question sent Jonas into a momentary silence. He knew the exact count because when one takes the life of another, it collects into the deepest reaches of the brain. That was a number he didn't share with many—perhaps there was a true account within the department, but perhaps also one or two may be missing for political reasons.

"Soccer to the number of people I've killed," Jonas stated. "Talk about a reverse in a friendly conversation."

"Still friendly," Carlos returned.

Jonas shrugged. "Too many."

"Ah," Carlos said while swirling the drink a bit in front of him. "Yes, one is too many, I believe."

Jonas did not respond.

"No disrespect intended, my friend." Carlos put the glass down on the table. "I am just making small talk."

"Really? Small talk would be about the weather or if I'm dating someone and not talking about death." Jonas decided there would be no more rounds after this one if he wanted to keep his temper in check. "As you stated, we haven't seen each other in many years but yet you head this meeting into the fields of poverty and killings. Explain the maze to me."

Carlos started hard across the table in silence at Jonas but then slowly nodded. "Again, I am truly sorry, and you are correct in that this is not the way old friends should meet after so many years. So, what may I assist you with?"

Jonas felt his anger slowly dissolving, knowing Carlos had just gone through some very trying personal issues and might have wanted to lecture a while like the old days bantering around random thoughts. Jonas didn't have the time.

"When we worked together outside of Iquitos, near and in Columbia, who were we really going after?"

A genuine look of surprise crossed Carlos's broad face. "I don't understand the question. It was a joint military and law enforcement action, trying to eradicate, or at least to curtail, the flow of illegal drugs coming from Columbia and into Peru. Rather simple really."

That was the synopsis Jonas recalled so many years ago when he had spent considerable time in the Amazon. The routine travel of illicit drugs generally headed north from Columbia and into the southern sections of the United States via small low flying aircraft or very fast and long range boats. Skirting the islands of the Gulf of Mexico offered wonderfully secretive hiding spots. But with increased surveillance from the DEA, FBI, CIA, and local American law enforcement, the warm waters of the Caribbean turned scalding, and new jungle routes were instituted by the cartels.

Southwest out of Columbia along new and some ancient paths through the jungles, the mules hauled their drugs and smuggled them into northern Peru. The confluence of the Amazon River near Iquitos was the ideal spot for the new operational trade route. It was especially ideal when the overworked Peruvian Navy was all that stood in the way of astronomical monetary profits.

Coincidently, it was also the time when the Shining Path or Sendero Luminoso was spreading bloodshed and fear throughout the heartland of Peru. The Maoist revolutionary para-military group attacked civilians and government personnel with the distinct intent of changing the face of the country. These terrorists wanted the country of Peru to match their particular ideology.

Led by Abimael Guzan, an ex-Philosophy professor from the Ayacucho's Huamanga University, the terrorist group desired a complete overthrow of the government, starting in 1980. The group started with the burning of ballot boxes in the town of Chuschi as a demonstration against then President Fernando Terry. The disorder was easily put away by the military and the election went on as usual—as usual when the military actually ran the country and this had been the first 'free' election in decades.

Guzman and his followers were not done, though, since he had been to China and believed the way to a healthy society was by following the teaching of Mao. He took the idea of guerrilla warfare from the great champion of human rights, Mao Zedong, and utilized it in the small villages and countryside of Peru.

The Shining Path created 'Liberated Zones' after ambushing and murdering Peruvian soldiers and local law enforcement, forcing any government protection from the areas. Then they went after the locals.

Martial law was the name of the game for these terrorists bringing their own sense of justice. Justice which meant villagers got the raw end of the deal. The members of the Shining Path did as they wished—murder, rape, theft, and anything else they desired.

This went on for years before the villagers started to counter-attack which threw the entire para-military group into dismay. How dare people want to rule themselves, Guzman's followers questioned? In retaliation, the Shining Path entered village after village murdering women and children. In one small and remote town, nearly all the pregnant women were murdered, their husbands forced to watch.

Their point was made. The villagers started to behave as they were expected to—slaves.

In stepped President Alberto Fujimori in 1990, and things began to go terribly wrong with the ambitions of Doctor Guzman and this gang of thugs. The military was given orders, both openly and secretly to 'wipe' out the Sendero Luminoso, no matter the costs.

Bodies piled up with the military personnel and the terrorists. But worse were the civilian casualties which numbered nearly 70,000 from 1980 to 2000. These were those missing or killed in the campaign brought on by the Shining Path but intensified by the Peruvian military.

President Fujimori resigned as president in 2000 after the Peruvian Congress labeled him as 'morally unfit' to continue as president. It was his overzealous campaign against the terrorists which was his downfall. Killing ideologues was one thing, but it was quite another at the amount of dead 'terrorists' that were turning up all over the country.

Not all were members of the Shining Path—or that's what was reported by the news outlets.

In 2003, the Truth and Reconciliation Commission, which met in the capital of Lima, released the facts that of those nearly 70,000 civilians either missing or dead only forty-six percent were due to the Shining Path. The remaining fifty-four percent were blamed on the military.

The military denied any wrong doing. Guzman was arrested and sentenced to life with no parole in 1993.

This was the historical timeline Jonas remembered. Now he was sitting across from the man who had led him and twenty other Americans through the jungles in search of drug dealers in the nineties.

Or was that what actually happened?

"Who were we really going after?"

"Drug traffickers."

"Not the Shining Path?"

Carlos pushed himself back a bit in his chair, slowly reached for his glass, and took a short sip.

"Were they the same?"

"Sometimes, but not always."

"I'm not ignorant, Carlos."

"The concept of you ever being ignorant would not cross my mind. But why the interest in the Sendero Luminoso?"

"It just seems they were more prevalent in the southern sections of Peru, correct?"

"Yes, around Cuzco and the locales near Arequipa perhaps."

"Then why north in the Amazon?" Jonas asked. "Why, if we were chasing drug traffickers do I have a sick feeling in my stomach that we may have been doing two jobs all the time?

"And those would be?"

"Ridding Peru of terrorists while believing we were taking down drug cartels. I hope I'm not being too blunt."

"Good men often are very blunt. History has taught us that many great men tell people what they want to hear but good men tell people what they need to know."

CHAPTER 13

Jonas stood up from his aisle seat once the seat belt lights went off and wondered if he had done the right thing. It had been on his mind the entire flight from Lima after his short but informative meeting with Carlos.

No time to think but simply react was what he kept telling himself during the short flight. He nodded at some of the passengers who were grabbing overhead bags and making their way down the aisle toward the rear of the aircraft and the exterior door. Since he wasn't exiting the flight, he decided to take a step out onto the movable stairway and take a look around.

The outside air struck him in the face like a blast furnace. Where Lima had been overcast and almost chilly, the beginnings of the rainforest were hot and humid.

"And I've got a few hundred miles farther to fly before I'm truly in the thick of it," he mumbled, feeling the beads of perspiration mounting on his forehead.

"Excuse me, sir," stated a pretty Peruvian stewardess who was wiping down a counter at the rear crew section of the Airbus.

"Sorry," Jonas stated. "Just talking to myself about the humidity. It's been a long time since I've felt it."

"And you're continuing to Iquitos?"

"Yes, I am."

The young woman put the rag down and smiled. "This is nothing yet—you have been to Iquitos before?"

"A very long time ago," Jonas returned.

"Then you will remember the true heat of the jungle, yes?"

He nodded and stared off into the distance over the tarmac toward the jungle which seemed to be encroaching on the airport itself in Cajamarca. "I remember all too well."

"Ah, but the jungle is beautiful and so healthy," the woman said, turning away, and started toward the front of the aircraft.

"Unless you get eaten," he replied.

Frank looked into Maggie's eyes but did not respond to her. It seemed like the safest thing to do. Though she was very pretty and very fit, Frank knew this woman was also a loving wife, mother, and sister. But the look in her eyes at this moment reminded him of a pit bull.

"Maggie," Frank said. "I haven't heard from Jonas since he left two days ago."

Maggie was fuming. "Frank Sanders—you are his friend, and if anyone knows where he is, it is you."

There was no way he was going to tangle with this fiery little blonde. "If I knew, I would tell you, besides you and he are close, and he told you he was flying to Peru."

Maggie nodded. "He did but not in great detail."

"Whenever has Jonas given anyone more information than he believes they need at that very moment? He's a private person, Maggie—you know that, and we should be glad that he told us he was going to South America in the first place."

Maggie took a deep breath and paced the hotel lobby where she had requested to meet Frank after trying for the umpteenth time to raise her brother on his cell. She knew Frank was correct. Jonas was just like her—stubborn. Stubborn to a fault, which sometimes would frustrate her husband, but Roger understood Maggie and let the hard headedness alone. Roger was kind, patient, and extremely good to her.

"Okay, say I believe you and Jonas hasn't tried to make contact with you," Maggie said. "How am I going to know if he's safe or not?"

"When he tells you he is."

"That doesn't make sense, Frank," Maggie felt the wind going out of her since it was like Jonas to do just what Frank had just mentioned.

"Maggie," Frank said quietly, retaking the chair he had been sitting in. "Jonas is fine and he'll contact us when he feels the time is right. In his mind, I'm sure the less we hear from him, the safer we will be. It's his nature."

"And now damn nature boy is somewhere in Peru."

Frank looked down at the floor but immediately brought his eyes back Maggie's. "He'll probably end up in the Amazon, speaking of nature."

"What?"

"I'm not sure, but he did mention an operation he was on in the nineties somewhere in northern Peru, but that was before we had become friends in the department."

Maggie stared hard and then let the smile slip onto her face. "I remember those days. He went off on a joint venture with some governmental agencies to assist in stopping drug trafficking or something."

Frank nodded. "Joint task force mission with the Peruvian government. That's about all I know since, like I said, we've never really talked about it until recently and he was not fully cooperative in all the past details. Then again, who knows if that has anything to do with the bombing?"

"Of course it does," Maggie replied.

"Can't be sure," Frank said. "Could be a wild goose chase, actually. He needs to keep moving, Maggie, that's what Jonas does when he's upset, and believe me, he's upset."

The past two days had dragged so slowly that Maggie had found herself looking at her watch, wondering if it had broken. She wasn't quite sure what she had expected from her brother. She had hoped he would notify her of his every movement—if not only for her state of mind but to check in with Sam's medical progress. Of course, there wasn't much to report except the brain swelling had decreased and the breathing seemed to be holding without support any longer by tubes and wires. That was a good sign, and Doctor Scarlet Rose had seemed extremely optimistic that the induced coma was doing the trick.

Maggie predicted that Sam would be up and about by the time her brother had returned from Peru, and life for them both could get back to normal—whatever that would mean after the trauma they had been through together.

"He knows you're looking after Sam," Frank stated. "That's why he hasn't called in to check on her."

Maggie looked down at the man sitting before her. "Do you read minds now?"

"Sometimes." He laughed. "Wish I could read the next winning lotto numbers, though. That's not working out so well for me lately."

"He'll be okay, won't he, Frank?"

"Yes, Maggie," Frank replied. "He'll be fine and home soon with mission accomplished."

"I hope you're right," Maggie said, collapsing in a chair opposite Frank in the lobby of her hotel.

"I am," Frank said.

I pity anyone who would try to stop him from finishing that mission.

The humidity struck him in the face like a large fist nearly taking his breath away. The flight attendant had been correct. It was much hotter and wetter farther north. Memories flooded back as Jonas stepped out on to the tarmac with his carry-on slung over his right shoulder. The beads of sweat built up instantly, dripping down his sides as he followed an older couple making their way across the steaming asphalt toward the airport entry.

Coronel FAP Francisco Secada Vignetta International Airport seemed like any back water airport Jonas had flown into in the past or present. Climb out of the comfort of the passenger jet and make your way down steep stairs, trudge across what seemed like miles of tarmac with throngs of tired travelers, and then into a long waiting line in the port of entry.

Same routine, no matter where he had flown. Just grin and bear it was his mantra. Otherwise, the person glancing at your passport may not enjoy your attitude and the secondary check-point may take hours to get through.

The world traveling game—endure the wait and shut up.

Jonas smiled, handed over his passport, got the complete once over with standard questions of purpose of the visit to Iquitos, how long would he be staying, and have a nice day.

Peru had to be one of the most insecure or security conscience countries he had ever traveled. From Lima to Iquitos was a domestic flight but international travelers had to have their passports at the ready at every entry and departure gate. Luggage was screened not once, but twice.

Then again, this South American country had seen plenty of terrorist attacks in the past, and this hyper-security was perhaps what all countries should be doing.

The taxi driver was pushed aside by a wiry young man speaking a mile a minute and trying to take Jonas's carry-on.

"Slow down." Jonas smiled evenly while slapping the man's hand away from his bag.

Competition for customers was at full strength, and Jonas looked around, seeing dozens of other tourists being harangued by taxi drivers and motocarro drivers. Jonas nodded and moved along the sidewalk toward a long line of the three wheeled motorcycles.

"Which one is yours?"

"This way—the best vehicle in all of Iquitos." The driver grinned and moved down the line, suddenly stopping beside a red Yamaha 125 CC motocarro with a large face of the devil painted on the rear luggage carrier.

"Nice paint job," Jonas said.

The man bobbed his head up and down. "Yes, I did it myself, though I don't really like the devil but maybe thought it would look okay—yes."

"Yes," Jonas replied.

"I am Fernando. I'll take you to a nice hotel in town for a very cheap price."

Jonas shook his head. "No, you'll take me to the El Dorado at the Plaza de Armas."

The driver was going to protest but Jonas simply waved a twenty dollar bill in the man's face. "Deal or no deal?"

"Do you want to carry your luggage or have me tie it down in the rear?"

Though it had been a many years since his last visit to this large city on the Amazon, his memory wasn't short enough in remembering his first encounter with a motorcarro driver. A zig zag race through the crowded streets of Iquitos to a dump of a hotel. Jonas didn't speak Spanish, the driver gestured he didn't speak English, and Jonas found himself spending the first night in a rundown hovel with no running water and electricity which worked when it wanted to.

The trick was easy. Drive an unsuspecting tourist into town to a hotel which couldn't draw an overnight guest and then leave with a large tip from the counterman. One time only did it take for Jonas to catch on.

The following morning when his contact from the Peru-vian Navy showed up, there were huge laughs all around about how the naïve American had been taken in by one of the oldest tricks in Iquitos. The dump and run.

No, Jonas had not forgotten his first trip at all.

The current Mr. Toad's Wild Ride took off in front of the airport with Jonas clutching the vinyl webbing that sepa-rated himself from the driver sitting on the motorcycle seat in front of him. As the man shifted gears and dodged this way and that way in the late afternoon traffic Jonas tried to lean back, enjoying the wide padded bench seat he was sit-ting on. Not an easy task as the under-powered motorcycle converted into a taxi sped its way into downtown Iquitos.

The rushing wind from the open vehicle felt wonderful to Jonas as the sweat cooled his overheated body. Closing his eyes seemed to relax him even more. He wanted to tell the young driver to continue on until all parts of him were cool and dry but, within a short twenty minutes, the bike shuddered and came to a stop in front of the hotel.

Jonas clasped Fernando on the left shoulder. "And all in one piece, my friend."

"Always," Fernando replied. "If you ever need another ride make sure you have the hotel ask for Fernando."

Jonas nodded as the doorman opened the heavy glass en-try door of the four star hotel in anticipation. "No one else, Fernando."

After checking into his room on the third floor with a view of the indoor pool, Jonas spent minutes beneath the pulsating shower head.

Stepping from the shower, he felt his core temperature drop to a reasonable measure. The autocarro ride had been fine in reducing the perspiration but each time the vehicle had stopped at a red light, the sweat just started up again. The humidity was intense, to say the least.

"How the hell did I make it for all that time in the actual jungle?" he asked, shutting off the valves in the light beige tiled shower.

Toweling off in front of the bathroom mirror, he immediately knew the answer. "I was a lot younger back then."

Within a half an hour, he was at the interior hotel bar across from the lobby pond—a large opaque body of water which seemed to stretch the entire length of the marbled lobby but, in reality, was no more than thirty feet long and ten feet wide. Still, the cooling effect it had for newly arrived guests was amazing. Towering walls and open skylights allowed the blue skies of the Amazon to reach down to the very pit of the hotel, giving a sense of being outdoors. The outside was hot and humid, while the cooling atmosphere of the lobby pond and ever-present air conditioning was the place to be.

Jonas sat on a bar stool and gazed over his shoulder as more tourists entered the hotel. He wondered if anyone had ever accidently fallen into the shallow infinity pond in the lobby. There were no safety rails or warning signs advising guests to be careful on the slippery tiled floor by the pond.

He took a sip of his Cusquena.

"We've lost a few guests in the lagoon," said the bartender

"Excuse me?"

"You were looking at the great mistake." The tall dark-skinned man behind the granite bar grinned. "People get mesmerized and just walk into it. Funny, but no one has gotten injured except for wet clothes and their personal pride."

Jonas nodded his head. "It would be interesting to see, though."

"Better if it is a young woman with a thin dress. The male patrons love that show as she wiggles and giggles out of the water soaked. Many applauds have occurred."

"You could charge for such a show."

The bartender nodded. "We've suggested it to the management who seem not to have the humor or business sense to take it up."

Jonas smiled at the young man and imagined the scenes of people falling into the lobby pond. No lawsuits—this was Peru. You fall and you own it. Responsibility belongs to the one who isn't watching where they are walking.

In the United States, you would have ambulance chasers parked out front of the El Dorado Plaza Hotel.

"Refreshing," Jonas murmured.

"The pool or young women in wet clothes?"

"Probably both but my mind had drifted someplace else, actually."

"And that would be?"

Jonas, for the thousandth time, wondered what he was doing in Iquitos. He was two years short of fifty, still in great shape but still rational enough to realize he was no child.

"Tell me, who owns the Yellow Rose of Texas?"

The bartender shrugged. "Same guy since eighty-one, Gerald. He's not going to leave unless in a bronze box. That place makes a fistful of money."

"Really, Gerald is still here?"

Silence for a moment while the bartender suddenly studied Jonas quite closely. "You know Gerald?"

"I did, from a long time ago."

Finishing his beer Jonas saw a new one placed in front of him. "No, I have to leave."

"In Iquitos, Senor, there is always time for on more cold Cerveza."

As Jonas walked across the Plaza de Armas by the large water fountain, he looked over at the beautiful Iglesia Mariz Church and remembered the time he had visited there. Not a religious man, he did find a sense of peace within the walls of the Catholic Church, though. Kneeling with his hands clenched, he remembered having nothing to say to the man on the cross behind the ornate altar.

"What do I say to a guy like you that gave so much for us sinners?"

After ten minutes, Jonas had stood up and walked from the sanctuary without uttering a prayer.

During that period of his life, he felt there had been nothing for him to say. His team was moving out to the jungle the following morning, and he realized what they may be forced to do to people he had not even met yet.

Those were dangerous days, he mused, looking to the right and left before stepping off the sidewalk and into the wide boulevard. Taxis, motorcarros, and buses sped by, swinging around the square as if they did not have a care in the world. Pick up passengers and drop off passengers was the only matter on the drivers' minds.

What a simple world it must be.

The tall man standing at the exterior of the Yellow Rose of Texas immediately smiled as Jonas walked up the sidewalk and entered beneath the canvas awnings covering the tables closely packed on the sidewalk. In Iquitos, if you owned a business, it seemed you also owned the public walkway in front of that business. Either that or no one really cared in this city of nearly six hundred thousand on the frontiers of the Amazon.

"Twenty years and you recognize me?"

"Could be forty years, and I'd still remember Jonas Peters," replied the heavily muscled man as he moved away from a table of guests and reached out his hand.

Jonas gripped the huge paw the man extended and felt the warmth in the touch. Even though he knew the owner was nearing seventy years old, he was still impressed how fit he was. Not an ounce of fat anywhere and, from the firm grip, Jonas realized the man must work out regularly.

"Gerald," Jonas said. "You look the same as you did the last time I saw you."

"And you, my friend, are a courteous liar." The large man laughed while slapping Jonas on the back. "But at my age, I will eagerly take such lies."

The two men stood there, laughing and making small talk, while the busy street beside them echoed with nearly deafening small engine noise. Though Iquitos was one of the healthiest spots on earth to live with the high humidity and unlimited fresh oxygen from the millions of square miles of rainforest, it was also one of the nosiest.

Being the largest city in the world which could only be reached by air or water, Iquitos was destined to have small motorcycles with two stroke engines. The locals depended on the fuel efficient bikes. With the thousands of small motorcycles humming around the city, the street noise was painful. The high decibels day and night could cause a person to lose their hearing in a matter of time, and many of the motocarro drivers actually did.

Jonas saw that nearly every outdoor table was full with young tourists looking for a taste of the Amazon and ex-pats, mainly from the United States and Great Britain. The fresh-faced tourists drank their fancy drinks with ice while the craggy faced ex-pats simply slugged back beer after beer. It reminded him of his last time in Iquitos. Nothing had changed in Jonas's mind.

"Does anything every change here?"

"Nope and that's the way I like it," Gerald replied, leading the way to an unexpected empty table. "Have a seat and I'll have Angelica grab a bottle of beer for you."

Jonas sat in a multi-colored padded chair with a high cane back and instantly felt relaxed, even though he was perspiring. "Still hotter than hell here."

"You get used to it," Gerald replied.

The young and very attractive waitress grinned when Gerald gave the order for a tall bottle of beer for his friend sitting across from him.

"Then why are you sweating like a pig?" Jonas asked, watching great globs of perspiration drip off of Gerald's forehead.

Wiping away the moisture, Gerald laughed. "I didn't say it wasn't hot or humid, but you just get used to being wet all the time. By the way, pigs don't sweat. It's actually a reference to pig iron, which is form of iron smelting."

Jonas didn't reply, remembering how Gerald was a font of little-known facts. He sat there watching his old friend and waiting for the cold beer.

"When pig iron is originally created from iron ore, the smelter needs to heat the ore to extreme temperatures and then move the liquid metal into the mold. Until the liquid cools, it can't be safely moved, as the extremely hot metal is liable to spill, burning whatever it comes in contact with. So, how does the smelter know when the metal is cool enough to transport? When the pigs sweat. As the metal cools, the air around it reaches the dew point, causing droplets to form on the metal's surface. Thus, sweating like a pig. It's a simile."

Luckily, Angelica returned with the Forest Pilsen secured within a wooden cozie made out of mahogany culled from the nearby forests privately for Gerald for exclusive use at the Yellow Rose of Texas. "I know what a simile is."

"Yes, but I bet you didn't know where that particular simile came from, did you?"

Jonas nodded and poured some of the beer from the bottle into his glassware. Careful not allow the locally made brew to form too much head, Jonas then sat silent while taking a long pull of the Pilsen.

It was cool and refreshing. Jonas wasn't a fan of most Brazilian beers but this extra hoppy tasting one did the trick. It moved down his throat like rich textured foam. The high humidity seemed like a thing of the past.

Gerald looked around the entrance to his restaurant bar and leaned forward a bit. "What brings you to Iquitos?"

Jonas again questioned himself. "Not sure really, just ended up here."

"Jonas, no one comes here by accident," Gerald replied. "You can only get here by river or by the air. It's not as though your GPS went funky, and you took the wrong off-ramp. No, to get to Iquitos one has to be chased here or needs to disappear. I haven't seen you in decades, but you're not the type to be chased anywhere just as you are not one to disappear."

"You forgot one more angle."

"That would be?"

"To gather information," Jonas answered.

Gerald smiled and laughed as a customer walked up the sidewalk and plopped down into one of the vacant chairs two tables from where Jonas was sitting. From the familiarity, the customer seemed accustomed to a waitress appearing like a ghost and delivering a tall glassy drink to the man without saying anything but leaving a large smile in her wake.

"Wow, that's what I call service," Jonas said as he glanced back at the man who was busy taking a long sip of his icy bar concoction and ogling the young woman's behind with all the power his eyes had.

"He's a regular."

"I gathered that as the drink magically appeared without him ordering anything."

"I clapped him on the back."

Jonas looked up at Gerald. "That's the new way to order drinks?"

Gerald smiled while shaking his head. "No, he's a loser who moved down here about three years ago. He comes in seven out of seven days and orders four of the same drinks. Most of the time, we have to pour him into a motorcarro to get his heavy ass home so he won't get hustled by the hookers on the next block or robbed by the local thugs who see him as an easy mark. I can't stand the guy, but he spends money here and the only harm he does is look at my girls."

"Well, I can't blame him there, Gerald," Jonas replied. "You do seem to have the monopoly on the most beautiful women of Iquitos."

"I pay the most and offer medical insurance after a year," Gerald said. "That's a deal not easy to find in Peru."

Jonas nodded, pulling on his beer, and glanced over at the bald fat man who had taken a seat twenty feet from him. He was alone with his drink but the brown tiny eyes beneath his puffy eyelids never moved much from the waitresses as they hurried here and there between customers. A cold shower would have felt good about that time. As he watched, the man seemed to drool when the young women passed his table.

"Yes, he's a pig but his money is good and, like I said, he's never done anything to annoy any of my employees except his staring, which most of them find pathetic."

"What's his story?" Jonas asked, wanting to just sit and idle away in nothing conversation for a bit.

He was enjoying the cold beer and getting cooler from the array of overhead fans beneath the colorful heavy canvass covering above the outdoor patio.

The sun was kept at bay, and that was good in the tropics.

Gerald shrugged. "I don't have much information and don't really care to. Seems he was a banker from California who got fired and then started stealing from his father's accounts to maintain a false lifestyle. Daddy dies and the whole thing unravels when the probate court investigates, and there you have it—a loser who got caught needing to get away from the law and his family. We have a lot of these here, Jonas. Ones like him who his siblings wish he had never been born. Sorry pieces of shit who head into the Amazon as though it were a sanctuary but it always turns out the same."

"And that is?"

"Their personal hell," Gerald replied. "They come to escape and sure, no one really chases these human scum here, but they are always looking over their shoulders and, when they realize no one cares, it's too late. They either venture into the jungle to be eaten during the night or they drink themselves to death like that old guy there."

"How old is he?" Jonas asked, casting a glance sideways at the man at the other table already ordering another cocktail.

"Sixty-four years old."

Jonas nearly dropped his beer. "What? He looks fifteen years older than that."

"He's a coward and that's what brings on the years—being a coward," Gerald said matter-of-factly. "How old are you?"

Jonas grimaced. "I'm almost fifty."

"And yet you look ten years younger," Gerald said. "That's because you are a man, and a true man does not age like that pussy sitting over there. You take responsibility and live life on your terms, but dogs like him look for others to make things right for him. Pathetic, but again, his money is still good, and my drinks give him hope for tomorrow."

"And what hope can that be?"

"That he may not wake up," Gerald said, excusing himself from their table and seeing to a guest.

Jonas, now sitting alone beneath the comforting shade offered by the Yellow Rose of Texas, looked over and studied the man downing his drink and actually felt sorry for him. To be young but look so old. What drove a person to steal from his own family?

He didn't have an answer as he tipped the cold beer into his mouth and enjoyed the coolness.

"He's a fucking thief," said a voice behind Jonas, and instinctively he reached for the weapon attached to his belt, but the gun wasn't there.

Different countries meant different rules.

"If I had meant to kill you, your head would be laying on the table," a stranger stated, taking a seat across from Jonas.

"That's a great way to introduce yourself," Jonas stated, relaxing a bit and trying a smile on the man who moved gracefully into the seat Gerald had relinquished a few moments ago.

"Sorry, but all the seats are taken and here are three that were remaining free," said the man as he looked around and then brought his gaze back to Jonas. "You don't have a problem with that, do you?"

Within a second, Jonas wanted to stand up, smash the man's face into the tabletop, and then drag his ass onto the sidewalk, but instead he merely nodded his head and returned a half meant grin.

"I didn't think you would."

Jonas took a long sip of his beer and set it down on the counter. "I'm new around here, but there's something you need to know about me. I saw the forty-five on your hip and your English is from the United States. You may be a bully here, but if you move an inch toward that weapon, I will as openly as possible drive my beer bottle up your ass and then unload your clip into what must be the dumbest brain in the Amazon. If you get my point, then order another beer for me, or if you don't, prepare to have a rectum exam as the last thing you experience on this earth."

"Why you little shit—" the man started but suddenly shut up as a ham of a hand came upon his left shoulder."

"Joseph," stated Gerald as he squeezed the man's shoulder as tight as he could, drawing tear drops from Joseph. "You just met my friend, Jonas Peters, and I just saved your life. You owe us both a drink."

"Thank you, Gerald," Jonas replied. "It is awfully warm here."

"It is warm, isn't it, Joseph? So warm you aren't only buying one drink for my friend but his tab for this evening. Got it?"

Jonas shook his head. "Gerald, it was just a misunderstanding. I can buy my own rounds and maybe would like to talk to this ex-vet."

Gerald released his tourniquet hold on Joseph. "If that's what you want?"

"It is," Jonas answered with a smile. "If that is all right with you, Joseph?"

"How'd you know I'm an ex-vet?"

"Your eyes," Jonas responded. "I can see it every time."

"You did time in the service?"

"None of your business," Jonas returned. "I'm not here to answer your questions but simply to enjoy a cold beer with an old friend but you tried to ruin that. I'm not happy, but I think we're over that, correct?"

Joseph looked angry but Jonas could see the man was having very serious second thoughts about starting any-thing. That was good—real good.

"Okay, buy me one beer, and we will call your boorish attitude a draw," Jonas stated.

With a wave of his hand, Joseph called the waitress over and made a call for two beers and a Scotch on the Rocks for Gerald.

"As they said in the film Casablanca," Jonas said, "this looks like the beginning of a beautiful relationship."

A loud laugh erupted from Joseph, and he slapped the table top with both hands. "I am glad to buy you a drink and know that I would be dead if I did not."

"What?" Jonas asked as Gerald looked over his shoulder a few feet away and merely shrugged.

The laughter didn't stop as the man slapped the table top again and then finally grabbed a cloth napkin and wiped his eyes. "Whew, that was rich and rather scary by the way."

"What was?"

"Approaching you the way I did," the man responded. "I was told you were over the hill and nothing to be afraid of but I have to admit the idea of a beer bottle going up my ass had those thoughts quickly disappearing when I realized you might actually enjoy doing such a medical procedure."

"What the hell are you talking about?" Jonas demanded.

Joseph looked around and stopped smiling. Leaning across the table, he stared Jonas in the eyes. "Arianna sent me."

Jonas felt as if he had been punched in the stomach by a professional boxer. He could barely focus on the man in front of him let alone notice that Gerald had suddenly turned pale and wandered inside the restaurant.

"Who?" Jonas eked out.

"Arianna," Joseph said without much of a smile. "She, for some reason, knew you would be coming here soon."

"How do you know her?"

"I'm not her lover," the man stated. "But I am her friend, and we've done things together in the past that binds us."

"That's her way."

"What do you mean by that?" Joseph asked in a harsh tone.

The drinks magically appeared, and Jonas waved a hand at the man across from her. "No disrespect but I, like you, know her. My case is from long ago when things were different here."

"Were you her lover?"

Jonas thought a moment. "Lover or confident—in those times what might have been the difference may be argued today."

"Okay," Joseph responded, holding up his large beer, and gestured toward Jonas. "I humbly beg your forgiveness for my boorish behavior but Arianna said if I didn't approach you as I did, I would have no respect for you."

Jonas lightly tapped the edge of his bottle of beer against Joseph's and nodded. "Do you have respect for me now?"

"Better."

"That is?"

"Fear."

"Why fear a guy like me?" Jonas asked.

Joseph shrugged. "You like killing people."

"No," Jonas declared. "I've killed a lot of people but hate ending a human life. They may deserve to die, but it always hurts me to be the one pulling the trigger."

Joseph shrugged. "I'm sorry I came across like an asshole but that's my nature."

Jonas nodded. "Fits you well, but you were saying something about Arianna?"

The man signaled for another drink. "Yeah, was talking with her two weeks ago up river where she has a place and she mentioned you might be showing up sooner or later."

Jonas stared hard at the man. "Why would she say that? I haven't seen her in nearly two decades."

Joseph merely shrugged his shoulders. "Sixth sense, I guess."

"There's more to it than a lucky guess or some voodoo fortune teller routine. She told you that I, a guy you don't know, might be showing up in Iquitos sooner or later?"

"That's what she said."

"And you don't have any idea why?"

"Nope."

"Where is she?"

"Got a lodge about an hour and a half up river by a small village," Joseph stated. "Does some tourist crap—you know, those folks who want to experience jungle life but generally end up doing nothing but bitching about the humidity and bugs."

"Wouldn't know," Jonas responded. "I like the jungle. The rawness and mystery of it always intrigued me."

"Yeah, Arianna said you liked it."

"She spoke of me then?"

"Yeah, a few hundred times over the years. Guess you kind of broke her heart or something like that."

"Something like that, I guess, but it went both ways," Jonas responded and then took a long pull of his beer. It wasn't as cold as a few minutes ago or as refreshing, just like this conversation. "So, why are you here?"

"She'd like to see you."

"Who?"

"Arianna, as though you didn't know who I was talking about."

Jonas smiled. "Just wanted to hear her name again."

"There's still a bit of a torch left, huh?"

"Nothing like that but I have to admit we had some fun times together years ago."

"Let the past alone, Jonas," Gerald interjected as he returned to the table where the men were sitting. "It can only get you into trouble."

"Can't be that bad, Gerald," Jonas returned, staring up at the large man.

"Get back on a flight and return home. There's nothing for you here."

"I need answers, Gerald," Jonas said. "That's all."

"And you think Arianna may have them?"

"Come on, man," Joseph argued. "She's a pretty smart lady—perhaps she does have something Jonas wants. In the way of answers, that is."

"Answers are all I want."

Gerald shook his head. "I'm afraid you may find more than you might be bargaining for."

"I'll take my chances," Jonas said.

Joseph finished his drink and stood up from the table. "Gentlemen, I will take my leave from the both of you and, Jonas, I'll let Arianna know you'll be traveling up river to see her in the morning."

"I'll need directions," Jonas said as Joseph was turning around.

"I have them," Gerald said. "I'll have one of the barmen take you in the morning."

"You knew where she was all this time?"

"Iquitos may be the largest river village in the world, but it's still a village. As Jimmy Buffet once sang about the coconut telegraph, we have the banana express. Things are known before they are even thought of here in the jungle, Jonas."

"I remember."

"Then remember the jungle wasn't kind to you once before, and this time may be a repeat or worse than you recall."

"I'll keep that in mind," Jonas said, nodding.

"You do that, my friend," Gerald returned as he walked away to greet five more customers entering the patio area from the street.

Jonas stood up, dropped enough soles on the table to cover his bill, and walked down the sidewalk into the warm evening air toward his hotel.

The Hotel had Wi-Fi, which gave Jonas a chance to contact Frank and give him an update.

To say the least, Jonas's friend was not happy. "What the hell do you mean you're going off into the jungle?"

Jonas stared at Frank's face on his laptop and shrugged. The Skype signal was sharp, and Frank shook his head in return.

"You tell me you're going to visit some mystery lady who lives in the jungle and then simply shrug to my question. What is she, the queen of some lost tribe?"

Jonas laughed. "No, no queen but simply a woman I knew once who may have answers for me. Somehow she knew I would be here, and I need to learn why she knew that. There's other issues also, but that I won't go into right yet."

"When?"

"Not sure but soon," Jonas replied. "Frank, I'm not being coy, but the less you and Maggie, especially Maggie, know, the better I will feel. This whole thing could be a wild goose chase, and I don't want to alarm anyone if there isn't any need."

Frank's face stared back at Jonas. "You wouldn't be there on a lark, but I won't ask anything further until you want to tell me."

"Frank, I appreciate everything you're doing—it's great news to hear about Sam."

Samantha's condition, according to Frank, had improved to the point that the doctors had been contemplating slowly taking her out of the drug-induced coma. Her injuries had healed faster than expected with the reduction of the brain swelling. The doctors would monitor her condition to ensure there were no further complications and judge the level of her motor functions if the coma was reversed. Frank was confident, and that made Jonas confident in his fiancée's recovery.

"Have you spoken with Maggie?"

"No," Jonas replied. "Not sure what to say to her. How about you?"

"At least twice per day, by phone mainly," Frank said. "Once about you and once about Sam."

"What do you tell her?"

"Nothing about you—I lie and tell her that I don't hear from you but promise I will tell her the minute I know anything what is going on."

"Are you going to tell about this current discussion?"

"No."

"Good." Jonas nodded. "Okay then—I'll get in touch with you when I get back from the jungle. Please don't forget to look into those matters for me."

"Don't worry I got it," Frank stated. "Don't get eaten by a jaguar, Jungle Boy."

Or by a woman by the name of Arianna, Jonas thought as he left the conversation on Skype.

Frank looked at the clock—did the time change calculation—and knew Jonas was turning off the light. He had an early morning wake-up call to head up the Amazon. Part of him was a little jealous of the adventure Jonas was on—not the reason, but the traveling.

Frank hadn't done much traveling, except somewhat local in California and the southwest. Once his family had been killed in the car accident, he hadn't felt like moving about much. Besides occasional business trips, he couldn't remember the last time he took a trip just for the fun of it. Perhaps he would in the near future, or perhaps he wouldn't.

Now wasn't the time—his friend had asked a couple of favors, and Frank needed to get to work. It might be late in the night in Iquitos, but not in Southern California.

CHAPTER 14

The skiff was six feet wide, fifty feet long, and had a six-horsepower outboard motor.

An hour and a half, my ass!

Jonas tapped the young man sitting cross legged on the bow of the brightly painted red and blue skiff.

"Si?"

"How long to our destination?"

A shrug. "Maybe two hours—depends on the river."

How about a bigger engine? Jonas wanted to ask but not sure sarcasm was called for. It was the way of the river—always had been since the Jesuits had started building missions along the length of the Amazon while forcing conversion on the local natives. Once under the thumb of the Spanish, the Port of Iquitos was discovered to be a profitable piece of real estate with Brazil, Ecuador, and Columbia as trading partners with Peru.

With the mighty flow of the Nanay and Itaya rivers moving westward to the Atlantic over twenty-two hundred miles, the Rio Amazon had the greatest volume of water in the world.

"With that much water flushing west, you'd think we'd move at the speed of a toilet emptying," Jonas mumbled while reaching into his knapsack for a bottle of water. Seven in the morning and already the humidity was nearing seventy percent. There weren't enough bottles of water to quench the thirst he was feeling as the blistering sun slowly moved over the jungle.

Even with the coolness of his hotel room back in Iquitos, Jonas had a restless night. His mind never had allowed sleep to enter his being. He felt guilt and a lot of anguish over his troubled thoughts.

Jonas felt he belonged back in Riverside by the bedside near Sam, but at the same time, he was in a quandary, knowing that wasn't his personality. She was in good hands, and he needed to be here to learn who had brought this misery to her and his life—not to mention the other innocent victims of the explosive blast—and punish them.

No, Sam would have been surprised and probably disappointed to find him glibly sitting by her and not out hunting.

He was a hunter, and she knew his nature, but still that nagging guilt of not being with her had kept the sleep from welcoming him.

Then again, there was more than enough questioning of himself as he recalled more than a few thoughts concerning seeing Arianna once again.

He had thought that not seeing Arianna was probably the way it would be when he had departed Peru so many years ago, but that didn't seem the case any longer.

Thinking back to those sweaty bug-infested nights sweltering in the god-awful humidity of the jungle was bad enough, but how was he to know he was going to fall in love—in love with an officer from the Peruvian Drug Enforcement Agency?

It happened, and it was good.

They were young, single, and spent twenty-four hours a day trekking through the thick Amazon with machetes in their hands and sex on their brains. The others on the international drug eradication task force knew of their dalliances once the teams had settled for the night in their makeshift camps, but no words were spoken about the romance. It was the jungle law—actually everyone was too miserable to care.

Arianna and Jonas first met at a four-day briefing held in Lima, Peru's capital city, at the Naval Headquarters. Intense daily discussions, lectures, and warnings by medical personnel, military experts, and drug trafficking officers from around South America left everyone exhausted at the end of the daily rituals.

Their friendship and romance started on the second evening when they nodded to each other when the teams were dismissed for the night. Tired, but young, Jonas wanted to get to know the green-eyed beauty on a more intimate nature. They walked to a small bar just off the naval base and, after the second beer, Jonas was struck.

"Your English is perfect," Jonas stated, staring across the small corner table.

"And yours is decent for an American," she said with a smile. "I was educated in the United Kingdom. so my English is probably more proper than yours."

"But no British accent," Jonas replied. "Rather disappointing, actually."

"You don't like the Peruvian side of me?"

"I think I'm going to like every side of you," Jonas stated.

Arianna leaned across the table and touched Jonas's right hand. "Where are we going with this?"

Jonas smiled, laying his hand atop hers. "The jungle, if the last two days meant anything with all that talk about poisonous this and poisonous that and use lots of Deet."

"You know what I meant."

"Yeah, I knew what you meant, but I thought my reply was rather clever," Jonas said.

"Clever, but clever may not get what you want."

"And that is?"

Her eyes stared softly at Jonas. "Me."

Instead of heading back to the barracks, Arianna led Jonas a few miles to the apartment of a friend who was on duty in southern Peru near Cuzco.

Jonas and Arianna were more exhausted the next morning than the night before, but as they shared secret smiles across the classroom where a lecture on the anti-government terrorist group Shining Path was being presented, both knew it had been worth it.

Tired or not, busy or not, they always found the energy for energetic sexual trysts. At first, it was just a physical thing between the two of them but after the first week in the jungle, Jonas was in love. Arianna was the most amazing woman he had ever meant—gorgeous, intelligent, and afraid of nothing.

Perhaps seeing her again is not the best idea, after all.

The puttering of the small engine ceased. Jonas stood up and shook to unkink his body from the uncomfortable position he had been sitting in for the past hour and a half.

"What's the problem?"

"Refueling," the young man yelled over his shoulder from the bow of the skiff.

"Do you ever move from that position?" Jonas stretched and looked toward the stern where an old skinny man was tipping a red plastic gas can into the tank on the top of the engine.

The young man didn't bother turning around but simply shook his head. "I like it here."

"I see that," Jonas replied, moving forward and taking a seat a couple feet from the bow keeper. "What's your name?"

"Ademir," he replied without turning his head.

"Well, Ademir, my name is Jonas and after being on this craft for over an hour, I thought it would be time to introduce myself."

"Yes."

"Not too talkative, are you?"

"No," Ademir replied. "My English is not so good but better than most here on the river."

Jonas nodded at the simple confession. "I see, so do you spend a lot of time on the Amazon?"

"Much but other rivers too," Ademir stated. "There are many little rivers that come to the big one—the Rio Amazon—and I go up and down those, delivering things."

"Things like what?"

"Many things. Medicine, foods, sometimes tools or even gas when people need it."

"Oh, I thought you worked at Gerald's full time."

"Yes, I do."

"But you're on the river most of the time, yes?"

"Yes."

"Okay," Jonas replied, staring at the young man's profile.

The old man finished topping off the gas tank on the small engine and, suddenly, with a cough and spurt, the long wooden skiff was once again plying up the brown river.

"Why's the water so muddy?"

"The flow of water is very great and pulls the soil from the bottom and makes it stay on the top."

"Makes sense, I guess."

"Yes, it does, does it not?"

"I said so," Jonas replied, wondering if he were on the way to a lodge or a rabbit hole.

The two men sat beside each other in silence for the next twenty minutes when suddenly the boat started slowing down and turning toward what appeared to be a very large island of green on the east shore of the river.

"Is this where the lodge is located?"

"Arianna's place."

"Do you know her?"

"She's my madre."

The question came out before Jonas could stop himself. "How old are you?"

"I'll be twenty-one in a couple months."

Jonas didn't say a word but started doing the math.

The man working the tiny outboard gave the long boat one more boost of gas, and the skiff effortlessly landed itself on the muddy river bank. A beach twenty yards deep and slightly uphill met Jonas as he unlocked his long legs and edged over the gunwale, stretching in the early Amazon morning.

"Adrianna's probably in the mess tent, thinking of starting breakfast for the river guests."

"Thinking of what to have?" Jonas asked as Ademir grabbed two heavy bags from the bottom of the skiff and headed up the beach.

"Every day is different here," he replied. "One day we have fish and perhaps the next day chicken. It is what is nearby and at hand."

"The jungle provides everything?"

"Nearly but what it doesn't, Iquitos does," Ademir mumbled and then disappeared into a nearly invisible path heading to the multiple lodges in front of them. The tall willowy grass was nearly shoulder height, and Jonas tried to keep up with his companion from the boat but as the boy moved gracefully over the now-soggy ground, Jonas found himself slipping and sliding.

"The puma versus the elephant," he moaned as, once again, his right foot stepped into a three inch quagmire of grayish mud. *I don't remember the jungle being like this.*

Within a minute, he was surprised to see a very well-manicured front yard stretching out in front of him. Jonas had a chance to look around the large compound and found he was impressed. Arianna had done well for herself as the place must have easily held forty or fifty guests at one time with six different buildings. Four appeared to be multi-roomed dormitories and one was probably the mess tent where Jonas could see people drinking coffee around a dozen tables. The last huge structure was built higher than the other buildings which had a marvelous unobstructed view of the wide river in front of the lodge.

This must have been a gathering room with deck chairs, hammocks, and what appeared to be a rather long bar in which to serve guests in the afternoon with cold drinks after a full day of adventure.

He took it all in within seconds and nodded his head as he looked south and saw a volleyball court and a semi-in-ground pool which must have measured twenty feet wide and sixty feet long.

"We found that if we had the pool wall off the ground by two feet, jungle wildlife had a little more trouble making it their private domain. Of course, we always remind our guests to look into the pool before diving in. Safer that way," said a voice which hadn't changed in two decades. "Ademir told me you just arrived."

"I didn't hear you coming."

"The years in the jungle have taught me to be quite stealthy, even in my old age," Arianna replied. "It makes an even older life more possible out here."

Jonas turned and found himself looking at the same woman he had fallen in love with so many years previously. A few more wrinkles perhaps, but the eyes were as shiny, green, and alive as they had been the first time he had met her. Long flowing auburn hair framed her beautiful face. She was still beautiful.

"What are you thinking?" Arianna asked from five feet away. Neither had made a move toward each other.

"Many thoughts."

"Want to share?"

"Not at this time, except to say you have built quite a place here, Arianna," Jonas responded.

Turning slightly and raising her right arm in a soft gesture, she said, "The camp was already here but in terrible shape. Took a ton of money and nearly three years to make what you see here."

"Three years?" Jonas asked. The place was rather impressive but in three years in the States, a city could have been built.

"Remember the jungle, Jonas," Arianna said with a smile. "Everything moves like a sloth—the seasons, obtaining materials, working out financial details with the local tribes to ensure they all get a piece of the construction pie.

Politics here in the Amazon are sometimes more dubious and exhausting than anything you have in the United States. Excepting here, if you upset a chief, your whole building enterprise may burn down in one fateful evening. I've seen it happen, but I worked very hard in getting the trust from all concerned—even the corrupt officials in Iquitos to ensure my supplies weren't hijacked at the docks. It's the only true law of the jungle and so, only three years from rebuild to this."

"Impressive."

Arianna smiled. "Thanks and you've only seen the front façade. I'll have your bag put away in one of the only empty bunks and then take you on a tour personally."

"Thanks," Jonas replied. "But I do have questions."

Arianna smiled, revealing a perfect set of white teeth, and laughed. "Jonas, you're down here to find answers which I hope I can assist with, but you also have to remember one must take it slow, too. Tell you what, go to your room and settle in and then meet me in the guest dining building in fifteen minutes for the beginning of your many questions. I have a few details remaining to take care of so my guests will have wonderful experiences during their stay in our jungle. How's that sound?"

"Good." Jonas nodded as suddenly a short older man appeared out of nowhere and reached down to take Jonas's small duffel bag. "No thanks, I got it."

"Jonas," Arianna said. "You're a guest and will be treated as so. Please follow Miguel, and I will see you in the dining hall in fifteen minutes. Take a shower or just relax—the humidity is just building up."

With that, she seemed to glide away across the neatly manicured yard toward the large gathering room where Jonas could see guests standing taking photos of the surrounding jungle and river. He nodded to Miguel who smiled and led the way to the accommodation lodge across from the pool.

The humidity seems to be rising already.

"So, Miguel," Jonas said, walking behind the man carrying his duffel. "What sort of animals have you found in the pool?"

Miguel pointed to the dense thicket about twenty yards from the pool. "Two days ago we had to pull out a very large Anaconda. The guests did not see it, which is good."

"So, I guess I should look in the water before diving in?"

"It would be wise, senor," Miguel replied. "That is what Ms. Arianna tells the guests."

"So she said."

The accommodations were modest with a single twin bunk bed, a small three-drawer dresser, and a rattan chair sitting next to the dresser where a single bulb lamp would offer the only light for the evening. Jonas shrugged as he tossed his knapsack onto the bunk and walked into a very tiny bathroom. Sink, toilet, and a spigot that seemed to flow onto the open floor.

Some shower, but it will work.

He kicked off his Columbia hiking boots and rubbed his feet, which were moist and itchy from the humidity in the air. There was no air conditioning, and already his room was stifling in the early-morning heat.

"Jesus, this is going to be lovely," he mumbled, stripping off his clothes and stepping into the shower. Even at full throttle, only drops of water splattered uselessly onto his naked frame. Ten minutes later and barely wet, he retreated back into the room, rubbed down with a towel, and donned a pair of olive-drab light-weight shorts, a white tank top that stated "I love Peru" in lime green letters, and a pair of flip-flops. He was still sweating miserably as he made his way out of his room and walked toward the kitchen tent.

"No bad things in the water, senor."

"Thanks," Jonas waved back at the man slowly pushing a broom through the water of the lodge's pool. "Maybe later."

Ademir nodded as Jonas entered the dining hall but didn't say anything. Jonas nodded back and smiled. That was it. The two men acknowledging each other without uttering a word as though they both knew a secret but were only waiting for the other one to broach the subject first, which wasn't going to happen.

The hall was pretty much empty except for a young couple who were busy discussing the day's events.

"You know I want to go to the monkey rescue island, and you want to swim with the piranha but perhaps we can do both?" the young woman said as she touched the right arm of the man sitting across from her at the wooden table.

"You'd swim in the Amazon?"

"I don't want to, but I will if you want me to," the petite blonde replied with a smile.

The man, rather muscular with short cropped hair, tapped her hand and returned the smile. "No, we'll go to the island and, if there's time on the way back here, I'll jump overboard for a swim. You don't need to."

"Make sure to tighten your bathing suit," Jonas said quietly while looking around the room for Arianna. "There's fish called bonefish which like to explore human cavities. They are very painful to remove since they're built like a fishing hook with barbs that tear when pulled out."

The man turned and stared up at Jonas. "I thought that was just a joke from that movie Medicine Man a long time ago."

"Perhaps, but take it from someone who has spent a lot of time in the waters around here, it's worth remembering the advice."

The young woman stared at Jonas with widening eyes. "Did you—I mean did you every have one of those things, uhmmm?"

A laugh erupted from Jonas as he waved at Arianna who came in a side door to the left of the large professional cooking area of the lodge. "No, but I always made sure to cinch up my drawers before going into the water. Gotta keep the privates really private."

Jonas walked off to where Arianna was standing by a short but wide refrigerator.

"Thanks, I think," responded the younger man as he turned his attention back to his partner. "Maybe I'll reconsider the swim—they have a pool here."

Arianna shot Jonas a smile and then said. "How do you like your room?"

"Hotter than hell."

"They all are," she replied. "Out here, we can only run a generator a few hours a day, or we'll run out of gasoline. We turn it on around four until the sun goes down so the guests can use fans in their rooms or come into the mess hall where we have a small but sometimes functioning air conditioner. It's remote and most are paying for the thrill of living in the rain forest. It's hot and humid—they get what they pay for, but the beer is cold and the pool nearly cool."

Jonas nodded. "I do have to admit the place is pretty pleasing to the eye. It's hot and humid but we have to remember where we are."

"I never forget where I am, Jonas." Arianna returned with a coolness that had come on suddenly.

"Arianna, listen—"

"Jonas, it's been twenty years and not a word from you. That was downright mean."

"I was busy," Jonas stated, knowing that comment would only enrage the situation.

"Busy? *Busy*—what the hell do you think I was? We were young and spent what I thought were some extremely moving times together—may I throw out perhaps we were in love but yet after a couple of months, you head back to the states and not a word!"

He stared into the same eyes he had stared into so long ago and wondered why he hadn't made the effort. It wasn't as though Jonas thought of what happened as merely a jungle fling because what he had felt for Arianna had been much more. It had, using her words, love. "I have no excuse."

"Well then, that makes it okay in my books," she shot back at him. "No excuse after twenty years—that's fine."

"Arianna that's not what I meant," Jonas held his arms out to his sides in supplication." I don't know why I didn't stay in contact, but I didn't. Time went by and I got married had a little girl who died and then I got divorced. After that, the years sped by, and I didn't care any longer how fast they went just as long as they went. It wasn't that I didn't think of you, which I did often, but you were here in Peru, and I was in the United States. I guess, after a while, things blurred and memories faded. They can still be mustered up when need be, though."

"And when would that be?" she asked. "Is it just when you need a favor?"

Jonas shrugged and let his arms hang by his sides. "I don't even know why I'm here, Arianna but something told me I needed to come back to Iquitos and perhaps I'd find some answers."

Arianna took a deep breath and exhaled slowly. She eyed the man before her critically and felt her heart leap. As hard as she tried to hate him, she could not bring herself to that emotion. Jonas was still the only man she had ever truly loved, and though she had known other men through the years, she had never married or even had a very long-lasting relationship with any other.

Jonas Peters had ruined that side of her.

"What answers do you need?" Arianna asked. "And, Jonas, I heard about your daughter and her death—I am so sorry for your loss."

Jonas sensed the feeling was sincere, and it touched him deeply. Arianna, even after all these years, seemed like the young woman who had meant so much to him at one time. He nodded. "Thank you."

"Okay, let's sit down, since all the guests are gone and doing what they desire for the rest of the day, and discuss what brought you back to the Amazon."

Jonas moved toward the table just vacated by the young couple and motioned for Arianna to take the chair opposite him. "First, at Gerald's, I met a man who said you knew I would be returning. In fact, he said you knew I was already here."

Arianna breathed heavily and turned her head to look out the mosquito netting toward the jungle less than fifty yards to the south. "I had a feeling you would come back some day, but then through the grapevine, I learned what had happened in the city in which you live in California. I knew then you would show up at my lodge any day. How is the woman that was injured doing?"

Jonas didn't respond right away. "How did you hear about all that?"

"I told you, the grapevine."

"I don't believe they grow grapes out here," Jonas responded.

Arianna only smiled. "I still have contacts, and believe it or not, they let me know what's going on in your life and don't get weird on me—I'm not a stalker."

"Wow, I'm pretty popular, I suppose, to have you thinking about me all the time," Jonas replied sarcastically.

Arianna shook her head. "Don't flatter yourself that much. Yes, I still care for you, but it goes a lot deeper than that."

Jonas stared across the table hard at Arianna. "What the hell is going on? Gerald knew more than he let on, and certainly the guy I met who told me you were expecting me also had more information than he shared with me. Arianna, I have a very close friend in a hospital and a lot of dead people back home, and I sure would like to learn why someone wanted to cause that much destruction."

"Your fiancée."

"Yes, Samantha is my fiancée, but there were a lot of others hurt horribly and killed," Jonas responded. "I need to know who did it."

"It's very complicated, Jonas."

"How?"

Arianna got up from the table, walked to the bamboo bar across the room, and poured two glasses of iced tea. "This room always seems so much cooler than the others. I think it's the fact the trees hang over the building until late afternoon affording much-needed shade, and the river is right out front with a slight breeze, which makes the room a little bit more comfortable also."

Jonas nodded as Arianna handed him his glass of tea. "Thanks and probably the four ceiling fans in here don't hurt either."

She smiled. "That's technology for you—a couple of solar panels on the roof give these fans more than enough energy to spin day and night. Well, perhaps not in the wet season but then the temperatures aren't as brutal as the rest of year."

"Very nice," Jonas responded.

"We have plans to increase the solar panels and, hopefully, have fans in all the rooms by the end of this year. Just takes money and time and the locals willing to help, which sometimes can be frustrating when you have to deal with village elders."

"Arianna, why did you move out here anyway? You had it all with your military background, United States education, and your damn fine looks."

"Ah, the circle has come complete now," Arianna said with a smile. "Am I still good looking?"

Jonas stared across the table and nodded. "You are as beautiful as the first time I saw you in Lima so long ago. Fountain of Youth or what other secret do you have?"

"I believe it's from all the moisture in the air. No need for creams or make-up which keeps your skin breathing twenty-four-seven. All this oxygen keeps the heart running at capacity and cleanses the soul."

"This should be a health resort and not an adventure port."

"Who says it isn't both? Honestly, Jonas, you look pretty good yourself. Sure, a few more wrinkles around the eyes and the hair has about equal gray to brown but, overall, you still can turn a woman's heart."

"Thanks."

"Of course, those baby blue eyes of yours are what caught me years ago the first day we met in class at the Naval Academy. Had me at one glance."

Jonas smiled, looked down into his tea, and knew this conversation was not why he flew so many thousands of miles. "Arianna, back to the point."

"Ah, and here I thought we were just going to sit here all day complimenting each other." She pushed out her bottom lip as though pouting but instantly her eyes were dark and cold. "Didn't it ever cross your mind why I didn't come and visit you in California? I had been to America earning my college degrees and truly loved your country, but after you left, I wasn't allowed to leave nor were any of my colleagues."

"What do you mean you couldn't leave?"

She sat back deeper in the rattan chair and looked across at Jonas with the darkness in her eyes ebbing away. "Shortly after you left, Peru had elections, and the political parties changed power, and things changed dramatically here.

Once, the military were the heroes of the people, but we suddenly found ourselves quickly on the outs with the new power in charge."

"What do you mean?"

"We were cast as criminals, or more specifically, war criminals," Arianna replied, tapping her right hand fingers on the table top. "I don't want to go into such history but, suffice it to say, we were tried and, though not put in prison, our tenure in the military was very short lived. Five years after our last tryst, sorry had to say that, I was released from service with a dishonorable discharge and meandered a bit, which is not easy for a single woman in Peru with a young child. I did stints as a teacher, a house keeper, and finally I knew I had to leave Lima and headed back to where it all started—the Amazon and Iquitos."

Jonas shook his head. "No, you're not going to get away with a two-minute explanation of what happened over the past twenty years. War criminals! We were going after drug traffickers."

This time it was Arianna who shook her head, causing her long reddish-brown hair to dance about her shoulders. "That's what you were led to believe."

Jonas felt his head spinning and wasn't sure it was the humidity, which seemed to have suddenly sky rocketed in the large room, or what he was hearing. "We were led to believe? This sounds like a bad movie script."

"Okay, we were looking for drug dealers as requested by your DEA and ATF, but on the back page we, the Peruvian military, were hunting members of the Sendero Luminosos or as you know them, the Shining Path."

"The Shining Path," Jonas uttered, leaning forward. "Arianna, I know about those people, but they weren't in the Amazon region but south toward Cusco. Am I right, or do I have my history wrong?"

"You're right," Arianna responded.

Searching his brain, Jonas couldn't make sense of what he was just told. True, he had been a rookie with just a half dozen years on the force when he volunteered for the assignment of the task force, but he recalled in great detail how the co-national drug force was going after those carting illegal drugs from Columbia through Peru. The northern route had become too costly with the beef up of law enforcement in the Gulf of Mexico. A new trade path had been created by the cartels through Iquitos and then west across the northern tip of Peru to the Pacific Ocean near the city of Trujillo, nearly three hundred and fifty mile north of Lima. Even to this day, large amounts of cocaine were being confiscated by federal law enforcement personnel of Peru and made headlines weekly around the world. Tons of the contraband moved across ancient trails, making it nearly impossible to stop all the illegal trade from moving through Columbia and Peru to its final resting place in the United States.

"Then what are you saying?" Jonas asked, even though he already had the answer.

"Unlike your country, we deal with terrorists—who at that time the Sendero Luminoso was—differently. We went out and engaged, but if they resisted a bit, we killed them. A dead terrorist is one who will not be able to murder innocents."

"Also not able to make political statements against the treatment of those who opposed your government at that time."

Arianna nodded and stirred her tea which no longer had any semblance of ice cubes floating on the top. "Yes, we are a democracy but not what you would recognize."

"I've been told Americans are ignorant with the term."

"You are not ignorant, Jonas," Arianna stated. "Americans are the most generous people in the world—Google that if you don't believe me, but even with your generosity, you are blind to what democracy is."

"How's that?"

"Americans believe that when a government holds elections and there is a clear winner, then that political person of the party runs the country. Well, that may be so in the United States or the United Kingdom, but most places who profess equal and binding elections are only stating that the party which wins better be the party that it wanted to win. That's why there are military coups or governments where certain people disappear without a clue and no one dares ask where they went. It is like that here in Peru every once in a while. For the most part, we are free but only to a certain limit. In Lima, for example, you noticed the haves and the have nots?"

Jonas pushed his "iced" tea away since it had suddenly warmed. "It's a large city, Arianna, and there are poor always."

"No, you miss my point." She tapped the table. "We don't have welfare or any of the other social benefits you do in your country so there are the miserably poor who the government does nothing for and there are the rich who control everything. We vote, yes, but it doesn't always turn out the way we believe it should."

"A political discussion on the Amazon, how cool," Jonas breathed. "Honestly, I could have this conversation at home over a few beers with a few friends but I need to know what you know."

Arianna slapped the table hard and stared at Jonas. "I'm trying to tell you, but you are not listening. We weren't hunting drug cartels when we worked with you but members of the Sendero Luminoso's. Our mission was to assist the United States in fighting the drug trade but the underlying issue for us was to kill as many terrorists as we could."

"Jesus!"

"He was not brought into the conversation."

"You played us," Jonas replied.

"Who played who?" Arianna questioned. "You Americans come down to third world countries—I'm sorry that's now politically incorrect—you Americans come down to developing countries and spread money around as though it is butter, and we are supposed to bend over and do any of your bidding."

"A little bitter," Jonas snapped. "It's not our fault that the United States is a rich and powerful country. Perhaps others should follow our lead?"

"And you never let any other country forget that, do you?"

Jonas took a deep breath since he had had these discussion years ago with the woman across from him. He may have loved her then but her politics drove him nearly insane—they would argue about this and that and then fall into bed into each other's arms making passionate love. A wonderful way to end political debates where neither party was willing to let go of their tenets.

"Arianna, I'm sorry, but again this is not why I am here," Jonas said. "I need to know and I believe you are leading me to what may have caused the explosion in Riverside. Why was I brought here as I believe I was?"

"Go home, Jonas."

Jonas shook his head. "That's what Carlos told me in Lima and Gerald in Iquitos. I'm not in the force any longer, and no threat to anyone, so why do I feel involved in some international espionage thriller."

"It's too dangerous for you here," Arianna said simply.

"Shit, it was dangerous back home when I was just walking down a street to meet Samantha and an entire block of buildings blew up in my face. Life seems pretty damn dangerous just on its own. Excepting for the humidity and the fucking mosquitos, this seems pretty tame."

"You didn't curse when you were younger."

"I'm not young anymore and getting rather tired with each passing year, which brings out the worst in me, I suppose," Jonas replied.

"Carlos is dead," Arianna stated bluntly.

Jonas stared without saying a word. The heat was getting to him as he felt balls of sweat rolling off his forehead. No matter how many times he wiped with a cloth napkin, the sweat just reappeared like magic. "What did you just say?"

"Carlos was shot last evening while leaving a casino near his apartment."

"Was it robbery?" Jonas asked. *Please, God, let her say it was a robbery gone bad.*

Arianna shook her head. "Professional hit—two in the back of the head while he was reaching for the gate keys."

Jonas sat back, felt his chest stiffen, and wondered if he could suck in the next breath. He remembered that Carlos lived in a small apartment in the Surco district of Lima about a block from a casino he frequented for the live music and a bit of gambling. He'd go there, have a drink or two, perhaps drop a few soles into the slot machines, and smoke a cigar on his way home. Carlos had joked that as he got older, routines got easier, and he liked walking and having a good Cuban while looking up into the Peruvian sky.

Carlos would not have that chance again.

"Who was behind it?"

Arianna just shook her head while leaning across the table and grasping Jonas's right hand. "Not sure as of yet, but we're looking into it."

Jonas stared at the woman across from him, his mind whirling with questions but knew he would not get any answers from her. "What do you mean we're looking into it? You own a lodge in the middle of nowhere, and now you're telling me we're looking into it! Shouldn't the local authorities be conducting the murder investigation?"

"They are and so are we," Arianna said, removing her hand from Jonas's. "Jonas, you may not be on the force any longer, and that is fine, but here in Peru, once you belonged, you always belong."

"Like the mafia," Jonas said.

"No, not like the mafia, but remember when I said politics changed and we were no longer free to leave the country—that's what I mean that I'm—we're—still part of the past since it can come back to the present."

"Seems like you're saying the past will kill. At least in Carlos's case."

Arianna remained silent a moment. "Carlos knew the danger of meeting you, and he also knew he had to."

"He didn't give me anything except the same as you are about leaving since it is too dangerous for me to be here. I was a flunky on an international team hunting for what I thought were drug dealers. Now it seems I was a dupe who was really hunting terrorists without my knowledge and fell in love with a team member."

"I fell in love with you too—remember?"

"I believed it."

"Twenty years, Jonas. That's a long time and not even an attempt at a contact from you."

"Arianna—"

"No, I don't mean about us being in love but a phone call or email asking how I was doing. I know life got in the way for you but here in Peru we long for lives worth living, and I had perhaps believed that may have been with you. After you left, things changed, and we couldn't leave the country and were considered some sort of criminals by the very people we swore to protect with our lives—our government. They turned on us, and I guess here we are."

Arianna stood up and walked behind the wooden bar bringing back a bottle of Piscolagia Acholado and two shot glasses.

"No thanks," Jonas said, pointing at the bottle. "I had enough of that last time I was Peru and it is not for sipping.

Perhaps with an egg white or some juice but by itself tastes like gut rot."

"Shouldn't malign a nation's number one alcoholic drink," Ariana replied. "It's not very diplomatic." She poured two healthy portions into the shot glasses. "Try it please."

Jonas shook his head but picked up the glass and sniffed the contents. To his surprise, a nice aroma of pecans and honey met his nose, and a tiny sip proved that he may have been mistaken."

"The mixture of Italia grapes and other ingredients makes it nice, yes?"

Jonas nodded. "Tastes like it has a hint of banana too."

"Probably—expensive but worth it since I agree with you that most pisco is hard to take straight but this one I found a few years ago and seems to be a hit with my taste buds."

Jonas liked the drink. It was fresh and cooling but then he knew his thoughts had to turn back to what the discussion was about. This was no time to relish in the moment.

"But, Ariana, back to the point. That was so long ago, and the Shining Path are a thing of the past so why would anyone want to bring up ancient history? What point would there be?"

She took another slow sip of her drink and momentarily closed her eyes, enjoying the rather earthy taste after she swallowed. *It is good.*

"Have you spoken to the other members of the team the United States sent after you went home?"

Jonas thought a moment and then shook his head. "There were only two or three of us from local law enforcement agencies and the rest were people I didn't know who worked the fed side of the action. We shook hands, said we would stay in touch, and went home. Unfortunately, we didn't."

"Longtime friends, yes?"

"Just the way it is, I suppose."

"What would you say if I told you that your entire team has been systemically murdered over the past two years?"

Jonas quickly took another sip of the pisco and stared hard at Arianna. "That this is really starting to sound like a spy novel."

"It's true," Arianna said. "But don't take my word for it. Look it up when you get back to Iquitos. All dead, Jonas excepting you and me."

"Carlos…"

"Once there were three and now there are two."

Jonas turned his head as the screen door to the kitchen opened. Ademir strolled into the room and actually smiled Jonas's way.

"Hello, Madre," Ademir said as he came over and kissed Arianna on the forehead.

"Good morning to you too," she said, giving her son a quizzical glance. "But we've already greeted each other already."

"Just felt like doing it again, I guess," Ademir replied, turning to Jonas. "Good morning to you too, Mr. Jonas."

"Jonas will be just fine," Jonas replied.

"Yes," Ademir said and suddenly sat down at the table beside his mother. "What are you two discussing so in depth that the need of pisco is present?"

"Ah, nothing much, Ademir," Arianna said. "Just catching up on old times."

"Good old times or just old times?"

Jonas didn't like the tone of the young man's words. Not rude but not friendly.

"Ademir," Jonas started. "I do need to finish this conversation and need to speak to your mother privately."

Ademir flashed a wide grin Jonas's direction. "Of course, I understand and will leave you two alone."

With that, the young man stood up and exited the eating area without further word.

"That was odd," Arianna stated, watching her son leave.

"I need to ask you something."

Arianna turned her attention back to Jonas. "Yes?"

"This sounds strange but…"

"He is your son, Jonas."

Arianna stood up, poured the both of them another shot glass full of pisco, and put her hand out as Jonas was about to start to talk.

"When you left, I discovered I was pregnant but things were moving so quickly I didn't know what to do. In this culture or at least in the nineties, a single mother was not looked upon so well. So, I had a heart to heart with my commander, explaining the situation and because he and I were good friends, he suggested I take an assignment in Puno on the shores of Lake Titicaca. There I could work a bit and have my baby out of the eyes of more stringent supervisors, and then I came back to Lima and Ademir was more or less raised by my parents and me."

"Why didn't you contact me?" Jonas asked, feeling his chest rising and falling with difficulty—*I have a son.*

"I tried but Jonas I was young and scared. My career was just starting and, like I said, being an unwed mother in a mostly Catholic nation was not something I had ever imagined."

"How hard did you try to find me?"

"I made some calls to others on our team but they weren't much help and, truly, we didn't spend much time talking about the exact city you lived in—I couldn't even recall what agency you belonged to—either federal or local."

Jonas was about to say something out of anger but decided not to. They spent their time together making love at night and hunting what he had thought were drug dealers during the day. There wasn't much time for small talk and, for the life of him, he couldn't recall if they had spoken of his home or even which department he worked for at the time. All members of the eradication team wore the same camouflage uniforms, making specific identities nearly impossible to know, and carried no hard and fast documents, in case they were captured.

"About four years after Ademir was born, I finally was able to get a location on you, but by that time, you were married and soon after that you had a baby girl," Arianna said. "At that point, I was not about to intrude into your life with the news you had a son in Peru. Probably wouldn't have set well with Mrs. Peters."

Jonas thought back and knew what his ex-wife would have done with that news. It would not have been joyful to say the least—Becky was a good woman and mother but once their child had been taken away from them so horrendously, she had changed. A moment never went by that Jonas wasn't blamed for the death of their daughter during that bungled convenience store robbery.

He would never forget that awful year after Stacy had been murdered beside him and the night after night screaming accusations by his wife. "You were such a big stud cop that you had to draw your gun on the criminal instead of just letting him rob the damn store! Jonas Peters you are nothing but a fucking coward and the worst father there could be on this planet—I hate you now and I will always hate you for killing our little girl!"

Jonas recalled in those few quick seconds the anguish he always felt for the loss of his only child. It took one short year of failed counseling sessions, meetings with the local parish priest, and finally divorce court to end the Peters' marriage.

Since the case was so well known, the *Riverside Press Enterprise*, the leading newspaper in the area, carried the divorce and all the dirty details on Detective Jonas Peters. The one piece of all those stories he still carried in his wallet was when his then ex-wife shouted to the reporter carrying the divorce: "Jonas Peters will find his perfect place in hell when he dies for the murder of my little girl!"

Though it was tattered, he often had taken it out through the years to remind himself he had once been a father and perhaps—if Becky had been correct—a bad one.

Now, he was a father again. That knowledge scared him greatly.

"Where are you?"

"The past and now the present," Jonas answered.

"It doesn't change anything," Arianna stated. "I mean it does but it doesn't really."

Jonas stared at her. "What the hell does that mean? Of course, it changes everything and by the look in Ademir's face he knows too."

"No, he doesn't."

"I can see it in his eyes."

"No, what you see is you looking back at yourself," she said. "That is all—he probably thinks something since I have never spoken of his father excepting that he left us before he was born."

"That's true but his father didn't know."

Arianna ignored the jab. "So, being a very smart young man, he is probably putting two and two together. He obviously knows of my history with the military and the missions I undertook against the Sendero Luminosos and figures that was about the time he was to become my son and you were in Peru at the same time. So, there you go."

"Yes, there we go." Jonas took a short sip of the pisco. "And where do we go from here? Do we tell him? Do I try to take you all home with me when I leave? What do we do?"

Arianna shook her head. "What right do you have to come here and start trying to figure things out? We have a good life, and it was you who interrupted it. Yes, Ademir may have been curious, but he coped very well all these years without knowing who his father was and it would be up to me to tell him not you. This is home—not the United States but Peru. Here in this hot and humid Amazon jungle is where we belong. Jonas, I loved you, but that was a long time ago and you left me with something I could never live without—a child to adore."

Jonas listened in silence, knowing Arianna was right. It pained him to know that he had a child but also realized that if Ademir found out the truth, it might ruin his entire adult life with confusion, and that was something Jonas would not allow to happen.

He had been the cause of another child of his not reaching adulthood, and this time he would not interfere.

"Of course, you are correct, and I'm sorry if it sounded as though I wanted to take control. You are very successful and safe here—so we will leave it just friends from the past for Ademir."

A smile stretched across Arianna's face. "Very close friends but thank you for understanding, and I am sorry it can't be something different, but, Jonas, you have a life in California with a woman who loves you lying in the hospital. I suppose I could scream and demand that you make amends for leaving your lover in Peru while you went home to the safety of America, but I'm not that way. I was a very willing partner in our love making, and though it saddened me with you gone, I got used to it and realized it would never had worked out between us."

"We could have tried."

"No, my love." Arianna reached across the table and again laid her hand upon Jonas's. "It would never have worked in the long run. We're from two very different cultures, and the thought of leaving my beloved Peru, even with all her faults, would have killed the very life I was carrying in my belly. This is home and always will be."

Jonas knew there was nothing to say.

"Don't be sad or angry with yourself," Arianna said after a moment of staring into Jonas's blue eyes. "The memories of your arms around me while making love still visit me often and bring a smile to my face. So find the answers you came for and kiss me goodbye forever this time knowing I hold no feelings of hate or loss but ones of knowing I truly cared for one of the best men I have ever met."

He couldn't help himself as a single tear dripped from the corner of his left eye. He did not wipe it away.

CHAPTER 15

Frank pounded his fist on the desk and screamed at the ceiling. "Goddamn, Jonas, can't you be near a fucking phone when I need you?"

He had just gotten back from the hospital and learned that Samantha was doing remarkably well, and her prognosis even surprised her doctors.

"We keep going over her vitals and test results and have to say that, for a person having such injuries, Samantha will be up and out of here within a couple of weeks," Doctor Scarlett Rose told the two people standing in front of her.

Maggie had let out a loud "whoop" in the hallway right outside of her friend's private room, and Frank stood a little more stoically next to her with a grin from ear to ear.

Maggie hugged the doctor and gave her a quick kiss on the right cheek. "Frank, I'll go phone Roger and the kids with this great news while you try to get a hold of Jonas—if you can."

With that, Maggie shot off as though she was in a sprint to the finish line.

Frank smiled at the doctor. "That is great news, Doctor. Should I hug and kiss you too."

"The hospital would probably frown on that, but I'll just imagine you did," Scarlett Rose replied with a smile.

"Seriously, Doctor," Frank said as the two of them started down the hallway toward the nurse's station. "You and your team have done an unbelievable job here, and there is nothing we can say that would be enough to express our gratitude."

Scarlett Rose nodded her head and then stopped, placing her hand on Frank's left arm. "Where is Detective Peters?"

"I don't know," Frank replied.

"But you just agreed to phone him with the news about Sam's health," she said. "You just told Maggie you would."

"Yes, I did tell her that, but she also added if I can."

"Are all cops minds that fast to remember the exact words and nuances of another's speech?"

"Not all," Frank said. "I did know some pretty dumb cops in my time, though."

"I do not believe you fit in that category, Detective Sanders."

Frank nodded. "I'll take the compliment since, at my age, they come slower and slower every day."

"And what about Detective Peters?"

Frank thought a moment before answering, not sure where this was going. "One of the brightest I have had the pleasure of knowing."

"He's a good friend of yours?"

"Wasn't always, but we worked well together on certain cases while on the force here."

"But not friends?"

"Cops don't try to make friends just in case."

Scarlett Rose looked into Frank's eyes. "In case of what?"

"Friends sometimes are taken away from us unexpectedly and quickly in the streets—so have a few beers together, solve a few crimes together, but don't ask for a home phone to set up a game of golf. Sometimes those golf games never materialize because the foursome has been cut to a threesome."

Removing her hand from Frank's arm, Scarlett Rose adjusted her white smock. "So, it is as dangerous out there as we read about in the newspapers?"

"No one reads about what really goes on within the heart of a police officer. It's our job to keep as many people as safe as we can from the wolves prowling twenty-four-seven. We are simply sheep-dogs running circles around our flocks just in case one of those wolves enters the fence. Sometimes we save the sheep and sometimes the wolf wins and eats them—it's a predatory world out there, Doctor—not good and not bad, just what it is. We're the only stop-gap society has to maintain some sense of equal balance between the two—unfortunately, it seems nowadays the wolves may be winning."

"And the reason for Jonas's absence?"

"He's the best sheep dog I have ever met and truly pity any wolves who run into him."

The glass filled quickly. Frank tipped the quart of Jack Daniels almost on its head. One more, and that would be enough.

Maybe not.

He had tried every number Jonas had given him in promised secrecy but nothing was working. The guy he was to meet in Lima, Carlos, wasn't answering his phone, the hotel Jonas had called from in Iquitos said they hadn't seen Mr. Jonas for two days, and that was it. Jonas's cell seemed to be turned off or in an out-of-service-area, which didn't surprise Frank since Jonas had told him he was going remote.

After doing some Googling, Frank realized that the northern section of Peru where Iquitos was located was about as remote as one would want to be. But knowing Jonas, it wouldn't be remote enough.

He imagined his friend—yes, he did consider Jonas his friend, no matter what he had said at the hospital to Doctor Scarlett Rose—would be jungle side. Frank wasn't sure what Jonas was after and the very quick briefing Frank had received was just enough to be totally confused.

Of course, he knew Jonas was hunting down whoever had blown the coffee shop up but exactly who or where he was wasn't clear.

Taking a long sip out of the tumbler and feeling the warm whiskey flow down his throat seemed to ease his anxiety a bit.

Yes, he wanted to deliver the news about Sam's almost miraculous recovery but there was something more pressing he needed to give Jonas.

He took another pull—tried the phone numbers again and threw the rest of the drink in the glass against the opposite wall.

"Damn it! Where the *fuck* are you?" he yelled again, looking at the note he had found below his office door on his return from the hospital.

His anxiety was back full force. The message had been simple: *I know who blew up the building!*

CHAPTER 16

hey T sat in comfortable silence for five minutes before Jonas started to talk. At first, he wanted to continue the conversation about his and Arianna's son but realized it would just end up in an argument, and that was something he did not want to endure.

Was he upset—that would be an understatement—but did he blame Arianna? No, at this time in his life, he did not blame anyone.

Damn, I'm changing. Jonas would not allow himself to discussing things that occurred twenty years ago. He had fallen in love for a short while with a very beautiful woman working beside him day and night, and they had episode after episode of passionate love making which was good.

Very good!

But he had returned home, and though he thought of Arianna constantly, life took over and, once back at work, the days, weeks, months, and then years came and went. He remembered her soft skin and the way she arched her back as he entered her but, with time, everything faded and so did that two-month romance.

Jonas didn't see himself as a user but an enjoyer of the time they had spent together—then again, if he had known about Arianna's pregnancy, there would have been nothing to stop him from rejoining her in Peru and trying to convince her to come back to the United States.

Looking across the table, he realized the last thought would have been a losing battle. As she had said, Peru was her home and where she belonged.

He understood that all too well. Riverside was his home but how many times he had wished he could move away and start over, but his baby girl was buried there, and no matter how much he tried to tell himself that it didn't matter, it did.

There was no way he could move—he tried it once to Scottsdale, but the thought of not visiting his daughter's grave once per week was unbearable.

He was the one who put her in the grave and the one who needed to visit weekly to say how sorry he was.

But listening to Arianna, he knew this was different and always had been. He may be Ademir's father, but it wasn't like he left the boy on the sidewalk without a caregiver. Arianna was his mother and had done a wonderful job raising the young man.

Jonas didn't feel any guilt—something he hadn't experienced in years.

"I love you," Jonas said as he looked across the table.

Arianna smiled. "And I love you too and will always."

"Thank you for being such a good parent to my son."

"Thank you for not making it more difficult at this time."

Jonas nodded. "He won't know?"

"He may guess but guesses are like those things people do with lottos—pray the numbers come your way, but they never do. No, Ademir will be fine and grow into the man I have prayed for. Strong, independent, and wise—much like his father."

"I am honored."

"You should be," Arianna said with a smile. "Here, have a bit more pisco, and I will put the bottle away before we have too much and end up in a hammock together."

"I could think of worse things," Jonas said.

"Aw, that is what we need—to have our son come back to the lodge while you are on top of me swinging in the breeze naked."

Jonas laughed. "Who said I would be on top?"

Arianna poured another shot and shook her head. "What we had was wonderful and let us leave it at that. We have much more serious concerns at this time."

"Yes," Jonas said as, suddenly, the screened door to the kitchen violently ripped open and Ademir staggered in.

"Mother," he said in a detached voice.

"Son!"

"I've been hurt," Ademir replied as his body suddenly lurched forward and fell face first onto the wood floor.

The cruel and hideous bloody marks across his back indicated he had been attacked by a machete.

Within seconds, both Arianna and Jonas ran to their son and slowly turned the young man over. Ademir's face was ashen from the loss of blood but he tried to smile as he gazed into his mother's face.

"Two men arrived after the tourists left at the dock and said they were looking for the whore who owned this lodge. I told them that only my mother owned this place, and they laughed and said she was the whore they were looking for."

Jonas knew the blood loss was great as Ademir's face went from white to deathly pale. "We have to get him to a hospital."

"There is no hospital," Arianna answered. "We're in the goddamn jungle!"

The short time he had been on the Amazon, Jonas realized that death was imminent unless Ademir could be seen by a doctor. "There has to be something."

"A full first aid kit behind the bar," Arianna shouted. "Get it!"

Ademir breathed slowly but steadily which Jonas took as a good sign. *Relax, boy, we'll make it through this.*

"Mother, when they said that, I told them you were a good person, and they were wrong. That's when they laughed again and I hit them with a paddle from one of the canoes," Ademir's speech was short and gasping. He was having trouble focusing and, as Arianna looked into her son's eyes, knew he was dying.

"Don't speak—save your strength."

A cough and a few blood bubbles seeped out from between his lips. "That's when they hit me with machetes but they also had guns strapped to their backs. They want to harm you, Mother."

"Stop talking," Arianna said quietly as she saw the light going out in her son's eyes. "Relax, my boy."

Jonas was kneeling with the first aid kit open on the floor beside Ademir and was fumbling with large pieces of gauze, tape, and antiseptic. "We need to roll him over."

Arianna simply raised her hand. "Don't. My—our—son is no longer with us."

Jonas stopped and looked at Arianna who was cradling Ademir's head into her bosom and crying softly. Suddenly, she started humming a soft melody to the young man lying in her arms as she rocked him back and forth.

"Arianna," Jonas started while still holding a handful of gauze.

"Shhh," she whispered. "This was Ademir's favorite ever since childhood. Let me sing it to him."

"But, Arianna," Jonas started and then stopped again as his former lover and mother of his child kissed the brow of the child they were never able to share together.

Arianna hummed a few bars and then gently laid her son's head onto the wood floor and slowly stood up. Jose had come into the kitchen and quietly stood to the side holding a metal rake in his hands as though it was weapon.

"Jose," Arianna said. "Please ask the village elders to come to the lodge and do me the great honor of placing my son into the holy ground."

"Ms. Arianna," Jose spoke quietly. "Are you sure they are needed?"

"This is their land that they allowed me to build my lodge on many years ago, and I must ask their permission. You do understand don't you?"

There was no reply as the old man left the dining area and headed north from the lodge toward the village which Jonas had been told was only a mile away.

Jonas was still staring at his son, hoping against hope that the boy's would flutter open suddenly.

The eyes remained closed and the chest remained motionless.

The son he had for only minutes was gone.

"Arianna—" Jonas started but was cut off.

"Jonas," Arianna interrupted. "Do what you do best."

"What is that?"

"Kill."

Jonas looked at Arianna who was only inches from him. "I'm not a killer or at least never wanted to be."

She touched his right arm and pulled herself into his chest. "My love, they have killed our son."

"I don't even know what this all about," Jonas whispered, inhaling the scent of her hair.

She gently pushed him away. "I thought I did but this is far beyond anything I would have imagined."

Arianna stopped talking and started crying openly as she fell to the floor grabbing her only child into her arms.

Suddenly Jonas felt the sorrow leave him, replaced with pure hatred. Bending down, he kissed Arianna on the forehead and then knelt farther while giving the son he had never known a kiss on the right cheek. "I love you."

Jonas stood and gave a glance down at mother and son. He turned and started from the room.

"The jungle can kill you," Arianna said between sobs as she watched Jonas barge through the screen door.

"Then the jungle better be wary of me."

Frank glanced again at the note in his hand. *Meet at midnight behind the CVS Pharmacy on Market, and we will tell you who was behind the bombing.*

He was standing beside his car, looking at his watch, when a man walked up from the left.

Within a second, Frank had his 9mm snug against the man's right temple. "And what is that you want?"

The man stopped in his tracks and started shaking.

"You're not here to meet me are you?" Frank asked.

The man only shook his head as a stream of urine ran down the right side of his pants.

Frank handed the man a twenty. "Sorry, mistaken identity."

Fifteen minutes rolled by, and Frank was getting a little bit edgy. He didn't like the secret private eye gig that was played out on television. He wanted answers and waiting around an area like downtown Riverside was not something he enjoyed as homeless people shuffled by pushing stolen shopping carts.

He wasn't without feelings, but with the amount of taxes he and all his friends paid, there shouldn't be any homeless anywhere. Mental illness might be one thing, but these others should be working.

Was he an unfeeling bastard when it came to the poor? No, Frank liked to think of himself like most Americans—

work and you will be free, but if you depend on the government for everything, you will live as a slave.

He was about to give up the vigil when a black SUV pulled into the parking lot, parked, and no one got out.

Three minutes later, Frank realized that he was supposed to approach the vehicle.

"I will charge Jonas three times my usual rate, I swear when he gets back," he muttered to himself as he approached the vehicle from the right rear with the 9mm conveniently tucked into his right hand.

Unlike Hollywood, there was already a round in the chamber.

He tapped on the passenger's window with his left hand and suddenly heard approaching footsteps from behind.

"What the hell?" Frank asked as the lights went out.

Jonas leaped off the porch of the front lodge and headed for the docks where Ademir had said the men had confronted him.

He had no idea what he was doing, but doing was something he had to do. The idea of losing a son he had just met was too much, and Jonas needed to move, to get the adrenalin jumping in his being to make it from one step to the other.

The parent within him screamed to sit on the ground and claw the earth in frustration and horror. Stacy and now

Ademir were dead—at least he had time with his daughter but not his son—even a son who would never know his father—at least they could have been friends.

Now there was nothing but emptiness.

Jonas hooked a left at the dock after seeing marks of a struggle in the thick mud of the Amazon and, within moments, found himself deep inside the fauna of the jungle. Though it was only past noon, Jonas realized within the canopy of the jungle it was at minimum dusk. The sun was shadowed by the large leafy trees and bushes which only allowed a few feet of visibility in front of him.

Within ten minutes, Jonas stopped with hands on his knees sucking in as much oxygen as he could gasp.

He estimated he may have only covered a few hundred yards in the dense undergrowth and wondered how much longer he could last.

"Killer? I can barely walk at this point," he muttered to himself as the sweat from exertion and the humidity had sweat running down his body like torrents from a thunderstorm.

His nearly fifty years on the planet suddenly came to Jonas with the realization he was no longer a young man.

"What the hell am I doing out here?" he asked as he found himself sliding down into a sitting position on the ground against a tree. His chest ached, and the sweat was clouding his eyes to the point he could barely see.

For the first time in his life, Jonas had doubts about his ability to accomplish what he had set out to do.

He was uncomfortable with that realization.

One thing Frank hated more than anything was being tied up like a pretzel.

He was now a pretzel in the back of a vehicle driven to who knows where and that really irritated him. Ten years earlier while on the force with the Riverside Police Department, he had been involved with saving a suicidal juvenile who had wanted to take a nose dive off a bridge that spanned the highway at Central Ave. As the distraught girl of fifteen made her best effort to make a splash on Highway 91, Frank leaped out and grabbed her while attached to rope guidelines from the fire department which were fastened to a rather large water tanker and his crotch.

Frank and the girl fell ten feet and then snap, crackle, and pop. He was a hero, and she was a disappointed teen who ended her life six months later with the use of her father's handgun.

That was the way of life and death, Frank figured, but the pain in his back had never decreased but increased. This situation, being bundled up like firewood, certainly wasn't helping the agony.

Early retirement had been offered at seventy percent, but Frank had thought, *Early retirement to what?* His family had been killed in an auto accident years previously, so what was he to do with the remainder of his years?

Full retirement finally came and, with that, a license as a private detective in California which usually involved divorce cases, employees stealing from the till, and more mundane issues like that.

Now, sitting extremely uncomfortably in the back of a vehicle was not what Frank had signed up for, and whoever opened the back door was going to be in a world of hurt.

As the vehicle slowed, Frank turned slightly. Even though the cloth bag that had been thrown over his face blocked out all sight, he knew which end was up.

He doubted his captors knew that as he painfully wriggled his handcuffed wrists below his waist and buttocks.

Within moments, Frank knew whoever had kidnapped him would be rather surprised. Very surprised.

The vehicle stopped and the engine went dead. Frank prayed that the rear doors would open equally.

He was sore and ready to beat somebody to death.

"I'm fifty and have to get used to it," Jonas mumbled, gulping in some air, and felt the ground below his frame starting to feel too comfortable. He stood up and grabbed the nearest branch.

The heat in the jungle was beyond belief, and the humidity must have been topping ninety percent.

I have to move.

Jonas straightened up with an effort and took another deep breath—it felt like sucking in water. When he was about to let it go and return to the lodge to be with Arianna and his son Ademir, a rush of noise no more than fifty yards to his left got his attention.

He couldn't make out the words but, by the urgency in the tone, he knew it must be the killers of his boy.

They had stopped too, but now they were up and moving.

Saddened, horrified, exhausted, and scared, Jonas took another deep breath and quietly followed the voices.

Unbelievably, within a few minutes in the dark green overgrowth of the jungle, Jonas found himself within ten yards of two men who were standing outside of a village hut. One of the local villages he had been told about with the guide when he had arrived and one that tourists visited on a regular basis.

Jonas sat behind a large ceiba tree and waited. He had no weapon, no cell phone, and no one knew where he was. There was this large forest, the killers of his son, and him. As he looked to his left, he noticed a short, thick, spiked branch lying on the forest floor as if it had been hacked off. A man with a machete must have cut this deadly branch off to use later…for what, Jonas wasn't sure…but he picked it up, very carefully, and broke off several of the three-inch spikes at one end to make a handle. The moment now seemed a little more in his favor. This might do the trick if needed.

It seemed the two men were trying to keep their voices down and also seemed upset that no one was answering the wooden door of the hut they were standing in front of.

"I told you just to ask the kid a question or two but, no, you had to grab him," said the smaller and older of the two men in fair English. "You scared him, and that's why he swung at you."

"He should not have done that," the younger man replied, again in passable English, bringing his right hand to his left cheek rubbing it gently. "I didn't mean to machete him."

"You swung and hit him hard on the back and then you swung again and again," Shorty stated, again pounding on the simple frame of the door. "Why does he not answer? We have to get back up river soon since you ruined our chances with the gringo."

The taller of the two men shrugged. "I'm not afraid of that man. He's old and not going to chase us. He's probably crying like a baby right now."

Shorty was about to knock again on the door when he turned and saw his partner's head explode into a mass of tissue and blood splattering the side of the hut. The man did not have a moment to utter a word before he was attacked, too.

"Call me old, huh, asshole?" Jonas yelled while quickly spinning on his heels and thrusting the short thick branch containing nearly three inch spikes into the other partner's chest causing him to stumble on the uneven wood deck.

The man grabbed the thick branch, but immediately snapped back his hands as the skin was torn to the bone.

"Hurts, doesn't it, motherfucker?" Jonas said as he leaned into the branch, forcing a few of the spikes to pierce the man's chest. "Wonder how my boy felt as that dead scumbag there kept swinging the machete, huh? Think about it for a moment before I kill you."

The man stopped moving as he looked down and saw the spikes slowly sinking deeper and deeper into his chest. "I didn't want him to do it."

"But he did."

"That wasn't the orders," the man squealed as the pain increased to the point he felt he might vomit any moment.

"But he did," Jonas repeated, leaning harder on the branch, forcing the three inch spikes to fully extend into the man. "He did and he died—like you are going to."

As if a switch of realization finally went off in the man's mind, he suddenly lurched forward trying to make a break from Jonas and the barbed tree branch.

He didn't make it far as Jonas moved back two steps, pulled the branch from the man's chest, swung it with all his strength into the man's groin and viciously tore it out leaving a streaming blood flow from all the holes punched by the spikes.

Deadly silence was in the air as the man simply stopped in his tracks and toppled to the wood porch.

Jonas leaned down and stared into the man's startled eyes. "Those tears running down your face will only last a minute or so since I'm going to kill you but how you die depends on how you answer my questions."

Recollection barely seemed to register behind the globes filled with water and, as Jonas looked down at the man, he only felt hatred. As the man slowly started to move his hands toward his crotch Jonas stopped him with a not to gentle tapping of the tree limb. "No, no—there's nothing left down there to touch so don't worry about it. I can tell you can hear me and you can probably speak, so first off— why did you kill my son?"

The man tried to speak but only a frothy red substance leaked out the side of his mouth.

"Okay," Jonas started. "I'll give you a couple of seconds to compose yourself."

Looking around the small village, Jonas wondered if it was deserted since no one had bothered to come outside to investigate the noise of the first man falling heavily to the ground, dead. Not a peep when the second man screamed with the thrust of the branch into his chest and neck. Jonas saw no one and heard no one. *Why were they about to knock on the door if no one was around?*

The jungle was eerily quiet as though it knew that death was imminent.

Jonas's attention was brought back to the man at his feet who mumbled something almost intelligible. "What was that?"

"I didn't know he was your son," the man whispered, wiping the spittle from his mouth.

"Actually, that should not have mattered—he was just a boy."

"He was running from us to warn those in the lodge."

"That would have been me."

"And the woman who owns the lodge."

"Arianna?" Jonas asked, believing he had been the only target but then he remembered what had happened to Carlos and the others Arianna had told him about. "Who sent you?"

"A man from Iquitos."

Jonas picked up the broken tree branch and felt a shudder of revulsion run through him as he eyed the blood and skin tissue sticking to the barbed spikes. "What man from Iquitos?"

"I don't know but he goes to a bar nearly every day where the gringos drink."

The man stopped speaking as Jonas laid the spiked branch at the man's throat. "Are you sure?"

"Yes, he said you were dangerous and must be forced to leave Peru, either alive or dead."

"Is the man's name Gerald?"

"No, not the owner but he knows the man. He's big and an American who has been living here for many years."

"Yeah, I know him," Jonas whispered, unsure if he believed the man or not. Gerald had pointed him out and said something about the man being ex-military from the states.

"So, what about the woman?"

"He said she had to go, too." The man moaned when finally reaching down and feeling the blood seeping out of his groin and realizing that he would bleed to death if he didn't get any medical attention. "That she was a bad person who took advantage of the people of Peru when she was in the military and killed many innocent villagers years ago."

Jonas's mind was racing, trying to put this all together, and slowly very slowly the puzzle pieces seemed to be coming together.

"So, you were hired to kill us?"

"Yes, or at least scare you enough to leave Peru for good, but killing you was what the man said would be the best."

"You killed my son," Jonas stated very flatly.

"He did." The man grimaced in pain as he rolled over a bit and pointed to his dead partner laying less than a dozen feet from him. "I told him not to but he went crazy and started swinging and then we got scared and ran away. We didn't think you'd find us in the jungle."

"You don't know me," Jonas whispered.

"Are you going to kill me?"

"I already have," Jonas stated.

The man nodded and knew the man with the broken tree branch had spoken the truth. Feeling himself growing cold from the loss of blood while his eyes began to grow heavy and the relief he knew he'd feel in a matter of minutes would be a good thing.

He was prepared but suddenly sorry for all the agony he had brought others in his life.

Jonas wasn't sure but there seemed to be a look of contentment on the man's face as he died.

CHAPTER 17

The doors of the van opened, and Frank kicked with all his strength at the first face that looked into the rear. A sickening sound of breaking cartilage erupted into the night sky as the head disappeared from sight, and Frank bounded out of the rear of the van.

Even though he was still handcuffed, Frank spun around and gave an additional kick to the side of the head of the man withering on the ground. The man stopped moving.

"Hold on there, Frank!" said a voice to the right.

Frank didn't hold on but only got angrier and lashed out with clenched fists at the first person he saw.

The iron bracelets he was shackled by found a soft target. With a loud groan, another man went down like a rock, dropping a heavy revolver onto the ground.

In an instant, Frank was down, grabbing the weapon and rolling quickly beneath the van looking for any target that showed itself.

It was dark. Extremely dark and quiet suddenly while Frank quickly tried to figure out where he had been driven. Remote and out of the way with no visible signs of lights or civilization.

"Goddamn it, Frank!" said the voice, which seemed to have moved farther away. "You're making this a lot more difficult than it needs to be."

"I do that when someone is trying to kill me," Frank yelled, slowly edging further up the frame of the van and scanning the area. Nothing was moving, and all he could make out in the dim moonlight was the bodies of the two men he had dealt after leaving the van.

Don't make assumptions.

"If we wanted you dead, you would be by now," the voice in the night replied. "I just want to talk."

"Then talk," Frank said, suddenly hearing someone trying to be very sneaky coming up on the driver's side of the vehicle.

He moved the weapon into the direction of a foot that was protruding from around the front tire.

The first round from Frank's gun tore off the front of the shoe while the second ripped the heel loose from the ankle and a third man fell to the ground with a shriek while a mean-looking semi-automatic bounced beneath the van and into Frank's outstretched hands.

He scooped it up.

"For someone not trying to kill me, you are making it hard to believe," Frank yelled and then turned the gun back on the man screaming in pain. The third round made the man fall silent.

"Frank, for God's sake, stop this!"

"Stop what?" Frank replied, quickly scanning all around him for any more unexpected guests.

Within seconds, he knew no one was about to try to sneak up on his hiding place any time soon. With the respite, he moved his hands to his right front pocket, dug out his car keys, and used the cuff key which he always carried to unlock himself from the restraints.

Never leave home without them.

He tossed the handcuffs out from beneath the van and smiled as they clattered nosily on the ground beside the now dead man by the front tire.

"I believe those are yours," Frank said. "Do you now want to tell me what's going on, or do I come out and make you tell me?"

"Frank, it wasn't supposed to happen like this," came the response. "A quick chit-chat and you would have been on your way."

"Like hell," Frank muttered, inching his way to the front of the van and carefully turning his body so he was looking forward instead of the direction of the rear of the vehicle. Even more slowly, he crawled out, and in a half crouch, looked around himself silently and quickly while keeping the revolver pointed with both hands, the semi-automatic now tucked snugly into his waistband.

He could see the road with its black asphalt nearly shining, indicating the use of very few vehicles, but beyond about twenty yards, the night encompassed everything else. The sliver of moon didn't allow him much of a chance to view anything, but at the same time, it must be working the same for his would-be captors.

"Okay, Frank," said the voice from the darkness somewhere to the rear of the van. "We'll have to do this another time."

With that, a roar of an engine exploded into the quiet night and, within seconds, Frank was blinded by a pair of high-beam headlights as a large SUV, obviously the one he had encountered earlier, roared by.

He spun and let the remaining three rounds from the revolver erupt from the barrel trying to find its mark but the night blindness won and the bullets missed by a couple of feet. The vehicle was gone, and Frank suddenly found himself in the darkness surrounded by only silence.

"What a hell of an evening," he said, while standing up and stretching feeling all the knots in his back screaming.

A fast reconnoiter told him the man by the front wheel was dead, the one with the busted face wasn't getting up any time soon, and the other one he had beaten with the handcuffs was coming around but not making much sense from a mouthful of broken teeth.

Frank toyed with the idea of just shooting them, but down deep, he wasn't a killer, just a protector of lives. Mainly his own.

"Mumble mouth," Frank said, leaning down to the man on the ground who was very slowly coming back to reality. "I'm not going to kill you but instead leave you out here—wherever out here is. Now, I could give you a ride back to town if you tell me everything I want to know, but realizing you are probably nothing more than a piece of shit stooge for the guy you're working for, I doubt you have much to offer. So, the offer of the ride is no longer valid. I'm beginning to think how all this is going to play out so, next time, I won't let you off so easy."

With a quick but firm kick, Frank sent the man back into dreamland.

The keys were in the ignition and, with a rumble, the large van started and Frank flicked on the headlights, driving slowly first down the road. Within moments, he rounded a bend and saw the city lights of Riverside below.

"I'll be damned," he said aloud.

The kidnappers had only taken him to a utility road alongside the dry Santa Ana riverbed just southwest of Mount Rubidoux, which had blocked all the lights of Riverside. Less than five minutes later, he was back to where he had parked his vehicle earlier in the evening at the CVS Pharmacy on Market Street.

Five minutes more and the van was wiped clean and parked discreetly on Fairmount Blvd. a block west of the store.

"No need for questions to be asked about the van," Frank said while climbing into his car and leaving the parking lot. He wondered about the cameras that were sure to be in the parking lot but knew whoever had taken him would have dismantled them in the first place.

By the time Jonas returned to the lodge, he was sore and saddened by what he had witnessed and done.

"I'm not a killer," he whispered, climbing up the few stairs to the boardwalk that circled the lodge. He could hear murmurings from within the kitchen area and knew that many people were in there but wasn't sure he wanted to join them.

This wasn't his world, and he suddenly didn't feel like he belonged. A woman he once loved was mourning the son he never knew existed. He had just taken the lives of two strangers in the middle of a jungle thousands of miles from his home feeling pleasure at their deaths. The puzzle pieces were falling into place but what the final picture would be could be very different than what he was imagining at this moment.

"Jonas." Arianna had come out through the screen door and touched him lightly on the left shoulder. "The village headmen are saying prayers over Ademir and have agreed that he can be buried here."

"That's good, Arianna," Jonas whispered.

"Did you find the men who did this?"

"Yes."

"And?"

Jonas shrugged. "They're dead."

Arianna said nothing but turned on her heels and re-entered the screened in dining room.

He wished he hadn't given up smoking a million times. A cigarette might have tasted good right then as he stared out across the grassy area sloping to the banks of the Amazon, thinking of his next moves.

Thoughts of Samantha came back to him like a steam roller, and all he wanted at that moment was to reach out and hold her hand—he wanted to marry her and just forget all the sadness that had overtaken their lives in the recent past. Perhaps move away or simply live on his tiny ranch in Phelan and hold each other day and night.

He was lonely and knew no one could fill that hole he was feeling but Sam.

Glancing one more time out over the dark colored waters of the great river he walked into the room behind him and into the mysteries of a death ceremony for a loved one he didn't know.

"Frank," Maggie said as the detective walked into the waiting room of the hospital. "Any news from Jonas?"

"No, nothing," Frank lied. Well, actually he hadn't totally been dishonest with Jonas's sister since he hadn't heard from Jonas in nearly a week but what he had just gone through definitely had Jonas in mind.

Being kidnapped and nearly murdered was big news—really big news, especially when you leave dead bodies out on a dark roadway as a way of paying them back.

Nah, nothing out of the ordinary happened lately, Maggie.

"What happened to your head?"

"What do you mean?" Frank asked, involuntarily wincing while Maggie poked him on the right side of his head just above the temple.

"Hurts, huh?"

"Well, yes, especially with you pounding me on the head," Frank responded, gently touching the half-inch swollen egg on the side of his cranium. He had done his best to conceal the bulge but ice could only bring swelling down a bit after being clobbered by whatever it had been that had knocked him unconscious.

"I barely touched you," Maggie said, eyeing Frank evenly. "What the hell is going on, Frank?"

Frank shrugged. "What do you mean?"

Maggie waved at a pair of faux-leather chairs in the waiting room and waited until Frank got the hint and sat down in one of them. She took the opposite one.

"I've known you for years, Frank Sanders," she stated. "Not well, mind you, but ever since Jonas left the force, you two have grown a bit closer, and I'm usually on the hearing end of the conversations with Jonas when your name comes up. He has a lot of respect and confidence in you."

Frank digested that a moment and then smiled. "That's nice to know."

"And I want to feel the same way, Frank."

Oh, boy, Frank thought as he gazed into Maggie's eyes. "And I would want you to feel the same way about me too."

"Then you need to be straight with me, Frank." Maggie reached out and touched his left arm. "Tell me what's really going on. I know Jonas isn't in country and probably looking for whoever did this to Sam and the others, but he's been gone nearly a week and not a word. That's not like him. You know it, especially with Sam still in the hospital."

"She's getting stronger by the day, and it won't be long until she's released."

Maggie took her hand away. "Don't change the subject. Where is he?"

"He promised me not to tell you."

"Why?"

"Jonas loves you and your family."

"I know that—" Maggie stopped, and her face turned ashen. "Wait—he thinks we're in danger?"

Frank nodded.

"Why?"

"That's what he is trying to find out."

"Why us?" Maggie asked, but suddenly, her thoughts turned to another time a few years earlier when Jonas was the focal point of a killer's revenge, which had ended horribly with her own family being tortured physically and emotionally. She could barely hold herself together as the memories flooded back to her about those horrific moments in Scottsdale.

"Maggie—Maggie, are you okay?"

She was silent a moment, catching her breath. "I was just thinking of Zachary Marshall."

This time, it was Frank who reached out and comforted Maggie. "It's not like that this time. Marshall was a homicidal maniac, but this time—"

"But what, Frank? He was just one man bent on killing as many as he could, but what's the difference here? These people behind the bombing killed dozens and wounded twice as many, so you see there is a difference. They make Marshall look almost calm. And now you say they are after us?"

"No, that's not what I said," Frank declared. "It's just that Jonas has an idea who may have been behind this and is trying to tie up the loose strings."

"Is that why you have a bump on your head the size of a walnut? They came after you last night?"

Frank was suddenly very tired. "Yes, they did, but I got the best of them, I think."

"Who is doing this and why?"

"I think I may have a lead on who but not on the why part," Frank answered. "I'm hoping Jonas will give us that piece of the puzzle when he gets back."

"And when is that?"

"When he's done is all I can imagine. Haven't heard from him in a week—he was in Iquitos the last time I spoke to him heading for the jungle."

"The jungle?" Maggie questioned. "Wait, he was in the Amazon decades ago doing some police work with other agencies. He went off as a lark but came back a changed man."

"How so?"

"I don't know, but much more serious than he had been before he had left, and he was only gone a couple of months or so if I remember correctly."

"Well, I didn't know him back then, but I'll take your word for it—those kinds of operations can have people thinking differently about a lot of things when it's over."

This time, Frank was being as honest as he could. All the specific details of Jonas's stay in the Amazon had never been fully discussed with him but only bits and pieces through the years. A story here and there over a cold beer. Nobody really paid attention, thinking of a tale which might supersede the last story.

"PTSD?"

"Not sure, but knowing Jonas the way I do he wouldn't admit it."

Maggie nodded. "Do you have any idea when he will get a hold of you?"

"When he does," Frank said with a shrug. "He goes by his own calendar, Maggie."

She held out her hands to Frank, who slowly wrapped his own hands around hers. "Would you say a prayer with me?"

Frank hadn't prayed in so long he wasn't sure if he remembered how. "If you say it, I will, surely."

"Of course," she said.

"Are we praying for Sam's health?"

Maggie shook her head. "I want to pray for all of us, Frank. I believe we may need it sooner than we want."

CHAPTER 18

The funeral was held the morning after Ademir's murder. It was quick, to the point, and not many tears fell as the small group of nearly a dozen people stood forty yards from the lodge and placed the young man into the ground covered only with a burial shroud.

Jonas had been aghast at such a rapid pace for a mourning and funeral but was told it was the way of the jungle. The boy had to be placed into the ground quickly so the spirits of the jungle could meet him as soon as possible, giving him immortality in the afterlife. He had heard different accounts of periods of mourning which could last up to three days and sometimes involved a pyre—to ensure the body would not decompose in the moist ground—or other elaborate shows of loss.

"This is the way they have offered me, Jonas," Arianna had told him during the preparations for the service the day of their son's death. "We're not natives, and the option the village elders are allowing me to bury my son here in the land he loved so is deeply moving. This is where he belongs."

"But, not even a casket—sounds barbaric," Jonas mumbled, looking over to the area being cleared in the nearby jungle where Ademir would rest.

"It's their custom," Arianna replied. "This is not our world, and things are done differently here. It wasn't that long ago that another Amazon tribe named the Wari would offer relatives a chance to eat the dead to keep the lineage intact."

Shaking his head, Jonas thought a moment. "Well, I suppose we've made progress over that custom."

"My love, let it be and let him rest in the ground."

"I don't have a choice."

"Not really, no," she said, turning away and walking to where a group of native women were huddled around her son's outstretched body as it was being prepared for the burial.

Ademir would now belong to the Amazon forever.

Jonas walked to the wide river's edge and stared across the breadth of one of the largest rivers in the world, wondering what secrets were hidden within the canopies of the great trees covering the millions of square miles of land which encompassed the Amazon territory.

"What secret are you keeping from me?" Jonas asked aloud.

Looking back over the past twenty-four hours, he realized he would never understand this land he found himself in.

A son he never knew had been murdered by strangers. Then he killed both men in broad daylight in a fit of rage and revenge.

As he had settled down back at the lodge, he expected the authorities from Iquitos to be called in to investigate the series of crimes and that he himself would be placed under arrest for murder or at least detained. But nothing had happened—things had happened but not what he expected.

Jose, the caretaker had calmly took him aside and explained how the village had agreed to bury Ademir on their land near Arianna's lodge and that there had been no reason for any law enforcement or military personnel to investigate. The boy had been murdered with a machete—anyone would have known that so an investigation was not called. Especially since Jonas had found the murderers and dealt with them accordingly.

Death was the sentence for such men and the father had carried the full judgement to the men who had taken his son from him. Justice had been served.

"You do not need to worry about those men," Jose had said to Jonas during their very surreal meeting. "The Amazon is wide, swift, and very deep with many creatures of the water looking for food. They will not be seen again, and no one will ever mention them being here, even if asked. The jungle holds its secrets tightly, as do the people who live here."

Jonas held her in his arms and felt the years melt away as his lips gently touched hers. Between the soft sobbing at the loss of their son Jonas could feel himself rise and knew his feelings for Arianna had never left. Softly and gently, he entered her and then stopped as he heard a large crashing sound outside of his screened room at the lodge.

"What?" he asked, shaking off the dream.

"Jonas, it's the boat to take you back to Iquitos," Arianna said softly from the porch that ran in front of his room. "Did I wake you?"

"No, I was just lying here waiting."

"For what?"

"I'm not sure." He threw his legs over the side of the narrow bunk and stood up, going to the door. "It's still dark," he said.

"The sun will be up soon," she said, leaning against the railing across from his room. "You need to get back to Iquitos and then back to America and find out what has caused all this horror and sadness."

"I'm not a magician."

Arianna shook her head and wiped a few stubborn strands of hair from her face. "No, you're not a magician but simply a man who gets jobs done."

"I really got this done well," he replied, realizing how real his recent dream had been and wondered for a moment if he should reach out for her.

"It's too late for us, Jonas," Arianna whispered. "We had our time together but this is no longer that time."

"Are you a mind reader?"

"No, just a woman who is very vulnerable at this moment after the loss of her son and now, for the second time, the man she loves."

With a nod, Jonas turned back to his room, gathered up his belongings, and stepped back out to the walkway. Arianna was still there.

"Do you think that if things had been different—"

"Things are what they are," Arianna interrupted. "The boat will be here in fifteen minutes. Come and I'll make you a breakfast you can eat and some hot coffee to take the chill of the Amazon off you."

"Thanks," was all he could muster.

"And, Jonas," she said. "When you do find out, please leave a message for me with Gerald explaining everything, so I can have some closure in my heart, but never come back here."

"I understand."

Arianna turned and gave him a hug. "I know you do."

The boat ride was quiet with the slight hum from the small-horse-powered engine barely stirring the water behind the long dugout. Jonas sat watching the shoreline slip by. He was alone, except for the silent man guiding the boat across the waters, and he suddenly felt very empty inside.

Looking at the bow, he imagined just for a moment a young man sitting there with crossed legs staring out over the Amazon. Jonas wished he could turn back the hands of time and get to know him as a father would a son.

Jonas felt the tears slipping down his cheeks but didn't wipe them away—a second child he had lost, and again he had been the cause of it.

The harbinger of death was what he was—he realized it now.

Then I will bring it down on all those who have wronged those I love.

A slight jab to his right shoulder brought Jonas instantly awake from the almost-comfortable slumber he had dozed off to on the long boat ride from the river lodge. Jerking up and looking around, he realized the engine was no longer running and the small old man was simply standing beside him pointing into the distance.

It didn't take a genius to understand that a very fast boat was pounding across the slightly choppy waters directly toward them.

"Who are they?"

The man motioned that he didn't fully understand Jonas's words but saluted.

"Military," Jonas guessed. "Great."

Within moments, the twin 250 horsepower outboard engine Peruvian Naval patrol boat roared beside the skiff and shut down its engines, almost swamping the low-lying boat

Jonas was now standing in. The captain looked scared, but simply shrugged at Jonas.

Two armed men pointed short nosed sub-machine guns at Jonas from the patrol boat but did not say anything as the two craft equalized next to each other in the currents of the Amazon.

Jonas smiled and waved from the skiff, wondering if he should jump from the craft and try to make it shore a quarter a mile west. He realized that, within moments of him hitting the water, it would be peppered with bullets, and even if he could avoid the lead, he'd have to swim against the current with the piranha and the anacondas. He waved once more.

"Are you Jonas Peters?" a voice asked from the interior of the forty-five foot boat, and then a man in a very crisp white naval commanders uniform came up to the deck.

"I may be."

"Ah, in this country it is wise to answer in full sentences with complete answers and not coy responses. I'll ask again, are you Jonas Peters?"

He had no choice. "Yes, I am."

"That is what I thought—you will come aboard then, and we will talk."

"About what?"

"Help him aboard."

With that, the commander disappeared into the rather small salon on the gun boat as Jonas was given a hand by one of the navy personnel and jerked up onto the deck. The old man on the skiff tossed Jonas his backpack, waved, and started the five-horsepower outboard. Within seconds, he was a hundred yards south of the gun boat on his way back to the jungle camp.

Jonas, with backpack in hand, headed to the salon being gently nudged with the gun held by one of the two men who had been standing on the deck. He didn't like being handled like that, but looking around at his current conditions, Jonas didn't think he'd much choice but to go along.

He was shown into a small but comfortable salon with a long settee on one side and two chairs on the opposite wall.

"We travel quite a bit on the river and sometimes need a place to relax instead of always being in the elements. Please, sit down," said the man who had ordered him aboard.

"Your English is perfect," Jonas said, tossing his backpack onto the floor and taking one of the chairs opposite the settee where the commander was sitting.

"It should be since I went to the University of California in Berkley. Marvelous school but very liberal for my tastes—then again, I received a full scholarship in Philosophy so liberal or not, I took advantage of the education."

"Smart move."

"Yes, it has rewarded me in advancing my career in the navy here in my home country of Peru. I am up for admiral next rotation."

Jonas nodded. "Congratulations."

"Thank you," the commander said, gesturing to a naval personnel who handed Jonas a cup of tea. "None for me, thank you."

Jonas sat quiet, not knowing what was expected, and sipped the tea. It had a hint of chocolate and mint, giving the tea a robust but pleasant taste which was a compliment from a man who rarely drank tea of any sort. "Nice flavor."

"The chocolate comes from Colombia and the mint from a local supplier not far from here—greenhouse, of course, since the weather on the Amazon isn't exactly suited for such a delicate herb."

"Yes."

The commander stayed mute for a moment and then reached out his right hand. "My name is Javier Guardio, and you are not under arrest."

"That makes me feel better," Jonas replied, actually feeling his breathing start to slow down a bit. Luckily, the tea cup wasn't shaking in his hands.

"Unless, that is, you may have done something unsavory in the jungle recently."

The thoughts of the two men he killed entered Jonas's mind, but he knew his outward appearance would show nothing. "Nothing unsavory at all."

"That is what I believe also," Guardio responded. "Things occur in the Amazon, but the mighty river cleanses anything that could be deemed unsavory, yes?"

"I would also agree."

"Good, now, the reason for the lift we are giving you to Iquitos," Guardio stated.

Jonas nodded, placing the empty tea cup on a small wood table beside the chair he was sitting in. "Ah, a taxi."

"An expensive but very safe taxi, yes?"

"Yes."

"Good." Guardio nodded. "Now, I understand from many sources that you have been here in Peru for only a short time period."

Jonas thought about making up a story but instantly knew better when he looked into the officer's dark brown eyes.

He knows.

"I came here looking for answers," Jonas replied.

"Did you find them?"

"Not completely and some I don't understand."

"What do you understand…completely?"

Jonas took a deep breath and then felt the strong outboard motors start to rev up as the boat moved ahead at a slow but steady pace. "I was here in the late nineties as a joint task force from the United States."

"We have had many of those."

"It was the height of the Shining Path."

Guardio shook his head. "No, actually, it was in the eighties those terrorists of the Sendero Luminoso reigned terror in the countryside, killing and torturing innocents. They even invaded certain parts of Lima itself—now you can still see splendid houses in Mira Flores surrounded by tall walls and barbed wire. A shame, but after Guzman, their god, was arrested in September of 1992 the whole business seemed to calm. Of course, there were scattered strong holds but through the brilliance of the military, we routed them."

"I understand they do a pretty good drug trade even now."

Guardio stared quietly into Jonas's eyes and then smiled. "Ah, there are drug traffickers everywhere, and if it wasn't for the fat market in your United States, most of these drug dealers would be out of business. There is no need for buying drugs in most third world countries, yes—I even admit my beloved Peru is such, but any farmer or peasant can grow enough cocaine to make a little money on the side. The Luminoso only grows it in the highlands in southern Peru like the Apurimac River Valley where no one wants to venture and then transports it to various ports on the Pacific."

"Why not?"

"It is remote, inhospitable, and many jungles that hide snipers. It is where, for now, it is believed the source of the Amazon begins. It is nothing but small villages but important to the citizens of Lima who rely on foodstuffs from the region and much of the hydroelectric energy comes from there. A perfect hiding place for small bands of terrorists."

"As you just said," Jonas said, nodding. "How many terrorists are still left?"

"I am not sure—maybe a hundred or so, but they are not interested in taking over Peru any longer but making money from the sale of their drugs. Though, there are rumors they have slave peasants who grow the cocaine and the women produce babies in a rapid way so child soldiers can be produced. Perhaps the rumors of them wanting to battle the Peruvian military isn't so far off, but then again, how long for those child soldiers to grow into fighting units?"

Jonas thought a moment before answering. "Maybe ten years."

"Maybe less, depending when their mommies were raped, producing them, but I will be retired then and living comfortably and unmolested."

"When I was here in the nineties, we were told we were hunting drug cartels in the north by Iquitos, but now maybe

I'm guessing it wasn't just drug dealers," Jonas said, thinking back to what Arianna had told him. He wondered if this Commander Guardio would validate her.

Guardio stared and then stood up from his chair, looking out a large glass window toward the shore of the Amazon. "We were after drug dealers."

"With political aspirations?"

"You did find some answers, didn't you?" Guardio replied without turning around. "We were being brutalized by these bastards and didn't have the technology or connections to fight both the cartels and the Luminoso. As you know, Peru and the country of Columbia have never been that close, so when the United States offered assistance in getting rid of the cartels, we agreed and thought what you didn't know wouldn't hurt you."

"Killing terrorists?"

Guardio turned from the window and stared down at Jonas. "Aren't drug dealers the worst sort of terrorists there are in the world? They bring their filth into communities, making people so desperate for their goods they are willing to murder their own family members to steal money to buy the drugs. People are so frightened of the drug users and sellers in their own neighborhoods, they try to be home before dark. Children become look outs for the drug panderers and then become addicts themselves or drug dealers as they grow older. Entire sections of cities are torn apart by these narco-terrorists. Look at your own Detroit, Chicago, and even your precious Washington DC. Aren't they dens of crime brought about mainly by these animals that do not care for anything but their own sick ideologies—be that religion, politics or simply money?"

Jonas didn't reply as his mind back-tracked over the years he spent as a detective for the Riverside Police Force. Replaying scene after horrible scene in his head, he couldn't find an argument against Guardio's statement. He didn't try too hard either. "Okay, say I buy into what you are saying and I truly can't find much fault in it, but did we really track down any actual drug cartels?"

"Yes, quite a few of them moving cocaine from Columbia through the upper Amazon and into northern Peru, but there were a few times those drug traffickers were actually members of the Luminoso moving the drugs themselves to the coast."

Jonas stood up and stretched. "Then there was no harm or foul, correct?"

"True, but we had not asked your government to assist in ridding our country of terrorists with an ideology of turning Peru into land of Mao worship. We were not like certain Middle East regions who gladly accepted help in destroying the groups known as Al Qaeda or ISIS. We were simply on the same page of trying to keep drugs out of the hands of the young people in the United States—and you assisted blindly."

"It was long ago."

"Certain people have long memories."

"That's what Carlos said a few days ago in Lima before he was murdered," Jonas replied.

"Yes, and a shame. He and I were friends?"

Jonas shook his head. "I wouldn't know."

"We served together for nearly fifteen years before he retired."

"He told me he was forced out for something he did while hunting the Shining Path," Jonas said.

"One man's retirement is one man's forced out," Guardio replied. "Anyway, a good man and a true shame being killed in such a way and just steps from his home. Probably a robbery is what I heard from some sources in Peru."

"Yes, a robbery," Jonas replied, knowing there was no robbery involved.

"So, there," Guardio said. "You have your answers to your questions, and we are only fifteen minutes from Iquitos. The taxi ride is almost complete."

"Almost," Jonas said, glancing around the boat's salon. "I said some questions were answered and some were not."

"That's all I know, and all I can offer."

"What went wrong when I was here as the joint task force? What was there that was so fucked up that someone tried to kill me and those I love in the past couple of weeks? Why was my son murdered and Carlos a couple of days ago and probably others I don't know? In fact, what the hell is going on?"

Guardio suddenly produced a small caliber semi-automatic from his right pants pocket and pointed it at Jonas's stomach. "You ask too many questions."

Jonas held his breath and then felt the anger rise. "You don't give me the answers I wanted." At that moment, Jonas swept out his left hand, caught the gun by the barrel, snatched it away from Guardio's hand, and directed its lethal barrel at the man's face. "A small twenty-five caliber but it will do the trick with the bullet entering your right eye and tearing into that piece of shit brain of yours. You'll be dead before I can get the second round off."

Any confidence Guardio had diminished. He peered at the gun in Jonas's hand and raised both of his. "I was told you were not to be fooled with—a dangerous man who didn't give a damn about his own life. Not afraid to die."

"I've died many times in the past but the damn of it all, I arise to die all over again—you hurt my loved ones, and I will hurt you and yours."

Guardio lowered his hands and retook the seat ge had prior to standing a few minutes earlier. "You can lower the gun. I won't try anything foolish again and will answer what you want as best as I can."

"You know, I once watched a movie about a guy hunting for his daughter who had been kidnapped by some scumbags, and you know how he got the information he needed?"

Guardio started to sweat but simply shook his head instead of answering verbally.

"He shot the guy's wife in the leg and then threatened to shoot her in the head. Let's go visit your family—you have a wife, a daughter, or a son? You see I've lost both a daughter and a son to assholes like you and, in this stage of my life, I can take yours as well to get what I need to stop this bloodshed from spreading. Do you understand me?"

Guardio nodded. "There was a small village in northern Peru that was supposed to be a center for training the Luminoso. Not a large place but one that needed to be taken out and, as long as the multi-national task force was present, we decided why not use it for our purposes? Intelligence, or at least what we called the information, we provided stated that there were possibly twelve to fifteen traffickers in that village ready to make a move toward the Pacific overland through the jungles. Our job, yours and ours, was to simply stop them, arrest them, and seize the drugs."

"That was how it was supposed to have gone down?"

"Exactly," Guardio stated. "But the day before we were to penetrate the village, orders came from Lima for an immediate and mandatory meeting for most members of the task force. It was something to do with new and true trafficking information that the combined governments wanted us to deal with and forego the village for the time being. It wasn't like the village or training base was going anywhere in the near future so most of us—I included, though I wasn't present with your detail but instead was serving near Cuzco in the south—left for the capital city and the three day briefing."

Jonas remembered the change of plans as though it was just yesterday and recalled the joy he had felt realizing it would be a great chance for he and Arianna to spend time together back at her apartment in Lima. Neither he, nor she, was supposed to attend the meeting at the naval base in Lima but somehow between his bullshit and Arianna's beautiful eyes they were allowed to escape the jungles for a few days together. It had been three of the most intense love making days he had ever spent—remembrances of actually eating or sleeping were only a fleeting thought. No, it was the sweet passion he remembered intertwined within damp sheets.

"What happened?" Jonas asked as he heard footsteps moving about the deck outside.

"That is a mystery still," Guardio said. "After Lima, I headed back south to Cuzco and I suppose the rest of the northern units returned to the village."

Memories of the return trip over the jungles of the valleys flooded into Jonas's brain as he recalled being miserable at having to leave Arianna's small apartment for the discomfort of a military transport. She had sat across from him and all he could think of was reaching over, pulling her tight against his chest and continuing where they had left off only hours earlier. Then suddenly those images left and other filled his thoughts.

"Or what was left of it," Jonas said, pocketing the gun. "If I remember when the main force returned, the village had been fired and the traffickers killed."

"Yes, that was the official story."

"What do you mean?"

"There were no drug traffickers or terrorists in the village," Guardio stated. "We had received the wrong information."

"That can't be true," Jonas started. "I heard that dozens of drug traffickers had been killed. I wasn't there, but it's what I remember."

Guardio nodded. "You were sold a bill of shit, as they say in your country."

"It's goods, but what do you mean?"

He motioned to get up from the chair and Jonas nodded. "You see, it was only villagers that were murdered during the raid, while most of us were in Lima. Twenty-eight to be exact and nine of them were children under the age of seven."

Jonas felt as though he was in some alternate universe at that moment and had to physically brace himself against the interior wall of the salon.

"It's true—nobody but simple peasants in a nondescript village eking out their living in the jungle. The task force, those that weren't in Lima, went in and shot them all—perhaps thinking they were drug traffickers or terrorists, and perhaps not."

"That's bullshit. We would have been told. I should shoot you right here and now!"

"You wouldn't get off the boat alive," Guardio said.

"Who gives a damn, after hearing the story you just told me?" Jonas turned around and then spun back again. "Why wasn't it made public?"

"That's not how we do it here in Peru."

"But we were Americans."

Guardio shook his head slowly. "True, but then you would have been part of the task force that committed murder."

"I was in Lima just like you."

"You were part of the task force, and it really didn't matter if you were there or not."

"I wasn't in charge," Jonas stated.

Guardio held out his hand. Jonas pulled out the weapon from his pocket and placed it in Guardio's hand. "It was thought best to hide that terrible secret forever."

Jonas felt sick to his stomach. Though he had not been present at the supposed killing spree, he was guilty by association. After all these years, he would be considered one of the prime suspects by not revealing what he did not know took place.

"You do understand that because of your silence, ignorant or not of the truth, you are guilty."

Jonas nodded his head just as the boat gently bumped up to the rubber bumpers along the wood dock.

"Why has it suddenly reopened?"

Guardio slid the semi-automatic back into his own pocket. "I am not totally sure, but I would believe and may be guessing somewhat, that a person or people do not want anyone alive that may have been a witness to such a terrible tragedy."

"It was murder not some train accident."

"Tragic homicides then," Guardio said, holding out his hands. "Secrecy seems to be the play here, and I truly know nothing else. You see I didn't learn of this event until a few years ago and never mentioned it."

Jonas nodded. "Am I free to go?"

"I wouldn't think of stopping you," Guardio replied.

"One more request before I leave?"

"That would be?"

"Can I get a list of everyone that was on my team from all countries included in the task force?" Jonas asked.

Guardio walked to the end of the salon, held open the door, and waited until Jonas walked through. "I'll see what I can do."

"Thanks," Jonas said, turning to jump down to the dock.

"Let me ask you something."

"Go ahead," Jonas replied.

"Would you have really killed my child if I hadn't answered your questions?"

"No. I would never take from any father what I have lost," Jonas returned.

CHAPTER 19

Frank sat at his desk with an ice bag stuck to his head. The bump Maggie had seen and mentioned had grown to the size of a nice half grapefruit, and he was wondering if a trip to the urgent care wouldn't be a bad idea. He had been punched pretty hard, and it hurt like hell.

He moved the ice a bit to the left, sipped on his shot of whiskey and prayed the throbbing would stop soon. He hated the thought of wasting hours inside a room with a bunch of whining sick people. A few more shots and everything would be fine.

Frank's real concern was what was to happen next.

He had already warned Maggie of what Jonas was doing and had asked a couple of buddies to discreetly keep an eye on the hospital where Maggie and Sam were so he was confident they were in capable hands.

Let anyone try to go through Buster, and the hospital will have a new patient or two, unless the coroner is needed.

The dilemma Frank had was what he had to tell Jonas seemed impossible. Perhaps he hadn't heard the voice correctly at the end of the encounter earlier. The bump on his head, being kidnapped, shooting a couple of people, and being left alone in the middle of nowhere might have played tricks on him.

No. The voice—he knew the voice—everyone knew the voice.

But it couldn't be.

"Would you fucking call me?" Frank yelled, feeling the bump pounding with intensity.

Jonas watched the navy boat slip away into the currents of the Amazon and waved at the commander who simply nodded in return.

After walking through the fish sellers and trinket mer-chandise, Jonas hailed a motocarro and gave the driver the address of the hotel he had been staying. He needed a drink and some rest but was not sure of how much of either he would actually get.

Tapping the driver on the shoulder, he yelled a change in plans.

"Didn't think I'd see you again," Gerald said as Jonas walked beneath the awning at the Yellow Rose of Texas.

"I was told that a man here who is a regular told a man I met in the jungle I would be at Arianna's."

"If it's who I'm thinking, he's gone," Gerald replied. "He was only here for a week or so—didn't know him person-ally, but he came in a couple times a day. He'd just sit there at a table near the street as though watching for something."

"What was he watching for?" Jonas asked.

Gerald shrugged. "Don't know, just something. Perhaps a ghost from his past and maybe you. I didn't talk to him much—some of the people who stop by here I don't want to know. They pay for their drinks, and I just leave them alone. Iquitos is a place where getting too comfortable with someone may not be a good idea."

Jonas stared at the large man and nodded. "I can see that, but you think he's gone?"

"Haven't seen him since the day you took off for the jungle," Gerald replied. "Came in, had a beer or two, and then left a large tip. I noticed a carry-on in the chair next to him."

Gerald gestured to a young and very pretty waitress. "*Dos Cerveza's, por favor.*"

"Make them tall, Gerald," Jonas stated. "Did you think I was dead?"

"And in my own purchased mahogany beer cozies," Gerald replied. "No, not dead but just gone. I haven't seen you in a while but the thought of anyone actually killing you didn't cross my mind—I'm sure someone tried, though, and they lost."

"Perhaps," Jonas said, stretching his sore back into the deep recline of the bamboo caned chair.

"You're like a real James Bond," Gerald said.

"He's fictional, and I'm not." Jonas turned toward the street and watched as half a dozen cars and bikes swept by the bar. "They killed my son, Gerald."

Gerald sat in silence and then leaned his large arms onto the table before him. "I know, Arianna called and told me. I'm so sorry, but I believe you were advised not to go into the jungle."

"You warned me, but did you really think I wouldn't go?"

"Of course not, or I wouldn't believe it was you."

"Why did they do that?"

Gerald shook his head as the two large bottled beers arrived at their table hidden in half inch thick wood cozies. "The question is who are they?"

"You don't know?"

"Jonas, the last time I saw you, didn't I mention that there are people who may not want to see you? That you weren't welcome in Peru? But did I ever say or even hint I knew of their identity?"

"No, I think you mentioned about bad things could happen in the jungle, and it was Carlos who warned me to leave Peru."

"My mistake, but the jungle *is* dangerous, and it means the same thing, doesn't it?"

"Of course," Jonas replied, taking a long pull from his beer. "I'm leaving tomorrow for Lima and then back to the states."

"That's good," Gerald said, waving at a new customer entering under the awning just as the afternoon rain started pounding.

"I like the rain," Jonas said. "Very calming."

"So is sleeping but a person can take only so much of either in a lifetime," Gerald replied. "Go to Lima, check around, and get your ass back on a plane for Los Angeles. That woman you left needs you more than Peru."

Jonas nodded. "It is time to go home."

"Have another couple of beers, walk the Plaza, have a bite, and hit the sack. The morning will be fresher than now."

"Is it me or do most Peruvians, even American born ones, speak with such quotable lines?"

"It is all we have—time to think of clever things to say."

Jonas smiled, stood up, and reached out his hand. "It was good to see you, old friend."

"You are leaving so soon?"

"I have arrangements to make and phone calls to return," Jonas said. "Thank you for your hospitality."

Gerald grabbed Jonas in a large bear hug. "I wish you could stay but understand why you cannot. Watch your back and remember that sometimes that which you are hunting will end up hunting you."

"See, that's what I mean," Jonas said with a chuckle and walked from the awning and into the warm rain.

"What did I say?" Gerald asked, watching the broad-shouldered man glide across the wet sidewalks toward the plaza across the street.

Stopping by San Juan Bautista Catholic Church, Jonas paused, looked up at the tall spire, and felt himself being tugged into the sanctuary. He couldn't remember the last time he had set foot into a church.

Yes, he did. Three days after his daughter had been murdered, there was a mass and services at St. Catherine of Alexandria Church in Riverside on Arlington Avenue. A large ornate Catholic Church that Jonas and his ex-wife had attended for years until the death of their daughter. One last time Jonas had entered that church, watched the little coffin of his five year old darling being wheeled down the tiled floor, and never returned after it was wheeled out.

Church, or God, didn't mean that much after that day—nothing truly mattered in the long run after watching the life run out of her on the floor of the convenience store after being shot by the junkie robber. The days were on the calendar, and Jonas crossed each off as a routine—he loved Sam with all his heart, but in that heart there was still a large hole—now two—a daughter he would never dance with at her wedding and a son he never had a chance to know. There was happiness but the darkness shaded the rest.

Suddenly finding himself on his knees in the back pew of the dimly lit church, Jonas stared down the length of the church toward the altar at a huge crucifix adorned with the bloody body of Jesus Christ. He felt a trickle of a tear edge down his right cheek.

"I need some assistance," he said, folding his hands and closing his eyes.

"What do we have?"

"The same as yesterday," replied the man wearing a smart and narrow dark blue Brionico suit. "There's nothing to worry about."

"Easy for you to say," replied the silvery-gray-haired man sitting across from the impeccably dressed lawyer. God, how he hated these morsel-eating hounds. "You don't know the man like I did—hell, he didn't even know I knew him."

"Minutes turn into hours which turn into days which turn into years."

"Listen, Mario," the reply came. "I'm not sure what the fuck you are saying, but I'm not paying you one thousand dollars per hour to hear something that seems like it's coming from Billy fucking Shakespeare."

Mario Hernandez stood up, moved away from the comfortable leather Wyatt chair, and made his way to the Mahogany bar at the end of the room. Looking at himself in the etched-glassed 1850s mirror behind the bar, he liked what he saw—a handsome and very highly priced attorney from humble beginnings in Baltimore. Mario had made his way to Los Angeles and was banking nearly a million dollars a year now. Not bad for a kid who had barely made it out of high school but through the kindness of government programs, AVID classes, free lunches, and student loans—he didn't have to pay back—which got his ass to Stanford. He didn't initially qualify, due to low grades and lower attendance, but he soon loved affirmative action when he had applied to the west coast ivy league university and was accepted.

But now he thought it was crap as he was often a guest speaker at colleges all over California and realized much of the taxes he paid from his handsome salary went to pay for students like him—those who wouldn't be there if there weren't enough handouts. Another frustration was he was smart—these others he spoke to at campuses had gotten into the game because of color or economic disparity tended to drool during his lectures.

He smiled, talked, and then walked to the nearest bar for a pure shot of Bourbon. He often questioned himself on his allegiances—being a liberal was a great way to sell oneself but the path it led to was not good for the community as a whole.

He liked his money, though, and he made a lot of it. Being a hypocrite didn't bother him at all.

"Billy." Mario chuckled. "I like that. I once had white professor who used to call William, Billy like the rest of us weren't allowed to—"

"You start that racist bullshit once again, and you are not only out of my office but stripped of your six-thousand-dollar suits!"

"This one cost nearly eight."

"How much did you donate to that church you say you attend every year when the paper comes a calling?"

"Five thousand."

"Then shut the fuck up. Do you realize that conservatives in this country always give three or four times more for charity than any of you goddamn liberals."

"Jeff," Mario said. "You seem angry with me but, yes, the statistics are clear. We are rather selfish but pretend not to be. We want the tax payers to pick up the bill so we always say the government needs to do more which means raise taxes for those who don't need it."

"Then why do it?"

"Ah, propaganda has its niche," Mario declared. "We like to pretend that we care but only if someone else picks up the tab. Its simple economics really—convince the insignificant people you care about their needs, and they will vote for you or someone else we are nominating. It doesn't really matter if we follow the desire of the people or not. We do what we believe will keep our party in power."

"You know, I don't belong to either party."

"Yes," Mario said. "And you can care less about politics, but here you are with tens of thousands of dollars being given to this candidate or that candidate. Some are conservatives and some progressives—why not all for one or the other?"

Jeff sat a moment and then placed his head into his hands atop his desk. "I truly don't know—I thought I did but, at this point in my life, perhaps I've made a mistake."

"What do you mean?" Mario asked.

Jeff shrugged his shoulders. "I turned sixty last week and we had a wonderful birthday party with sons, daughters, and grandchildren. A marvelous time. Then, as they were leaving, the doubts came to my mind on who should really run this country and would it benefit my children and grandchildren."

"My answer would be us progressives," Mario said with a smile. "We're all about sharing the wealth and making sure that people who have made fortunes know it was on the backs of others."

"That's bullshit."

"Of course," Mario said. "If it wasn't for the likes of inventors and innovators who have brought us the wheel, the hydra-electric plants, the buggy, the automobile, the telephone, the internet, and thousands of other ideas, we'd be in the dark ages. We hate that, I mean, I don't, but I'm a hypocrite, and the progressives want people to think that, without the workers, there wouldn't be any of the things I mentioned. The problem with their thinking is that no one truly believes it any longer.

Jeff stood up from behind the eighteenth-century ivory-inlaid desk and walked around to where Mario was standing with his drink in his hand. "Okay," he said. "Am I in trouble for ghosting donations?"

"Nah, no one will know," Mario stated, slowly sipping his drink.

"What about Dinesh?"

"Dinesh d'Souza," Mario replied. "He was a target by the last president's men, if you ask me. Many have done what you've done with giving contributions to candidates using different people without getting in trouble or simply paying a fine or at the max getting a few months' probation—a slap on the hand really. Dinesh got screwed by the courts because of the power of the White House. Presidents don't like being ridiculed in public by writers or film directors and Dinesh fit both categories."

Jeff filled a glass with Jack Daniels, very little ice, and then retook his chair behind the large desk in his home office. "I have another issue."

Mario liked the sound of that. It meant more hours to bill. "And that would be?"

"Did you hear about an explosion in a city called Riverside a while back?"

"Yes," Mario said. "Nasty affair if I remember, leaving dozens dead and twice that injured. Gas pipe ruptured or something, correct?"

A long pull on the Daniels by Jeff had Mario thinking in a different track. "Is there something you'd like to get off your chest?"

"Not sure I should and not sure I shouldn't."

"You sound like an attorney and here you are simply a bundler for political campaigns."

"Well, you made that sound trivial."

Mario shook his head. "Not at all—if it wasn't for the likes of you, the poor idiots out there in the real world would never hear about the politicians we want them to vote for. No, Jeff, it's men like you who do a lot of work getting everyday people to donate small amounts of money, turning those small amounts into huge tubs of cash which can be used pretty much how the political party wants to. It's a glorious system and one you are well paid for."

"Okay," Jeff said, waving his hand for Mario to sit across from him. "I was approached about a decade or so by a political hack who wanted me to bundle campaign funds for a guy wanting to run for state senator."

"State, that seems hardly in the realm you deal with, Jeff."

"I know but I like the way this guy told me his candidate thinks and perhaps I found a soft spot since the guy's a vet and all that. Anyway, I agreed but I'm not so sure I made the correct choice."

"What state?"

"California."

"What party?"

"Democrat, and he won the seat."

"That was an easy call for sure out there, but what makes you think you may have made a poor choice?"

"I think I know who was behind that explosion in Riverside, and it wasn't a ruptured gas main as has been reported."

Mario smiled. "My fee just went to two thousand per hour."

Jonas made his way across the plaza toward the hotel with his emotions at the lowest he had felt in years. The love of his life lay in a bed in a hospital thousands of miles away. A son he had never known had died in his arms two days ago. The woman he had loved decades ago was all alone in the depth of the jungle with their son buried only yards away from her abode.

Stopping for a moment, he watched a young couple kissing beneath a large sparklingly water fountain. The streams of water plumed upward twenty feet, and the numerous spot lights seemed to make the fountain shimmer in response. It was both beautiful and touching as the young man smiled at the girl and then, hand in hand, they walked across the plaza.

His mood deepened into an almost pitch blackness.

As he walked by the marble reception desk, a young woman called to Jonas.

"Senor, something was left for you."

Jonas stopped, turned, and walked to the desk. "Who left it?"

"I am not sure, sir," the woman replied. "I was off duty but it was here with your name on it."

Jonas was handed a simple brown business sized envelope with his name clearly and neatly imprinted on the outside. He didn't open it. "You have no idea who left this?"

The woman shook her head. "Not a clue, as you Americans say, sorry."

"That's fine," Jonas replied and then smiled. "Thanks."

He didn't open the envelope until he entered his room.

"It's about time you called," Frank said, holding the phone to his left ear while looking out his office window to the street below. He wasn't nervous about his safety, but he wasn't nonchalant about it either. An attempt on one's life was, in fact, a wakeup call on how precious time on the earth was.

"How's Sam doing?"

"Jonas, she's getting much better and the doctors have been slowly taking her off pretty much everything since she's so strong. I would think in a day or two she'll be out of the coma. That's what I think when talking with Maggie."

"How's my sister holding up?"

"You know her," Frank said. "She's tougher than her brother."

"That is true," Jonas replied. "I need you to do something for me."

"Just name it, but tell me when you will be home first so I can get Maggie off my back," Frank said.

Silence for a moment. "I'll be flying out tomorrow afternoon and should be back in Los Angeles sometime in the late evening—can you pick me up?"

"Of course," Frank replied. "We have a lot to catch up on."

"Yes, we do," Jonas said.

Frank decided not to mention the activities that had occurred in the last two days since he wanted his friend to rest a bit and then he could unload on Jonas on the hour and a half drive back from LAX.

"I just received a list of names," Jonas stated. "Maybe twenty or so, and I need you to check them out if you can. I was told by a friend that most of them are dead, though."

"You have friends in Peru after all these years?"

"There was a lot more down here than I expected but not sure it will lead me any closer to what actually happened."

Again Frank remained silent. No harm waiting until Jonas got back to inform him of the near murder of himself, the implied threat to Jonas and his family, or the fact that the voice he heard sounded very familiar.

The worst part of it was that, even though he recognized the voice, he couldn't put a face or name to it. There was no doubt he knew the man who had ordered him kidnapped and killed.

"Anything I need to know before I try to get some sleep and fly out of here tomorrow?"

"Nothing that can't wait until you get back," Frank said.

"Thanks," Jonas said. "I truly mean that."

"I know you do."

The flight from Iquitos to Lima was uneventful and on time. Jonas was relieved. He'd had enough excitement and sorrow the past few days to fill his soul for many years to come.

He felt a terrible guilt about Arianna and the son he never knew but realized there was nothing he could have done. He hadn't known and, if he had, what then? There wasn't enough time in the world to rethink the events of two decades. Answers probably wouldn't have come to him anyway. That was the way of life, he recalled Arianna saying to him just before he had left the jungle.

She was correct—the way of life and death, he surmised, sitting at the gate waiting for his return flight to the states.

Grabbing his carry-on Jonas walked over to one of the many bars spread around the airport and ordered a beer. The bartender gave him a curious glance while handing over a draft of Cusquena.

"You look tired, my friend."

Jonas sipped the beer and nodded. "I am and feeling rather morose at this point."

"Ah, woman problems?"

"You could say that," Jonas answered.

The bartender smoothed out the right side of his bushy mustache. "Women—who can understand them or want to probably?"

A smile came to Jonas's face which felt unusual but welcomed. "I agree."

"You see, bartenders do not simply pour drinks for customers but instead are secret doctors of the minds, making sure those customers leave feeling good. We are not shrinks—that is the term used, yes?"

"Yes for psychologists or psychiatrists."

"Instead of shrinking the brain, we want our customers, our clients, our patients instead to expand their brains with thoughts of a better future for themselves. Does that make sense?"

Jonas took a long pull of the beer, smiled again, and nodded. "You make perfectly good sense."

"Are your troubles from the present or the past?"

"The past but the present also," Jonas replied, wondering why he would open up to a man he didn't know but, then again, maybe he needed to open up so why not a stranger?

"The present will work its way out if you let go of the past," the bartender said. "You see, many people let what has gone before rule what is to be. That only harbors resentment, intimidation, doubt, and a lack of self-assurance to ensure a positive and fruitful future."

"Damn," Jonas responded. "You should take up an office and give advice for a living."

"This is my office and you are my patient," the man said. "Enjoy your beer and plan only your future since the past is of no consequence now, since you cannot change one tiny aspect of it. What happened, happened, and nothing can change that, but the future—it is like a beautiful and voluptuous woman we just met. The aspects of what is waiting us is like nothing else."

An announcement made Jonas finish his beer. "That's my plane."

"And thank you for your patronage and remember the words of your country's famous humorist Will Rogers, 'Don't let yesterday use up too much of today.'"

Jonas smiled. "I won't, and thanks."

He over tipped but knew it was rather cheap for the therapy.

CHAPTER 20

Jonas grabbed his carry-on as the plane coasted to a stop and the seatbelt light went off. He hurried out of the airport, bypassing luggage and getting only a cursory glance by Customs. A passport stamp and a limpid smile welcomed Jonas back to the States.

"Good to be home," he muttered, making his way to the exit and ground transportation at the Tom Bradley International terminal.

Frank was curbside, smiling at Jonas right on time. "What's the special privilege?"

"Yeah," Frank said, shaking his friend's hand. "Showed them my identification and advised them I was picking up a very important man from Peru. Said I had ten minutes—you made it in eight."

"Two minutes to spare," Jonas said.

Frank nodded. "Get in the car. I think our time is up. The traffic is brutal."

Two uniformed Los Angeles police officers strolled up to Frank's vehicle. "By our watch, the time is up."

"Your watch is correct," Frank said, slowly pulling away from the curb being extra careful not to lunge onto the crowded roadway. "Man, they are punctual."

Jonas looked into the passenger side rear view mirror. "Yes, strangely so."

Frank looked left, accelerated, and headed for the exit toward Highway 101. "Is this another conspiracy, Jonas?"

Remaining silent for a few moments, Jonas turned toward Frank. "Tell me if anything strange has happened since I was gone?"

Frank knew it was coming and wasn't really prepared to answer the question. Hell, yes strange things had happened in the nearly two weeks Jonas had been out of country, but how did one explain it and not sound deranged?

"I'll share mine, if you share yours."

Jonas just shook his head. "Coward."

"You didn't ask about Sam, and now you're calling me a coward?"

"Spoke to Maggie while walking to the exit and really happy she's coming along so well and in the next two days will probably be able to look at my ugly face on her own."

Frank nodded. "That mug may put her back into a coma."

"You're probably right, but it's a chance we'll have to take," Jonas said. "Okay, my story first and then yours."

"Deal," Frank responded. "Besides, I hate this traffic down here and wouldn't be able to give my perspective without a lot of cursing in between concerning the bad drivers."

"Fine, you concentrate on driving, and I'll do the talking."

For the next forty-five minutes, Jonas related his experience in Lima and Iquitos while Frank managed the various freeways heading north and then east back to the city of Riverside. Frank asked a few questions for clarification purposes, posed a comeback here and there, but for the most, just listened, running Jonas's dialogue through his head.

It was quite a story—but Jonas hadn't heard his yet.

"Jesus, you had a son?"

"Yeah, and I lost him as soon as I found him."

Frank didn't reply as he stared at the road in front of him. "I can't think of anything to say."

"Nothing would be appropriate since I haven't fully dealt with it and have no idea if I should relate this to anyone else."

"You'd keep it a secret from Sam and Maggie?"

Jonas had played many scenes a thousand times through his mind on the eight hour flight from Peru. He didn't see a win-win in any of them. What would be the point of adding to their burden of misery with his tale of having a son whom he watched die in front of him? No, this might be a secret he took to the grave.

"Not much choice actually," was all Jonas said.

"Probably for the best," Frank replied, not really sure if that were true or not. Jonas's soon-to-be wife and sister should know everything about Jonas, but Frank knew his friend had thought this through. Jonas was dealing with the devil in his soul. Frank would not want to have to make that call. "So, this all boils down to when you worked on the multi-international task force?"

"As we said before, it all had to with something going wrong in Iquitos, and now with the death of my son and Carlos, I believe the slate is being wiped clean."

"Not many more marks on that white board, my friend."

"You haven't told me of your adventures while I've been gone and perhaps what you've learned will enlighten the both of us."

Frank smiled. "Yeah, about that."

"What?"

"Oh nothing except someone kidnapped me and tried to kill me."

Jonas shot straight up in his seat. "What the hell! You didn't tell me that over the phone."

"Didn't want to worry you," Frank commented. "You had enough on your mind."

"What the hell did you do?"

"I killed them back or at least a couple of them before the main man got away."

Jonas sat back, took a couple of deep breaths, and then slowly turned toward Frank once again. "What the hell is going on?"

"I don't know, but I think I know who is behind all of this."

"Who is it?"

Frank flicked the turn signal while changing lanes. "That's the problem."

"What?"

"I recognized the voice—I've heard it before on the news—distinct—one you wouldn't mistake."

A slight jolt of disappointment erupted through Jonas as he sat back once more and stared silently out of the windshield. "Okay, tell me all the details."

"I may have time," Frank responded as they passed the city limits sign for Corona about twenty minutes from the hospital where Frank was taking Jonas. "Barely."

"Use short sentences," Jonas advised.

Jonas knew his sister was in great physical shape, but he had no idea how truly strong she was until she threw her arms around him as he entered the hospital.

"Don't break my neck, Maggie." Jonas teased as he held her out a foot or two from him. "You look great."

"You haven't been gone that long, Jonas," she returned while releasing her brother and smiling. "Though it does seem forever."

"Forever is a long time," Frank stated, watching the re-union.

Maggie walked over, gave Frank a quick hug. "It hasn't been that long since I saw you last but it's always good to have you around."

"Ah, you have my friends here also," Frank stated, pointing out the couple of security men he had arranged to be around the hospital.

"Yes," Maggie replied. "They hover like a pair of drones."

"But unlike most civilian drones, these guys are plenty well-armed and willing to use their firepower at the least provocation."

Jonas smiled, excused himself from Maggie and Frank, and walked over to the two men standing a short distance from them. "Just wanted to say thanks for all you're doing keeping everyone safe," he stated.

The larger of the two men simply nodded. "It's what we do for friends."

Jonas nodded in return. "Well, thanks again. Talkative couple of guys," he said, rejoining his sister and Frank.

Frank laughed. "Quiet but deadly—worked with them on some tough cases, and we began a sort of friendship."

"Sort of?" asked Maggie.

"Yeah, those kinds of guys aren't big into close relationships. A beer once in a while is the extent of friendship they're interested in."

"Whatever, I am sure glad they are on our side."

"Okay, let's go see Sam—I'm sure she'll be happy to see you."

Jonas stared at Maggie. "She's awake?"

"Only an hour or so ago," Maggie replied. "Awake and wondering where you were."

Jonas started walking down the hall toward Sam's room. "What did you tell her?"

"You went out for a bit on an errand," Maggie answered. "I thought I would let you tell her everything once she's feeling better. She believes you were here all along."

"I was," Jonas said, speeding up his steps.

"You look beautiful," Jonas said softly, staring into the eyes of the woman he loved.

After going through what she had, Sam did look beautiful. The induced coma had allowed her to heal almost effortlessly, and there wasn't a bruise or swelling to be seen. It was as if to Jonas she had just woken up from a restful night's sleep. "I'm very groggy, but I think you said I was beautiful—so groggy or not, I'll take the compliment."

Tears welled up in his eyes as he took hold of her right hand and sat in a chair closest to her bed.

"You cry?" Sam whispered, looking into Jonas's face.

"I have feelings, contrary to the strongly held rumor that I don't," Jonas replied, not caring if a tear or two dripped down his cheeks.

He was so relieved she was going to be well, he suddenly was overwhelmed with emotion. A couple of deep breaths, and he felt more in control. He hoped that Sam hadn't seen the moment of weakness. She needed him to be strong for her.

"I think you're a softy down deep."

"Don't let anyone know that, or I would have to rebuild my reputation."

She smiled but then looked sad in an instant. "What happened?"

"What do you mean?"

Sam shook her head. "I mean Maggie sort of told me what occurred, but I had just woken up and wasn't understanding what she was saying. Something about a bomb?"

Jonas nodded. "It's a long story, but I'll tell you what we know as of now."

"Good but make it a short story since I can feel the medicine begging me to fall asleep again."

Jonas explained how they were to have met at the coffee shop but he was running late from the meeting with Frank when all of a sudden there had been an explosion and she was seriously injured. He neglected to tell her why the explosion happened, letting her believe it had been a terrible accident caused by a gas leak inside the shop. At this point, Jonas felt she needed to heal one hundred percent before realizing that he had almost been the cause of her death from his past. It was hard enough to deal with the fact that over a dozen people had died in the terrorist explosion—more nightmares he would have to deal with the rest of his life.

"Was anyone killed?"

"Quite a few," Jonas said. "Many more injured like you and some not so badly. The investigation is still ongoing to learn what triggered the explosion, but I am so happy you're getting better by the day.

"How long have I been here?"

"Nearly two weeks," Jonas replied. "The doctors decided to place you into an induced coma so your body could heal slowly, and it seemed to have worked. You appear to have just woken up from an afternoon nap. Doctor Scarlett Rose has taken a special interest in you because of the pressure from my sister, I think. Seriously though, she's good doctor."

Sam nodded. "I don't feel like I've been here that long, though."

"The induced coma."

"Yes, that must be it…" With that, Sam quickly fell back to sleep, her breathing very soft and rhythmic.

"It's the medicine," a voice said from behind Jonas. "I've ordered just enough sedatives to induce sleep on a regular basis but not enough to render her unconscious the whole time. She needs to periodically awaken to gather her strength."

Jonas turned and smiled at the very doctor he had just mentioned to Sam. "Doctor Scarlett Rose, good to see you, and thank you for the wonderful job you have done with her. She looks marvelous."

"She is one tough girl," Rose stated, holding out her right hand to Jonas. "She healed quicker than I thought, and we started physical therapy a week ago so there wouldn't be any muscle atrophy. She's lost a few pounds, but I've upped her IV to ensure she is receiving her daily requirements of nutrients. Once she's up and around, she'll be just as she was before the explosion."

"That's great to know," Jonas replied.

"Speaking of that," Rose started. "Did she ask about the explosion?"

"Of course, and I lied and told her no one knows why it happened as of now."

Rose nodded in agreement. "That's what I would have recommended. She doesn't need to know the truth for a little while. When she returns home, I'd say that would be the time to let her in on all the details—that is, if you would let anyone in on all the details."

"He won't," Maggie said as she and Frank entered Sam's hospital room. They had remained outside to give Jonas time to be alone with Sam but after the doctor entered believed it was safe to enter. "He likes keeping things close to his chest."

"He's a stubborn one, that Jonas Peters," Frank said.

Jonas just smiled, shaking his head. "I'll tell her what happened—I will."

"All the details?" Rose asked.

"What she needs to know."

"See, what did I say?" Maggie said.

Jonas turned but didn't respond. He knew what he was doing, and Sam—or Maggie, for that matter—didn't need to know every detail of his trip to South America. He wasn't sure they could or would want to handle the information he had.

They were both tough individuals but, at this point, even Jonas wasn't one hundred percent sure what was happening. With the extended conversation he had with Frank on the way back from LAX, it was sure looking more and more like a strong conspiracy with deadly results.

A recognized voice was a start, and Frank had started listening to all the news he could, trying to find the person connected to the voice. It wasn't an actor, but someone who had been in the news lately and a lot.

"Perhaps that is best," Rose responded, noticing the detached look in Jonas's eyes. This man had a lot of secrets and probably pain, she thought, studying the ruggedly handsome man's face. "With the event she has gone through, the healing process will also include her mental state which might take some time. We need to remember that nearly two weeks have past and that time is missing in her memories. One moment she was sitting waiting for you, Jonas, and the next thing she recalls is waking up here in the hospital a short while ago."

"I understand," Jonas said. "I'll be there for her."

"Twenty-four-seven?" asked Maggie.

"I'll try to be," he replied.

Frank patted Jonas on the left shoulder. "We'll all be there for her, Jonas."

Maggie shook her head. "I'll be here ready to take her home when the chance arises, but you two still have work to do."

"What do you mean?" Jonas asked.

"Jonas, I love you dearly as my brother, but your job isn't over yet, is it?"

Frank looked over at Jonas and shrugged his shoulders. "You're right, it's not over."

Rose held up her hands in front of her. "I think this is when I leave since I don't want to know what is going on with this discussion. Sam will be fine, given rest and understanding with her emotions, but I do have other patients to administer to."

Rose turned and walked out of Sam's room.

"All right, you stay with her but call me the second she wakes up again, okay?" Jonas asked Maggie, bending over and giving the sleeping Sam a kiss on her forehead.

"I'll do that of course," Maggie replied as Jonas and Frank left the room.

CHAPTER 21

Ie's a politician," Frank said as the two men walked out of the main doors of the hospital.

"Who?"

"The man who thought I'd enjoy a ride into the boonies to kill me," Frank said. "I just figured out the voice."

"How?"

Frank was silent for a moment and then turned toward Jonas. "He was on CNN the other evening discussing the financial situation in California."

"What show?"

"I had it on for most of the evening so not really sure," Frank replied. "I have it on for background noise most of the time but it just occurred to me now as we walked out the door—he's a politician."

"Do you know who?"

Frank shook his head. "No, like I said, I wasn't really paying attention and didn't catch his name or see his face."

"Californian?"

"That I'm sure of since he sounded so sure of himself about the economy of California getting stronger with all the new taxes. I caught the message but not the messenger."

Jonas went back to walking toward Frank's car. "That's a good starting place."

Frank took out his key FOB and unlocked the doors to his car. "You know why they call this a FOB?"

Jonas shook his head while climbing into the vehicle. "Frank, really?"

"It's called that because it is a finger-operated button," Frank finished as he crawled behind the steering wheel. "Strange, isn't it? All these years I thought it was some high technology acronym and it turns out to be the simplest of terms, in reality. A finger-operated button—imagine that."

"What's that got to do with who is behind the bombing?"

Frank started the car and began to back out of the parking space. "Not really sure but maybe what we're looking for isn't all that complicated—like this key FOB. Wouldn't that be surprising?"

"Nothing surprises me anymore, Frank." Jonas shook his head. "By the way, did you ever get a chance to look into that guy Yuri for me?"

"Yeah, called Marla Gaines. Remember her?" Frank said.

Jonas nodded. "Of course I do. Great person and a sad day when she left the department."

"She retired, Jonas and moved to Texas," Frank stated. "She's married and all."

"But?"

"Yeah, she was rather nervous after she looked into this Yuri friend of yours—in fact, she hung up on me, stating she had been on a secured web site for too long. Who is this guy?"

"Just a guy I met in an airport one day. I didn't realize it was the guy who helped those school kids up in San Bernardino County until later on," Jonas said. "I just thought perhaps he might be able to help, since this case seemed to be about terrorism, but no contact, huh?"

"Nothing and Marla was scared, I think."

"Huh, that is strange," Jonas said. "I'll check in on her when this case is over—I'm sure it's nothing."

"Nothing could be further from the truth, Jonas," Frank returned. "This is one strange case and it ain't over yet."

"I'll call her today," Jonas stated.

Jonas didn't go back to Frank's office but, instead, headed north on Interstate 15 toward his home in the tiny town of Phelan. He needed to look some things up and felt the need to wander his acreage to clear his head.

A little over an hour from his home, Jonas would be ready at a moment's notice to jump into his vehicle and race southbound if Maggie called with any news concerning Sam. At this juncture, as Doctor Scarlett Rose had said though, Sam was coming along fine and would need rest for the next few days before the staff would allow her to leave. Jonas would keep his phone handy and his gas tank full, but he needed time to think.

As was his usual modus operandi, when he was in Riverside, he had taken a few minutes to visit the grave of his daughter, Stacy. He stood there, looking at the green blanket of grass covering her site and said a silent prayer—not for her since she was always an angel but for Sam and the job he needed to finish.

"You know something, Stacy," Jonas said, kneeling down and removing a weed that was encroaching on the marble monument with his daughter's name etched onto it. "You had a half-brother. I know, it surprised me too, but perhaps you've met him now. Some bad people hurt him, and he had to go to heaven. If you do see him, please tell him Dad loves him as he loves you. I just wish we all could have met years ago, though."

He wiped a tear from his eye and walked back to his car.

Man, I'm getting too old for any more tragedies—it's tearing me up constantly.

Pulling the sedan onto the half mile of dirt road, Jonas waved at a neighbor and then pushed the button to engage the sliding gate to the entrance of his property. He felt a sudden relaxation as he took in the sprawling twenty acres of desert sprinkled with large Joshua Trees and Mesquite. The house itself was modest in size but suited Jonas, and he knew that Sam liked the remoteness of the place.

Climbing from his vehicle, he entered the four-bedroom home through the garage, turned off the alarm system, and grabbed a beer from the LG side-by-side in the kitchen. He hadn't bothered stopping for the mail two miles away, thinking he'd do it later—he had something he needed to do first.

He exited the west side of the house, walked to the eight-foot-by-forty-foot metal shipping container, and took a key from his pocket. Inside the container, he flipped on a light switch and instantly the darkness within was brimming with illumination from the rows of fluorescent lights near the ceiling. Opening a large gun safe, Jonas withdrew a 9mm Smith and Wesson Shield and inserted the twenty-round magazine, which was lying beside it.

Donning a pair of ear protectors and safety glasses, he proceeded to run out a new body silhouette, stopping it thirty feet from where he was standing. The image on the silhouette was his own design—it was a man holding a gun staring back at you.

It was the image of the man who had killed his daughter so many years earlier. Jonas's memory was dead-on, and he never wanted to miss the chance for revenge on the person who had murdered Stacy.

He had hundreds of the silhouette.

When he had mentioned building the indoor gun range to Frank, his friend almost went ballistic.

"Are you nuts?" Frank had told him over a beer. "That's too short for anything but small arms—the chance for a ricochet would be astronomical."

Jonas wanted one, and he built it himself—lining the walls in heavy plywood, restructuring the rear wall with heavy one-inch boiler plate with plywood over that and in front of the boiler plate two rows of hay from floor to ceiling. He had a shooting range of not much more than thirty feet at the max but, in his line of work, most shootings were within ten. It worked well.

He closed his eyes, bent his head, and took a deep breath. Exhaling, he jerked the semi-automatic pistol into a shooting stance and emptied all twenty rounds into the silhouette.

The criminals head was nothing but tattered shreds.

"Asshole," Jonas said, removing the now empty magazine and putting the pistol back into the safe. He would come back and clean the weapon—it was his gun of choice—it was the one he carried most often.

But at this moment, he needed fresh air and, as the Aussies say, a walk-about was called for. He needed time alone to think.

With his nearest neighbor over fifty acres away, Jonas never worried about the sound of the gunfire, if any did actually exit the container shooting range.

It was Phelan, and people kept to themselves. His privacy would not be disturbed.

While Jonas was walking and thinking, Frank was sitting behind his PC in his office near the Mission Inn. For over an hour, he'd been going through interviews CNN had done in the recent weeks and was about to give up when an anchor introduced a California State Senator who may or may not be throwing his hat in for a possible vacant seat in the United States Senate in the next election.

Rumors had been going around that one of the current sitting senators may be thinking of retiring at the end of her term.

The Democrat who had served from the most populace state for nearly thirty years said she was considering moving on and letting a younger person take the spot.

Frank froze as California State Senator Greg Renn was introduced. He almost shot the Scepter monitor when the senator opened his mouth.

"I got you, you son-of-bitch!"

The questions were typical and light, seeing if Renn was seriously thinking of running for the possible open United States Senator seat. Renn would smile and state the obvious, that if he had a chance to assist the United States Senate in making the correct decisions for the citizens of the United States, he would be honored to serve.

He was currently sitting on the California Senate Budget and Finance Review Committee and boasted how the Golden State was turning golden again. With the recession far in the rearview mirror, Renn assured the anchor that California was no longer fearful of states like Texas and New York stealing businesses from it.

"No, in fact, we have seen a swelling of business interests in our state in the past two years," Renn stated. "Our budget is strong, and we have ample workforce for any organization to come to California if profits are their bottom line."

Both men went on for another three minutes. Frank was no longer listening but simply staring at the man's face as he answered question after question about the state's and the country's fiscal shape.

The voice was the same, and Frank knew he had his man.

But the question was—and it was a good one—why would a state senator try to kill him in the middle of the night near a river bed in Riverside?

Frank had never met the man—didn't even know anything about him until a recollection of hearing an interview on CNN had come to his attention.

It didn't make sense. A person who was thinking of running for the United States Senate didn't generally go out of his way to have someone murdered. It just didn't make any logical sense.

"That's the real issue," Frank said. "When does anything in this crazy world truly make logical sense?

Just then his phone rang.

"I was just thinking of you," he stated into his phone.

"Good," Jonas replied. "Any more news on the guy was who tried to have you whacked."

"I know who his name now," Frank replied. "I just spent the last hour listening to interviews from CNN and got him."

"Who is it?"

"Greg Renn," Frank replied.

"That's him? What the hell is this about?" Jonas asked. "He's thinking of running for a United States Senate seat if what's-her-name retires, isn't he?"

"You mean Senator Rosalind Webster. I think she's going to pull the pin, and he'll run for it."

"Okay, and again, why would he behind the attempted hit on you and the terrorist attack at the coffee shop?"

"That, my friend, wasn't because of the bad coffee but because you were going to be there, and it needed to look like a random act of terror. There's enough going around anyway so one more would be a shame but not earth shattering. He tipped his hand when he texted you about Iquitos, though, and you were late on arriving for your destination."

"We can't prove it was him who texted me, and a voice in the darkness is hardly proof. Maybe we're trying too hard."

Frank shook his head. "No, I never forget a voice, and trust me, when that action went down the other night I recall every painful moment. It was him, but I have to agree that it doesn't make any sense."

"No, it doesn't."

"Was he there with you in Iquitos during your drug-busting days?"

"Nope, never heard of him, and he's not on the list that was given me before I left either."

Weirder by the moment. "When are you coming back down?"

"I've shot my silhouette, walked around the property, and gotten the mail," Jonas responded. "I'll be down first thing in the morning and can meet you at the hospital if you have time?"

"I always have time for you," Frank said. "Do me a favor and fax over the list of names you have will you?"

"Most are dead."

"And some aren't—just do it okay?"

"Yep, right away."

"By the way, Jonas," Frank said.

"What?"

"One of these days you're going to shoot your eye out in that death trap shooting range you created in the middle of nowhere."

"By the way, talked to Marla today, and she's fine," Jonas stated. "Got a little spooked when she read the whole dossier on Yuri. I think she watches too many spy movies over there in Texas. Told her also to stay off of restricted sites, even if she still has the passwords."

"Thanks for checking in on her," Frank said, feeling relieved about Marla. "Too bad about not finding this Yuri—maybe he could have helped."

"Yeah, maybe," Jonas said. "See you tomorrow."

Frank smiled and hung up his office land line.

CHAPTER 22

California State Senator Greg Renn smiled and then stood up from behind his desk in the spacious office which was his in the Capital Building in Sacramento. Looking out the window toward the massive rose garden in front of the main portico, Renn felt very proud of himself. Not yet fifty-five and he was being fast-tracked for a possible US Senate seat. That was, if that old fool Rosalind would give up her seat and finally retire. Over thirty years in Washington was long enough for anyone. The senior senator, in more ways than one, would be seventy-five years old next March.

"Jesus, Mary, and Joseph," Renn snarled. "She should be dead by now."

"Who should be dead, Greg?" asked his assistant who was sitting on a brown leather settee on the other side of the room from the window Renn was looking out of.

"That doddering old fool who sits in Washington and does nothing."

"She'll retire," replied Randy Noble.

"Not soon enough, Randy—not soon enough."

Renn continued looking out his window and marveled at the many varieties of old growth trees that complimented the stately white Capital Building. He loved the trees from around the world and would often walk by them in awe and then give the gardeners a pat on their backs for the great job they were doing. He was a man of the people—he understood the little guys.

Senator Renn loved everything about being in politics. Quite a change for him when he left his previous employer nearly fifteen years ago and found his niche. He could communicate with people—they trusted him.

He reminded himself of the Roman goddess Minerva who graced the Great Seal of California. The mythical goddess who was fully grown at her time of birth—much like the state of California, which never had to be a territory before being ratified a full state on the west coast on September ninth of 1850. Fully grown at birth.

One of the strongest economies in the world, and Renn had been there for the past twelve years. He, like Minerva, had never felt the growing pains of reaching adulthood. No school board membership and then leap frogging into a city council and working his way up to the state capital. No, with his charm, wit, and knowledge, he had easily defeated the six-term senator from the Thirty-Fifth District during a contentious but invigorating contest. He had enjoyed pointing out the defaults of the sitting senator and then relished the results on election eve. He recalled walking into his office in Costa Mesa after being sworn in and immediately ordered a complete renovation.

It was his office now and, as the old saying went—out with the old and in with the new.

He felt that way with that idiot Rosalind Webster. She needed to go, and he needed to be in Washington DC—the real seat of power of the United States. Of course, being almost fifty-five wouldn't make him a young senator but young enough to enjoy a decade or two of unlimited power. With his silver tongue, it wouldn't be long before he was the head of some major influential committee.

He held the power on the Budget and Fiscal Committee in California, which was a powerful tool to use when he would run for the committee chair of any of a dozen committees he might desire.

Patience was needed at this time until Webster announced her retirement from the US Senate—everything else was falling into place nicely. A couple of hiccups but nothing that shouldn't be taken care of before he would announce his candidacy.

"Your donor's secretary contacted our office this morning and is willing to back your run into the senate next year," Noble stated, not looking up from his Blackberry. "They'll bundle a minimum of thirty million for you."

Renn let out a slight whistle. "Thirty million? I was hoping for maybe five or six million."

"Boss," Noble said. "You've got to keep up with the times. Back in 2012, it cost over ten million for the six-year spot. Inflation and your possible competition from Roosevelt will at least double the cost."

"Andrew Roosevelt is a frigging moron," Renn said. "He's a two-term senator from San Diego. I'll beat him hands down."

"He's got name recognition."

"I understand but he's not even related to the Roosevelts, simply shares the family's last name."

"Not that the public will make the difference," Noble said, turning from the Blackberry. "I'm sure you will win the seat but it won't be easy. He has a lot of juice farther south, and he'll have money too."

Renn nodded and turned back to look at the roses. "The trees are really beautiful this time of year, aren't they? Changing color as they do."

Noble caught the buzz on his phone and his attention drifted away. "Hadn't noticed really."

"Randy, you really should," Renn replied. "You never know when you won't be able to take in the glory of nature—life is short."

Frank sat behind his desk—seemed like that was all he had been doing for the past few hours—and rechecked the list of names Jonas had faxed from his home in Phelan.

Two ten-person teams equally divided by Americans and Peruvians. Late nineteen nineties and the mission was referred to as Operation Elimination—rather ominous sounding. But, to rid the influx of drugs coming out of Columbia to Peru and then making their way into the United States via the Pacific, any name would do.

Frank had been on numerous multi-agency operations in his time, though never with international members, and someone always came up with a catchy title. Operation Catch-Them was his all-time favorite, except the teams had never caught Them—an organized city gang running heroin and young girls through the east side of Riverside. The teams had caught a lot of late nights and empty houses, but after two weeks, the operation was called off. A month later, the suspects they had been hunting had been located executed by a rival gang near Rubidoux. It didn't really matter, the criminals were gone, and their operations had been stopped.

Whatever it took, he mused, going through the list for the third time. Jonas had been correct when he told Frank that nearly everyone on the list was dead. Three fatal car accidents which took out four of members, one sky diving incident where a parachute didn't open over the desert of Arizona, one drowning when the person was on vacation in Bermuda, five of the Peruvian military gunned down by remnants of the Shining Path near Cuzco, three suicides—one Peruvian and two Americans—and most recently Jonas's friend Carlos murdered during a supposed robbery.

That only left five people still alive from the original twenty.

"This is insane," Frank said, staring at his computer screen. "Didn't anyone take notice of all these deaths?"

Jonas was still alive, as well as Arianna; a retired copper from Boston, who was living in Boca Raton; a Peruvian captain, who was doing life in a pit of a prison outside of Lima for murdering his girlfriend and three children; and an ex-agency person by the name of Kevin Jennings.

Frank had found it strange that the Central Intelligence Agency had only one personnel involved in this eradication operation and instead used mostly outside police agencies. Jonas had briefly mentioned that it was really an excuse for a training exercise for law enforcement and the CIA agent was only there for introductions.

In fact, Jonas had stated that Jennings was here and there during the two months period in Peru. "He'd show up for a day or two and then disappear for a few days and then come back again when we went in for an operation. None of us thought much of it since we knew his real job was being a spook throughout South America. A little odd, but what agency spook isn't?"

The explanation sounded plausible but still he couldn't find anything on this Jennings person. It seemed as though his trail went cold and Frank could find no records about him. Frank didn't have any contacts with the agency but he still had some friends from the Federal Bureau of Investigation and had spoken to one of them about an hour earlier about this Jennings.

Frank called Jonas, who was on his way back to the hospital to see Sam.

"I have my blue tooth so don't nag me," Jonas stated.

"My friend, if I didn't nag you, who would?"

"My sister."

"Got me there," Frank responded. "Doesn't it seem a little strange that nearly everyone on your teams is dead? I mean really, drownings, sky diving accidents, and the like. The only thing weirder would be if someone had been eaten by a hippopotamus."

Jonas laughed. "Didn't I tell you that, when Sam is fully recovered, we're taking a photo safari in Africa?"

Frank moved the phone from his left hand to his right. "Okay, be funny but try as I might there is something wrong with this list. You, Arianna, a guy doing life in a shit-hole, a retired cop living large in Florida, and some spook by the name of Kevin Jennings are the only ones still alive."

"Frank, it's been over twenty years," Jonas responded. "People die."

"Sure, the only gift we get at birth is death but come on, "Frank said. "None of these people have even reached the old age of sixty. It's not heart attacks, but accidents that's killing them."

"They lived dangerous lives."

"Three were killed in car accidents while driving home from work or from the market. That is not really dangerous."

"Roads are the greatest killers in the nation, as far as I know."

"Okay, say I go along with your stupid logic which I don't."

"I can hear that."

"What about this Jennings guy?"

"I told you that I didn't know him well and we kind of avoided him. A rather strange guy who kept to himself. But, Frank, he worked for the agency so what do you expect?"

"That I could at least get a lead on him."

There was silence over the line for a moment or two before Jonas spoke again. "What do you mean?"

"I've got a bead on everyone but Jennings. He dried up—nada since the early two-thousands."

Another silence. "That is strange. Think he's deep cover and the agency has a lid on him."

"For twenty years? That would be a world record. He wasn't that kind of spook was he? I mean working the field himself?" Frank questioned.

"No," Jonas said. "What I recall was him being a handler. He recruited and ran local agents to infiltrate drug cartels and the like. I don't believe he was undercover, excepting the usual of being a businessman conducting whatever he conducted in South America."

"That's what I thought, so this doesn't make sense. People don't drop off the face of the earth with no record. I've gone through every system I know, and I can't pull up anything on Jennings."

Jonas didn't question Frank's tracking method. He knew Frank had, as he did himself, the passwords to do backgrounds on pretty much anyone they wanted to. They may not be active law enforcement any longer but the tools of the trade didn't go extinct once they turned in their retirement papers. No, ex-cops still had their methods of finding people using all the latest technology and if they didn't at their fingertips they knew someone who did.

"That doesn't make any sense," Jonas replied.

"I know so I put a call into a buddy of mind from the Bureau, and he said he'd look into it a bit deeper for us. Said he'd get back today on whatever he could dig up."

"Good," Jonas said. "Hey, I'll be at the hospital in about twenty—can we talk there?"

"On my way," Frank said, hanging up the phone.

This case makes no sense and is not logical in the slightest.

Frank and Jonas met up in the lobby of the hospital and were surprised to see Maggie nearly leaping for joy.

"She's up and about!"

"Who?" Frank asked.

Jonas just looked at his friend. "What do you mean, Maggie? I thought the doctor wanted a few days more rest before Sam was supposed to try anything that strenuous?"

Maggie gripped both of her brother's arms. "She's like you—too stubborn to listen to doctor's orders. This morning when Sam heard you were coming in to see her, she insisted on doing her hair and a bit of eyeliner. She wasn't content with me doing it for her but got out of bed and walked to the bathroom to look at herself in the mirror."

"She's a tough girl," Frank muttered.

"Come on," Maggie said. "She's waiting for you."

Frank's phone rang. "I'll get this and perhaps catch up with you two later. I doubt she wants to see this old face and only has eyes for Jonas."

Jonas nodded and patted Frank on the shoulder. "Catch up when you can."

As Maggie and Jonas walked down the long hallway toward Sam's room, Frank slid his finger across the face of his phone.

"Sander's."

"Got that information you asked for."

It was his contact from the Bureau. Though Frank had wanted the information to share with Jonas before seeing Sam, it was welcome news anyway. He could always tell Jonas what he had learned.

"I really appreciate this, Jason," Frank said.

"You may not when I deliver what I got."

"Shoot."

"The man's gone cold."

That certainly wasn't the reply Frank had wanted. "Gone cold? What does that mean?"

"It means, my friend, that your Kevin Jennings has slipped off the face of the earth for all intents and purposes."

"How is that possible?" Frank asked, his head swimming in disbelief at the words he had just heard.

"Seems he was drummed out of the agency back in two-thousand and showed up once in a while as a contractor for some pretty dubious characters around the world and then the agency lost track of him for good in two-thousand and three. Nothing since then."

"How could the agency lose someone?" Frank asked. "They're the agency and that's their business."

Silence was met for a moment. "Frank, it's not Hollywood. These are real people who are not perfect. It's an organization, given a pretty good one, but mistakes happen or things are not followed up in a timely fashion. Issues or people can fall through the cracks."

It made sense to Frank, but he didn't want to believe one of the premier law enforcement agencies in the world could make mistakes. But with humans running things, mistakes would sometimes occur.

"Okay," Franks said. "What was he drummed out for?"

"Here comes the tricky part," Jason said. "Very little detail but something like this happened in ninety- nine while your Jennings was working out of Venezuela. A contact he had made as a handler turned on him and the agency. Hugo Chavez had just been elected the sixty-fourth President of Venezuela and the US State Department knew this guy was bad news from the beginning."

Frank's mind was like a computer when it came to world history, especially somewhat-modern history. He did remember when the Chavez, the supposed fighter for the people, took over as president for the South American country who later turned into one of the worst tyrants of the era. A sigh of relief was heard from most truly democratic countries when the strong man passed away in 2013 from a heart attack following a long battle with colon cancer.

"It seems the agency wanted Jennings to find someone deep within Chavez's party—not too close to the man himself but just close enough to get some intel."

"Why? He was elected and was supposed to be what the people wanted, wasn't he?"

"That's what he and his followers led others to believe, but the truth was he was a strict Marxist who believed the government needed to tell the citizens how to breathe and think. The guy was a punk, and we, as in the United States, wanted to keep an eye on him from the beginning."

"Thus bringing in Jennings."

"Yep, it seemed to be Jennings job to recruit insiders and learn how the Chavez government was funding FARC in Columbia."

This was starting to sound like a spy novel to Frank. He knew that FARC or the Fuerzas Armadas Revolucionarias de Columbia, had been fighting the legitimate government of Columbia since around 1964. It had been the longest running so-called civil war in South America's history or probably the entire world. The communist terrorist group was known for attacking police stations, civilians, and anything else which would get their name and cause in front of the public—nationally and internationally.

"The agency knew that Chavez wanted nothing more than to spread Marxism or pure communism like the FARC in Columbia and funneled money into training camps in the jungles of Columbia and probably Venezuela alike. A big problem for the rest of the countries in South America who had their own problems with active terrorist groups."

"Like the Shining Path in Peru?" Frank asked, recalling the mini-lecture Jonas had told him about the terrorist group which had haunted Peru from the early eighties.

"Just like the Shining Path in Peru," Jason said.

"So, what happened?"

"Not too sure of all the details since even my contact at the agency wasn't technically allowed to talk about Jennings, but it seems he went on a killing spree."

Frank took a second to digest that one. "A killing spree? He wasn't a field agent, right?—a handler was all I thought he was."

"Titles and lines get blurry in the field," Jason responded. "Especially when Langley is over four thousand miles to the north."

Frank was afraid to ask. "Who'd he supposedly kill?"

"The guy who turned on him. Seems when Jennings first hired the guy—someone by the name of Raul Dominguez— it worked for a couple of months, but then Jennings found himself being tailed everywhere he went down south. Didn't matter which country he went to, but he knew he was being followed and the information Dominguez was giving him never turned out to be true. The agency put increasing pressure on Jennings, who one day, I guess, lost it and shot his man in the middle of the street in Caracas. Broad daylight— one shot to the back of the head."

"Shit!"

"Worse, after the murder, the police located Dominguez's entire family shot dead in their home in Caracas—wife and two kids. Chavez put the hit out on Jennings, and the man fled the country. Two months later, he was fired."

"Jesus, he killed the guy's family and there were no charges sought from the Venezuelan government? You just can't go around shooting people in foreign countries and get away with it."

"You got me there," Jason responded. "I guess some deals were made or whatever, but to this day there is an indictment against Kevin Jennings for murder in Venezuela—that is, if he ever returns there. The agency wanted to wash their hands of him and they did, I suppose."

"Chavez could have used that incident for years against the US—why didn't he?"

"Again, you got me there. I've never worked in the south but with politics, maybe we were able to scratch a back or two for the promise of no noise on Jennings. Perhaps the guy who was murdered wasn't that much loved—maybe Jennings did Chavez a favor without knowing it. Still a shame about the man's family."

"Yeah, sure is, but there still seems to be a lot of unknowns," Frank said.

"Isn't that the way of the spook world? Someone who is someone's friend one day may be the enemy the next. Strange life my brothers and sisters live over at the CIA."

Frank nodded. "Like you guys at the Bureau don't do the same?"

"Frank, we're home grown and not international," Jason said. "Domestic is where we stay, minding our own business."

"Now that I don't believe."

"It is what it is. Did I give you enough to chew on with your Kevin Jennings?"

"No contact since two-thousand and three?"

"Not that I know of and that was just rumors he was playing with some dangerous fellows from the Middle East— he's probably dead, Frank, just not officially."

"Thanks for all the intel," Frank replied. "If there's anything I can do, I owe you."

"I'll remember that."

The phone went dead, and Frank found himself sitting on a chair, trying to figure out the conversation he had just had.

It wasn't easy digesting.

Jonas smiled as he walked into Sam's room and saw his fiancée sitting in a wheelchair. "You've never looked more beautiful," he said as he walked over and knelt in front of her.

"And you never cease to amaze me with your compliments," Sam said. She returned his smile and reached out to touch his face.

"I haven't shaven."

"I don't care."

"I'd make him shave," Maggie said as she stood by the doorway.

Sam shook her head. "No, I just want to touch his ruggedly handsome face is all."

"Now who is spilling the compliments?" Jonas returned, gently brushing away a loose hair which hung over her right eye. "You do look beautiful."

"Keep this lovey-dovey talk up, and I'm leaving."

Jonas turned to his sister and pointed behind her. "The door is wide open."

With a humph, Maggie turned on her heels and strode out the door. "I'll get us some coffee."

"Jonas," Sam said. "You shouldn't have chased her away."

"I didn't, and she's still standing right outside," he said. "Isn't that right, Maggie?"

A laugh and then Maggie poked her head back into the doorway. "Sam, do you want anything besides the coffee I'm getting Jonas?"

Sam shook her head. "I've got all I need right now in front of me."

"Ah, Gad," Maggie said as she actually walked down the hallway toward the cafeteria. She caught Frank by the elbow as he was walking toward Sam's room. "Nope, not yet—it's sickening sticky with love talk in there. You won't be able to take it."

Frank stopped, looked at the doorway, and then at Maggie. "I'm buying."

Sam straightened her back up in the wheelchair and smiled. "Not sure how long I'll be able to stay awake but I'm too tired to go back to bed."

"That made a lot of sense."

She shook her head a bit before responding, "The nurse told me that it was too early to get out of bed and I may feel a bit queasy or dizzy."

"Do you feel any of the two?"

"No."

"Oh," Jonas responded. "Now I'm totally confused."

"Sorry, my Love," Sam said. "I'm a bit ditsy but it could be the medication but I just couldn't lay there any longer. How long have I been here anyway?"

It was hard for Jonas to say. He'd been so busy on his own that he'd lost track of days and time. "I'm not sure but I think a little over two weeks. You were very lucky you know."

Sam nodded. "I know we both were but I keep forgetting the whole story—I know you've told me as well as Maggie but I seem to forget what exactly happened."

"It's the pain medication, I assume."

"Probably but tell me again how bad it was."

"You sure you want to hear?"

"Yes, and this time I promise to remember."

"If you don't, it's okay—I'll remind you when you ask any time."

"I do love you so," Sam said.

"As I you," Jonas responded.

It took nearly ten minutes to explain the explosion at the Common Grounds and the destruction had taken place. The dead and wounded were especially hard for Sam to hear about, but with a stiff chin, she listened to Jonas and asked few questions. She didn't need to—his telling the story was descriptive enough.

Then the two of them sat in silence a couple of minutes just holding hands. There was no need to talk—their silence was warm and comfortable.

"You two love birds done in there?" Maggie asked from just outside the room.

Disturbed from their serenity, Jonas gently let go of Sam's hand and stood up from the chair he had been sitting in beside her. "Yes, come in and I hope you have a cup of coffee."

Maggie was followed by Frank holding two cups of coffee. "Sam, you look great."

"Thank you, Frank," she responded. "I'm actually a bit stronger now than I was a few minutes ago."

"That's good, that's real good," Frank said, handing Jonas one of the cups of coffee. "Black with nothing."

Jonas nodded and waited.

"I think now that Sam is solidly awake and feeling better, I'm going to push her into the bathroom and see what I can do with her hair."

"She's fine the way she is," Jonas said.

"It's just my way of saying that Frank needs to talk with you, and I was trying to be cute and give you a clue. For a wonderful detective, you don't always figure things out quickly, do you?"

Jonas smiled and kissed Sam on the forehead. "I'm like the turtle, Maggie. Slow but always knowing which direction I'm walking."

"I would have said like an Owl—perched and always waiting."

"Don't use similes, Frank," Maggie said.

"Not good, huh?" Frank asked.

"Not even close, but Jonas's wasn't much better," she said, stepping behind the wheelchair and moving it toward the bathroom. "We won't be long."

"Got anything?"

Frank nodded. "Yeah, but not sure what. This is getting weirder by the day."

"You telling me," Jonas replied. "Come on, we'll talk while we walk."

"Like a couple of turtles?"

Jonas simply shook his head and moved toward the hall-way. "Yes, a couple of slow-moving turtles."

CHAPTER 23

Y ou said things were getting very weird, Frank." Jonas stated, sipping on the tall, cold Stella Artois.

He and Frank had decided to get away from the hospital after an hour and seriously ponder what they were both thinking. Frank's office was the logical location but both agreed that where this case was heading, it might not be the optimum place for a brainstorming session.

The Cellar was the place chosen. Two blocks from Frank's with a clear view of the coming and goings around the Mission Inn. Frank sat on the outside patio looking north-east while his partner kept his eyes looking south-west.

"We're paranoid."

"A bit."

Frank wagged his finger in front of the Firestone Bravo—a brown ale Frank had picked up drinking since its release in 2017. He liked the rich chocolate malt taste. Though he didn't generally enjoy beers as robust at the Bravo, this one he did.

Frank knew Jonas usually stuck to only a few beers and today's choice was his standby Stella—a lighter lager with a crispness that Frank rarely found refreshing.

Then again, on hot days he could find anything refreshing.

"You're thinking about beer again, aren't you?" Jonas asked, taking another taste.

"Makes me think," Frank returned. "Mundane things make me think and wondering why you have, like, four choices in beer unnerves me."

Jonas looked across the small table. "Unnerves you? What the hell does that mean? Me drinking certain beers unnerves you."

"It does," Frank replied. "I mean, there are literally dozens upon dozens of beers out there waiting to pass between your lips, and you stick to four."

"To tell the truth, I only drink two different kinds of beer," Jonas said. "I do this to impress you."

"Two." Frank shot a look across at his friend while also watching a man strolling past the outdoor patio of the Cellar. "That unnerves me more."

"What if I told you that I only shave four times per week? Would that unnerve you more?"

"You toilet habits are yours and only yours. Why would that interest me in the least?"

"But only drinking a limited amount of beers does?"

Frank nodded. "Now, you understand my dilemma."

"You are one strange person, Frank Sanders," Jonas stated, keeping his eyes peeled down the street toward Frank's office, suddenly feeling the hairs on his neck rise a bit. A moment and then he relaxed. Simply a jogger stopping to bend down and tie his shoes.

"As I said, we're paranoid," Frank mentioned, tipping the Firestone up for a quick gulp. "I've noticed we have been eyeballing every person walking down Orange Street as if every human is a suspect."

"They could be."

Frank set his beer down on the table. "No, Jonas, they can't be. This is a screwed up set of circumstances but yet the key is in front of us, and we just can't figure it out. That's all."

Jonas smiled. "You're right. Tell me how easy this all is."

"I didn't say it was easy but let me put the pieces together if you don't mind."

Without a word, Jonas leaned back in the wrought-iron chair, picked up his beer in his right hand, and gently waved his left. "Explain it to me then."

"I'll use bullet notes to make it really simple."

"By all means—I like bullets."

Frank eyed his friend for a moment before beginning. "First the coffee shop gets blown up—"

"No," Jonas interrupted. "First, the person who destroyed the coffee shop and those within know that I'm supposed to meeting Sam there."

"Corrected," Frank stated. "First, the person responsible knows you are meeting Sam at the Common Grounds and detonates the bomb by some method—probably cell phone but I don't have that information. You, unknown to the perpetrator, decide to be romantic and stop to buy your lady a ring—romantic but doesn't fit into his plan. You're not killed."

"So far spot on."

"Then you for some reason figure out that you need to flit away to Peru in search of what is going on because the murderer mentioned Iquitos. A place you haven't seen in decades."

"I didn't flit, I flew and it was two decades not decades—don't make me feel older than I already do."

"See," Frank said. "You are more pleasant after a beer or two. Usually, you are so serious and dangerous."

"I'm serious now and enjoying the outdoors and your bullet points."

"Good," Frank responded. "Now, this is where it goes dark for me, and I'm sure a lot more for you. You meet a few people in Peru who lead you back into the Amazon where you make acquaintance with a woman you once loved. You find out that you had a son with her but were never told. Should I keep on?"

Jonas finished his beer in one swallow and ordered another. Frank got a shot at the look which passed over Jonas's face and realized this was where his comrade could be dangerous—the blackness behind the blue eyes was there only for a second but the darkness was there and very lethal.

"Go ahead."

"While you are there doing what you did, I get man-napped. I didn't like it much and surely didn't like shooting a couple of fellows but it was either them or me—it was them, and I'm okay to a point, but what I don't like is not really knowing why I was man-napped. All I learned was that I recognized the voice of the one in charge. Now, here's the hard part—I still don't know what the hell is going on. You came back from Peru—after, and excuse me, losing a son you never knew, and killing the two men who killed him. A guy you knew back in the day gets whacked on the way home from a casino, and everyone else you knew tells you to forget about it and return home. Am I missing anything?"

Jonas looked down the road while draining half the beer and shook his head. "No, you got most of it but I think I can add to it—call it a hunch or what, but it makes sense."

Frank nodded and motioned for another Bravo from the waitress sauntering by their table. "Tell me."

"You have everything in a nutshell but the person behind this is a lot bigger than we thought."

"Meaning?"

"It's not some narcotics dealer or anything like that but someone who was in charge of the mission or at least some person who had a lot to lose about those missions."

"Taking bribes, a piece of the action, or what?" Frank asked.

"No, I don't believe it had anything with the drug dealers we were supposed to be hunting nor the terrorists that Arianna told me about. Perhaps we were pawns used by the Peruvian government at the time to help rid them of the Shining Path but I don't think that is what this is about."

"Why not?"

"Because, Frank, that was twenty years ago," Jonas stated. "That's a long time for a grudge or whatever this is about to lift its ugly head. No, this is now and what happed then could affect now."

Frank nodded. "A politician?"

"You said you recognized his voice."

"I did."

"Then that's the mastermind," Jonas stated and leaned forward. "That's who we are after."

Both men sat in silence for a few minutes, reflecting on what was shared.

Frank broke the silence. "Then I feel we're at peg one and starting over."

"Seems like it, doesn't it?"

Studying the man across from him, Frank knew that Jonas had not been totally forth coming with him. "What are you keeping from me?

"What do you mean?"

"I know you, and you have not told me everything—I knew at the airport after yapping for so long there was something you were keeping close to the chest."

Jonas looked down Orange again and then back at Frank. "No, I haven't been honest with you and there's a reason."

"To keep me safe?"

Jonas looked at Frank with a steady eye. "Why would that worry me? Keeping you safe."

"Because we're friends."

"Right," Jonas stated. "No, it was because I had to do some digging, and I think I may have come up with something earlier today that I couldn't share with you since we were at the hospital, and I didn't want to alarm Sam or Maggie."

Frank didn't like the sound of this but, then again, he hadn't liked the sound or actions of anything in the past couple of weeks. "What do you have for me?"

"Does the My Lai Massacre ring a bell?"

Sitting in silence for a moment or two before answering, Frank clearly remembered the small villages of My Lai and My Khe in the Quang Ngai Province of South Vietnam. Over four hundred innocent civilians had been murdered by American troops fighting in Southeast Asia—call it evil or whatever, people who should not have died were butchered by United States soldiers. There was a cover-up but eventually twenty-six men were tried for the crimes against these men, women, and children—only Lieutenant William Calley Jr, was sentenced. A life sentence reduced to three and half years of house arrest. A stain on the United States to say the least but still—over four hundred innocents were murdered by the very ones sent to save them.

"Yeah, I know a bit about My Lai."

"Good," Jonas said as he opened his brown leather briefcase and withdrew the envelope he had received at the hotel in Iquitos. "Order another beer for the both of us."

"You know, I've never told you how much I like the new briefcase," Frank stated.

Ignoring the statement, Jonas moved the coaster away from in front of him and laid out the envelope. "It's made from leather and Aguayo cloth."

"And the last is what?"

"I don't know, a fabric of some sort made of wool," Jonas responded. "You like it?"

"Yes, but I just mentioned it to make small talk while you get ready to explain what's in the folder."

Jonas almost looked disappointed—he'd bought the satchel when he had first landed in Lima and believed it was well made, manly looking, and a hell of deal. He let his feelings go at this point, though Sam had thought it was very chic when he showed it to her on his return. "You'd never know classy things like this satchel."

"True," Frank said. "I'm a Neanderthal and only believe leather should be worn on the body and not as a tote bag."

"It's not a tote bag."

"The envelope, please."

Jonas undid the hasp and moved out a few sheets of paper which he had received the last night in Iquitos. "Don't say a word until you finish reading."

Frank said nothing but took the sheets from Jonas. He concentrated—reading each line like it was the last one in a long overdue story. He didn't even take a sip of his beer while reading.

"You are shitting me!"

"That's what I thought when I read it but it proved what Admiral Guardio told me on the boat when I was leaving the Amazon," Jonas said. "But I re-read and re-read the documents you have before you. It didn't make sense until I got back to the states."

"Why not?"

"You had to tell me your story of being kidnapped—"

"Man-napped," interrupted Frank.

"Yes." Jonas nodded. "When you told me the voice you heard, then I knew these papers meant something—until then it sounded like some conspiracy theory out of a poorly written novel. Perhaps I wanted to believe Guardio was just a blow-hard. Someone who wanted me to think he was more than what he was."

Frank couldn't deny Jonas's assumption. If what he held currently in his hands was true, then My Lai would be a good comparison. Perhaps worse actually since My Lai and the other village occurred in an armed conflict where emotions and judgments get all screwed up in the moment. My Lai was wrong but the village of Chaca near the southern border of Columbia and a few miles west of the Amazon in Peru was almost as bad. Not the amount of casualties but the murder of civilians, in any case, was beyond shameful.

Frank put down the paperwork and looked across the table at Jonas. "Is this shit for real?"

"As far as I can tell."

"Jesus Christ," Frank said with a sigh.

Jonas took a sip of his beer and slowly shook his head. "He, apparently, was not there that particular day."

Frank finished his beer in two gulps. "Order me another while I try to read through this once more."

"Take your time," Jonas responded.

"We drink too much."

"Perhaps we don't drink enough to erase what we've seen," Jonas stated. "The average person lives their lives generally in peace with moments of indecision or moments of personal tragedy like the death of a loved one. Terrible, but that is the extent of their misery."

"That's very cold."

"No," Jonas stated. "It is tragic, but you and I do this for a living. We investigate and truly see how horrendous humanity is—don't know why we do it but we do it."

"Makes me want to quit."

Jonas smiled while waving over the waitress for another round. "No, Frank, you and I won't quit on our own. We will continue to solve cases and wonder how humans can treat fellow humans the way they do, but we won't quit."

"We have to someday."

"Maybe, but it will probably take a bullet to stop us."

Frank didn't like the look in Jonas's eyes. "From a suspect we happen to be chasing?"

"Yes." Jonas nodded. "Or perhaps from ourselves when we've had enough of humanity."

"Goddamn, Jonas," Frank stated. "Nothing but sunshine and roses from you all the time."

Jonas laughed quietly. "That's me to the point. Read."

Frank did not respond but picked up the sheaf of papers and re-read what he had already read believing it had to be fiction but knew it wasn't.

"Is Jonas here?" Sam asked, sitting straight up in bed.

Maggie looked at her watch and wondered what was keeping her brother. "No, he and Frank went off to have a man talk about this case."

"They're drinking and trying to solve the world's problems," Sam said, looking at her best friend and the sister of the man she loved. "What is it between those two?"

"I couldn't tell you," Maggie answered. "Jonas really never mentioned Frank's name much while he was on the force. Of course, once in a while Jonas might talk about this case or another that he worked with Detective Sanders but that was about it. What I did know about Frank was that he lost his entire family in a car accident years ago."

"How horrible," Sam stated.

"Yes, and the worse part was that his wife really didn't want to drive to Indio where Frank was working for overtime for the department during spring break. She relented and said the kids and she would join Frank for the weekend. She never made it, nor did the children, dying on Interstate Ten just east of Palm Springs. A drunk driver hit them head-on driving the wrong way."

Sam inched herself a bit on the pillows at the head of the bed. Feeling much, so much, better than she had in the last couple of days, but suddenly she felt tired. "Is that why they drink?"

"What do you mean?"

"Sometime, oh, I don't know, Jonas will be fine but then a look comes over his eyes—not mean but distant. He'll have one to many and then go silent. Maggie, he has never been cruel or abusive—Jonas would never be like that, but it seems sometimes his mind goes places I don't want to follow."

"Then don't," Maggie replied.

"How can I not when I love him so much and want to be a part of everything that makes him who he is?"

Maggie smiled and reached out for her friend's hand. "Then be the listening post when he's talking or the silent witness when he's not. Jonas, as well as Frank and most of the people in their field, have seen things they can't or won't' talk about. What we see is tragic or heart rendering is what they see or saw on a daily basis. Sometimes the best they can do for themselves and others is to go silent and live with the memories."

"But those memories are horrible."

"And they own them," Maggie replied.

Sam let go of Maggie's hand. "That's cruel, Maggie. If we love them, then we have to get them to talk to us about those demons that revisit them in those memories."

"No," Maggie said softly. "What would be crueler is to force them to tell us things we don't want to hear and they can't explain."

The papers were dated nearly a quarter of a century earlier and then ended about twenty years ago. A simple package of six single typed pages outlining the encroachment of drug cartels moving massive amounts of cocaine from the southern tip of Columbia into the northern sections of Peru. Iquitos seemed the area concentrated by the cartels in the nineties. Remote and rather lawless with criminals, expats—probably criminals—and a drug trade knowing no bounds as the appetite in the United States was insatiable.

The northern routes from Cartagena had run dry as the United States Coast Guard, Border Patrol, United States Navy, and every law enforcement officer from Texas to Florida were on the lookout for fast boats carrying drugs or the ganga planes flying below radar. Transportation of illicit drugs and illegal weapons was getting too hazardous and costly for the various cartels shipping northward. So, to compensate for losses, they went southward and then northward along the Pacific coast all the way to west coast of Mexico and California. What meant more delays in moving product meant more product getting to its destination.

Capitalism at its best. Supply and demand was the way of the global market.

What Frank wasn't sure about was where the paperwork had come from. No headings of an agency present and nothing to indicate this material was official. There was nothing in the least incriminating about any one person or agency. It was a dossier that simply outlined certain activities which occurred doing specific time tables in a foreign land.

"It's all accurate," Jonas said, watching his friend. "You've read it—anything that doesn't sound true?"

Frank shook his head and hit the second page.

Detailed account from an agent—the way it was worded indicated with no doubt that an experienced drug enforcement officer or other legitimate agency officer wrote the work-up. It was, to Frank's mind, almost as though this was being written by someone who believed that this information might be needed at a future date. All intelligent reports were in duplicate back in the nineties and immediately forwarded to supervisors—this paperwork had no headings, names of those writing it, or any supervisor it was sent to.

That made it the more interesting. Frank knew it was legit, and it didn't take two readings to understand that but it took two readings to fully understand the scope of what the paperwork laid out.

Jonas sipped his beer and texted his sister to inquire about Sam's progress which came back immediately that Sam was doing great, awake, and wondering where her fiancé was. Jonas typed back that he and Frank were trying to figure what was going on and Maggie texted:

~ Liar, you're drinking beer.

~True—but that is how things are accomplished.

~ I'll give her your love.

~ Thanks.

"Holy shit, again!" Frank said as he laid the sheaf of paper onto the table top. "Should we be ducking from sniper bullets?"

Jonas nodded, taking a sip of beer. "I don't think that is needed now but within a short time perhaps."

"You're very calm."

"I've been shot at before and hit actually."

Frank smiled. "Yeah, you took one for the team in your ass."

"It hurt like hell."

"Probably since you don't have much cushion back there."

"Really, you are going to attack a wounded officer of the Riverside Police Department? The shame."

Frank placed his right hand to his brow. "I salute you. You deserved the award you got back then for getting shot in the rear end."

Jonas smiled. "It probably would have been better if it hadn't been from one of the officers following me into the building."

"I didn't want to mention that."

"Do we duck or not?"

"What do you think?"

Frank mulled over the question a moment before answering. "If what I've read is true, then this will make front page news, which would not be good for our country."

"Seventy-six civilians murdered—yeah, not good front page for any government."

"Is it accurate?"

"A lot of people lost their lives in Peru and other South American countries during that time period. Maybe it's true."

Frank thought—really thought. It was crazy the idea that an American officer—be that who he worked for at the time—would authorize what he had just read in the paperwork. "No fucking way," he uttered. "It had to be when you and the rest of the American team were back in Lima. Someone else did this."

Jonas looked down the street and suddenly thought about what he had visited in the Amazon not more than a few days ago. "What we see and what truly happened does not always coincide."

"What the hell does that mean?"

"I was there," Jonas stated. "And then Arianna and I left for Lima for a de-briefing which was really just a way for the two of us to spend some quality time together."

"Screwing."

Jonas shook his head. "No, making love."

"That's sounds better. Now, while you were in Lima, did anything come up on the radar about bad incidents up north?"

"No, in fact, we were told to stand down for three days," Jonas said. "We liked that."

"I bet you did."

"Don't be an asshole, Frank," Jonas stated. "I loved her. Of course, it could have been led by tons of lust, but I did and still do love her."

"I believe you."

Jonas stared across the street toward the Mission Inn. "Did I ever tell you that the years the inn was boarded up I used to sneak into the basements?"

"No."

"Yeah, there are passages everywhere down in the basements," Jonas said. "The catacombs. We'd jump the fence and wander down below, looking for things."

Frank had heard of the catacombs beneath the historic Mission Inn but had never visited them. What he knew was they were not the same catacombs in Italy or any other country used for burial and thus possibly haunted. These were simply tunnels and rooms that Frank Miller, the original owner, had devised as meeting and storage rooms. No nefarious undertones—just places to be used when needed.

"Did you find any bodies?"

Jonas stared at Frank. "Of course not, but man was it fun running through the hallways in blackness and then having some slim light coming through basement windows."

"The point of this boyhood recollection?"

Jonas smiled. "Just memories but, then again, memories often produce thoughts that may serve as fodder for the moment."

Frank didn't reply. This was interesting.

"When Arianna and I were in Lima, that agent Kevin Jennings sailed through one evening and then we didn't see him for a week.

"Okay."

"Like I've said, we didn't know much about this guy, but as we discussed things—"

"Under the sheets?"

"And above," Jonas said. "We realized he was truly dangerous. He was not some handler but the caller."

Frank shook his head. No more beer for him this day since he had no idea what Jonas had just said. "Caller?"

"In the business, at least back then," Jonas said, "the handler simply handled the people who had turned but the caller was the one who told the handler what to do."

"The caller?"

"He or she was the organizer," Jonas said, "the person giving the orders."

"And this is the person you believe is the one responsible for the coffee shop and all the rest?"

"No."

Frank was really confused at this point, and it wasn't the beer. "What do you mean?

"I think the handler and the caller are the same person."

"That doesn't make sense," Frank replied. "How is one person in charge of different aspects of an operation?"

"He isn't."

"Okay, I'm leaving the beer behind and going for the hard stuff." Frank said. "Explain that to me like I'm a five-year-old."

"He has an alias."

"Jesus Christ!"

"That's not the alias."

"What the hell are you talking about?"

"He passed himself off as just a mid-level government agent," Jonas explained. "He was at the operations but not in the field with us but maybe once or twice. We saw him in Lima for a moment on our down time, but he didn't say anything. In fact, he looked rather nervous that we had seen him talking to a captain from the Peruvian Army at a restaurant where we were eating."

"Strange coincidence you two bumping into him."

"We didn't think anything about it since the restaurant was one of the only good ones near the base where we were stationed. But as soon as we sat down, he looked over and then left within minutes, leaving the captain alone."

"Did you know the officer?"

"Never had seen him before, and he didn't look particularly upset but just nodded when—"

"Why did you stop?"

Jonas didn't respond but looked west down the street from where they were sitting.

"You see something?" Frank asked, putting his right hand on the butt of the revolver holstered in the small of his back.

"No—his name was Elias Leland."

"Who?"

"The agent—I've been plaguing my brain trying to remember but just then when I recalled his leaving in such a hurry, it came back to me."

"After all these years? But I thought his name was Kevin Jennings?"

"That was his real name but one time when we did meet up with him in the jungle, he had a couple of shots of pisco and joked that he used the name of Elias Leland when he traveled outside of Peru."

"That doesn't make sense," Frank responded. "Why would he use an alias? The agency didn't know anything about that name."

"I don't know and perhaps he was just drunk and screwing around but that's what he told us."

Frank slipped out his phone and texted the name to his friend in the Bureau.

Jonas grinned. "You must owe that guy a lot of favors."

Frank nodded when his phone buzzed. "I do but I generally pay him back with family fun packages for Disneyland or something like that when he travels out here with his wife and kids."

"Fair enough."

Frank looked down and then suddenly up. "Dead end, and I mean that."

"What does that mean?"

"Leland was a name he used once in a while when he wanted to go missing and another reason the agency distanced themselves from him."

Jonas nodded and waited for Frank to scroll up the next message.

"Seems it's the passport he used when leaving Venezuela," Frank read. "That's why the government couldn't nail him since no one knew the name, including the agency at the time."

"I thought your friend just looked Jennings up?"

"He did," Frank said. "But this is brand new, and he had to make another connection—no one wants this information out."

"Why is it so secret?"

"Leland or Jennings is dead."

Jonas sat up straighter. "What?"

"He's dead."

"How?"

"My friend is looking into it and will get back to me later," Frank responded. "I'm surprised he was able to get that much to me with just texting."

Jonas took a long pull of his beer. "Something is just not right here."

"You can say that again," Frank replied. "Guess we can cross his name off of the list."

"Nope, not yet."

"He's dead."

"Someone is dead but we don't know who."

"I have a headache."

At that point a large and very black Chevrolet Suburban pulled up curbside in front of where Jonas and Frank happened to be sitting.

"I think that headache may turn into a migraine," Frank said as the front doors opened and two men in suits approached their outdoor table.

CHAPTER 24

Unlike in the movies, the men took a table next to where Frank and Jonas were sitting and were very pleasant. No sinister stares.

"Special Agent Ramirez, and I'm Goff," said Goff as he waved the waitress off.

"You know who we are," Frank said.

"Yes," Ramirez nodded. "Nice to meet you."

"Is it?" Jonas asked, not smiling.

Goff didn't like the looks of Jonas and knew the dossier had been correct. This man could be a danger to others. "There is nothing sinister happening. We have been working the bombing and knew you two were also investigating it but from a different angle."

Frank nodded. "And that angle would be what?"

"More personal than it is for us, understandably so."

The men looked at each other in silence until Ramirez broke it. "Okay, you and we know this wasn't some terrorist group with connections in the Middle East. It was a domestic wanting everyone to believe it when the target hadn't been neutralized."

Jonas and Frank shot each other a look, and then Frank nodded. "The department mentioned to the news that they believed it was terrorist driven."

"And the public was terrorized," Ramirez replied.

"That's not what he meant," Jonas retorted.

Goff held up his hand. "No disrespect was intended by Special Agent Ramirez but simply that the department thought that was the best way of handling it until the full investigation was concluded."

"Okay," Frank replied, "but why the interest in us?"

"You're looking into who bombed the coffee store, yes?"

"You already know that," Jonas replied.

"Then we were wondering if we could share what we know?"

"And if we refuse?" Frank asked.

"Then Special Agent Ramirez and I will stand up, return to our vehicle, and move at the pace that our investigation allows us, which is pretty damn slow at this point."

Jonas smiled for the first time, but Frank saw the looks on the agents' faces—they weren't taken in by the gesture of comradeship. They shouldn't think such things with Jonas.

"What do you have?" Jonas asked as he sat back into his seat.

Frank was visibly relieved at the sudden relaxation of his friend. "Wait a minute, Jonas. How do we know we can trust the feds?"

"I didn't say we'd trust them, but we have to start somewhere, and we're up against a wall at the moment."

"Okay," Frank agreed. "How'd you know where to find us right now?"

Goff looked at Ramirez and merely shrugged. "We pinged your cell and knew you had contacted one of our agents in DC."

Before Frank could reply, Ramirez reassured him that the agent's name would go no further than the four of them. Investigators received information from wherever they needed, and it wouldn't do to burn someone who they may need in the future. Even if that agent happened to be in the same agency.

Frank nodded his approval.

"We know the bomber was an expert in explosives, he used a cell for detonation, but probably wasn't anywhere near here when it went off," Ramirez explained. "At first, we thought that he'd be a sick bastard and stick around, but nothing turned up on surveillance or anywhere else that would lead us in that direction. Your department—"

"Ex-department," Jonas corrected.

"Of course, has been helpful but they are in the dark as much as we were until Lieutenant Smythe mentioned something about you, Frank, coming into the office with Jonas's phone. He told us it was nothing but a text Jonas had received moments before the explosion about some place in South America."

"Iquitos," Jonas said.

"Yes, Iquitos," Goff replied. "Smythe thought nothing of it since it could have been just a message about a potential trip Jonas and his girlfriend were going to take in the future."

"I fed that to him."

"He ate it up then—that is, until we asked more details about it."

"Smythe didn't have any details," Frank said. "He brushed it off immediately."

"Can't blame the lieutenant," Jonas said. "He'd—hell, no one had handled such a deadly explosion like that in the department, and he wasn't thinking clearly. Probably hoping to find out it was a busted gas line, to be honest."

"Anyway, that's why we felt the need to contact the two of you," Ramirez concluded.

"Why two weeks?" Frank asked. "Shouldn't you have caught up with us a while ago instead of just now?"

Ramirez held up both his hands in front of him. "Yes, we probably should have but with Jonas in the hospital, badly hurt, we thought we would try to tie things up here. And then suddenly he's out of the country and Frank…well, you don't let moss settle under your feet either."

"Just a couple of movers and shakers—that's us," Frank said with a forced chuckle.

"True," Goff replied. "Well, besides the fact that against doctor's orders Jonas not only left his bed but the country, we thought we'd track you down once he returned. And here we are."

"You don't have much, do you?" Frank asked.

Goff shook his head. "We've got squat, really. We know Jonas was on a team in the late nineties in Peru hunting terrorists or drug traffickers and that most of the people on the list are dead, except a few. And that you almost got whacked the other night by some nefarious fellows. Two who are lying in the morgue—good shooting by the way."

Frank didn't reply. There was nothing to say.

"For having squat, you seem to have plenty on us," Jonas mused.

"Which again isn't going anywhere—that you have our word on," Ramirez stated, flagging down the waitress. "I think it's time for a drink or two if you guys don't mind?"

"That's why we're here," Frank replied, feeling much better all of a sudden knowing he wouldn't be answering for those two stiffs at the coroners. He suddenly loved the power of the federal government.

"Then tell us about Kevin Jennings or Elias Leland."

"Unfortunately, not much to tell, from what we can gather and, this time, we are as honest as we can be. Our cousins at the Agency are pretty tight lipped about that guy as your texting friend has already informed you, Frank. We can't get much out of them either except this guy—by whatever name he went by is probably dead."

"Probably?" Jonas asked.

"Shot doing something naughty down south is what we've been told but then again no body was ever brought north for identification. Supposedly, he fell off a fast boat just off the coast of some island I can't pronounce. He had run afoul of some bad dudes and floated away as fish bait."

"Yeah," Jonas scoffed.

"That's all we have," Goff replied. "Now it's your turn to show your hands if you would?"

Frank glanced down at the envelope and Jonas just shrugged. He was tired, and if they could get the assistance from the FBI, so be it. All he really wanted was to get this thing finished up, go back to his life with Sam, and maybe retire. He'd seen too much and, as he grinned at his friend across the table, knew Frank felt the same.

"I've got to use the restroom," Jonas said, sliding the papers over to Goff. "Read these and then let Sepcial Agent

Ramirez read them. Digest what's on the pages and then perhaps we can come up with something together."

"What about your personal reports of the actions you've taken since the bombing?" Ramirez asked while Goff reached for the sheaf of papers.

"You two seem to know what we've done since then and the little details are not that important right now compared to what's in those documents," Jonas said, standing and leaving the table.

"I like him," Ramirez said. "He's a straight shooter."

"That he is, my friend, that he is," Frank responded. "In more ways than one."

Jonas stepped outside the restaurant and called Sam to let her know what was happening. He explained how the feds were now working with him and Frank and, hopefully, they could put this thing to rest soon. He promised he wouldn't be much longer before he'd go back to the hospital. Sam reassured him that he could take his time since she wasn't going anywhere and that Maggie was keeping her company. She too, she stated, wanted this whole thing behind them so they could go forward again.

"She is a keeper," he said aloud as he re-entered and headed for Frank and the others.

"This can't be accurate," Goff said, handing the papers to Ramirez.

"Why not?" Jonas asked, resuming his seat at the table.

"Because I don't want to believe this," Goff snarled.

All four men looked at each other in silence and then laughed.

"Must be the beer," Frank declared. "But I thought you just said you didn't want to believe it so it can't be true?"

"Must be because I'm thirsty and my beer isn't here yet." Goff wiped a tear from his left eye. "I know it's not in the least bit funny, but for God's sake. We may have been involved in a village being wiped out in cold blood?"

"Not any of the four of us here," Frank said, watching Ramirez skim through the papers quickly.

"I was there," Jonas stated flatly.

The momentary levity dropped, and three heads turned to Jonas.

"I was there," Jonas repeated.

"At the village?" Frank asked.

"No, I was in Lima, like I said, but I was there all the same and should have known something had gone wrong."

Ramirez threw the papers down hard onto the table top. "Gone wrong? You mean like when you forget to change the oil in your car or forget to pick up the dry cleaning—that kind of wrong or the kind of wrong where seventy-six civilians get gunned down on a sunny day in the jungle?"

"Take it easy," Goff said, looking between his partner and this guy named Jonas. The tension had risen like a clutch play at a ballgame. "If it's true, then this is bad—very bad."

"It's true." Jonas nodded. "I meant I should have known that something like this could happen."

"How could you?" Frank asked.

"I was a detective, wasn't I?"

"Sure, but that doesn't mean you would know when a mass murder went down when no one, and I mean no one, said a word about it. The victims certainly couldn't begin to be witnesses for you, now could they?"

"No, I suppose not," Jonas replied.

Ramirez gathered up the papers neatly and handed them back to Jonas. "Sorry about that—I shouldn't have said what I did, but I guess looking at those it just seemed unbelievable."

"What now?" Frank asked. "Do you guys take this back to DC?"

Goff looked over at Ramirez but then back to Frank. "I'm not sure."

"That's a confidence building statement," Frank said, shaking his head. "When the Bureau doesn't know what to do, that's crazy."

"Let's just continue on the way we're going," Jonas stated. "You two were only going to talk to us but that doesn't mean you have to mention anything to anyone at your home office of the big bosses in Washington."

"We have to account for our time on the investigation," Ramirez said.

"I'm not asking you to do anything that would jeopardize the investigation but simply let us continue on the path we're moving and you on yours. Then if we happen to assist each other, so be it."

"Partners?" asked Goff.

"Sounds good to me," Frank replied. "We'll share information as we get it as you will, and we'll get this sucker solved soon."

"God, I hope so," replied Ramirez.

"This isn't quite like we usually conduct business but I suppose this isn't like any other case we've worked on either."

"True dat," Frank said and shrugged his shoulders when Jonas shot him a pained look. "I heard it last night on a talk show—just wanted to be hip."

"You're not," Jonas said.

"Thanks, but now that we four may put our brains together, which of course, you're getting the short end of the stick—"

"Speak for yourself," Jonas interrupted.

"Well, of course, I meant only me, old wise one," Frank said with a smile. "But as I was saying, the fed boys can get us information, and we can tell them what else we've learned."

"There's more than what is in those papers?" asked Goff.

"Yes," Jonas replied. "Frank will fill you in. I'm heading back to the hospital."

With that, Jonas stood up, dropped forty dollars near his empty glass, shook hands around the table, and left.

"Not much for goodbyes," said Goff.

"Nope," Frank returned. "Now are you two ready to hear who we think is behind this whole thing?"

Neither Goff nor Ramirez said a thing.

"Yeah, not sure I would either," Frank stated, starting in on what he and Jonas had been speaking about prior to the black Suburban pulling to the curb.

"Don't you think this is rather awkward?" Frank asked Jonas as they were sitting in Sam's hospital room.

Frank had stayed at the restaurant for another hour after Jonas left and then bid goodbye to their new FBI friends and walked to his office. Another half an hour scanning a dozen emails and responding to three found Frank back at Riverside Community Hospital.

Sam had been up, dressed, and looking like she was ready for the evening. The bruises were barely visible, and her breathing was fairly normal, Frank thought as he smiled at his friend's fiancée.

After a few minutes, Sam told them she was tired but they could stay and talk but she needed to lie down again.

"And here I thought you two were going out dancing," Frank said. "You look beautiful."

Sam smiled. "And I felt that way but standing up for nearly thirty minutes doing my hair and a bit of makeup was all I could handle. I feel that now, sorry."

"No need for apologies," Maggie said, helping Sam back into her bed. "The boys would just as soon sit here and muddle through their detective stuff. Isn't that correct?"

"I'm not leaving," Jonas stated.

Frank nodded. "I'm with him."

"Settled then," Maggie responded pulling the sheet up a bit on Sam. "We won't listen to any confidential information being spoken."

"Big ears won't miss a thing," Jonas said with a smile. "With what we've all been through, I don't think there's anything we can't share."

Frank sat in a chair farthest from the bed, allowing Maggie and Jonas the closer ones. "Sam, seriously when are they going to be able to release you?"

"The doctor says in less than a week," Sam replied. "I just have to show that I can handle being on my feet for more than thirty minutes before getting weak. I'm doing well but I don't want to rush—everything else is just fine."

"Healing better than expected," Jonas stated. "Sam's strong like that."

"Only sweetness coming out of you," Maggie retorted. "Sounds like you're talking about a horse."

"Now, Maggie," Sam said. "I know what your brother means and it is sweet."

"Thank you, my dear."

"Welcome."

Frank laughed and then pulled out some papers from his briefcase. "Jonas we do have to discuss what happened after you left me with the feds."

"Yes," Jonas replied. "We do."

"Well, both Goff and Ramirez were astounded with the information we shared—especially the stuff you learned in Peru."

"That we weren't privy to before," Maggie said. "When will we get the full story of both your adventures?"

"There'll be time for that later," Jonas responded. "Well, if that surprised them and you're information while I was gone, did they give up anything?"

"Actually, they are handling it as a terrorist attack, though they've been very tight-lipped about it to the press."

Jonas nodded. "Yeah, haven't seen anything much in the papers or local news."

"It made it to CNN and FOX News the day it happened, but Roger says he hasn't seen anything on it since."

"That's because no one has laid claim to the explosion," Frank stated. "If ISIS or Al-Qaida had taken credit, then it would still be in the news. Once in a while I see something coming off of my Twitter feed with this or that but nothing substantial. Hard to believe, though, that with that many dead and wounded, more news isn't coming out."

"That is strange," Maggie said.

"Well, the FBI and the department do hold combined news conferences a couple times a week but nothing new, and no one is asking questions from the news reporters," Jonas returned.

"The public has short memories," Sam stated, lying on her bed with her eyes closed. "Don't forget there have been other terrorist attacks internationally in Belgium, Germany, and France with a much higher number of casualties than the coffee shop."

"True," Frank replied. "And both groups claiming credit for the bombings."

"One ups-man-ship," Maggie said.

Sam sat up in bed. "Though I've been with the living again a short while I have heard you all talking the past few days. What if what the FBI told you today wasn't the truth?"

Frank looked at Jonas and then at Maggie. "What do you mean?"

"Perhaps it's the medicine, but what I heard you say is they didn't have much to offer and you two had quite a bit."

"A lot more than we received from them," Jonas said.

"Well, why is that, since they have unlimited resources and—no offense to either of you—you don't?"

"We're just better snoopers than the feds, I guess," Frank replied.

Jonas stood up from his chair, walked to the window overlooking the hospital parking lot, and then turned around. "Perhaps, Sam is correct."

"For once," she replied.

He simply smiled and then continued. "It did seem Frank and I had a lot more information to share than they did."

"The agents did say they would get back to us after checking some of the details we gave them," Frank said.

Jonas nodded. "We'll see how long it is before they get back to us before making any more judgements about their motivations. How's that?"

"Sounds reasonable," Frank said with a nod.

"Want to hear another weird idea?" asked Sam.

Maggie smiled. "You don't have weird ideas."

"She's in love with Jonas," Frank replied. "At least that's a weird thing—so a weird idea isn't too far-fetched."

"Very funny," Jonas replied. "Go ahead, my love."

"It is really a strange thing I'm going to say," Sam said.

"You heard the man," Frank said. "Go ahead, my love."

Maggie slapped Frank across the right shoulder. "You are impossible."

"Thank you, my dear," Frank said with a bow.

"Okay, the strange idea is this. What if the person Frank heard the other night is a politician who just came onto the scene."

"No, the guy I think I recognized has been around awhile in Sacramento but that doesn't make sense why he would want to do me harm."

"Harm," Maggie said. "It seemed he wanted you dead."

"Well, permanently harmed—how's that?"

"Yes, anyway," Sam said as she shifted a bit more on her bed. "What if the man you heard had another identity—a previous life and somehow he made his way back."

Jonas walked to the bed quickly. 0000. "Goddamn, why didn't I think of that?"

"Think of what?" Maggie asked, suddenly concerned by the look on her brother's face. Such an intensity had come over Jonas she barely recognized him.

"You are a genius," Jonas said as he bent down and kissed Sam on the lips.

"Wow, I'll come up with other weird ideas if a kiss is my reward."

Frank already had his phone out and was walking into the hallway.

"Could someone tell me what is going on?" Maggie asked as she turned her head from the smiling couple to Frank's disappearing back.

"We were too close to the action and looking for answers in the present when the answers were in the past."

"Peru," Sam stated.

"Yes, Peru," Jonas replied.

"What the hell are you talking about—" asked Maggie.

"We've got a meet," Frank interrupted the trio as he walked while placing his cell into his pocket.

"When?"

"Fifteen minutes at the office."

"Again, what is going on?" Maggie asked.

Jonas again bent down to kiss Sam on the lips and whispered he'd be back soon.

"You'd better be," Sam said.

"Is anyone going to answer me?" Maggie asked yet again, turning and facing Frank.

"What Sam said wasn't weird," Frank told her. "In fact, it makes all the sense in the world. We're looking for a man we thought was dead a long time ago."

"He's not dead?"

"Probably not," Jonas responded. "It's a long story and a longer hunch but if the path Sam just laid out for us becomes true, then we will solve this issue once and for all."

Maggie turned from Frank and looked down at Sam. "Do you know what he's talking about?"

Sam merely shook her head. "Not really, but it just dawned on me laying here that perhaps something the boys were chasing from the past is still here in the present."

"God, you all sound like something from a confused episode of *Dr. Who*."

"I thought they were all confusing," Frank uttered.

"*Dr. Who*?" Jonas asked.

"Exactly," Maggie responded.

"We'll be back shortly," Jonas said and walked from the room with Frank in tow.

When the two men had left the hospital room, Maggie just stared after them in silence for a moment.

"Will you please explain to me what is going on, Sam?" There was no answer as Sam had drifted off to sleep, leaving Maggie the only one awake in the room. "I'm going crazy," she uttered, taking a chair by her friend's bed.

CHAPTER 25

"In two-thousand and two, one Elias Leland flew from Rabat, Morocco, to the Dominican Republic."

"For what purpose?" Frank asked as he sat in front of a metal table on the second floor of the Riverside Police Department.

The meeting had been decided to be held at the police department instead of the feds' office on Vine Street. There was much more foot traffic on Orange Street, and all four men thought that would be a better fit for the somewhat clandestine meeting. Their comings and goings wouldn't be given a second thought by anyone who might be watching. The chance of outside surveillance was something they would not discount.

"Not sure, but it is a place where a person who wants to change identities may go," stated Goff.

Ramirez nodded. "There's a doctor in the Dominican Republic, Dr. Jose Garcia, who is known to be able to erase fingerprints by surgically removing skin from the feet and then reattaching it to the fingers."

"That sounds gruesome," Frank said.

"No more than sanding fingerprints off or using acid to alter them," Ramirez responded.

"John Dillinger did it once," Jonas replied. "Probably more than once since he was able to stay on the run for so long."

"A historical note, everyone." Frank laughed.

"So," Goff started. "We think he went, had the surgery, and left, and suddenly a year later, rumors hit the streets that Kevin Jennings is dead. Of course, no body so no solid proof he actually is, but since there was no chatter concerning him in the following years, he was officially written off as being deceased."

Jonas looked down at his clasped hands. "When did you know this?"

Silence for a few seconds entered the room before Ramirez broke it. "We had a feeling that may have been the case, even when we met with the two of you earlier but I just received the confirmation from the Bureau about thirty minutes ago."

"I didn't think the Bureau had any information on him since he was a spook," Jonas stated, turning his eyes to the man across the table from him.

"I didn't either but a few twists of the arms and I learned that we do have a backdoor with the Agency that contains very restricted materials."

"Kevin Jennings or Elias Leland isn't truly dead," Jonas stated.

"We don't think so…well, those guys are dead, but he's around in a different persona," Ramirez finished the thought everyone in the small room was having at the same time.

"Who is he now?" Frank asked.

"We're starting to narrow it down but it's rather difficult since we don't have the new guy's fingerprints or anything else to identify him."

Frank looked puzzled for a moment. "He wouldn't necessarily have any fingerprints, right? They'd just be smudges."

"No," Goff started. "Dr. Garcia has really done some remarkable work—brand new prints and new identity for his patients. He also is famous for making slight alterations in a person's face that cannot be detected by the most sophisticated facial recognition software."

"Geez, the Agency should hire him," Frank said, shaking his head.

Ramirez and Goff turned toward each other and smiled.

"Wow, you guys too?" Frank asked.

"Sometimes the witness protection program needs a few extra steps to ensure the safety of those assisting the justice system," Ramirez replied. "We can't do that in country but must find sources we can deny from without."

"So, this Garcia told you about our man?"

"Of course not," said Goff. "He and those who utilize his offices need the assurance of confidentiality—we just knew Leland went there and put two and two together."

"So again, I ask—where is he?" Jonas asked.

Ramirez shrugged as Goff responded, "We don't know, but the belief is he's been back in the country for at least ten years and maybe longer. Not sure what he's up to, but it can't be good."

"Okay, he's not a good guy," Jonas agreed, "but what does that have to do with the bombing?"

Ramirez looked at Goff who simply nodded his head.

"We checked up on some of the details you mentioned about your time in Peru and the package you let us read was a real eye opener," Ramirez said. "In fact, when you were in Lima on your R and R, Jennings returned to your base camp near Iquitos. From there, he went into the jungle with a group of Peruvian soldiers and entered a small village."

"Chaca—we have that information," Jonas stated.

"You didn't know Jennings was there and orchestrated the massacre of the villagers, did you?"

"I learned of the murders when I was taken onto the gunboat by Guardia and that package which was delivered to me at the hotel in Iquitos."

"But Jennings name wasn't mentioned by Guardia or wasn't in any of the paperwork you received either?" Goff asked.

"No," Jonas agreed.

"He's the one who went in with the soldiers on the premise of hunting the terrorists for Peru and ended up killing dozens of innocents."

Frank stood up and retrieved the glass coffee pot, refilling three out of the four cups on the table. Ramirez waved Frank off politely.

"Seventy-six to be exact," Jonas stated.

"Maybe someone in the village actually opened up on them and the soldiers returned fire," Frank said. "I'm just playing the Devil's Advocate here."

Jonas shook his head. "No, it was uncalled for and why would they go in to kill everyone in a remote village?"

"Ready for my theory?" Goff asked.

"Theory or somewhat backed up by your connections?" Frank questioned Goff.

"Both, actually," Goff said. "I think that village was hit intentionally on orders of a now defunct cartel from Columbia."

Ramirez took over. "In the late eighties, there was a small but dangerous cartel running drugs, guns, and women across the border. Not far from southern Columbia and into the northeastern corner of Peru. Not very far from the southern border of Ecuador. They were brutal—had to be, actually, since in numbers the traffickers couldn't compete with the other groups trying to do the same thing. But murder, rape, and torture were everyday activities for the members of the Rosaria's Cartel."

"Sounds like a Mexican restaurant," Frank quipped.

Jonas sighed and took a sip of coffee before Ramirez continued. "No, it was a nasty-assed cartel run by a guy by the name of Jose Rosaria. Ex-commando for the Columbian military but he got tired of the small paychecks he was picking up and decided to go into business for himself. Everyone did rather well—that is, except villagers who didn't want these *el cabrons* running amuck through their territory."

"Bastards," Jonas stated as he saw the quizzical look on Frank's face.

"Yes, I know they were bastards to do what they did but I was wondering—"

Goff interrupted. "The name Ramirez means bastard."

"I knew that," Frank said with a nod.

Jonas held up his right hand. "What's this got to do with the village that got wiped out years later?"

"Probably remnants of the Rosaria gang," Goff replied. "In ninety, he and seven of his men were caught in the cross-hairs of a Columbian and Peruvian pincher movement. They lost and both countries thought they were done…well, at least with one cartel."

"Shit," Frank said. "The nineties is when we saw the influx of massive amounts of drugs from South America. How did they think it could be over with the killing of eight bad guys?"

"Ignorance," Ramirez replied. "And don't forget the feelings between the two countries weren't exactly friendly. I mean they weren't going to go to war like they did in the nineteen-thirties but each blamed the other politically for the increase in drug trafficking and murders that come along with that trade."

"Hand ringing and blame was the battle cry of the day," Goff said. "Of course, both countries truly thought the fault lay with us."

"Us? As in the United States?" Frank asked.

"Yes, think about it," Ramirez started. "If it hadn't been for the voracious appetite of the United States for cocaine, then perhaps these cartels would not be so powerful. It's true that the people here in this country, as well as other fully developed nations, do have an impact on the drug trade."

"Of course," Jonas stated. "But they should take care of the illegal activity in their countries and then there wouldn't be any product to ship north to the idiots buying it."

"You forget one thing," Goff replied. "These countries are notoriously corrupt."

"Back to the Rosaria cartel," Frank suggested.

"No, they were pretty doomed when their leader died but soon more and more peasants saw the hunger for drugs in America del Norte. Why eke out a living scratching in the forest floor when with some pharmaceutical smarts a wonderful financial profit could be made. Dangerous, yes, but the returns were worth the risks," Ramirez finished.

Jonas nodded. "So, that's why there were periodic joint force exercises with our people and those from Peru and other countries? To make it look like they were trying."

Goff took a sip of his coffee. "You got it. Now, the real issue became when many, and there were many, who wanted nothing to do with the drug trade. They'd rather be poor than grow plants that could possibly neutralize entire generations."

"The cartels killed them if they disagreed?" Frank asked.

"Usually, they would kill one or two as a warning," Goff said. "But if the village wouldn't budge, then the village would be wiped out."

"And the governments?" Frank asked but thought he already had the answer.

"Looked the other way." Ramirez shook his head. "Probably ten or fifteen thousand villagers have been murdered in such a way since ninety—of course, it got worse when the Sendero Luminoso were battling with the government of Peru."

"That's right," Jonas stated. "That's what I learned and you read in the reports I wrote up in the file. But I also learned they really worked out of the south near Cuzco."

"That's where Guzman brought the war to the Peruvian Government but they had to have money, so up north near Iquitos, where the drugs were being funneled, became a favorite hunting spot. Guzman would order a few soldiers to rob or negotiate with some of the smaller cartels for donations."

"Donations?" Frank said. "Extortion would be a better word."

"Exactly," Goff replied. "They'd go north for a couple of weeks and return with enough funds to buy weapons, food, and whatever else the crazy former professor said they needed. It worked well until he was arrested in ninety-two."

Jonas rubbed his head. "I am so fucking confused."

"And I thought I was the only one," Frank returned.

Jonas sighed. "I know Abimael Guzman has been locked up since ninety-two and the Shining Path is really nothing more than a faded memory, but sometimes the hardliners resurface. Once in a while they pop a cop or someone in the government, but a threat to the government of Peru? Not a chance. But what does this have to do with my time in Peru in the late nineties? What does this have to do with Chaca? How do those seventy-six murdered people have anything to do with the Rosaria cartel, Guzman, or any of the other shit you're talking about?"

"Ditto—my thoughts," Frank added.

Goff suddenly laughed. "Very confusing to say the least but there is a point to what we've been talking about."

"I can't seem to find it," Jonas said.

"I'm sorry," Ramirez said. "I know this is not what you guys are used to dealing with but, for us, it is."

"We're not stupid," Frank replied. "Well, I may be but Jonas is as smart as a whip. Where did that saying come from anyway—smart as a whip. A whip can't be smart."

Jonas turned toward Frank and snarled. "The whip smarts when you are struck by it. Get it now?"

"See, I told you," Frank replied. "He's smart like a whip."

"Goddamn, Frank," Jonas said.

"Jonas," Frank said and then clapped him on the left shoulder. "I'm just screwing around. We're very tense in here, and you know I say stupid things to reduce that tension, but hear me out."

"Go ahead," Jonas said, shaking Frank's hand from his shoulder. He stood up, started to pour a cup of coffee, thought better of it, and just stood, trying to make sense of everything.

"Gentlemen," Frank said. "If you'd allow me. I think this whole round-about bus ride we've been on for the past forty-five minutes is really quite simple."

"Like you," Jonas said.

"Perhaps." Frank smiled. "The reason for the tales concerning drug cartels and those dimwitted people starting peoples armies is you two are building up to something."

Goff and Ramirez shot each other a quick glance but gave nothing away.

"Ah, a nerve was struck," Frank said and then continued. "The United States Government works with nearly all the countries in the world, isn't that correct?"

"Probably," Goff said.

"And there's nearly two hundred countries on this globe. Well, Uncle Sam isn't going to worry too much about many of them, in reality—perhaps with a speech or two—but our politicians don't have the time for every president, dictator, or whomever is running each and every country. We have to pick and choose our friends—and our enemies, for that matter. So, we—the government, executive branch or legislative branch since they are all the same really—must decide who to help and who not to. I believe this whole meeting can be boiled down really simply."

Jonas had returned to the table with his mood much calmer. Frank was onto something and that was what he sometimes forgot. Frank had an uncanny way of looking at things. To make jokes when no one else would see any humor but it was his friend's way of reducing matters into small little boxes in his mind. The attempt at humor allowed him a chance to focus. Strange but Jonas had witnessed it dozens of times when they worked cases together.

He focused on what Frank was saying.

"We know that many countries are corrupt as you both have mentioned earlier and, with that corruption, comes a dilemma for the United States. Who do we help first? The most corrupt or the one who is just as corrupt but keeps it on the down low? My druthers, if I was a politician would be the latter."

"Makes sense," Goff said.

"Thanks. Now, all through the eighties, nineties, and probably today, Columbia still grows and exports much of the cocaine we see on our streets. I think it was back in two-thousand and eleven that they did rank as number one in the world for producing cocaine. I'm sure they're still in the top three, but I digress."

"Wait a minute," Ramirez stated. "Peru is right up there in the top five if not in the number two spot."

"That may be true," Frank stated. "But which country do you hear about the most when it comes to producing cocaine? Columbia. Peru isn't even on the radar for most people. I'd wager if you asked people in Los Angeles to say something about Columbia they'd say cocaine. Ask those same people about Peru and they'd say Machu Picchu. See, one country keeps it on the down low."

"And what is your point?" Goff asked.

"That's why Jonas and the others were on a joint exercise in the late nineties. Peru promised us they were on the verge of eradicating the cocaine production, knowing they weren't."

"Okay, but if that's the case, why does the United States give Columbia a hell of a lot more money that it does Peru each year?" Jonas asked.

"I wouldn't give any money to any of them," Frank retorted. "But that's not my place to say. For whatever reason it's not working to our benefit, especially from Columbia who receives about four-fold more than Peru. We're talking hundreds of millions of dollars per year."

"And again, what's your point?" Goff repeated his earlier question.

Frank sat back and smiled. "I think you know."

"Jesus Christ," Ramirez nearly shouted. "Maybe you are a simpleton."

Goff raised his hand, and Ramirez settled down. "What do you mean, Frank?"

"You said that Kevin Jennings or Elias Leland is not dead," Frank said. "You told us that he dropped off the radar in two-thousand and three but new information says he may not be six feet under."

"True," Goff said quietly.

"So, he's been around under a new identity," Frank continued. "If this doctor Garcia is as good as you said he is, then Jennings or Leland has new fingerprints. This guy got a brand new lease on life."

"And what do you think this new guy is up to, Frank?" Jonas asked.

"You'll think I'm crazy."

"I already do."

"I think he blew up a coffee shop a couple of weeks ago," Frank replied.

Ramirez was in the hallway outside of the glass-enclosed office, fuming. Goff was on his phone. The tension within the room had escalated like a too-taut string on a Les Paul guitar. Jonas was sitting back, sipping on a bottle of water, while Frank toyed with his phone.

"Did you know that Prince Charles may be cheating on his wife, Camilla?"

Jonas shook his head. "Are you going to tell me why you made that statement?"

"So, you're not interested in the news I'm viewing on my phone?" Frank replied, sticking his cell into his pants. "No, because they are going to tell us."

"When did you figure this out?"

"Not sure, really," Frank replied. "But I don't trust the feds—I've had a few lie to me in the past, so I keep a real sharp eye on their movements. I like these two guys, but they are under orders."

"Orders from whom?"

"Their bosses," Frank stated. "Like you and I were once upon a time when we worked for the department. We rarely showed our cards, even when we told everyone we would play with an open deck. It's our nature, Jonas, to be sneaky and only give out as little as we can or want."

"We had a deal."

"Did you tell them everything, and I mean everything, about this case?"

"Most."

"Everything?"

"No."

"My point," Frank said. "I predict they'll come in and tell us pretty much everything at this juncture."

At that moment the door to the conference room opened and a rather-cool-appearing Special Agent Goff walked in with a rather-stern-faced Special Agent Ramirez behind him.

"Okay, let's clear the air, shall we?" Goff suggested.

"You first," Jonas demanded.

"Frank, you kind of gave a shot there a moment ago," Goff replied. "'That's who we believed blew the place up.' Hang on a minute—we didn't suggest it earlier since Ramirez and I thought you'd think we were crazy. This guy—this Jennings or Leland—was supposed to have died back in two-thousand and three. We didn't know the department had information that he may or may not have. I feel like I've been lied to also. By the people we work for."

"Is that why you are so upset, Ramirez?" Jonas asked the well-muscled man sitting beside him.

"That's one way of putting it." Ramirez huffed and clasped his two hands together tightly on the desk top. "I don't like being played. Not by you guys, though I sort of understand the trust issue. But not by my own department."

"Mutual feelings," Jonas replied.

"Yeah, we're sent here to investigate a possible terrorist attack, since the world is worried daily, and what do we get? Nothing from our people. They were sitting on some hard evidence that we had to pry out of them day by day."

Goff held up his hand. "Let's not go any further with this."

"Why not?" Ramirez shouted. "Jesus Christ—this guy was almost killed, his girlfriend seriously injured, and dozens dead and wounded. This wasn't ISIS or Al Qaeda—this was just a nut case who used to work for the agency."

"Ramirez!" Goff shouted.

Jonas held up a hand. "Wait—the puzzle is fitting together. You and Goff have the missing pieces. Tell us now what you know."

"I am not at liberty."

"I'd tell him," Frank said. "If you don't, he will probably shoot you. I've seen him do it before."

Goff turned to Jonas and then back to Frank. Finally, he turned his head to his partner Ramirez who only looked away.

"Goff," Jonas stated. "A lot of good innocent people lost their lives and dozens more were seriously injured besides Sam. I take that very personally—to the point I don't give a fuck what I have to do to find the person behind it. If you don't believe me, leave this room and ask any one of those detectives out there. They will tell you the same—I will shoot you to get the information I need."

"Are you threatening me?"

"It's a promise."

"I've had enough of this bullshit," Goff yelled. "You can't threaten an agent of the Federal Bureau of Investigation."

"Shut the fuck up, Goff," Ramirez stated, looking at his partner with a look that spelled he would back up Jonas. "I've had enough. Let's get this bastard."

Goff looked around the room and then put his head down into his palms on the desk. A few moments passed and then he pulled his head up. "I'm really sorry. Really, I am, but this came down from the top of the Bureau, and I mean the top. But, and I'll probably lose my career, I agree with you gentleman. I'm not a hundred percent sure, nor are my superiors, but we believe that the identity of the bomber is known."

"Who is it?" Jonas asked, holding his breath for the answer.

Goff took a deep breath. "Someone here in California—a person planning to make a run for United States Senate next election."

"Bullshit!" Ramirez stated.

"I second that," Frank replied.

"It makes sense," Jonas said. "That's why I got the message I did."

"What message?" Ramirez asked.

"Oh, yeah, that part of not always telling everybody everything," Frank replied.

Jonas looked at Frank and smiled. "Just before the blast, I got a text message that said—'Remember Iquitos' and then a second later 'Of course you do.' That's it, and the next thing, I awoke in the hospital. It makes sense."

"How?" Goff asked.

Frank tapped Jonas on the sleeve. "If I may? This is the same crazed loon that was down in Iquitos with Jonas and the task force. This Jennings guy. And I think when Jonas and the rest were in Lima for a bit of R and R, he decided to head back to the jungle and talk with some villagers who didn't like the idea of cocaine. They didn't like it growing near their village. They didn't like it being processed near their village. And they surely didn't like the assholes coming and going near their village carrying it to the coast. They objected, and he went to discuss it with a few other fellows, probably those who wanted a taste of the business financially. When cooler heads couldn't prevail, this Jennings decided to teach the village a lesson like the old boys of the Rosaria cartel used to. There were seventy-six dead and no one alive to tell the deed. Drug production went on and the task force returned none the wiser."

"Goddamn," Jonas said. "But why blow up the coffee shop?"

"Because, my friend," Frank said. "He knew the list of most of those present who could add two and two together were gone. The last thing he could do was make a hit on one of the famously crazy ex-cops of Riverside. That would lead to in-depth investigations, which could lead back to him. But by blowing up the coffee shop, some crazed ideological fringe would eventually take credit, and there'd be no looking into why one Jonas Peters got cooked alive in a bombing. You'd just be one of the innocents."

"Then why text him?" Ramirez asked.

"Because he wanted Jonas to know who killed him," Goff said. "It would fit into the psychological profile we have on Jennings."

"Let me guess," Frank started. "A narcissistic sociopath?"

"Bingo," Goff replied. "Think about it—the diagnosis fits him perfectly, and now that he has a new identity? He would believe himself unstoppable, except for one thing."

"That would be?" Ramirez asked.

"Jonas is still alive," Goff replied. "That's why Frank was abducted the other evening and nearly killed."

"I look at it like a joy ride gone bad, and I won, by the way," Frank retorted.

The four men sat quietly for a few moments before Goff started again. "Frank, you stated that the voice you heard the other evening was one of a politician you had heard on television."

"Yes, I did but just couldn't put a face to the voice."

"And, Jonas, it doesn't surprise you that this person may want you dead if they are planning a run for a bigger office in the country of politics?"

"Makes sense to me, and what I know is the list is down to me and Arianna."

Goff coughed into his hand. "No, the list is only down to you now."

Jonas heard the words but they didn't register until his stomach reached for his throat. Frank grabbed his friend's arm and rushed him out of the room toward the restroom at the end of the hall.

"When did you find out?" Ramirez asked—his own face felt pale, watching Jonas rushing from the room, ready to vomit.

"A text message while Frank was talking," Goff said while rubbing his eyes. "Yesterday—found her hanging from a tree just south of her lodge."

"This is fucked up."

"We got to get this bastard, Ramirez."

"Yeah," Ramirez returned. "Before Jonas gets him first."

CHAPTER 26

What had he brought down on all those he had loved in his life? Jonas mopped his brow with a wet paper towel after throwing his guts up in the second stall. Frank was gracious enough to leave the restroom so he wouldn't witness this weak act of retching.

Frist, his daughter, then the nasty divorce, then the loss of his son, his lover—the mother of his son, friends, and Sam trying her damnedest to get better. He was a cancer. No, he was an unexpected heart attack lurking in the shadows like the grim reaper.

"Goddamn!" he blurted, straightening up and staring into the mirror above the sink. "Do you have to destroy everything you have ever loved or that has loved you back?"

"It's not that way, Jonas," Frank said as he reentered the restroom.

"What the fuck do you know?"

Frank slowly leaned against the door, to ensure their privacy was not interrupted, and folded his arms. "Yes, my friend, it does seem that death follows you, but you are not alone."

Jonas took a deep breath but didn't reply.

"We live in a tough world, Jonas," Frank said. He looked down at his shoes and was silent a moment or two. "I lost my entire family—not my fault—a drunk driver, but I blamed myself. The worst part for me to deal with was that my beautiful wife didn't want to drive down Interstate Ten for the weekend when I was doing extra duty at the Date Festival. I insisted, joking that it could almost be romantic except for the children tagging along. I never saw them alive again. You know the story since you and the others on the force helped me through it. But, Jonas, things happen, and sometimes they are really ugly."

"Arianna was happy in her silly little jungle, Frank," Jonas replied. "She just wanted to be left alone but no, I show up and now my son and my—"

"His mother," Frank interrupted. "You've been through a lot—more than me but once I lost my family, I sort of went underground with relationships. It was my way but it wasn't yours. Not your fault—it's who you are and you fell in love with Sam. Who could have known a nut job would suddenly be hunting the entire task force?"

Jonas nodded and took another deep breath while running his hands through his hair. "This just gets worse by the day."

"Well then, let's end his days—shall we?"

Jonas stepped past Frank who was holding the door open. "I'm going to kill him, Frank."

Never a moment of doubt, my friend.

"Does the name Greg Renn mean anything to either of you?" Goff asked as soon as Frank and Jonas returned. Goff was hoping they could keep on the path and not get sidetracked with the news he had just delivered. It was bad enough to be the messenger, but he never had liked the look in this Jonas's eyes. A very dangerous man when confronted, he assumed.

Frank nodded. "Yep, that's the guy I swear I heard the night I was Frank-napped. I had heard him before but didn't have a name and then I saw him on the news about a run for a possible opening in the United States Senate. The more I thought about it, the less it seemed a reality. A California politician systematically wiping out a group of law enforcement and military personnel from over twenty years ago. Seemed pretty bizarre, so I put it down as 'sounding alike.'"

"Makes sense," Ramirez responded. "But there's an issue we've been playing with the last couple of days."

"And that is?" Jonas asked. His stomach was still upset as he thought of Arianna alone in the jungle and what she must have gone through in the last moments of her life. He purposely had not asked for any details from Goff. At this point, he couldn't take it. Later maybe—but only maybe.

Ramirez looked at Goff who merely shrugged. "One of our agents back east got contacted by a guy who knew a political bundler."

"That's mysterious," Frank quipped.

"Yeah, like the news reporters who keep telling everyone they have an unknown source—we all play that game. But, anyway, this source told the agent there was a politician who needed someone who could garner funds for a possible run for a seat in the United States Senate."

"Doesn't that happen all the time?" asked Jonas.

"Sure," Ramirez continued. "But this time the bundler met with the player and felt pretty uncomfortable. As though this guy wasn't of sound mind."

"Renn?" both Jonas and Frank asked.

"The one and only."

Jonas stood up from the table. "That doesn't make sense. If this Renn is Jennings or Leland, he shouldn't need any cash. If he wiped out a village because they were standing in his way, then he should have plenty of funding for his own run at the seat."

"Maybe he needed the legitimacy," Frank added. "You know, having a big-time bundler get money for your campaign from donors makes you look a lot more legit than just showing up with suitcases of cash tainted with cocaine."

"Exactly," Goff said. "With a bundler, he could funnel in his own cash through fraudulent parties, and perhaps no one would be the wiser."

"So, did you do any snooping on this Renn?" Jonas asked.

"A bit, but nothing," Goff stated.

"Nothing?" Frank looked confused. "Why bring him up then if there was nothing?"

Ramirez took over. "What my partner meant was that we ran his fingerprints which we have because of his position in the state of California and found no records on him."

"That's a good thing, right?" Frank stated.

Goff shook his head. "That's a strange thing, in reality. A man in his mid-fifties, and we can't find any record on him past ten years ago. I mean we got nothing."

"That's impossible," Frank nearly shouted. "The government knows when I go to the bathroom."

"Actually, we don't," Goff said with a smile. "I checked and we stopped counting the midnight trips to the john you take."

"Well, that makes me feel better."

Ramirez smiled and shook his head. "No, we don't have the records everyone assumes we do and when, at first, we turned up nothing on this state senator Renn, we thought it was a dead end. But then it didn't make any sense. There's no record of him at all. It was as though he just showed middle-aged nearly a decade ago."

"How's that possible?" Jonas asked.

"We're not really sure," Ramirez commented. "I suppose when his fingerprints were run and nothing came back, the technician signed off on it. No past crimes so no issue, is what I'm thinking."

Frank raised his hands up. "That seems pretty lackadaisical."

"Not really when you think about it," Goff explained. "He had just won an important seat in the senate of California and his fingerprints are sent off to the lab. The technicians who have more than they can handle didn't see any blips on the radar and gave the newly elected senator a clean bill of health. They are not trained to look into a person's past like we are to see if he or she ever existed. Also, since the guy was middle-aged and had won an important office, there should have been past records so—two and two equals four. The guy has clean fingers and shouldn't he, if he's going to be a state senator?"

"So, is this our guy or what?" Jonas asked, taking a seat and slumping down. He was tired, he wanted to see Sam, and he wanted this nightmare to be over.

"We don't know," Goff returned.

This time, Frank stood up and kicked the door. "Goddamn, that makes me feel better. We've just spent the last twenty minutes hanging this piece of crap out to dry and now you tell us you're not sure if he's the perp or not."

Ramirez stood up. "Look, we're all tired and it's been a long day. Perhaps we should call it and let everything we've discussed sink in. I admit, it's as confusing as hell but we—like you—are against a wall. Who is behind this bullshit? We need to find out and can only take one step at a time."

Jonas held out his hands for silence. "Yes, I agree we're tired, but we're also professionals. If your unknown source stated that this bundler was uneasy with the request from Renn, then maybe he's our best shot. If a person can murder an entire village, then wiping out anyone who can say he was there decades ago is not a big deal. He has money, we're assuming, so paying off goons to do his dirty work is not out of line. Now, we need to go see this guy."

"What?" all of the other three men uttered at the same time.

"What choice do we have?" Jonas said with a shrug.

Silence registered in the room for a few moments.

"Where is he?" Jonas asked.

Goff shook his head. "Not sure, but give me an hour or so and I'll have an answer for you."

"Call me, I'm going to see Sam," Jonas responded.

"Call me too, I'm going to see a bartender," Frank quipped.

"I'm going with Frank," Ramirez stated.

Goff stood there, suddenly alone. He took out his cell phone. "Great, left alone again to do the digging."

CHAPTER 27

Jonas almost physically bumped into Doctor Scarlett Rose as he entered the main lobby of the hospital. He was   looking at a couple of text messages, and she was directing a nurse on a procedure for a new gunshot patient who had arrive a couple of hours earlier. Neither was looking in the right direction.

Reflexively, Jonas stopped his forward motion when a shadow came across his frontward view, and he put his right hand out. As Scarlett Rose turned, she suddenly was stopped by Jonas's hand against her right shoulder.

"Should have signals here," she said, smiling at Sam's fiancé.

Jonas stopped and stared at the young doctor. This woman saved the woman he loved. He wanted to hug her, but he knew that wasn't his style.

I'm tired and my feelings are getting the better of me.

"Sam is fine," Rose stated, noticing Jonas's hand had not moved from her shoulder. Though he was twenty years her senior, she couldn't help but noticing how blue his eyes were. A stern face with just a couple of wrinkles but he must have been a lady killer in his earlier years. He made her look twice and this wasn't his earlier years.

I'm tired, and besides there is the doctor-patient oath. Then again—he is not bad and not my patient.

"Thanks," Jonas answered as he noticed he hadn't removed his hand. "Sorry."

She shook her head, making her long blonde hair bounce around her shoulders. "No apologies needed. We're all very tired, I'm assuming."

"Exhausted."

"Want to grab a cup of coffee?" she asked and immediately regretted it.

Jonas paused a moment to look into her face. "Thanks, but I need to see Sam."

"I understand."

"Doctor," Jonas said. "This has been a harrowing couple of weeks. I've lost friends and those I never knew I had in my life—it's just been tough."

She looked at his face, his eyes, and then smiled. "I don't know what you have been through but I've been around your sister long enough and heard stories."

"God," Jonas said and then sighed. "What lies has Maggie been spreading?"

She reached out and touched his left arm with her right hand. "No lies, Jonas. She told me stories of years back when you lost your daughter to the present. You've been through a lot in your years."

"A hell of a lot of years by the way," Jonas commented.

"I don't want to be forward but with all you've been through you still look pretty good for a middle-aged guy."

Jonas suddenly found himself chuckling. "Thanks, and I'd like to say it's the daily two hour workouts but being a doctor you'd know I'd be lying."

"Yes, I would," Rose returned.

The moment passed, and they both looked at each other as friends. Jonas was in love with Sam, and Rose knew that this would not be someone she would ever want to get involved with. He was dark and his past darker. There were demons floating around in Jonas's head, and she hoped the most for her patient, Sam.

"I believe Sam may be ready as early as tomorrow or possibly the next to leave the hospital," Rose stated. "Though that means she still needs to watch herself, and I'll need to see her at a minimum of once per week."

"That's fine. We'll be staying in my place in Phelan, and I'll drive her down here anytime you need but I may require a favor."

Rose looked questionably at Jonas. "And that would be."

"Give me three days before you release her."

"She wants out now."

"Three days."

"Why?"

"Police business."

"I'm sorry, I'm the ruling party here," Rose stated firmly. "Why?"

"I'll tell you in three days."

"Deal." She hated making it but, at this point, she was as much interested in getting a closure on this murderous rampage as anyone. She'd dealt first hand with the dying and the severely wounded. It was time to close this thing. If anyone could do it, perhaps this Jonas Peters was the person.

She had no doubt he would. It was his character.

No wonder her patient found him so appealing. This was a no nonsense guy. One who would find answers, no matter the cost! That was what made Jonas so dangerous and, at the same time, exciting.

"Thanks," Jonas replied. "I'll go see Sam now."

Rose nodded and held out her hand. Jonas shook it, nodded in return, and walked down the hall toward her patient's room.

Rose shook her head. *I envy her, while at the same time, I'm terrified for her.*

"Doctor says I can leave in the morning," Sam stated. She was standing by the window looking as beautiful as Jonas had ever seen her.

"That's what she told me," Jonas stated.

"You don't believe it, though," Sam replied, walking over and giving Jonas a kiss on the lips.

Jonas shook his head. "No, she said you could leave tomorrow."

"Then what?"

"I asked her to keep you another three days." Jonas said flatly.

"But I want to go home. To our home. To be with you." Sam looked at Jonas with tears in her eyes. "I don't have to stay here if I don't want to. I'm strong, and you can't make me."

Silence for a moment and then the warden walked in on Sam and Jonas. Maggie had arrived.

"Maggie, a moment please," Jonas implored.

Maggie let out a breath loud enough to be heard in Arizona. "Like that would happen."

"Seriously," Jonas implored again.

"Jonas Peters," Maggie started. "You may scare everyone in the world but I'm your sis. You scare me nada. I love you and I love Sam, so there you are. And the answer is that Sam will stay in the hospital for three more days or until you call us."

"What?" Sam asked.

"What?" Jonas said, echoing Sam.

Maggie edged over and sat on the edge of Sam's bed, facing both Sam and Jonas. "Sam, you are my best friend, and Jonas you are my favorite sibling."

"I'm your only sibling."

"How I often wish I had more," Maggie quipped. "But what I mean is that if Jonas says he needs three days, he needs three days. Remember Scottsdale, Sam? If Jonas hadn't told us what to do, we might be dead now. My brother may be a bore sometimes, but he knows his business, and I'm sure he hasn't explained why you need to stay here, has he?

Jonas looked at the floor rather sheepishly while Sam looked from Maggie to Jonas. "No, he has not."

"Nor is it in his character."

"That's not fair," Jonas said.

"What my loving but daft brother is trying to say is that he loves you very much and wants to keep you safe," Maggie said. "You have two goons secured by Frank outside your room twenty-four-seven. No one is getting past those guys—trust me, they are scary, and I *know* them."

Jonas shook his head. "They're nice guys. And we're not paying them."

"You're lying, or as you liked to say when younger, embellishing a bit on the truth. I'm sure they are receiving a healthy stipend then?"

"Okay," Jonas agreed. "She's worth it."

"Damn right she is, and, Sam," Maggie said, "you need to listen to Jonas. I know the hospital is very dragging on you at this time, as it is me. I haven't seen my children in over three weeks except for the occasional overnighter when Frank would sit in for me. I'm not complaining but three days? Really, is it too much to ask at this point?"

Sam walked to Maggie and kissed her on the left cheek and then turned toward Jonas. "Why is that a girl like me can love someone like you?"

"That's a heck of a thing to say," Jonas said, but a smile crept across his rugged face.

"I have a successful business and love to be the boss, but I look into those blue eyes and I lose myself."

Maggie made a retching sound. "I'm going to be sick."

Jonas held out his arms and Sam melted into them. "It's because I will always love you, your independent spirit, support every endeavor you venture out on, love spending every moment with you through-out-our lives, and will kill any bastard who tries to harm you."

Sam brought a hand to her right eye to wipe away a tear. "What more could a woman ask for? You have your three days."

"God, that's one for a romantic novel," Maggie retorted. "I will love you and kill people along the way."

"Jealous?" Sam asked as she walked over and gave her best friend a squeeze.

"Roger makes a lot of money," Maggie stated. "But even with all his finances, he knows no one would ever fuck with our family as along as my brother is around."

Sam brought her hand to her mouth while laughing. "Oh, my God, Maggie. I don't think I've ever heard you swear."

"Yeah, potty mouth," Jonas chimed in. "And I truly love my brother-in-law. He's a nice man."

"You're a nice man," Sam said.

Maggie laughed. "No, Sam, Jonas is a good man, but not a nice man. Nice people don't generally go out hunting bad people and killing them. They find excuses to forgive them."

"Is that true?" Sam asked, though she knew what Maggie was getting at.

Jonas nodded. "My sister first started saying that a million years ago when I had to choose between taking the life of a dirt bag or taking the risk of him not letting the hostages go during a bungled clothing store robbery. I didn't wait to see if he had mental issues but simply saved a lot of people. I live with the memory of killing that young guy but that is trumped with the knowledge that many more walked out alive because of what I did. Nice, probably not, and I also question the good analogy also."

"Did he deserve forgiveness?"

Jonas shrugged. "That's up to God. I knew he had to die, and I killed him. Pretty simple really except I'll always remember the look on his face for the rest of my life."

Sam was afraid to ask but she did anyway. "What was that?"

"I could see it in his eyes. He believed we were supposed to negotiate," Jonas responded. "I didn't have time to negotiate. I asked him to put down his weapon, he refused, and my first request was the warning. Seven people went home to their families that evening. It was a win-win as they say."

Sam looked into Jonas's eyes. "You are dangerous."

"I'm realistic," he said and then shrugged.

Maggie had walked out of the room. She wanted the love-birds to have a moment.

"Then, my good or not so good man," Sam said. "Go find out whoever did this and do what must be done."

Jonas nodded. He kissed her lips and then her forehead while embracing her. "I love you. I'll be back."

"Corny," Sam said, "That was used a million times in Hollywood."

Jonas didn't smile. "They're make believe but I live in the real world. I *will* be back, and then we can be together with no worries."

Just as he was almost at the door frame Sam stopped him. "Honey, whatever you do, I'm not sure I want to know."

"Nor would I ever tell you," Jonas stated, stopping two feet from Sam's room. "What I carry is my burden and will always be."

Sam watched Jonas walk down the hallway and Maggie came right in.

"He's a jerk," Maggie said.

Sam straightened up and looked at her friend. "I know you're joking but this isn't funny. What he's about to do is really dangerous, isn't it? Tell me the truth!"

Maggie took a hold of Sam's hands and guided her to the hospital bed so her friend could sit down. "Okay, I love my brother, but he is also one of the most dangerous people I have ever met. He's not psychotic or anything like that, or I wouldn't have introduced you two. He just has this way. This black and white way. If people are harmed—no matter their color, race, or religion—my brother will bulldoze his path to ensure justice is served. And if one of those people happens to be his family or friend, pity the person standing in his way."

Sam didn't want to ask the next question but needed to. "Maggie, is what Jonas does all legal?"

Maggie did not respond for a few moments. She wasn't sure how to answer the question.

"Just tell me. It's not going to make me love him any less."

"I can say that anything Jonas does is strictly correct," Maggie stated with a nod. "He would never do anything that would indicate otherwise."

"I can live with that, as his spouse," Sam stated. "That is if he'll be returning."

Maggie smiled. "Oh, he'll be back. Maybe not in one piece, but he'll be back loving you. And thanks for under-standing my brother."

"I don't, though."

"Me neither, darling," Maggie replied, bringing a pint of rum from her purse and a bottle of Coke.

"Maggie," Sam protested. "In a hospital?"

"It was Doctor Scarlett Rose's idea."

"I like her," Sam finished while Maggie got ready to pour out a couple of rum and Cokes. "Do you think she's pretty?"

Maggie pretended to be preoccupied with mixing the alcoholic drinks but she heard every word. "I think so. But being a doctor would anyone else even look?"

Sam nodded. *Would anyone?*

CHAPTER 28

"Where do we go from here?" Frank asked as he and Jonas met up again with Special Agents Goff and Ramirez at Frank's office.

Goff replied, "He's the one we believe—I mean Ramirez and I believe—is behind all of this. So we have to come up with a plan."

A photo was handed over to both Frank and Jonas. A handsome man in his perhaps early fifties sporting a light gray pin-striped suit smiling into the camera. It was a PR photograph which had the caption, *State Senator Gregg Renn from California.*

Frank handed the photo back. "I told you that it was dark. All I heard was his voice which reminded me or at least sounded like the politician on television. I agree it's probably him but my saying I think that's his voice isn't enough for court."

Goff nodded. "And the fact that a grand jury is not going to go for an indictment—if we got that far—on a guy's word who had a shoot-out and probably killed a few people and neglected to inform the authorities. We'd be laughed out of court."

Frank shrugged. "I told you law-enforcement types."

Ramirez shook his head. "Yeah, and there's that. We never told anyone either. The Bureau would never dream of going in front of a jury with those little tidbits. I think we can all agree that we have violated every conceivable procedure in this investigation."

"Agreed," Goff replied.

Jonas had been silent, just staring at the photograph he still held in his hands.

"What do you think, Jonas?" Frank asked.

"Goddamn," Jonas said quietly. "I don't know if this guy is Jennings or whoever I met in Peru so long ago. The age is right but the facial features are different. This person seems a bit heavier—Jennings had a long thin face if I remember correctly."

"Age adds on weight," Ramirez suggested.

"No, it's more than that," Jonas responded. "This Renn seems to have more of a—I don't know muscular face."

"Muscular face, what's that mean?" Frank asked. "You think this guy does chin lifts each morning to get a more muscular face?"

Jonas laughed for the first time in a long while and stared at his friend. "No, sorry—I meant a different facial display. Cheek bones look more pronounced. I didn't mean muscular."

"Good," Frank returned. "I was going to start getting up earlier each morning and work out my face. A muscular face, I like that."

"Anyway," Jonas continued. "Earlier, before learning about Arianna, we discussed that this Senator Renn was probably our person. But he has no criminal record, in fact, nothing, and he is a state senator who has passed all sorts of background checks for the various committees he's on. He's planning on running for a US seat next. Are we sure about him? And if I'm not mistaken, we've already been around this hedge once before."

Silence hung in the air of Frank's office for nearly a minute while each man looked at the others.

"God, I don't know," Goff said.

"We were so sure," Ramirez stated. "We've got Frank knowing the voice is that of Renn."

"Now I'm just thinking I do," Frank corrected Ramirez. "Nighttime and I was pretty busy trying to save my fat ass—the defense would shatter me in court. My gut tells me it's the guy I saw on television, but that won't get a conviction."

"There's nothing in his record to indicate he was ever in any agency within the United States and me saying I think that was him twenty years ago won't sell either," Jonas followed up. "If he had plastic surgery as you've mentioned Jennings may have, it was a hell of a good job."

Goff nodded. "I feel rather stupid here. We all think it may be Renn but there's not enough to do anything with. I guarantee that if we check your text messages they were sent bouncing from tower to tower and whoever sent it used a throw-away, and it *was* too."

"Yeah, probably deep in the Pacific Ocean," Frank responded. "I did a little digging when the department didn't seem too interested, and you're right. Nothing at all on who sent it or from where."

"We know whoever sent it though was not in the vicinity," Ramirez stated. "But we've covered that already."

"How can we be so sure? Just because we can't locate the signal or any cameras with a fishy dude running away from the blast?" Frank asked.

"Because if that person was there they would have known I hadn't made it to the coffee shop yet. He or she at this point would have waited a moment or two longer to ensure there was a better chance of killing me."

"That makes sense," Frank said with a nod.

Goff stood up and made his way to the window in Frank's office that looked over to the Mission Inn. "I have an idea."

"That would be?" asked Ramirez.

Goff shook his head. "No, it's dangerous and stupid."

"I like dangerous and being stupid," Frank piped up.

Jonas gave Frank a concerned look and received a wink back from him.

"Tell us anyway," Jonas responded.

"We set up Senator Renn," Goff stated.

Ramirez shook his head. "The Bureau won't allow that on the shallow evidence we'd have to present in Washington."

"You're right," Goff agreed. "But what if we don't go to Washington?"

"Run a rogue investigation?" Ramirez stood up and faced Goff. "Jesus, if we're wrong, we will certainly lose our jobs and may end up with charges against all four of us."

"What sort of charges?" Frank asked.

"Oh, I don't know," Ramirez stated. "I can think of at least three or four under US Code Eighteen to start with. Tampering, threatening, hindering, or concealing testimony, and perhaps with Jonas, killing someone."

"That hurt," Jonas replied, giving Ramirez a sad look with his eyes downcast.

"Thought I'd lighten it up for a moment before agreeing to Goff's idea," Ramirez stated.

"What?" Goff asked. "We can't go through with this without the blessing of the Bureau."

Frank held up his hand. "May I speak?"

"This isn't a school classroom," Goff snapped.

"Ah, true, and true, but aren't you forgetting something, Special Agent Goff?"

"Will you refresh my memory?"

"Of course," Frank replied. "Aren't you the person in charge of this investigation from the federal level? Aren't you the one who can decide on which way to go with that ongoing investigation? Why contact Washington at all? We have Washington right here in the person of you."

"Ah, Jesus Christ," Goff said and plopped down into his chair.

"That one person is not at this meeting—perhaps in spirit—"

Jonas interrupted Frank. "Frank's onto a point. Can't you advise your superiors that there's been a twist in the case, and you need to expand the investigation? Where it will take you, you're not certain. We've done that in the past on cases we were working. One trail leads to another and sometimes we are not sure what path to follow so we follow them all. Sometimes you're lucky and sometimes you end up with nothing."

"He's a state senator and if we're wrong?" Goff asked with a loud sigh.

"Then we can ask for adjoining cells and dream of the retirements we could have had," Frank mused.

Jonas nodded. "He's also possibly a homicidal maniac who isn't afraid to kill again and again. Being a senator does not make him immune to the law."

"That would be news to ninety-nine percent of our elected officials," Frank stated. "Jonas is right. Let's say we are wrong, but my gut is telling me that four men in my office right now have a hell of a lot of years under their belts solving some sticky crimes. We all believe it's this Renn who used to be Jennings and this Jennings may be responsible for wiping out a village of innocents and walking away with millions of dollars of drug money. I'm for taking the chance."

Ramirez was following Frank's reasoning. "And if we *are* wrong, I think we can say we're sorry but there was some information which led us to believe he, the senator, may have some information on a case we're working. It's not like we're going to Sacramento and arrest him tomorrow. He may not be our man at all."

"It deserves a little snooping," Goff said, resigning himself. "I'll ask permission to expand the case without details."

"Good," Jonas replied.

"Anyone up for a drink?" Frank asked, pulling a bottle of Johnnie Walker from the bottom left drawer of his desk.

"Maybe just two," Ramirez stated and received nods from all those in the room.

The men met up the following day for breakfast at a local IHOP, grabbed a booth in the rear of the restaurant, and just ordered coffee for the moment. "Give us a few minutes to check the menu," Frank said, flashing a smile at the waitress.

"Sure," she replied, returning the smile and leaving a carafe full of black coffee for her customers.

Goff cleared his throat. "I went a little beyond what we finished with last evening with my boss in DC." Before any of the other three could say anything, Goff held up his hand. "Listen, I know what we talked about but, seriously, this is not how an operation is run by us. We have to obtain clearance so our superiors know what we're up to. It's one thing to stretch a bit on an investigation, but we're opening up a new one with a possible suspect who happens to be a sitting state senator."

"We already discussed this," Ramirez was the first to voice his complaint that his partner had broken the deal they had agreed to the night before.

"I know," Goff stated, "but lying in bed, I knew our asses had to be covered. It's one thing to be almost nonchalant, but this could be deadly serious with deadly serious consequences. I don't know about the rest of you, but doing time or losing my job is not something I relish."

Jonas nodded. "Point taken."

"Jonas?" Frank asked, turning and staring at the man seated on his left in the booth.

"Let, Agent Goff finish," Jonas stated quietly while topping off everyone's coffee mugs. "I'm sure he's not going to disappoint."

Goff allowed a smile to creep across his mouth. "Thanks, Jonas. I got a hold of Rudy Patterson—not exactly my senior but senior enough to garner his blessing. Took nearly an hour but after laying out our case and our hunches he put me on hold for ten minutes. He came back and said the department would back us."

"That's great," Frank nearly shouted. "Where's that waitress—I'm in the mood for a sausage skillet and gravy."

The men ignored Frank.

"Patterson told me to ensure everything is written, taped, photographed—in other words make sure every frigging T is crossed and I dotted."

"The local department here in Riverside?" Jonas asked as the waitress returned to take their breakfast order.

"He said that's up to me," Goff started and then waited while orders were taken and the waitress left. "Since this could be dealing with a man who may have been involved with the murders of innocents in another country, may have been transporting drugs, now may be impersonating someone who he is not, I believe it's a federal case. You two are private detectives and no longer have any relationship with the Riverside Police Department."

"Well, we do get a healthy retirement from them," Frank responded. "That's sort of like a relationship."

"Sounds like a divorce to me," Jonas returned.

"What about the Agency?" Ramirez asked Goff. "This could be their long-lost man who I'm sure they would want to talk to very badly."

Goff nodded. "I'm sure they would, and will, once we close the case and bring Renn in if he happens to be the mastermind behind all of this. I'll let our cousins know we have him when we do."

"Don't trust them, huh?" Frank asked.

"Of course, we do," returned Goff. "So, now that we're okay with my tattling, the next move was to be Jonas's if I recall."

"Learn anything last night?" asked Ramirez.

Jonas nodded as he cleared his coffee cup out of the way as the waitress returned with their orders. He waited until the four of them were alone again. "Senator Renn had a speaking engagement last night at a fund raiser at the Democratic Club in Woodland Hills but returned early this morning to Sacramento. His schedule states he's there for the next few days."

"It's really that easy to learn if a representative is in their office or away?" Frank asked as he scooped up a forkful of scrambled eggs with bits of sausage slathered in gravy.

"Transparency in government," Jonas stated. "Actually, I called his office this morning and told one of his aides that I was a constituent and wondered if the senator would be in his office today. The guy was more than pleased to share the senator's calendar with me."

"Wow, good thing you're not hunting him to be given that much information," Ramirez said. "Oh, wait we are hunting him. Forget I said what I did."

"Forgotten," Jonas returned. "Anyway, I'm thinking of grabbing a flight out of Ontario early this afternoon and calling the senator personally when I land."

Frank put down his fork. "What are you going to do? Tell him that you think he's an ex-CIA agent who went very rogue and now is playing in politics and you want to arrest or perhaps kill him?"

"Arrest please," Goff replied.

"Yes, that would be much more beneficial in the long run," Ramirez agreed with his partner. "There's a lot this guy could tell us what has happened over the past couple of decades. That sort of intel would be a hell of coup."

Jonas simply nodded while taking a sip of his coffee. He had taken a few bites of his Denver Omelet but wasn't really hungry. It wasn't lost on Frank.

"Not feeling well?"

Jonas smiled over at Frank who had by now devoured his entire plate. "Just thinking about the case and when I do that there's not much of an appetite."

"That's why you're in such good shape," said Goff as he polished off his eggs over easy with a side of bacon and hash browns.

"It's a hell of a diet plan," replied Frank. "Are you going to eat your sour dough?"

Jonas turned his plate to Frank. "No, I'm not going to be quite that open but I will let the senator know I know who he really is. I'll arrange a meeting and he'll show."

Goff studied Jonas a moment. "How can you be so sure?"

"I'm going to advise Renn that I am a reporter for the AP—don't worry I do have such identification in my name."

"That wouldn't be fake news would it?" Frank asked

Jonas just shook his head before continuing. "Then I will inform the want-to-be United States Senator that I have just come up with very personal information on him. Namely that he is not who he says he is."

"How much will you give away?" Ramirez asked.

Jonas shrugged. "Not much to lose if I rattle off everything we think we know about him. He'll take the bite if we're correct. This egomaniac isn't going to let some two bit reporter take him down before his glory days. No, he'll come to the meeting."

"We'll be there as back-up," Frank stated.

Frank finished his coffee. "You better all be there. He'll try to convince me that I have my information wrong and when he knows I don't believe him—well, you better be there."

"To protect him or you?" Goff asked.

"Just keep me in sight at all times," Jonas responded. "I gotta go—plane takes off in three hours."

"What about us?" asked Frank.

Jonas slid a piece of paper across the dining table. "Here's my flight information and the next one after that is at three. I thought it would be better if all four of us don't fly together. Keep me not knowing you, in case this Senator Greg Renn has eyes everywhere."

"He may certainly have," Ramirez stated, suddenly looking around the restaurant.

"Perhaps," Jonas said, standing and getting ready to leave. "I'll be staying at the Hyatt Regency on L Street. I'll text Frank before I come out to go to the meeting."

"Hate saying this," Goff said. "Be careful and don't do anything dangerous."

"Now, you've ruined Jonas's day," Frank said, watching his friend leave the restaurant. *You have a very special lady waiting, Jonas, do as Goff suggests.*

CHAPTER 29

The flight to Sacramento took nearly an hour—of course, going through TSA screening and waiting by the gate added another hour and a half to Jonas's day, but that was the way with air travel.

Be at the terminal hours early and then stand around and wait. Jonas traveled in his business but never got used to the waiting part. He remembered the days when a person could bang on the cabin door when a moment or two late and the steward or stewardess would open up, allowing passage. Those days were gone.

Now it was stand in a long line, take off shoes, remove your belt, put everything in a plastic carton, and watch it as it traveled its way down through an X-ray machine. Jonas always declared his 9mm and checked it into the cargo hold with the rest of the luggage. Even as an ex-cop and current private detective, it was too much of a headache to argue that he was licensed to carry and much easier to follow the federal rules. Declare it at baggage ensuring it was in a locked case unloaded and it was checked.

A few moments were saved when he showed his papers indicating who he was and the ammo was also locked in a separate container, but the process was carried out each time. He could travel without his weapon but they had become old friends through the decades, and it had saved him a few times from returning in a casket in the belly of the airliner.

Sometimes Jonas played by the rules and sometimes he didn't. Flying, he did—he could always kill a bad person on the plane with a fork if needed.

Jonas put those thoughts out of his mind as the wheels touched the tarmac at the Sacramento International Airport.

Killing someone with a fork—for God's sake

Frank, along with Ramirez and Goff, arrived at Ontario International Airport exactly two hours after Jonas's plane had left Ontario.

It had taken the three men nearly an hour and a half to travel the twenty miles from Riverside. They used dead-end streets, highway exits, and even a fifteen minute stop so Frank could get a Tazo Peach Green Tea from Starbucks to kill time.

They had not been followed and, arriving at the airport, felt confident that the three men would just appear as friends heading to Sacramento. They only had carry-ons so had nothing to check into luggage.

"We're going empty handed?" Frank had asked when the two men had picked him up at his office.

"Yes," Goff replied. "Less suspicious if we don't check any baggage."

"Don't worry," Ramirez chimed in. "We'll pick up some weapons from the local office in Sacramento."

"I know you guys can carry on planes—flash your badges and whammy we're on and protected. Why not now?" Frank asked. "I've carried before when transporting prisoners and the like."

"Exactly," Goff stated. "Yes, we can by law but standing by the ticket booth explaining who we are and why we have to carry could be tricky. Things have changed since nine-eleven, Frank. A fulltime law enforcement officer can carry for official business but right now we don't want to draw attention to ourselves. So, we go unarmed and pick up pieces in the Sacramento office."

"Well, not exactly the office but a parking lot a mile away," corrected Ramirez. "Everything is hush-hush."

"Got it and makes sense to me," Frank returned. "Besides, Jonas once told me he could kill someone with a fork if he didn't have his gun handy."

"A fork?" Goff asked.

"Why not a spoon?" asked Ramirez.

"It's rather sticky." Frank smiled as the sedan pulled into the light traffic on Mission Boulevard. "I think he said that once when we had been drinking on a return flight from Dallas on an investigation we were working on."

Ramirez smiled. "Many drinks?"

"It's almost three hours."

"Plenty of time to get liquored up, I guess," Goff said.

"Yep, it was," Frank returned, advising the driver, Ramirez, to take a slow drive through Fairmount Park. The thirty-five-acre park was beautifully green with trees and bushes on the shore of Lake Evans glistening in the sunshine. It was also a road that could be traveled at a very slow pace to take in all the gorgeous views of nature that had grown there since it was commissioned in nineteen-eleven. Frank had always loved this park and now he loved it even more since he could casually look out the rear passenger window to make sure no one was on their tail.

"So far so good," Frank stated from the rear seat.

"Nice to hear," Goff returned.

"This is a pretty place, Frank," Ramirez stated. "Very peaceful."

"Yeah, I like it. But it was really in two-thousand and one that it came back to its grandeur. Before that it was home to the homeless, the druggies, the pimps, and to say the least any dirt bag that wanted to hide out a bit. It's been cleaned up and now is a really nice place for families to spend relaxing days."

"You sound like a city spokesman trying to get visitors," Ramirez said.

"This is my city, boys," Frank said. "I love Riverside and Riverside loves me—gotta show mutual respect."

"True—true," Goff replied.

"Okay, next right take it and head west," Frank said. "We'll grab the Sixty for a few miles and then wander through some back streets. Never can be too careful."

"Again, true—true," said Goff.

Jonas retrieved his bag from the carousel, walked into the nearest restroom stall, loaded his Glock 9 mm, and tucked it neatly into his interior hip holster. He walked back out of the restroom, exited the airport, and hailed a taxi.

Twenty minutes later, he was dropped off at the Hyatt Regency. He tipped the driver, looked at his watch, and knew he had time to settle into his room for a quick shower.

The farce was about to start and Jonas hoped Renn was their man. He wanted this to be over one way or another.

"What's on the agenda this evening?" Senator Renn asked his assistant.

"Let's see," said Randy Noble as he passed his finger across his Smart Phone and scrolled through the senator's busy schedule. "Actually, I believe you have about three hours for yourself before you meet with Senator Robinson for cocktails at seven to discuss the education bill he's trying for."

"Oh, God," Renn replied, putting his head into his hands at the dark brown mahogany desk in his office. "I'd forgotten that I was supposed to look up some budget items so we could run through them."

Noble laughed. "They're on your desk marked *budget proposal for meeting with Robinson.*"

Renn looked up at the young man on the other side of the desk and smiled. "Dude, what would I do without you?"

"Not get elected to Washington, I would think."

"Very funny but I will, of course, keep you on as my number one assistant once we get elected."

"I'm actually honored to work with you, Senator," Noble stated. "It's been a great experience, and I'm looking forward to the move to Washington after the next election."

"How's your wife feel about the move?"

Noble shrugged. "Not really thrilled to take the kids out of their school but I already told her that we'd keep the house here and I could commute on a weekly basis."

"No," Renn said. "That would be a disaster for you and Terri. If I get elected, and I don't see why I shouldn't, we'll do some school shopping for the children. Great schools in the DC area."

"Thanks, Teri would appreciate it, as I do. I really didn't like the idea of commuting for six years."

"Six?" Renn looked at his assistant with a quizzical expression. "I plan to stay in Washington for a long time, Randy. One term is not going to do what I want to do as a US Senator."

"I know your ambition is to make things right for the people, but I expect there's something else in the horizon for you. Am I correct?"

"Perhaps," Renn replied and stood up from his desk.

"Chief of Staff at sixteen hundred Pennsylvania Avenue sounds very appealing, Senator."

"We must all have our dreams, Randy," Renn stated as a knock on his office door interrupted the two men.

Alicia Keene, Renn's secretary, poked her head into the office. "Sorry to disturb, gentleman but there's a man on the phone who says it is urgent he speak with Senator Renn."

"Who is he?" Noble asked.

Alicia shook his head. "Very polite but would not tell me his name. But he told me the senator would be very interested in hearing what he had to say."

"Randy, if you wouldn't mind?"

"Don't worry," Noble started. "I'll take it in my office. You need to go over those budget numbers for when you deal with Robinson this evening."

"Does it never end?"

"Not when you're doing the great job you are for the people of California, Senator," replied Alicia as she turned and left the two men standing in the office.

"Was that sarcasm I heard?" Renn asked, smiling.

Noble shrugged. "I can never tell with that woman but, without her, I'm afraid you or I couldn't function here in Sacramento."

"She is a Godsend," Renn replied, sitting back down behind his desk. "Thanks for taking care of the caller, Randy."

"It's my job, boss."

Jonas was sweating. He tended never to be nervous but as he hung up the telephone from his suite at the Hyatt he was actually trembling. "What the hell is wrong with you?" he asked aloud as he checked his Glock for the third time in the last five minutes.

The call to Senator Renn's office did not go as planned and instead of being forwarded to Renn himself it was his personal assistant Jonas ended up speaking with.

He could tell the guy was probably in his mid to late twenties. Sure of himself from the tone of his voice and did his best to dig out as much information from Jonas as he could. Jonas kept with the story of being a reporter and had some dirt on the senator he would like to discuss first hand. He even let it slip that it was well known in the press circle that Renn was planning a run for the US Senate and this information may stop that idea in its tracks.

"Big deal, a threat," Noble replied into the phone. "As a reporter, you must realize that leaks are a common symptom in politics. Senator Renn would have liked to make a well planned announcement, but we hadn't thought it would be until the current California US Senator announces her plans to retire. That would be the classy thing."

"So, you're not going to let the public know your man who is planning for a run has some dark information?"

"I'm sure, in due time, everyone interested will realize that a young man such as Senator Renn has larger plans to help his country than just stay in the state of California. He's a man of the people. Whatever you have would probably be nothing to his constituents. I think you're just a jerk who wants to make a name for himself."

"I've been called worse," Jonas stated.

"Well, it's been nice talking to you, Mr. Henry, but if you are not going to discuss the dirt you say you have, then this conversation ends now. Please do not call back, I'll have your number blocked and will advise security that you are a potential risk to the senator's person if you bother to show up at the capitol building."

"Sounds fair," Jonas said. "Just tell your boss that I know about Iquitos."

"Iquitos?" Noble asked. "What the hell is an Iquitos?"

"Ask him and then have him call me back. I'll wait around for ten minutes and then I go with the story. He can have his say or not—I don't really care at this point."

Jonas found himself listening to a dial tone.

Senator Renn stared at his assistant. "What the hell is an Iquitos?"

"That's what I wondered and just looked it up," stated Noble, sitting before the large desk in Renn's office. "It's a city in Peru on the Amazon. Sounds horrid—bugs, snakes, nothing but jungle, and very crowded."

"I've never been to South America," Renn stated. "What's this fool up to?"

Noble shrugged his shoulders. "Not a clue but he says he's running with the story, about you and Iquitos, I presume."

"This doesn't make any sense." Renn stood up and moved to the windows facing the park below. "I've got an important meeting with Robinson discussing some actually important stuff and now we have a crazy loon saying I did something in Peru that could hinder my run for the senate. Goddamn, there should be a law about crazies making up shit anytime they want to and the problem is the public will believe it."

"Of course, and he'll use the catchall of unnamed sources," Noble stated, noticing how upset his boss was. But why shouldn't he be? A million things on his mind and now out of nowhere a person threatening an untruthful expose. "You want me to call him back and threaten litigation if he proceeds?"

"And what?" Renn said, turning from the window and flexing his fingers on both hands a dozen times. "He'll run whatever crap he thinks he has, and it will be weeks before we can get an injunction against him. The damage will be done, and we'll spend months denying the shit he made up. Who's he with?"

"Stated the Associated Press."

"Did you look him up?"

"He's listed but can't find any stories he's written."

"Probably a newbie and this is his chance to pretend he's a real reporter."

"What do you want me to do?"

"Call him back," Renn stated. "Let's set a meeting for the Other Office in Old Town after my meeting with Senator Robinson."

"You're going to meet this asshole?" Noble asked. "Why don't I set the meeting and just have the police arrest him as a threat? Let the courts figure it out."

Renn nodded. "That would be fine but if this guy is serious about printing a bunch of lies about me, the story is already written and he's just buying some time. If he's arrested, look how that would appear. He'd say it was a set up so the truth about Senator Renn wouldn't be released."

Noble thought a moment and came up with a couple of different scenarios but in the end knew his boss was correct. With instantaneous social media, the news of the reporter's arrest would be nationwide, and all this reporter would have to say was he simply wanted to find out if his information was reliable. In the end, all that would be accomplished would be that he would be held a few hours and leave the police department pissed off.

"He probably has an accomplice waiting to ensure we handle this meeting correctly," Noble offered.

"Exactly," Renn stated. "Call the idiot back, tell him to meet me at ten at the Other Office, and I'll smile and convince him that I know nothing about Taquitos."

"Iquitos," Noble replied and chuckled.

"Taquitos or Iquitos," Renn said. "I have no idea what this moron is talking about."

"You sure you want to go alone?"

"Yes, Mommy, I think I can handle it but knowing you," Renn said, "you'll be there in the shadows anyway."

"I'll call Teri and tell her I'm working late."

"No, you make the call and set up the meeting," Renn said. "And then you go home, have dinner, kiss your kids when you put them to bed and kiss that wonderful spouse of yours. Meet me at the Other Office ten to ten. Then you can hide and keep an eye on me and this master reporter with the story of a lifetime."

Noble nodded and headed back to his office but before leaving the senator's company, he stated, "I know this guy is nuts but I meant what I said earlier."

"And that was?"

"I would like the chance to head to Washington and work for a United States Senator."

Renn smiled. "Thanks for your support."

"You'll always have it," Noble finished and left the room.

"The meeting's set for ten at a place called the Other Office," Jonas said into his cell to Frank who was parked across the street from the Hyatt. "It's a bar on Second Street in Old Town."

"Okay, got it," Frank replied, jotting down the information in a small notebook. "Do you think he'll come alone?"

"Doubt it," returned Jonas.

"We'll check it out and make sure no bogey men are hanging around."

"Take it easy, Frank," Jonas stated. "If this is our guy, he's very dangerous and so are the people he's hired. Make sure you have plenty of back up. See if Goff and Ramirez can secure a few more pairs of eyes."

"They're trying, but it seems the office here in Sacramento is rather a skeleton," Frank returned. "Most of the agents are at a briefing in San Francisco on some latest intel about possible threats concerning a homegrown terrorist out of the Eureka area."

Jonas asked, "How about the locals?"

"No can do," Frank said. "A double homicide on the eastern edge of Sacramento, cop shooting and suspect still hold up."

"When it rains."

"Yeah, but we got this, Jonas," Frank said with confidence. "I'll cover the interior, Goff on the rear and Ramirez in front. Anything kinky and we're drawing and shooting somebody."

There was moment of muffled discussion but Jonas couldn't make it out. In a few seconds, Frank was back on the line.

"I was just told that we can only shoot someone if it's a clear and present danger to you, us, or a bystander. I think that opens up a lot of options personally."

Jonas found himself smiling. No matter what anyone would say about Frank Sanders, Jonas knew he could trust the man with his life. His wisecracks and silly sense of humor only masked the realization that this was one dedicated lawman. Of course, his jokes were a bit stale and sometimes out of sync with what was going on, but Jonas loved the guy. He was a good friend. "It certainly does," Jonas responded.

"Okay, now you call Sam and tell her how much you love her and that you'll be seeing her real soon."

"You think she needs that reassurance?"

"No," Frank returned. "You do."

"And who are going to call, Frank?"

"I called you."

The phone went dead.

Jonas swiped Sam's number.

CHAPTER 30

Senator Renn sat at a rear table at the Other Office, awaiting the arrival of this James Henry, wondering what it was that he wanted.

A couple of drinks, a few laughs, and Renn knew the man would leave the bar in Old Town realizing he had made a mistake. He would have to. The vibrant charisma Renn could dish out made everyone instantly like him.

Jonas nodded as he made his way through the crowded bar and saw the senator sitting at a table alone. Jonas was hoping for a moment of recognition from the past but there was nothing. Something, just something from the past but it didn't appear. He had never seen this man in his life, except for the couple of times he had recently looked him up on the internet or a photograph.

Frustrating, to say the least.

"Mr. Henry?" Renn asked as he stood up and pointed to an empty chair.

Jonas nodded and took the offered seat. "Thank you, Senator, for seeing me on such short notice. I really appreciate it."

A large smile spread across Renn's face, allowing his very white teeth to sparkle. "Not a problem and thank you for agreeing to meet me here. I didn't like the idea of meeting at my office since I felt what you had told my assistant seemed to need a bit more privacy. Unfortunately, my office seems to be always filled with people, from those who work with me, those who work for other senators, and people who just stop by to see the one who represents them. I have an open-door policy even though sometimes I wish it would close more often so I could get more work completed."

"I understand completely," Jonas replied, watching Renn very carefully to see if there was anything that reminded him of who this man really was.

A waitress showed up and Renn ordered a Vienna for himself and one for Jonas. "Hope you don't mind but it's a locally brewed amber lager. Just a titch sweet but pretty smooth, if I do say so myself."

Jonas shook his head. "I'm not from around here so I'll take your advice on crafts."

"Good, then it's settled," Renn said with a smile at the waitress. "Any appetizers?"

"I'm fine."

"Thanks then," Renn said as the woman left and the two men were once again alone.

"So, Mr. Henry," Renn said. "My assistant, Mr. Noble, told me that you had some juicy dirt on me about Iquitos. I Googled it earlier and must say it sounds simply horrid."

"No," Jonas replied. "It's hot and very humid but the people are very friendly, considering where they live."

"Considering where they live?"

"I wouldn't be so friendly if that was my outlook every day I suppose. Waking up sweaty and knowing that it was only going to get worse as the sun sailed through the sky."

"I see your point."

"Yes, the Amazon is an amazing thing, but being so close to the Equator, it is so hot—especially in the jungle," Jonas stated. "Like if you were working for an agency that was intent on stopping the flow of drugs from, say Columbia, and into Peru. Imagine staying in the jungle, dripping sweat twenty-four-seven while hacking your way through almost impenetrable growth."

"Yikes, that sounds horrible," Renn said, giving a fake shiver. "Did you do that?"

"You did that."

Renn stared at the man across the small table from him for a moment. "Now, Mr. Henry, I was nice enough to meet with you, but I don't understand what this is all about. I'm a state senator—an important person—and I've gone out of my way to be kind. Perhaps you have mental issues or something, but I can assure you that until this very afternoon I did not even know what an Iquitos was."

"You were there."

The waitress brought the two pints of lager and placed one in from of each man at the table.

"I've never been to South America so I don't think I could possibly been to the Amazon, now could I?"

Jonas was about to believe Renn but a slight movement caught his eye. As Renn picked up his glass his little finger curled beneath the bottom of the glass. A strange placement since most, if not all, people tended to grip a glass with their pinkie firmly at the bottom of the glass so it didn't slip—not below as if holding the glass.

It was such a minor gesture but Jonas did not miss it.

"Did I do something out of the ordinary just then?" Renn asked.

"I just noticed the way you held your glass," Jonas commented. "I haven't seen anyone do that since I was in Lima twenty years ago."

Renn stared across at Jonas for a few seconds and then laughed. "Really, are you that astute to remember those sort of details from two decades?"

"It was the business I used to be in."

"Law enforcement?"

"Yes."

"And now a reporter, Mr. Henry?"

"Yes."

"So, as an investigative reporter what have you suddenly learned?" Renn replied, putting his glass down.

Nodding, Jonas took a sip of his beer, placed it on the table top, and then intertwined his fingers. "That I once had a few beers in Lima during a weekend briefing run by an agent from the Central Intelligence Agency. After the briefing, about ten of us went out to a local place, and I noticed this field officer from the CIA had a peculiar habit of curling his little finger of his right hand beneath the glass of beer."

"Is that strange?"

"No, not strange, but not common," Jonas responded. "We were trained to look for these little quirks in our line of business."

"The cop business?"

"Yes, I was a detective dealing with homicides, so every little bit I could learn about human nature assisted me in solving cases."

"Sounds impressive," Renn stated, taking a drink from his glass. "See, my little finger was around the glass and not on the bottom. So goes your theory."

"Not at all. You know I'm watching and, like any other person who may be guilty, will try to look nonchalant."

"As stated earlier, Mr. Henry, I'm guilty of nothing since I was never in Lima, Iquitos, or Peru."

"You know," Jonas stated. "When I walked in here, I knew I had made a mistake."

"So, you agree that I'm not the man you believed me to be?"

Jonas nodded. "At first yes, but then with the glass and now the shape of your eyes—almost almond but a lift on the right a bit higher than the left. Also, the way you pronounce the letter S as though slurring a bit. It's those little things that make me sure you are Kevin Jennings."

Renn laughed and then took a long draught of his beer. "So, master detective turned newspaper man, you've concocted one hell of a story. I'm an ex-agent for the CIA who is now a state senator. How's that happen?"

"You want me to tell you?"

"Yes, please," Renn said.

For the next ten minutes Jonas ran down exactly what he, Frank, Goff, and Ramirez had come up with on Jennings. From the man's time in South America to his sudden disappearance and presumed death. Then a rebirth, like the Phoenix from the ashes, Renn showed up in politics and after a few years had a plan to run for the US Senate. The grisly details of the bombing at the coffee shop and the subsequent murders of every member of the task force Jonas spent the most time on.

"Wow, I'm quite the character," Renn said, flagging down the waitress for another beer. "This time, we'll try the Sactown Gold Pilsner."

"I've had enough," Jonas replied.

"One beer is your limit?"

"No, your bullshit is my limit," Jonas stated. "I know what I know and it is you that has been causing all this hurt."

Renn stood up and almost shouted. "You are beyond your pay scale, Mr. Henry. I will not allow you to talk to me like this. This meeting is over and forget me paying your tab!" Other patrons looked over at the two men, and suddenly Renn put a smile on his face. "Sorry, folks. A disagreement between two friends over a football game."

"You are smooth," Jonas said as he tossed a twenty on the table. "The beer is on me."

"Look, you think I am someone I'm not, and I know you are not a real reporter," Renn stated. "Sure, you have some credentials with the Associated Press but we couldn't find one story you have ever written. I thought I would be kind and let you know that the story you want to run will ruin any chance, if you ever had one in the first place, of you being a real reporter. Mr. Henry, give up, but if not, run whatever you want, and I will destroy you in the press."

"I'm not afraid of the press."

"Then what are you afraid of?"

Jonas sat a moment and then stood up. "I didn't think I was afraid of anything but now I know what it is."

"Enlighten me."

"Bastards like you," Jonas said. "Sociopaths who will destroy anyone without concern of conscience."

"That scares you?"

"Wouldn't it you?"

Renn shrugged while picking up a pair of reading glasses from the table and tucking them into his left jacket pocket. "I suppose if I was a sociopath or in the company of one."

Jonas nodded and then started to leave.

"Mr. Henry—or should I say Jonas—I'm not the sociopath here."

Jonas turned on his heels and stared at Renn. "What did you call me?"

Renn laughed. "You didn't recognize me? Shit, I knew you the minute you walked into this bar. Jonas Peters—the guy from Southern California who was tough, smart, and got the girl everyone wanted."

"Arianna?"

"No shit, Sherlock," Renn stated. "She was hot but only you got next to that. How was it by the way?"

Jonas's head was spinning. What was going on? "What are you saying?"

"That you were right all along, dumbshit," Renn said as he gestured with his right hand and a man suddenly appeared out of nowhere. "Have you met my assistant, Mr. Noble?"

"Hey," was all Jonas heard as a blow came to the left side of his face.

That was it.

"Good God," Renn said in a rather loud voice. "My friend has had too much to drink. Can we have a couple of volunteers to help me get him to my car? Wow, this is rather embarrassing."

A few chuckles and then three patrons hefted and pitched Jonas into the rear seat of Renn's vehicle parked in front of the Other Office.

"Thanks everyone, I have to get him home before his wife thinks he's dead."

Laughter followed and soon the sidewalk was vacant.

"Asshole," Renn whispered. "You should have died."

Noble looked around the establishment not really catching what his boss had just said. "We need to go."

"Yes," Renn replied. "But first we have to get rid of this person first."

"What do you mean?" Noble asked. "Just dump him in the park. He'll wake up scared and with a headache. He won't bother you again."

"Not that easy, my friend. I'll take of this piece of garbage for good. He won't bother anyone ever again and you know what? " Renn stated as he started walking to the driver side of the vehicle.

Noble didn't like the look in his boss's eyes. They were sparkling in the dim street lamps outside of the bar. "What?"

"No one will even miss him." Renn stated. "It will be nice when Washington greets us, won't it be, Mr. Noble?"

"Yes, it will be," Noble responded as the sedan sped away from the curb with the reporter crumpled up in the back seat. He watched the taillights disappear into the night.

Noble thought hard. He enjoyed the perks of his job but now knew his boss was a cold-blooded killer. He knew his dream of being Chief of Staff had just driven off like that sedan. *What have I done?*

"What the fuck just happened?" Goff yelled into his microphone and was hoping someone on the listening end would have an answer.

None came.

Frank was watching the front of the bar and knew the shit had hit the proverbial fan. Jonas being carried out like a sack of potatoes was not good.

He jumped from his spotting post and ran to the bar. By the time he got there the sedan was gone and everyone else was heading back inside. Everyone but one.

"What just happened?" Frank asked.

"Not really sure but I think someone got pretty drunk and his buddy had some of us carry him out."

"I didn't see you carrying the guy."

"Okay, I was just watching."

"Then you spoke to the driver of the car."

"So?"

"So, I think you are lying to me."

"Who the fuck are you?" Noble asked but knew his resolve was quickly slipping away. He was in trouble—big trouble.

Frank shot out his right hand grabbing the man by the throat and pushing him against a pole a dozen feet from the entrance of the bar. "Not your worst nightmare—that was just taken away in your boss's car."

"Senator Renn?"

"You got it, sugar," Frank replied. "Now I'm going to ask you where they're heading and you'll give me the answers."

"I won't tell you shit!" Noble blurted out in a last ditch attempt of defiance.

Suddenly a dark SUV arrived at Frank's location and two men jumped out.

"Oh, you will tell Frank anything he asks," said Goff.

Ramirez grabbed Noble's left arm and started to leap frog him to the SUV.

"I have rights."

"Tonight, you have none," Frank replied, smacking Noble square in his face. "Your boss has my friend—pretty much my only friend—how does that make you feel?"

"Not good," Noble replied, feeling the blood seeping down from his broken nose.

"Smarter than your boss."

It took Frank nearly ten minutes to learn the location of where Renn was taking Jonas. It was a long time but he knew it seemed longer to Noble who was sitting in a chair pale as a ghost.

Noble looked up at the man with the pair of black leather gloves on. "You do realize that you've kidnapped and beaten the assistant to a state senator? And I don't know what you are asking."

"Sounds like your mumbling," Frank replied as he stonily stared back into the man's battered face. "I hated this almost as much as you but information has to be gotten and you were the safe that information was hidden in."

Goff shook his head. "This wasn't what I had planned."

"Not much of a choice," Ramirez stated. "I don't like this either but a man's life is at stake."

"He's probably dead already," Noble mumbled through a slight frothy red foam. "At least I bet he is. Senator Renn had a crazy look in his eyes that I had never seen before."

Frank sank down to his knees and looked Noble in the face. "If my friend is dead—then I will come back here, and you too will die, but with unbelievable slowness."

"I was only trying to help my boss. I have children!"

"So did he, but your senator didn't seem to care," Frank whispered. "Jonas's last child was murdered in the jungle by your precious senator just a few days ago."

"Oh, my God! I don't know anything about someone named Jonas or what you are talking about," Noble screamed. "I thought he was just a crazy, and I was doing my boss a favor."

"Now, do yourself one and tell me where they are," Frank said.

Noble got a hold of himself and stopped shaking. He knew he was a dead man at this point unless he answered the question honestly. If he lied…well, he didn't want to think what this man would do to him once he found out.

"You have thirty seconds," Frank stated, taking the man's chin in his left hand and cocking back his right fist. "The first punch will put out the right eye. The second—may put you out forever."

Noble shook his head, causing Frank's hand to fall from his chin. "Okay, okay—Senator Renn has a house out of the city. A weekend getaway—about twenty minutes on the Sacramento River. A place called Courtland, but I don't know if he's going there. I don't even know what's happening. I think he may just dump the guy somewhere. You have to believe me, I don't know anything else."

"Address?" Goff questioned.

As Noble gave the address to the house where Renn was going, Goff jotted it down, ripped it from his spiral, and handed it to Frank.

"Think that's where's he's going?" Ramirez asked as Frank wiped Noble's blood off on a rag.

"Seems to be the kind of guy who would want to take time and torture someone. If he's our man, it would fit his MO," Frank replied. "He'd want someplace he's familiar with and, at this point, probably thinks Jonas is alone and he has all the time in the world."

"Go," Goff commanded. "We'll take care of this piece of shit."

"You want company?" Ramirez asked.

As Frank started from the garage where Noble had been sequestered he shook his head. "You guys are probably in way too deep at this time and no point in going any further. I can handle this but just make sure you book that asshole for as many felonies you can."

"Will do," Goff replied.

"He shouldn't have resisted arrest," Ramirez surmised.

"Nope," Frank replied and was gone.

"Let's clean you up," Goff said. "You have to look pretty for your booking photo."

Noble stared up into the agent's face. "What about my family?"

"I'm sure they'll be very disappointed in you and a divorce attorney will be contacting you very soon."

CHAPTER 31

A bucket of ice water splashed into Jonas's face, and he came back to conciseness with a shudder. Disorientation invaded his brain but a couple of deep breaths forced him back into the reality of the moment.

Every part of him hurt. He knew he had been beaten—beaten badly, and he knew he was screwed. Bound to a chair in what looked like a basement and the smell. A strong pungent odor as though they were near a river—perhaps a river with trees alongshore or even parts of them in the water's edge. The room had two single hanging bulbs from the ceiling giving off a soft white light but plenty to see.

His reflections were suddenly knocked from him as a hand slapped the back of his head jolting him forward painfully. He had extremely limited movement.

As he had first thought, he was screwed.

"Sorry, but before I kill you, Jonas," Renn said as he walked into Jonas's view, "thought I would tell you why I did what I did."

Jonas took a deep breath and let it out slowly. "Confessions of a psychopath?"

"I hate that term," Renn stated. "They once referred to me as such when I was still employed with the Agency."

"Before or after you murdered the guy in Venezuela?"

Renn stopped directly in front of Jonas with his right hand scratching his chin. "You know, I can't really remember in which order. Doesn't matter though. Just hate that term."

"What would you call yourself?"

"An opportunist," Renn replied with a shrug. "Yes, an opportunist."

"How so?" Jonas asked as he tried to move his head to get a more accurate layout of his prison. His movement was very limited so not much to take in at this point.

"Well, in Peru," Renn said, "that part of Peru you were involved with, I came across a village that didn't want to allow cocaine trafficking and manufacturing. I wasn't involved in that part of the business as of yet but when I learned how much money could be made—I was all in. The problem was the villagers, especially the man in charge. Hard-headed and…well, wouldn't listen to reason."

"Your reason?"

"Only one being offered at the time," Renn replied. "Anyway, tried coaxing him with humor, reasoning—yes, mine, and bribes, but nothing seemed to work. So, I thought what to do, what to do?"

"I'm sure you came up with something."

"Sure did," Renn said with a smile. "While all of you were on a short furlough in Lima, I decided that I would not take no for an answer."

"And you murdered seventy-six innocents."

"They weren't really innocents."

"Men, women, and children?"

"No, they were people standing in the way of progress."

"Progress?"

Renn shook his head. "For a man who spent so many years in law enforcement, I would think you'd understand."

"Please enlighten me."

"The United States likes cocaine," Renn offered. "We're the number one buyer from around the world and when I saw a chance at my own entrepreneurial enhancement, I had to jump onto the band wagon. I couldn't allow people with no progressive sight to stand in my way."

"So you killed them?"

"Actually, not all of them, and I surely didn't act on my own," Renn stated. "In fact, I had help from a small group of drug producers who were being chased out of the jungle by the larger cartels."

"How did these guys succeed when, as you said, they were being chased away by more powerful people?"

Renn chuckled. "Well, let's just say we introduced them to our way of staying and growing in business. Took out the leaders along with their entire families. Bloody but a great business technique. I should really write a book on how to succeed in business by truly eliminating the competition."

"You're a sick bastard."

Renn shook his head. "No, I feel quite fine, thank you, and knew my father. But back to the point of this story which is actually enthralling me, if I say so myself. While you were out fucking your girlfriend in Lima, I and a bunch of the losing side took revenge on the villagers. We left just enough alive to spread the word to the other villages that we needed compliance for a thriving business. It did the trick and for nearly eighteen years we were making more money than I could count."

"What happened?" Jonas asked while straining his eye sockets to get a look around the room. He knew they were alone but that was about it. He was secured very tightly.

"After making millions per year, there is only so much to do with the money," Renn replied. "I traveled on fake documents for years here and there and no one was the wiser. Especially with the help from the Agency who actually thought I had died. An official death announcement, no matter how quiet it was, helped in more ways than they could ever imagine. I was free to do what I wanted."

"Even becoming a state senator?"

"Wasn't that brilliant?" Renn asked. "A long visit to a great plastic surgeon and I knew I could pull off that caper. You didn't recognize me even though I knew who you were the minute you entered the bar. By the way, a few gray hairs and a couple of winkles here and there but you are still the dashing Jonas Peters I remember from two decades ago. You take care of yourself."

Jonas ignored the compliments and wondered how long this egotistical maniac would continue his rambling.

"Anyway, you didn't know it was me until that stupid little finger thingie," Renn said. "Who would have thought that would give me away? I'll have to remember that in the future."

"So, after all the money you made you just wanted a change?"

"Simple as that," Renn said in agreement. "I shook hands with my partners of so many years, packed my millions, and moved to California to start a new life. Being a millionaire is great but gets boring really badly. You know what I wanted more than the money, Jonas?"

"Tell me."

"Power," Renn replied. "According to Gaham Green in nineteen-sixty-four, which I agree with totally, power is the great aphrodisiac. Money can purchase things but with power you can do anything. Look at socialist countries around the world today and yesterday. Most are poor but the leaders wield power like a God. The Soviet Union, China, North Korea, and Venezuela. Anyone gets in your way and they are gone permanently. You try to pay someone with all your money to kill someone and you end up in jail for soliciting for murder. Socialist countries, no one goes to jail. That's real power."

"So, California?"

Renn laughed. "No, I don't want power like that—it would be nice—but no, I want the power to change laws, to rule people's lives, and politics has given me that ability. I like strutting around being a state senator but wait until I become a United States Senator or even the President of the United States. To be feared around the world as the leader of the most powerful nation. Now, that is sexy."

"Then why didn't you just go on with your plans and leave all of us that were with you alone? I had no idea who you were and probably would have never made the connection."

"I couldn't take that chance, Jonas," Renn replied. "What if just one of you found out through a most unfortunate coincidence my true identity? Think of the ramifications?"

"You'd go to jail," Jonas said.

"Worse, my ambitions would the throttled. That would be the most terrible thing for me," Renn stated. "My plans of being powerful would be shattered. I couldn't let that happen."

Jonas couldn't believe what he was hearing. All this so this sick bastard could be a senator. Who cared? "Why everyone on the team?"

"Can't leave any stone unturned."

"Even my son?"

Renn shrugged. "That was just a bonus and besides those two idiots aren't around anymore anyway. I'm sure you had something to do with their disappearance at the water's edge."

Jonas didn't reply.

"I just needed a clean sweep. I sure you understand, Jonas," Renn said.

"Not at all. You just like killing, that's what I see."

"No, you're wrong," Renn corrected. "I don't mind killing—killing in itself is not a joy. Though there have been times when watching someone pass away was rather fun."

Jonas had to get out of here soon. "So, I'm the last?"

"You were but I think your girlfriend and perhaps your sister too. Of course, your partner Frank and those idiots from the Bureau—yes, that should do it. That's about all who know you were looking into me."

"Sam and Maggie know nothing of you!" Jonas yelled. "You leave them alone. Don't go near them!"

"Sorry, no can do, and let me tell you," Renn replied. "Both your sister and girlfriend are mighty fine looking. It may take time before I introduce them to their maker."

Jonas was blind with fury but he knew he could not release it as of yet. No, that moment would come and all hell was coming with it.

"You seem at a loss for words," stated Renn.

Jonas sat upright on the hard chair and stared at the man standing a few feet in front of him.

"Ah, but your eyes look at me like cold steel." Suddenly Renn laughed. "I could just about imagine what you would do to me if I let you loose. You'd likely try to tear me apart with your bare hands, huh?"

Jonas remained motionless—including his eyes as they bore into the target he wanted so badly.

Renn approached and slowly pulled a sharp ice pick from his rear pocket. "Let's see if your eyes will change as I drive this into one of them, shall we?"

Nothing in the outward appearance of Jonas changed—not his eyes—his ramrod like sitting posture but within his mind something did snap. It was all those memories of his loved ones being hurt and killed while he was still alive. Albeit, perhaps for not much longer but it was those recollections of all those he had lost in the past that gave him one last push. The fury unleased upon the man in front of him like a lightning strike.

Pushing with all his might, Jonas forced himself up out of the chair and, with a quick move, spun the chair, which was still half clinging to him, around and into Renn who received the full force of the assault in the chest as he had been walking toward Jonas.

With a loud and painful grunt, the ice pick slipped from Renn's hands and, as he tried to regain his balance, the chair struck him a second time.

"Goddamn!" he bellowed, ramming into the wall a few feet from where he had been standing. "No, fucking way!"

With the furious attack on his captor, the ropes came loose enough so Jonas managed to free his hands and, with another quick motion, pulled the knotted rope from around his head. The release of the pressure was like a gift from God. But he knew what he was about to do had more to do with the devil than the Almighty.

"Yes," Jonas snarled. "Fucking way!"

Renn had regained his balance and the ice pick. "Nice move, Jonas, but you're not leaving this basement with either eye or anything else really."

The men watched each other warily as Jonas dodged and swerved while Renn poked and swung the eight-inch ice pick dangerously close to Jonas's face. A feint here and there were tiring Jonas out but all the movement didn't seem to be phasing Renn one iota.

The rage was still there, and Jonas had only one thought on his mind—Renn's death. But even with the anger carrying him along, the pain of being tortured and tied so securely to a hard backed chair for so long had taken a huge toll on

Jonas. With each side-step and breath, he could feel his body struggling just to stay on course of staying alive and winning.

"Slowing down a bit, are we?" Renn asked with a laugh and stopped his attack. With a smug look he just shook his head. "I'd thought you'd be tougher—the great Jonas Peters—too damn tough to die. Seems you were over-sold."

Jonas used those few seconds to rest, if that's what any reasonable person would call it. He was panting, sweating, and felt like shit. Every inch of his body was screaming to succumb to what appeared to be the inevitable.

"You know, when this is over, and you're dead, I may finish the job on that girlfriend of yours the same way I'm doing with you, except for one exception," said Renn. "She is damn good looking, Jonas. I think I'll fuck her to death through her eye sockets."

An unworldly scream emitted from Jonas's throat as he pushed himself for one final lunge at his captor. As the two men collided Jonas threw his arms in a bear hug around his mortal enemy but could feel the cold steel of the ice pick enter his left shoulder and knew instantly that it had gone through all the tissue completely. But the pain which should have been collapsing him wasn't there.

The slight pause as Renn tried to release the hold Jonas had around his chest was all Jonas needed. With all the strength he had left, Jonas pulled his head back and slammed it suddenly into Renn's face.

With a blood curdling howl, Renn reared back and grasped the broken cartilage that once was his nose. Blood erupted into the air and all he could see was white flashes through his eyes and nothing but incredible pain.

Jonas gritted his teeth and yanked out the ice pick from his shoulder blade. In what seemed like minutes, he approached the now-kneeling and wobbly man a few feet in front of him. "You know what?" he asked, doing his best to stay on his own feet.

"Jo—Jo—Jonas, don't," Renn cried as he struggled to see out of his bleary eyes. "I can't even see yet."

"You would have made a shitty United States Senator anyway," Jonas finished, driving the ice pick into Renn's left eye socket up to the hilt.

A large gasp escaped Renn as he jolted backward onto his feet fiddling with the weapon protruding from his bleeding eye socket.

Jonas stumbled forward and hammered it home one more time.

As the thin blade slipped past the pupil and entered the retina the rest was elementary. Renn was dead within a matter of seconds as the frontal lobe was ripped open and he collapsed to the floor.

Jonas looked down at the last of the man's death throes and felt no remorse.

A large crash from the door at the top of the stairwell which led into the basement and footsteps pounding down the stairs stopped as Frank took in the scene in front of him. It was horrific at the amount of blood splattered everywhere and more ghoulish was the man lying on his back bleeding out from his face with an ice pick sticking out of his left eye.

"Jonas," Frank gasped. "Sorry I was late to the party but are you okay?"

"Yeah, he's dead and I'm not—game over." With that, Jonas turned toward his friend. "Frank, I think it's time I passed out."

"You do that, buddy," Frank replied, catching Jonas in his arms.

"How's Jonas?" asked Goff as he met up with Frank at UC Davis Medical Center.

"Unconscious, but he did come to a bit when they put him in the ambulance."

"What did he say?"

"Something like there was trash to pick up in the basement, and we better get to Riverside as soon as possible."

Ramirez laughed. "Sounds like him but, unfortunately, from what I've heard, he's not going anywhere for a few days."

"You better make it happen," Frank warned. "Or there could be other basements with our remains."

"I'll put in a few calls in once we know his status," Goff said. "If he's stable, we'll arrange a medivac to the south."

"He'd appreciate it," Frank said.

Goff shrugged. "No, I'd appreciate it if I didn't do it. I don't want your partner's wrath after me. Jesus, Renn looked horrible."

"Jonas doesn't look so good either," Frank retorted.

"He's breathing," Ramirez stated.

"Yeah, there's that," Frank said in agreement. "What about Noble?"

Goff held his hand up. "I think he's going to cooperate. We have some people talking to him and, so far, it seems he had no idea that Renn was Kevin Jennings. Noble was probably an ambitious asshole, trying to save his boss's butt, and thought Jonas was really just a crazy reporter. Noble hit him upside the head to get him away from Renn. I actually believe the asshole. He'll tell us everything we want to know, and he'll get probation and told never to look for another government position."

"Will he write a bestselling tell-all book about this?" Frank asked.

"Nope," Ramirez stated firmly. "He's so scared that he asked about the witness protection program for him and his family. And the truth be told, probably not a bad idea since we don't know how long a reach Jennings, sorry—Renn—

had. We'll look into various options but as of now he's a non-entity."

"I don't think there'll be any problems, really, of any further hits," Goff stated. "We know that Renn had others do his dirty work for the most part. Hired thugs and now that the wallet is gone, those cockroaches will retreat to their tunnels, never to be heard from again. Doubt we can chase them down since most are probably ex-government hires."

"Good training ground for assassins," Frank replied.

"Yeah, we do our best," Ramirez said. "They get tossed out of this or that agency, and the only thing these people know is dirty tricks, so they hire themselves out to the highest bidder. One thing to be trained in IT and another how to pull a trigger on a foggy night. A very limited field of employment. It's a nasty business."

All three men looked at each other without uttering a word until Goff nodded.

"Okay, my turn about the late Senator Greg Renn of California. He was fishing near his house on the Sacramento River when his boat capsized. Unfortunately, he was alone and wasn't discovered for about a day by some joggers."

Frank stared at Goff. "You guys are good. He has no family that we know of, and he liked fishing after looking through the residence in Courtland. Fishing poles and tackle everywhere."

"A tragic ending for a tragic man," Ramirez stated.

"To say the least," Frank said. "What about Riverside?"

Ramirez nodded. "One of the directors is working on that with your chief of police. It'll probably be a new and unknown terrorist group trying to make a name for themselves. The problem will be that they left enough information for the Bureau and locals to track them down. The entire terrorist cell will die in a gun battle out of sight of the public. We have to close that one the right way. Can't let the voters know it was a fucked up psychopath who wanted to be president someday."

"That's a little too close to home," Goff said.

Frank nodded, wondering how many things were truly fake news in the world these days. "You guys okay with the Bureau?"

"Never better," Goff replied. "In fact, we may get promotions since our cousins in the CIA are very happy we found their wayward son. Turns out they didn't want to talk to him and are very happy he is truly dead this time. No, we're good, and this case is closed as far as we're concerned."

"Wow, amazing how you make things disappear," Frank uttered.

"That's what we do," Ramirez said, reaching out his hand to Frank. "It's been a great honor working with you."

Frank shook Ramirez's hand and then Goff's. "The honor has been both mine and Jonas's."

As the two agents started down the hall, Frank yelled out to them. "Make sure Jonas gets home tomorrow."

"And what, have that crazy bastard chasing us down?" Goff responded. "Not a chance in hell. He'll be back down south as soon as we can arrange that, and that means now."

Ramirez turned and nodded. "I don't want him after me if I do something he doesn't agree with."

"I knew you were smart guys the moment I met the two of you," Frank returned.

EPILOGUE

Sam sat on a chair beside Jonas and rubbed his right hand gently between both of hers. She was concerned, Very concerned, but knew she would be when Jonas had failed to call her. He had promised to call once per day.

That had been two days ago and suddenly here Jonas lay in a hospital bed for the second time in a month. He was bruised, stabbed, and overall looked like death warmed over. But thankfully he wasn't, and she had shed many tears the past twelve hours.

After Frank had found Jonas in the home owned by Senator Greg Renn, aka Kevin Jennings, Jonas had been transferred to UC Davis Medical Center but that was short lived.

Jonas, against all the doctors' orders demanded to be transported back to Riverside Community Hospital. UC Davis denied his request but suddenly a request to honor his wishes came through from the Federal Bureau of Investigation.

One day later, he had been transferred back to Riverside.

Of course, Doctor Scarlett Rose had taken charge as soon as he had gotten out of surgery in the ER for some minor patching up here and there and now saw Jonas on her rounds every twenty minutes.

"I'm starting to feel like part of the family," she had said to Sam and Maggie when Jonas was wheeled into his present room. "Strike that—this guy is around trouble too much for my liking."

Staring at the unconscious love of her life, Sam wondered if those words of the doctor's were in anyway prophetic.

Sam wanted nothing more than marriage, possibly children, and a quiet life, but could Jonas guarantee her that? She knew of most of his ghosts that haunted his every waking moment but could he release them in the future? Their future? Ever?

Long talks with Maggie over the past two days reminded Sam that Jonas was a very complicated person. First and foremost a loving man whom she knew loved her as much as she loved him but secondly—and it was that secondly that confounded her so—he was a man of action and would never back down from a fight. Most times it seemed as though Jonas searched diligently to deliver the first blow and that was why her soul searching ached so much.

Could she bring herself to marry such a man? A good and honorable man but one that put himself in harm's way too often. A man who felt it was his mission in life to right the wrongs others did—even to strangers.

He was a cop. That's who Jonas Peters was, she chided herself. She knew that from the very first time she had looked into those beautiful blue eyes of his years ago in

Scottsdale. Sam had known the type of man he was when she had fallen in love with him.

"Damn it, Jonas," she said, continuing to rub his hand. "Why can't you let the world take care of itself? You don't have to be the hero every time."

"He doesn't know anything else," came a voice from behind her.

Turning, Sam smiled at Maggie who had just returned from Frank's office.

"But why?"

Maggie pulled up an extra chair on the opposite side of Jonas's bed and remained silent for a few moments, looking into her lap. Finally, she raised her head, gave a loving look at her brother, and then turned her attention to Sam.

"We've talked about Jonas for years, Sam," Maggie stated. "I've told you his story over and over again."

"Tell me again, Maggie." Sam pleaded. "Tell me again to reassure me that I am making the right choice in loving him."

Maggie smiled. "I'm biased toward my older brother so of course I think it's the right thing for you to love him, but there is a risk."

"What risk?"

"Him."

Sam stopped rubbing Jonas's hand and gently moved it on top of his lightly breathing chest. He had been sedated for the pain a little over an hour previously but was still sleeping off the torture he had endured at the hands of his captor.

"Sam, Jonas feels the need to protect those he loves and those he feels need protecting. That's why he became a cop in the first place."

"You've told me that before but I just want to know why now you say the risk is loving him."

Shaking her head. "I didn't say it was risky loving him since he will love you back with all his heart—which I will guarantee."

"Then what?"

"He is a risk to himself."

A puzzled look came over Sam's face and Maggie held her hand out as though asking for a pause. "You see, when our parents died Jonas believed it was his job to protect me."

"You were both teens when they were killed in the car accident."

"True but Jonas was seventeen and didn't buy into the notion that he was a child. He got a job—actually two to help out our grandparents who took us in after Mom and Dad were killed. He had always wanted to go to college to earn a degree in law so he could become a prosecutor. I can still remember my dad getting so frustrated with Jonas when they'd have one of those serious father-to-son arguments like it was yesterday. 'God, Jonas,' he'd say, 'you should become a lawyer since you like to prove people wrong all the time,'" Maggie said with tears in her eyes. She missed her parents terribly, and a day didn't go by without her remembering the wonderful family time they had had together.

"Well, college was out the question since we didn't have much money and the insurance we received from the accident claim barely was enough for the burials. Dad had never thought much of life insurance—called it usury, in fact, but that's not the point and I'm wandering down memory lane."

"No, go ahead," Sam stated. "I don't know this part of his history—or yours, for that matter."

Maggie managed a smile. "Well, Jonas did go to community college while working full time and received his associates in criminal justice. He was now twenty-one and felt badly since it had taken three years for a two year degree but he worked and worked and could never get a full school schedule—anyway—he was accepted by the Riverside Police Department and entered the police academy. When he graduated from the academy he made sure I had a four year college education, paying it all on his own. That's where I met Roger, he was studying business. He never allowed Roger or me to pay him back."

Maggie stopped a moment and wiped away a tear before she continued. "To make a long story longer, he got married a few years later, made the rank of detective, and everything looked promising to the rising star. Oh, by this time he had finished his Master of Science in Criminal Justice, hoping to move up the ranks in the department."

"He never told me that—that he wanted to be a higher rank than detective."

Maggie shook her head. "No, he wouldn't have told you since that dream faded away the night Stacy was murdered. That was his personal turning point, and from then on all he wanted to do was hunt down criminals and put them away. Sitting behind a desk as a lieutenant or captain did not have the same appeal it had when he had his daughter."

"It changed him?" Sam asked and then felt rather foolish. Of course the murder of your daughter would change a person. *That was unthinking and uncaring.*

"Jonas was still the same loving brother he had always been but the edge to him was sharper and more pronounced. From that day, he felt it was his duty to protect those who could not protect themselves."

Sam sat quietly and took in what Maggie had just told her.

"So, when you said he was a risk to himself, is it because—"

"What's she saying is that I will kick anyone's ass who tries to hurt the innocent even if that means putting myself in dangerous situations," Jonas interrupted.

Both women turned toward the man lying on the bed.

It was Sam who spoke first. "I thought you were still sedated."

Maggie was second to speak. "Okay, brother of mine, how long have you been listening?"

Jonas inched himself up into a more of a sitting position on the hospital bed. "God, wasn't I here not long ago?"

"Just answer the question, Jonas," Maggie demanded.

He smiled. "Long enough to hear some of what you were trying to explain to Sam but not long enough for the whole story. Thank God for the drugs."

"Jonas, I was just discussing with Maggie—" Sam started but stopped as Jonas gently took her left hand into his right.

"I know—sometimes I can't explain myself, Sam," Jonas said. "It's who I am—the great protector of the masses who happens to get himself physically beaten sometimes. I don't like it—it hurts and I really don't like hospitals."

Sam laughed and kissed him on the forehead.

"You missed my lips."

Sam re-aimed and scored a perfect shot.

Maggie feigned disgust. "This isn't going to get messy, is it?"

"Hope so," Jonas responded.

"Okay, I'll leave now," Maggie stated, standing up. "You two have a lot to talk about."

"Stay, Maggie," Sam said. "There's nothing to talk about now—I'm willing to take any risk to be with Jonas, even if that means him himself."

ABOUT THE AUTHOR

John R Beyer spent nearly a decade in law enforcement before moving into the education system for three decades, while earning his Doctorate from Pepperdine University. His writing includes fiction, non-fiction, blogs, and has won numerous literary awards. He divides his time with his wife, Laureen, in Southern California and Southern Nevada

9 781967 192670